MOONSHADOWS

A NELLIE BURNS AND MOONSHINE MYSTERY

MOONSHADOWS

JULIE WESTON

FIVE STAR

A part of Gale, Cengage Learning

GALE
CENGAGE Learning

LIBRARY OF CONGRESS CATALOGING-IN-PUBLICATION DATA

Weston, Julie W., 1943–
    Moonshadows : a Nellie Burns and Moonshine mystery / Julie Weston. — First edition.
        pages ; cm
        ISBN 978-1-4328-3073-1 (hardcover) — ISBN 1-4328-3073-2 (hardcover) — ISBN 978-1-4328-3081-6 (ebook) — ISBN 1-4328-3081-3 (ebook)
        1. Women photographers—Fiction. 2. City and town life—Fiction. 3. Interpersonal relations—Fiction. 4. Criminal investigation—Fiction. 5. Idaho—Social life and customs—20th century—Fiction. I. Title.
PS3623.E872M66 2015
813'.6—dc23   2015008076

First Edition. First Printing: July 2015
Find us on Facebook– https://www.facebook.com/FiveStarCengage
Visit our website– http://www.gale.cengage.com/fivestar/
Contact Five Star™ Publishing at FiveStar@cengage.com

Printed in the United States of America
1 2 3 4 5 6 7 19 18 17 16 15

For Gerry

ACKNOWLEDGMENTS

The seed for this book began on a full moon night at Galena Lodge in central Idaho. My husband, Gerry Morrison, and I and two friends strapped on snowshoes and ventured out into the dark, lit by the light of the moon, round and the color of bone. Alongside the trail, wheat grass appeared, casting shadows that rivaled those of a sunny day. On our way home after a delicious dinner following our adventure, we drove past a cabin, also lit by the moon. A story line began to weave its magic when the moon set behind the Smoky Mountains. Only starlight remained to dazzle the darkness.

For over two decades, Idaho has been the subject of my writing. Most of that time, I lived in Seattle. Now, I have returned to Idaho, a world as different from the city as can be imagined. We are surrounded by high desert—sagebrush and rabbit brush, native grasses and wildflowers. The sun shines most days; snow piles high in the winter. We ski, snowshoe, and play in the snow. Elk and deer populate the meadows and mountains behind us. Around our house, rabbits and ermine and fox leave their traces, winter and summer. In winter, the white trunks of aspen stand guard. In summer, their leaves rustle a soothing outdoor melody, accompanying meadowlarks and magpies.

A combination of writing groups, both in-person and online, have supported and advised me, critiqued my work, and read many permutations of the chapters in this book: Mary Murfin Bayley, Charlene Finn, Belinda Anderson, Gina Vitolo, and Anjali Banerjee. Without their good advice, I doubt if I would have finally brought this story to a close. With their encouragement, I still write about Idaho, and the adventures of Nellie Burns and Moonshine will continue.

I thank Five Star Publishing and Tiffany Schofield for believing in the fiction of the West and recognizing that Idaho is an integral part of the West. Hazel Rumney is a star editor with a keen eye and perceptive mind. Michael Seidman helped me with structure and character. The Regional History section of the Community Library in Ketchum, Idaho, and Robert A. Lonning's book, *Hailey* (Arcadia Publishing, 2012), gave me pictures and narrative to bring 1920's Idaho to life.

My husband is my first and best reader. He is also the photography expert who has informed the pages of this book and Nellie's vocation. His photographs inspire and he has made Nellie's efforts reality.

PROLOGUE

Rosy sank to his knees, gulped in shards of icy air, and rolled his burden out of his arms. A crust blanketing the snow cracked and broke. The stalking wind flung solid pellets against his face, across his shoulders. No time. No shovel.

He groaned and leaned back. Slow down. Time made no difference now. Standing, pulling one leg forward and then the next became an exercise in wading through sugar. Damnitall. How could he dig a hole in a bowl of drifting snow?

Nothing to do but to do it. He had stopped sobbing when he crossed the snow bridge to the grove of trees, but tears froze on his cheeks. Ashamed, Rosy rubbed them off. His winter gloves felt like sandpaper.

He waded and crawled toward a slight rise, backed off half a dozen steps, and began to dig. With each sweep of his hand, the snow slid back to its beginning. He crouched, legs apart, and scooped snow between his legs and back. Like a dog. Where was the dog? He could do it better.

"I won't . . . forget . . ." he mumbled and panted, ". . . you." A trench began to form. "I . . . know . . . what you . . . did." Snow slowly piled behind him. Good enough. Aspen branches clacked against each other like dancing bones. Dead leaves, still clinging, sighed, as if a soul wandered past.

Her pale face floated just out of reach, a ghostly presence in this haunted space. He shut his eyes, held back a sob. Goddamn weakling. He needed a drink.

The sun, a white pebble behind clouds, shed no warmth. But

his efforts did. Sweat spilled off his face. His shirt was wet. The wind blew through him, making a hole of his middle. He crawled back to his burden and pushed and pulled and laid it out in the trench, gently. What else could he do? Nothing.

"Take away my pain," Rosy pleaded. Opium. The word was a raven's screech. The wind calmed. He stilled his rising gorge, knelt a few moments over the body, not knowing what to say or even think. Then he raised his head and yowled. A magpie, dressed for a funeral in its black, blue, and white feathers, answered him with a "Cr-r-uuk." Two of them swooped down to land on branches, croaking, then dropped to the snow, strutting.

"Git! Git you blood-suckin' banshees!" Rosy staggered up and waved his arms like a blasted scarecrow. The magpies retreated two steps, and waited.

Where was the damn dog? He, Rosy, was the dog. He reversed his stance, and scooped snow back into the hole. If only he had a shovel. Tired, Rosy lay down next to the hole, scooping and patting, scooping and patting. At last, the white berm held. He could leave. Or, he could lie there and sleep.

Get up. He shivered like a sinner at St. Peter's gates. Get up!

The trip back across the river took less time, less effort. Hillocks and humps of snow where the struggle began and ended remained. Half a dozen magpies pecked and poked like ghouls fighting over gristle. The wind had sifted miniature drifts in every direction. The birds flew off, leaving scattered bloody patches, pinking and blacking the snow. With the coming of nightfall, winter would erase the fall of man, the craving, crying need of man. Rosy kicked the snow in a frenzy, hatred still simmering. Out of breath, he stopped and then forced his legs to step and step again.

A bottle of hooch and the devil called from Last Chance Ranch.

CHAPTER 1

Snow and a full moon. Nellie waded through heavy powder almost as deep as her high-topped boots. The man leaning over the automobile didn't look like he could guide her anywhere, let alone into back country to find a night scene worth capturing on film. He scraped at the back window. She smelled liquor on him, more like old liquor than new; maybe he'd been out drinking the night before.

Prohibition had seriously affected people's drinking habits in Chicago by the time Nellie left; everyone talked about how to get liquor. In Idaho, no one even mentioned Prohibition. A drinking man was not something new to her, and she tried to hide her distaste.

"Mr. Kipling?" she asked as she neared the car. "Mrs. Bock, my landlady, told me you carry people for hire." His Oldsmobile roadster was dented, had peeling paint and two cracked side windows, and what looked like scrawny tires under metal grippers. The man himself wasn't in much better shape.

"Where you want to go?"

"North of town, I think. I need a place where the moon will shine full on and create shadows on snow. I'll be carrying camera gear on a sled, so I can't hike too far from the road. I need time to set up all my equipment. And I need several hours to photograph different angles of light." His hands were red and gnarled, and he coughed several times while Nellie talked to him. The noise of his scraping made her wonder if he heard her.

She was ready to try again when he answered.

"Don't want much, do you?"

"On my way north in the train, I thought the area around Shoshone was right except there was no snow." The memory of the stark, flat expanses of sagebrush and the monster shapes of lava rock and trees that looked like grasping skeletons in the night still made her shiver. "But as we neared Hailey and Ketchum, the scenery closed in. Where can I find the kind of scenes I saw farther south, but with snow?"

Her enthusiasm didn't appear to be catching.

"Doubt you'll find what you want, but I'll take you there. Charge a dollar out and a dollar back." *Scritch*. He succeeded in clearing frost from the glass.

Two dollars for one trip! "That's too much." She had her nest egg, but she couldn't spend it willy-nilly. "If I hire you now and again when the moon is full, would you lower the price?"

"Might. Depends."

Nellie waited. To break the silence, she asked, "Depends on what?"

"On how much I need the money. What do you want to do at night? You can't take pictures then." Mr. Kipling stopped scraping to stand up and look down at her.

"I believe I can." In the portrait studio where she had worked in Chicago, most of the faces had been regular—made up if they were women to look as pretty as possible and clean-shaven if they were men.

This man's face appeared split down the middle. On the right side, his eye was milky blue and a scar near his temple pinched the skin around it, giving him a wizened appearance. On the left side, his eye was brown and his skin smooth, although he had not shaved in days and the stubble gave him a dirty look. All of his skin, smooth and pinched alike, had the rosy sheen of a common drunk.

12

"Staring at my bad eye, ain't you?"

Embarrassed, Nellie looked away. "I'm sorry. I didn't mean to."

He moved around to the front of the automobile. "You gonna hire me? Get in. Let's go."

The scraped place on the front window was a narrow gap all the way across it, hardly wide enough to see through, but there was really no other choice. Nellie couldn't hire a car and drive herself. Another one of her things to do—learn to drive—along with find a job, make a name for herself, and get enough money to buy an enlarger and other equipment for a darkroom. She opened the passenger door and climbed in. No ice clung to the side windows.

The road north followed the Big Wood River for several miles, and the windshield cleared as they motored along. Cottonwoods and scrub brush edged the rushing water, which peeked out from behind snowbanks. She wished she had her camera and could stop to try several landscape shots, but she had to be chary with her film, as no more was available in Ketchum.

"Why do you want to gallivant around all alone?"

"I want to find unusual subject matter." Why should Nellie tell a stranger? She had hardly told herself why she was doing this. "Nobody pays much attention to a woman in a man's field. If I do something no one else is doing, I can open doors." I hope, she added to herself.

"Why don't you get married like every other woman?"

"You sound just like my mother, Mr. Kipling." Nellie's mother had warned her she was attempting the impossible; she should instead find a man, get married, and have children. Nellie had to restrain herself from making a smart remark about drunken husbands and slaving wives.

"Nobody calls me Mister. I'm just plain Rosy."

"Rosy? That sounds like a girl's name. Why are you called Rosy?"

"Now that ain't none of your business, is it?"

Nellie turned her face back to the landscape passing by the wide window. She'd been rude twice, and his name was obviously related to the color of his face.

After a few bumpy miles, the river swung out of sight and the automobile passed between rolling snowy meadows. A snowfield at night without a foreground to attract the eye would merely appear gray. It was the contrast between black and white and pattern that she wanted.

It wasn't long before Rosy pulled a brown bottle from a sack on the floor beside him and took a drink. "Want a taste?" He held the bottle toward her. "Some of the best moonshine around."

Nellie edged closer to the door. "No thank you. I don't drink."

Rosy drove in silence, sipping from time to time.

The hillsides to the right of the road were white in the brilliant sunshine and bluish gray where clouds shadowed them. Without trees, they resembled pillows cut across with what looked like narrow terraces. "What makes those parallel lines on the hills?" Nellie asked, hoping to divert her driver's attention to something besides his bottle.

"Sheep."

The odor of whiskey in the automobile grew—a strong, almost antiseptic smell. Nellie took her handkerchief out of her bag and held it to her nose. The aroma of carnations, her mother's scent, replaced the whiskey and Nellie felt a pang of homesickness.

"Sheep," Nellie repeated. "I don't understand. How can the lines be so straight?"

"The Basques run 'em all summer into the canyons and gulches around here. A straight line is quickest and easiest for the animals 'stead of climbing up and down, so that's what they follow."

"What's a Basque?"

"You don't know nothin', do you? They's people from Spain. They come here to take care of the sheep for the rich ranchers, who don't want to get theirselves dirty. The mine owners hire us miners, and the sheep owners hire them Basques. 'Course, none of us'll work with sheep, so the ranchers got to bring someone in to do it."

"I suppose the mining pays better," Nellie offered. "But aren't most of the mines around here closed down?" Mrs. Bock had lamented the failing of one.

"Damn sight better. And sheepherding is nigger work."

Nellie stiffened. The memory of the riots of 1919 in Chicago when so many colored people were killed was still strong. The Negroes there were a proud people, by and large, and her mother and she would have starved if one of the Negro professors at the University of Chicago hadn't found her mother work at the school library. The same man had found Nellie a part-time job in a portrait studio, setting her on her life's work.

"Tell me what kind of mining you do." She wanted to concentrate on possible photographs. Riding with Rosy Kipling was a big mistake.

"Did. See this eye?" Rosy tapped his right temple with the bottle. "Blasting cap went off and did that to me."

"Oh, dear. I'm sorry." Mrs. Bock had warned about Rosy Kipling's "weakness." Maybe it was his eye, rather than drinking.

"What for? You didn't do it." Rosy lapsed into silence again.

The car's motor rumbled and bumbled, but seemed steady enough. The grippers clanked in the snow, which wasn't very deep. Other autos had traveled this way, leaving ruts. One appeared in the distance, a dot that grew larger and puttered past them going back to Ketchum. Mr. Kipling didn't comment so neither did Nellie. The road crossed over the river and the mountains on either side narrowed the valley. At last, they were close to the kind of terrain she was looking for—meadows, mountains, river, and trees. Along with naked cottonwoods and aspen, there were stands of almost black evergreens. A small white creature bounded across the snowfield.

"Stop!" she shouted. "What's that?"

Rosy stomped on the brake, throwing Nellie forward and down. "You b—!" The whiskey spilled on the seat.

Nellie pulled herself back up. "That little animal, what is it?"

"It's a weasel, you flatlander."

"But it's white, not brown."

"Ermine, it's called, in the winter." The disgust in his voice was so thick, Nellie could feel her face warm.

"I want to get out here. This looks like a good place."

Her driver stared at her as if she were crazy. "Suit yourself." He pulled the car to the side of the road, stopped the motor, wiped off the bottle top, and slumped back.

Nellie looked at him a moment. She had hoped he might get out too, help her break trail maybe. Her boots were tall enough, she hoped, that snow wouldn't fall in; if it did, her legs would get very cold because she wore a skirt. She stepped out, closed the door, took one step, and sank up to her knee in snow. From the car, a muffled laugh. She kept wading, poking one hole after another up to her knees. Rosy continued to chuckle and she felt herself blush again.

Ten yards into the meadow, she could see the area might work well. In the distance, an apparently abandoned house nestled in the snow near the river. It was two stories with a long porch across the side facing the road. Cottonwoods lined the riverbank with a sprinkling of silver aspens winding in and out. Closer to where she stood, fir trees clumped together, and red

16

willow bushes, their branches heavy with snow, bowed to the wind. Three magpies whined, as if she were an enemy invading their territory, and clots of snow dropped from the willows with whispered *phuts*. The air, smelling of cold steel, was such a contrast to the oppressive atmosphere in the auto that she hated to return. On the other hand, she was freezing.

"You need snowshoes if you're gonna scout around like that," Rosy said, when Nellie climbed in.

"Does anyone live in that cabin back there?"

"That ain't no cabin. It's a house. Last Chance Ranch." Rosy put the car in gear and began a U-turn.

"I want to explore some more. Won't you drive farther out?" Nellie really wanted to return to town and take a hot bath and sit in front of the fire in Mrs. Bock's dining room, she was so cold. But maybe there was a better place. "I'm not paying two dollars for this trip unless you do. I've hardly seen anything."

"I'm thirsty, and my bottle's empty." Rosy completed the turn and headed back to Ketchum. "And we got to wait for more snow to melt. Can't get through." Automobile tracks extended up the road, giving the lie to his words. "I'll throw in the second trip for free."

Satisfied with her bargain, Nellie stared back at the house. Last Chance Ranch. A strange western name. Whose last chance?

"A family lived there—wife, husband, two boys. Wife died, boys went back East, man drank himself to death." Rosy's voice was matter-of-fact for the economic telling of a tragedy.

Snow fell that night and again the next day. How could Nellie photograph a full moon and its shadows if the sky kept shedding bits of white? Her planning would go for naught if the snow didn't stop. She couldn't afford to wait another four weeks. Until her train ride across the Idaho desert and then north to the mountains, she had not known how bright the moon on snow could be, or that it could cast shadows deeper than those from sunlight. All the light she was familiar with came from electricity or candles. In Chicago, the stars and the moon counted for little.

But the stormy weather gave her time to prepare for a night out. She needed pants and snowshoes, as Rosy advised.

"We don't get much call for pants for ladies, Miss." The man at Jack Lane's dry goods store didn't laugh, although his eyes flashed a merry spark. "We're a sheep and mining town. All the ladies I know wear skirts." He didn't add, like they're supposed to, but she heard it in his voice.

"Ladies in Chicago wear pants," Nellie said, sorry the minute the words were out of her mouth. He didn't comment. Instead, he found the smallest pair of wool pants in the store and the shortest belt to hitch them around her waist. In the mirror, she looked like a little girl dressing up in her father's clothes.

"We'll take 'em up for you—have 'em to Mrs. Bock's tomorrow first thing. Anything else?"

"Snowshoes." As she hoped to spend time out in the snow, night and day, spending money on snowshoes felt like a necessity.

"What does a young girl like you want with pants and snowshoes?" He placed his hands on the counter and peered down at her.

Nellie mumbled about exploring in the snow. He shook his head and led her to the back of the store. At twenty-five, she didn't feel so young. Her acquaintances in Chicago considered her an old maid. She knew she looked younger. Maybe it was her dark curly hair that never seemed quite tidy, no matter how careful she was about fastening it at the back of her neck, or the fact that she was smaller than most western women she'd seen so far.

The clerk held up a pair of snowshoes. "These're used, but small enough so you won't trip over 'em. They're broke. I won't charge you for 'em. I'll get 'em patched up and deliver 'em along with the pants." A calendar sat on the back counter with a picture of the clerk. He stood in front of the store's sign: "Eat Lamb. It's Delicious!"

"You're Jack Lane."

"Yep." Mr. Lane held out a pair of wool socks. "You'll need an extra pair of these, too. I'll throw 'em in for free."

Nellie didn't ask Mr. Lane how to use the snowshoes, nor even how to fit them to her boots. The shoes seemed so big and wide. She would have to walk bowlegged to tramp through snow. With socks in hand, she paid, thanked him, and left.

Late the next afternoon in her room, Nellie checked her camera pack to be sure she had everything necessary for a night out. "Miss Burns." Mrs. Bock's voice from the hall was followed by a knock on the door. "Rosy said he's ready any time you are." Mrs. Bock knocked again and then opened the door. None of the doors had keys for the locks, a peculiarity of Idaho. A peculiarity and an irritation.

"Thank you." Nellie tried to sound polite. "I see it's still snowing."

"Humph. It'll stop 'bout five. This storm has had its day. A few patches of blue are peeking out now. Can't keep the sun hidden for long around here."

"Did Mr. Lane bring by my pants and those snowshoes for me? He promised they'd be repaired by now."

"Just been having coffee with him. He's mighty curious what you want with snowshoes. Mostly he sells them to hunters and prospectors and the like."

Nellie had already told Mrs. Bock about her plans. Her landlady offered the use of a small sled to carry camera gear, an offer Nellie had gratefully accepted. Nearly everyone during her trip had remarked on her traveling alone and with so much luggage. What was a city girl doing in a small mining town in the middle of the Wild West? She knew she intended to become an artist, known for her photographic landscapes, able to sell her work so she could live independently. But saying so seemed presumptuous and slightly mad.

"If you still have some hot coffee, Mrs. Bock, I'll come down shortly."

The collection of wrinkles on Mrs. Bock's face took an upturn. "If it ain't hot now, it will be in two shakes of a lamb's tail. And I'll fix you up some supper, too. You can't go out hungry."

If Nellie had ever been hungry, she had ceased to know what that meant. Every meal was planned to feed miners after a long day underground. Two miners lived at Mrs. Bock's boarding house, along with an old-timer who spent most of his time rocking in front of the fire and talking to the landlady. The working men shared an auto to drive to the Independence Mine when work was available. The last boarder was another woman who disappeared each morning and returned after dinner each night. Mrs. Bock kept a plate hot for her in the oven, saying she worked harder than any man around there and for less pay, too.

If only Mrs. Bock were right about the snow stopping. The clouds would break up and dissipate, leaving a clear sky, a pattern she'd already observed in the time she'd been in Ketchum. "The bathroom is empty and the water reheated," Mrs. Bock said and turned back to her kitchen. "You need to dress warm if you're still set on tramping around in the snow tonight." By now, the whole town probably knew what this "young girl" was doing there.

★ ★ ★ ★ ★

In the snow north of town, Nellie was alone in the world. All she saw and felt at that moment belonged to her and to no other soul. Although she could not yet see the moon, she beheld its effects. She had identified Jupiter, Saturn, Orion's Belt, but they paled in comparison to the dazzle on earth. The snow meadow at her feet glistened like an ever-shifting dune of stardust. Tufts of long wheat-like grass cast precise, narrow shadows on the snow, as did the crooked reaching arms of aspen trees.

All the difficulty of persuading Rosy to accompany her at night, strapping on the wood frame and gut snowshoes, wading with her feet apart through snow light as powder so that each step sank to the depth of her boot, and pulling a sled as heavy as a body might be—all were worth it, if she succeeded in taking the kind of photographs she wanted. Even if Rosy drove away, as he had threatened to do.

The silence alone was worth the effort. She wished she could photograph it, so that anyone viewing the photo would feel drawn in and given respite from the noise of the world, the same way Nellie felt. For a long moment more, she gathered in the night, the snow, the shadows, the quiet, the cold. Then she turned to work, sorry to disturb the serenity of scene and self. Setting up her equipment took time. Waiting for the moon to rise above the eastern mountain took patience. Waiting for it to move would take more. The six sheets of film in her pack should be enough.

She untied the sled's rope from her waist and plowed in her snowshoes closer to the grass tufts. Yes, the grass in the foreground, the aspen trunks white in moonlight against the dark fir background. Until the moon rose higher, this would do. She stepped in her own trench back to the sled and moved it another dozen feet closer to her envisioned photo. Where she had trampled in the snow looked as if a battle had taken place.

The moon topped the mountain and was so white, so astonishing, Nellie gasped. The man in the moon beamed down at her and she grinned back. Really, she wanted to whoop with joy, but Rosy might think she was in trouble.

With her tripod on as firm a footing as she could manage with her large 4×5 view camera attached to it, she retrieved her black cloth and covered her head and the camera to look at the scene reflected on the ground glass, then opened the shutter and moved the bellows on its rails to focus. The scene of wheatgrass, aspen, and snowy background was upside down and inverted, allowing her to see pattern and composition rather than objects. After a few more adjustments, as the light grew brighter and the shadows deeper, she set the aperture and shutter, slid in the film holder at the camera back, and removed the dark slide that protected it from light. From her pocket she drew a round timepiece, a present, her mother had said, one that had been intended for a son. Her mother's statement had been tinged with embarrassment, but also, Nellie liked to think, a smattering of pride.

The light was strong enough to see the second hand. At the hour, Nellie opened the shutter and followed the sweep hand around once, twice . . . A sound somewhere off to her right caused her to look up briefly, but she didn't lose her place. Five minutes. That should be enough, she guessed, and closed the shutter, replaced the dark slide, extracted the film holder, wrapped it with velvet cloth for protection, and placed the bundle in the film case with the unexposed sheets.

Nellie peered toward the direction of the sound, but heard nothing more and saw no motion. A still night. A forest critter, perhaps, watching her. That gave her a queer feeling, but she shrugged and went back to work.

Silver light bathed the meadow and the cabin she had ignored while focusing on the first photo. Last Chance Ranch, but this time she was on the other side of it and much farther from the road. The moon and the abandoned building might work to convey what existed in the West side by side—beauty, dereliction and hard work, disappointment and riches. An idea about photographing miners at work blossomed at the sight of the house. Even Rosy would fit into such a series.

Moving the sled with her heavy camera gear and tripod to a better vantage point used up so much energy, Nellie wondered if she could complete her task. After a short rest on her sled, she set up the tripod and camera and focused again. To complete a photo with the moon in it, she would have to take one picture of the cabin first without the moon in it, then wait for the moon to rise higher, and take the same picture on the same sheet of film with the moon. Otherwise, during the time the shutter would have to be open to capture the cabin, the moon would move, creating a blur. So she would take two photos of the same scene—one without and one with the moon. She snowshoed back to the sled, pulled a film holder from the pack, stood next to the camera, and inserted the film in the camera. She set the aperture at f8 and exposed the film by pulling out the slide and opening the lens. The click sounded loud. After another five minutes, she replaced the dark slide. Now she would have to wait for the moon to arc higher in the sky.

To fill time, she ate half the sandwich Mrs. Bock insisted she take and absorbed the shadowed beauty around her while she thought about her last confrontation with Sebastian Scotto, the man she had worked for at the portrait studio in Chicago. Even now she cringed at his words when he tore two of her photographs in half and dropped them on his desk.

"If you have time to waste on this . . . this foolery, you aren't working hard enough. I should never have hired a girl. Bah!" He pointed to one-half of her photo of buildings along Lake Michigan, drenched in sunbeams after a storm. "Sentimental drivel. You waste my film. Just as you waste my paper in the darkroom. You re-print too much."

"But you've told me adjusting a print is learning." They stood in his office and she walked to a bin with photographs and pulled out one of an elderly woman, wrinkled as a witch but with an ancient wisdom blooming from every line. "This one. You liked this one." It was one of the few Nellie felt was art, not just a photo of a person.

"That one is mine." He grabbed the photo. "Don't you dare take credit for my work!" His voice dropped and his eyes half-closed, like a snake's. "I've had enough of your incompetence and emotions. Leave now."

Stunned, Nell struck back. "That is my work. See this brooch." She pointed to an intricately wrought piece of jewelry at the woman's neck. "Your photograph had no brooch."

"You stupid woman. You have no eye. You have no art. Get out!"

Nellie left his office, afraid she would cry in front of Scotto, but not so afraid that she didn't collect her own portfolio first and gather her book of notes and her scarf, hat, and purse from a shelf in the darkroom she shared with two men. Even if Scotto would say the portraits in her portfolio were his, and she had nothing to prove otherwise, she wanted samples of her work. Somewhere, somehow, she would take photographs that were all hers.

She scouted toward the river to hear the whooshing sound muffled by snow, similar to a train on tracks in the long distance. A series of sharp yips from across the river raised gooseflesh on her arms. Coyotes? Wolves? Her trip alone at night became a foolish venture before the echoes died away and all was quiet again. This night, this place, belonged to the creatures of the dark. The moon's expression became a leer. She wished she had a lantern. What if she lost her way back? She could freeze and be covered with snow and no one would know.

The photo, remember the importance of the photo. The moon's arc traveled above the cabin. Nellie approached the camera again and this time set the shutter speed for $1/30^{th}$ of a second in the moon's bright light and exposed the same sheet of film again. The photos she took of moon on snow were hers. If the scene wasn't as bright as daylight, it seemed so because of the surrounding snow. With full moonlight illuminating the cabin, that should be enough to bring out the flat cut logs of the side wall and the pattern of river rock in the chimney. Perhaps it would also catch the tendril of smoke as a white line against the dark firs behind. Nellie caught herself. Smoke? No, she must have imagined it. She lifted her dark cloth, watched the chimney, and saw nothing.

The moon slid behind a cloud and Nellie shivered. She had been photographing for several hours. It was too cold and too late to take another photo with and without the moon. A full moon lasted two nights; maybe she could talk Rosy into bringing her to this place again. After a glance at the sky, she realized there was only enough time left to return to the road before her heavenly light dropped behind the western mountains. She carefully secured her exposed film holders, wrapped her camera in its case, and folded the tripod. It was during a last look around, when she had ceased making noise herself, that she heard a tapping, over and over, so soft it might have been background noise for some time.

What was it? She studied the cabin again. This time, she saw at the side window a reflected gleam that came and went, a flash, and not regular. The sound was a tapping on glass.

The road was too far away to see. Was Rosy there? She'd better hike out, sled and all, and seek his help. He might have a lantern. Her knees shook. She didn't want to admit she was afraid. Instead, she began to re-trace her snow trough. Then the snowshoe thong holding her boot broke. The moon was slipping toward the trees. Yips began again. *Tap, tap, tap.*

Nellie debated trying instead for the house. There were no such things as ghosts. The distance was hardly a hundred yards, and it was much farther to the auto. Coyotes, not wolves. She had told him hours. Scrambling to the house was going to be difficult with only one snowshoe. "No ghosts." Her own voice reassured her.

Pushing her sled to break a path, Nellie struggled toward the cabin, arriving at the door as the moon dropped to the line of mountains. The *tap, tap, tap* sound moved from the window to the door. When she turned the handle, the door opened and Nellie fell forward.

A black shape leaped up on her, grunting and squeaking, and a tongue slathered her face with saliva as she dropped to her knees. A dog. He wiggled and squirmed and then barked, a half-bark, half-yip. Nellie sat back on her heels and pushed the animal away. "You're not a ghost!" Then, in the last glow from the moon, she saw the form of a man splayed out on the floor, his face a mask of ice, one hand visible, his fingers curled around an axe.

CHAPTER 2

Nellie opened her mouth to scream, but the dog pushed against her, whining. It was real, not a ghost. Black, not white. And the dead man wasn't a ghost either. What should she do? The cold inside the house felt danker, more intense, than the cold outside. A whiff of something lingered. If she yelled for Rosy from the porch, would he hear her? Maybe he was growing anxious about her long absence and would look for her. More likely, he was probably passed out in his car, and even with the sheepskin he had pulled around himself was at risk of freezing to death. She began to shiver.

Matches—that was what she needed. Everyone was shocked when she smoked a cigarette in public, part of the reason she did it. "Nice women don't smoke," she was told repeatedly. After long practice, she could blow smoke rings, and that was always her answer to her critics—a series of O's in the air. She found the matches in her jacket and struck one on the metal hinge.

Light flared. The dog yipped. Nellie avoided looking at the body on the floor and scanned the room for a candle or lantern. A table was overturned, and beside it, the glass chimney of a lantern broken into pieces. Just as the flame reached her fingertips, she spotted a candle in a bottle with cold wax in a drip down its curve on a sideboard. With another match, she made her way to the candle, stepping carefully out of reach of the iceman on the floor and lit the wick. The steady candlelight illuminated more of the room. At the other end was the fireplace, empty of anything but ashes. At the end nearest her was an old cookstove. Maybe that was where the smoke had come from. She touched the top surface. Cold.

Beside the stove was a neat stack of kindling. Someone must live there after all. Or rather, Nell thought, with a sideways glance at the man on the floor, did live there. She took a stick, opened the stove top with the iron handle, and stirred in the ashes. A single remnant of an ember, almost gone, rewarded her search. Again, she scanned the room and saw a bundle of what appeared to be newspapers and magazines at the end of the counter. She grabbed one, tore off several pages, and crumpled them. As she used the candle to start a fire, the date on one page jumped out at her: January 31, 1923. It was a weekly from Ketchum, only one day old. She looked back at the man. He must have frozen to death. The ice on his face was thick. If he'd been there that long, should it have been thicker or almost gone? And who lit a fire in the stove in those two days?

The moon dog crowded against her leg, maybe trying to warm himself. His tongue hung out, then retracted, and he closed his mouth. Had the dog been licking him? Water, probably the dog needed water and food. A shudder lodged in her throat. Maybe the dog would have eaten the man if she hadn't appeared. A pump at the edge of the sink yielded water after a couple groans. Nellie wondered why it wasn't frozen. She filled an empty dish gathered from the floor, then walked back to her pack on the sled and retrieved her camera, her plate case, and the half-sandwich she hadn't eaten, and fed a piece of the sandwich to the dog. He almost took her hand with it, and then looked pleadingly at her.

Warmth seeped into the room from the fire in the stove. Now what to do? The man on the floor wasn't the first dead person she'd seen. He must have passed out and then frozen to death.

Still, the ice on his face was unsettling. It looked like a death mask.

In Chicago, people wanted photos taken of their loved ones in caskets. As low man in the pecking order, that had been one of her duties. After the first few corpses, she had lost her distaste for the work and treated the subjects as any other paying customer. The lighting was a bit trickier, as was the angle of the photo, but she had become expert at it, even moving a head slightly, or a hand, not something she liked, but was willing to do. Maybe firelight would work to photograph this one.

Before the thought was fully formed, she was dragging the body by its boots toward the cooler end of the room. Carrying camera gear had strengthened her arms, but she was unnerved when the axe in the man's hand caught on a board, flipped up, and clunked back. She hurried out to her sled, looked toward where she thought the road might be, and saw in the last of the moonlight fading behind the mountains, nothing but smooth snow around her single labored track.

As she set up her tripod and camera, Nellie calculated how much light she might need and how long an exposure should be. Chicago newspapers printed ghastly news and pictures all the time. They might pay well for a photo of a man's face covered with ice. Already, it seemed less thick. She would have to hurry to finish before the ice melted. Scotto couldn't call this sentimental.

Carefully, so as not to disturb the ice mask, Nellie sat the man at a slight angle, leaning against a couch that had seen better days. She focused on his face and shoulders in the dusky light of the candle. The dog paced to the stove and back again, slurped from the water dish, and then sat down by the man as if protecting him. He licked the man's face once.

"Don't do that, Dog! Come here, boy." She clicked her tongue and he crept toward Nellie, as if he understood the man no longer could take care of him. To confirm that impression, she gave him the remainder of the sandwich.

Once the camera was ready, Nellie piled torn paper, kindling, and a couple pieces of wood from the stack by the fireplace onto the grate. She struck a match on one of several loose stones. It flared and died. She tried another and the paper caught briefly. She sat back on her heels. This wasn't working and she needed the warmth as well as the light. Her shivering didn't help—from cold, she told herself, not nerves. With trembling fingers, she tried again. Only two matches left. Again the paper caught, and this time a plume crept toward the kindling, which began to crackle.

Nellie warmed her hands while she waited for the light in the room to brighten, hoping the body was far enough from the flame to retain its mask and pose. Flames reflected off something metal at his waist. She found a belt buckle—a large tarnished silver clasp bumpy to her fingertips—and pushed it down so no light glimmered. She slid in her film holder, removed the dark slide, opened the shutter, and waited. Five minutes, ten minutes, how long? The flickering light from the fire, over time, would appear to be steady light on the face. At the same time she noticed the ice melting, she heard a call from a distance. Quickly, she closed the shutter, pushed in the slide, took out the film, and wrapped it.

At the door, she thought she saw faint movement across the meadow, but the night had grown dark with only starlight on snow to illuminate it. "I'm here," she shouted. "In the cabin!" Then a light shone from the place where she had first stopped to take a photograph.

A few swear words preceded the next call. "Girl, are you all right? I can't get there without some goddamned snowshoes!"

"Mine broke. I'm all right." She ran back inside to move her camera and tripod away from its position by the fire. Not certain why, she only knew she didn't want Rosy to know she had been photographing a dead man. The body had slumped sideways and the ice was gone. The dog was once again licking his face. "Stop. Leave him alone."

Back to the door she went. "I'm all right. There's a dead man here." A breeze was beginning to sweep the snow along the surface of the meadow.

The words ". . . back . . . morn . . ." drifted to her. The light disappeared and she closed the door.

Alone again, Nellie felt abandoned and cold. At least Rosy hadn't frozen to death. If only the body hadn't been there in the room, she might have been able to feel a little comfortable. She looked around for something to cover the body or at least his head and shoulders. There was little furniture, except the couch, the overturned table, and a willow rocking chair near the fireplace. A makeshift cupboard perpendicular to the kitchen sideboard held several cans of food as well as empty Mason jars lining the lower shelves, as if they had once held preserved fruits, or perhaps moonshine, like Rosy's. Along the side of the room, two bunks flanked a door. One bunk's rope underpinnings were rotted through, but the other one contained blankets and a pillow, neatly arranged. Nellie spied something under the bed that reflected firelight. When she investigated, she saw it was nothing but a broken toy, small wooden wheels on a metal axle.

Nellie pulled the blanket off the bunk, but saw only a stained and ruptured pallet under it. Now that she was warmer from the fire, weariness dragged on her. All the slogging in snow, pulling her sled, setting up and taking down her equipment, and the shock of almost falling on a dead man threatened to knock her out. She would need the blanket herself. She wanted to lie down, but shuddered over sleeping next to the body. The dog nosed around the cupboard. With her bottle and candle, she searched the shelves and found a can opener, selected a can of kidney beans from the shelf, opened it, and poured the contents, lumpy with frozen pieces, into a dish for the dog. He gulped it down in ten seconds. She righted the table and picked up the glass pieces, stacking them on the counter, found the lower end of the lantern, still intact with kerosene in it, and pumped more water for the dog and took some herself, drinking long and deep, even though it tasted rusty.

"Moonshine," she said, her eye on the empty jars. That was a good name for a black dog.

Nellie sat on the bed with her feet up. Morning was still hours away. What if the body thawed and woke up? An impossibility. Still, she found the axe and rested it on the blanket pulled around her shoulders. She would rest, not sleep. "Curl up with me," she said. The dog leaped up, crawled across her, and settled against the wall.

The silence of night was broken only by her own loud heartbeat. Then wood creaked and she grabbed the axe and sat up. She was alone with the dog. The candle had died, and the room was inky in its blackness. Deep quiet again reigned while she waited to hear something else. The dog slept as if drugged, so she relaxed. Her eyes felt scratchy; she closed them briefly.

A door rasped. A board squeaked. Nell opened her eyes and tried to see through the Stygian dark. Wind moaned down the fireplace flue. Or was it her dead man? Again, she grasped the axe and touched the dog, which didn't move.

"Who is it?" Her whispered question echoed like a shout. An answering silence roared in her ears. Stop it, she told herself. She had dozed off and only dreamed of sounds. Minutes, maybe hours later, she heard a groan—was it hers? A cold, faceless moon shone on ice in her dreams. She wrapped herself tighter and held the axe and the dog.

CHAPTER 3

If Rosy had known he'd end up at Last Chance Ranch with the snippy little photographer from Chicago, he would never have agreed to take her out into "back country," as she called it. Anyone who would pay one dollar each way had to be twice a fool, so he couldn't resist. He needed drink and gasoline.

Last Chance Ranch, when he first saw it years ago, was a tumbled-down wreck. The hammered plank door sagged from one hinge. Pieces of warped floor had been fed to the fireplace— a butt end lay in the hearth. The river rock structure was as solid as the cottonwoods along the river. Maybe more so. It was a fall day with cottonwood fluff swirling everywhere, giving a glimpse of the winter to come. His panning for gold days were at an end, but not by choice. He was broke, hungry, and needed shelter.

He repaired the front door with fingers like sausages trying to grip the screwdriver, so the door wouldn't fall in. After he slept in one of the two bunks along the side wall, he decided to stay awhile. The thrift shop in Ketchum yielded a rope to repair the bunk and he scrounged some lumber to brace the outhouse, a doorless shed that slanted with the wind, and mended the floor. The town wasn't quite on its last legs in those days. Over the lintel, carved letters on a pine board announced past and future: Last Chance. Everyone in Idaho knew a Last Chance mine. Rosy had had a few first chances, some good and bad chances, a second chance or two, which he mainly muffed. A last chance was as good as any. He'd take it.

The journey to the Independence Mine for work took some doing, but he managed. Rosy discovered he liked being around other miners; many of them had tried mining alone too, with a mule, a gold pan, a sourdough starter, and a gun. The world was changing, though. He hadn't gone to war, but the younger men did. The ones that lived brought back a knowledge of life and death and misery that he thought he would never have; they also looked to each other for friendship and company, something Rosy hadn't needed. He'd left home in Missouri at sixteen and never looked back to a drunken father and a mother who'd given her last love to a baby that died. The only person he ever missed was his younger sister. He heard from her about once a year, but only if he wrote first. He had decided he could manage alone and he did for years.

He allowed as how mining gave him a working man's dignity and friends. One or two of the other men bunked with him from time to time, until they could sort out their own ways: Tater Joe, who married a farmer's daughter and left for Pocatello; Jack Bee, who played his horn and set dynamite until an avalanche ended his working days; Stumpy Skinner, who made more money selling furs than mining.

Rosy had grown proud of his Last Chance, and when he made enough money, he found the owner—an eastern dude down on his luck—and bought the place for a song. At one time, life was good.

Between then and now was a different world. Some men were lucky and others weren't. The first pile he could count on one hand. The second, starting with him at the thumb, would need ten hands or more to keep track of, and two more just joined the stack.

Now, gnarled hands rested on the steering wheel and Rosy saw his blind eye in the front window. Here was this girl excited about the scenery and the snow and Idaho. He kept his snort to himself. All that landscape and two bits would buy you a shave and a haircut. That's it.

At least this Nell Burns had given him a good laugh when she stepped out into the snow. He needed one, the devil knew. By the time she returned, he had finished off his last jar of moonshine. Only her dollars would satisfy his craving.

"Can we go back out tonight? The moon isn't quite full, but I'll get plenty of light anyway."

"Nope. It's gonna snow and I got things to do."

When Nell didn't answer, Rosy played a silence game. Her smile had disappeared and she looked out the window.

"Tell you what. If it clears tomorrow or the next day, I'll take you out again and you can take all the pictures you want," he said, "even in the dark." He shifted gears. He could feel her smile at him. "But I need the money now. Got to get gasoline."

Maybe a pretty lady would change his luck, just like before.

"Are you all right, Mr. Kipling?"

Rosy tried to grin, but it didn't work. " 'Course I'm all right. Get in and let's go on your fool's trip. I ain't got all night."

Nell Burns stopped in the middle of loading her gear in the boot. "But I told you. I need several hours to do what I want. You said—"

"I know what I said. Things come up the last day or two. You think a man don't have a life of his own and can just stand around waiting on a city girl to freeze her—hands off?" Rosy motioned to Nell Burns to finish loading. He stomped around to the driver's side, letting her climb in on her own. If she wanted to act like a man, dressed in pants, she could be treated like one.

"I'm taking you, ain't I?" He slipped his hand under the seat to be sure his bottle was still there. Not as good as his own stuff, but it would do.

Rosy did not want to see Last Chance Ranch again, so he stopped short of it, but still in the same general area. There were trees and snow and already the moon lit the top of the back mountains as it was rising. It was light as a cloudy day. That would make his passenger happy, he figured. Not seeing Last Chance Ranch would make him, if not happy, at least content to sit for several hours. He had his bottle and a sheepskin robe to keep him warm and drunk. He needed a rest.

The moon came up. Rosy drank, trying not to remember old friends and enemies and life and death. He'd had his fill of those subjects. He decided to see what the girl was doing. Maybe she was a witch. He didn't want her exploring too close to the ranch. All it did was represent trouble and tragedy and unfinished business. He walked around through trees where the snow wasn't so deep. He could see her camera in the moonlight and her putting a cover over her head, just like a real photographer. Maybe she did know what she was doing. He shivered and trudged back to the auto. There he covered back up, took several long swigs. As tired in body and mind as he'd ever been, he slept.

When he woke up, the moon was down. Still no girl. Rosy climbed out, stumbled on the robe, and fell down. "Goddamnit." Where was she? He waded out in the field, this time in her trough. The snow was deep.

"Hey! Girl! Where in hell are you?" He couldn't see her, but he did have a light with him and he waved it around. It was too small to give light beyond the first few feet or so. "Hey!"

". . . at the cabin . . . ," the girl's voice called. A breeze was picking up and he lost most of the words. "Snow . . . broke."

Rosy began to wade toward the house. He sank to his knee. Damned snow. He called out again. He couldn't get there on her trail without snowshoes.

". . . all right." Then nothing for a second or two. ". . . here."

Rosy debated. If he waded out there, he'd probably kill himself with the effort. Not that he cared, but she'd still be stuck. What a hell of a fix, and he was so addled he could hardly think straight. "Stay there," he shouted. "I'll go get shoes and come back in the morning. Stay warm!"

But first things first.

The trail from the north didn't need snowshoes. Rosy drove his auto up around the corner. He could find his way in the dark, he'd traveled the route so often, but he carried his light anyway. His feet knew where to tread; it was his head that had the trouble.

On the river side of the cabin, Rosy stopped. No candle or firelight showed through the windows. Was the girl asleep? Passed out from fright? It was only then Rosy remembered the dog, Lily's dog. Lily would not have been afraid, especially with a dog by her side. She never was afraid, even in the worst of times. He couldn't say the same for himself.

Rosy eased up the steps and opened the back door by the kitchen to peer in. No sound. No light. He sat on the top step and pulled off his boots. His grunt, the sound of leather against sock, broke the quiet. He waited. Then he stood up, flashed his light inside, and turned it off. His old friend, stone dead, lay propped by the couch, not where Rosy last saw him. The girl slept as if dead in one of the bunks. The dog beside her snuffled but didn't move.

His heart tripping like a hammer, Rosy stepped over to the body. No friend, no enemy in there now. He managed to sling the dead weight—no lie there—up and over his shoulder. This time, the belt buckle cut into his neck and he had to shift the body, nearly falling over. Where was the dog? Maybe the girl hadn't noticed the dead man.

"Who is it?"

The girl's whispered question startled Rosy. He almost dropped his burden. Again he waited, afraid he'd burp or sneeze or breathe too loud. He closed his eyes. It didn't matter; it was black inside his head and out. The bed rustled and all was quiet again.

One slow step after another, Rosy crept back to the door. He groaned when he remembered his boots were waiting. What in hell was he going to do with the body? He gently pulled the door shut and dumped his burden in the snow. By the time he had his boots on, he had an idea. The dark of night held a different quality, not yet light, but anticipating it. He would have to hurry.

CHAPTER 4

Boots pounding on the porch and Rosy's gravelly voice wakened Nell. Moonshine didn't move a whisker until she threw off the blanket and sat up.

"You in there, girl?" Light shone through the side window and filled the cabin when Rosy pushed the door.

"Here I am." She never thought she'd be glad to see the grumpy old miner, but his split face looked sweet to her. Her head ached, as if it had been pounded on during the night. She slipped the axe under the pillow.

"If you ain't a carcass of trouble."

Another man followed Rosy into the room. His tall silhouette filled the doorway, a cowboy hat shading his face, and he moved with long, springy strides. "We're pleased you are all right. Goldie Bock worried, but when Rosy said you were at the Last Chance, I knew you would survive the night." Each word was carefully enunciated, different from any of the accents she'd heard in Chicago. He glanced toward the fireplace. "You found matches. That's good. The night turned cold. Rosy used a bottle of whiskey to unfreeze his joints." He laughed, a pleasant, friendly sound.

"Moonshine here provided most of the warmth—"

She stopped, remembering the dead man, and turned to the fireplace and the couch. "What—?" She walked around the couch while the two men watched. The body was gone. Did she dream him? No, of course not. Moonshine tilted his head, looked at her, and looked at the men.

"Lose something?" Rosy stomped over to the sink, pumped some water out, and touched the stovetop with a wet finger. "Any food left in here?" He poked through the cans on the shelf. "Liquor's all gone." He fondled the jars.

Could someone have come in during the night and taken the body away? Was he not really dead and he'd walked out on his own? She knew he had been dead. No live person had an ice mask closing off his nose and eyes. When she had pulled and then propped him up, he'd been dead, dead, dead.

The old miner's activities gave Nellie a moment to push down her confusion. Rosy already thought she was stupid. The other man might think she dreamed everything. She hadn't. But where was the body?

"I'm Nellie Burns." She held out her hand. He didn't know what to do with it, then, belatedly, shook it with a warm, firm grip.

"Rosy said this place was abandoned, but here's this dog."

"This here is what we got for a sheriff in the county, Charlie Azgo. One of them Basques I was telling you about and nobody can't say his last name. Goldie insisted he come with me."

The sheriff removed his hat to reveal dark eyes, olive skin, a Roman-type nose, long earlobes, and black hair down his back. With many small wrinkles, his face looked older than his robust frame, as if he'd spent his life looking into the sun. Nell wondered if he had been a sheepherder. An officer of the law laughing at someone drinking. Prohibition indeed was no problem in Idaho.

"I didn't get back to you, Rosy, because the strap on my snowshoe broke and the moon was going down. I decided to hike here instead, and found Moonshine—"

"Alone?" the sheriff asked.

"That's what I can't understand." She sat on the couch. How

much to tell? But this was the sheriff. "There was a tapping at the window—"

"The ghost," Rosy said, as if he knew one. He tromped to the fireplace. "Where'd it go? Up the chimney?" He cackled at his joke. "Musta dreamed it."

"I didn't dream it. There was a man here." Nell glanced toward the door she hadn't opened. The sheriff followed her glance and crossed to open it. A stairway led to the second floor. He shouted, "Hey, up there!"

Moonshine ran to the door and up the stairs, barking. He put up the kind of racket Nell would have expected when she fell into the room, or, later, if someone had come and taken the body away. Then she remembered her dreams. Both men followed the dog, making enough noise to scare anyone up there. No one could have crossed the front porch without making the same kind of noise as when Rosy and Charlie came in, waking her and the dog. Their boots pounded back and forth, causing dust to sift down from the ceiling. Nell walked to the stairway and looked up. She stepped back to the kitchen area and saw a door to the outside.

Boots clomped down the stairs. "Nothing up there," Rosy proclaimed. The dog padded after them and raced out the front door.

"No one there now," Sheriff Azgo said, "but someone has been, smoking cigarettes."

The implications of what he said made Nell's skin crawl. A dead man in the living room. A live one upstairs, waiting. And all the while, she had been below, taking a photo, watering and feeding the dog, sleeping in the bed. Why hadn't Moonshine made a ruckus?

"There was a man here, Sheriff. But he's gone now. I don't understand." To cover her confusion, she picked up her jacket and took out her own cigarettes. The sheriff watched while she lit one, his forehead creasing.

Rosy snorted. "You can't understand ghosts, now can you?"

"Those were your cigarettes, Miss Burns?" the sheriff asked.

"Mine?" She realized what she had done and snuffed the cigarette out on the rocks near the fireplace. "No. I didn't even look for stairs. I forgot this place had two stories. I was too tired to explore anything last night. Sheriff—" she said, and then Moonshine came back into the cabin carrying a sock. He brought it to her and dropped it at her foot with a clunk. She picked it up and realized there was a rock almost the size of a baseball tied in the toe. A dog toy. "No, Moonie, I can't play now." She turned back to the sheriff. "I came to the house because I thought I saw someone tapping on the window. It turned out to be this dog. But there was a man on the floor. Frozen to death."

Rosy and the sheriff looked at each other. She half expected them to make the crazy sign.

"You don't believe me." She walked over to her camera. "I have a photograph."

"If there was a man, where did he go?" The sheriff didn't ask rudely, but disbelief colored his words and the corner of his mouth twitched.

Rosy laughed. "Let's get outta here," he said. "I gotta get back to town. There's another storm comin' in. I can smell it. Where's that snowshoe? I'll fix it good enough to get you to the road." He headed out to her sled, mumbling about women smoking, seeing ghosts, and the world coming to an end.

"I'll need to pack up my gear," Nell said. More than one man had laughed at her in the past few years. Besides, she did have a photograph to prove it. A man who froze, then thawed and walked out, but only after smoking cigarettes in the upstairs of an abandoned house. Or maybe he smoked the cigarettes first and then froze to death.

The sheriff picked up her tripod and pack after Nell filled it with her camera and film case. "Be very careful," she warned. "That's my livelihood in there." He used two hands to convey the pack to the sled and watched while she secured it. By then, Rosy had attached a new strap to the snowshoe and waited to help her into it. The sheriff's manners were rubbing off on him.

"C'mon, c'mon." No, not manners. Rosy was in a hurry.

So was she, but she decided she wanted to check the house again. Moonshine stood in the doorway. "Wait. I'll be right back. I left . . . my cigarettes." The sheriff gave her an indecipherable look.

Inside, Nell glanced around. There was still no body. She walked to the door between the beds and opened it. The hinges worked without a sound. The rumpled bed reminded her of how neat it had been when she arrived, so she smoothed out the blanket, felt the axe under the pillow, but left it there. The dog picked up the toy and brought it over. "Not now." She grabbed at it and he pranced backwards and dropped it, waiting for her to throw it. She stuffed it in her jacket pocket, then realized she had crushed her cigarettes. Maybe that was why the sheriff looked at her so strangely. He probably saw her replace the pack. Damn.

"Get a move on!"

Nell rolled her eyes and left the cabin. With her snowshoes fastened, she followed behind Rosy and the sheriff, the latter with the sled tied to his waist. Her awkward bowlegged walk of the night before had improved, although she still couldn't move as rapidly as the two men. The dog brought up the rear.

A second night of photographing was out of the question. Rosy certainly wasn't in the mood for another evening's foray, and Nell felt as weary as she'd ever been. Flakes drifted down as they snowshoed back toward the road in the trampled path. Gray clouds painted the scene in gloom, nothing like the magical black and brilliant white of the night.

While she walked, the mechanics of developing negatives in a makeshift darkroom took over her thoughts. The bathroom at the boarding house should be dark enough. She hoped the water came from a well and not the hot springs piped into town from the source at Warm Springs where a spa stood. The minerals in the water might be medicinal and good for ailments, but it wouldn't be good for photography. The thought of a good long soak in hot springs appealed to her. Muscles she never knew existed ached along her legs and in her buttocks, although pulling the sled hadn't seemed so difficult the night before.

Moonshine ran back and forth between the two men and Nell, an ever-widening space. The weight of the rock-sock in her pocket reminded her it was there. She threw it for Moonie to retrieve. He barked and grinned at her, galumphed through the snow, retrieved the toy, and brought it to her to throw again. "Good boy!" She tried to pull it from his mouth. He pulled back. "Drop it!" This he promptly did. Who had trained him so well? This time, as she picked up the toy, she noticed a smear of black and brown on the end, then tried to look in the dog's mouth to see if the rock had scraped the animal.

"Goddamn it, will you move along, girl?"

"Coming." Nell stuck the toy in her pocket again. Snow was falling thicker and faster. The two men ahead of her looked hazier and hazier. The wind picked up. She turned for a silent goodbye. Indeed, Last Chance Ranch was an abandoned place, and behind the curtain of snow, it looked more and more like a ghostly image floating in the distance.

With her next visit, she would come with food, a lantern, matches. She wished she could circle the house and see what tracks there were in the back. A brave thought after her dismaying night. With another snowfall, any trace of activity might be gone. But something would be there. Ghosts did not exist.

Somehow that body was taken away, even if neither she nor the dog had seen what did it. *Who,* she meant. Seen *who* did it.

When Nellie reached her room, she took the sock out of her pocket and placed it on her dresser. Then she carefully unpacked her camera, film case, and the three wrapped film holders. These were precious. Two of the sheets of film might hold her future, and the third—it could affect her future too. Art and money.

In the kitchen, she approached Mrs. Bock. "Will it be all right to develop my film in the bathroom?" Goldie was her first name, Nell remembered. She wondered where the name had come from as there was nothing gold about her landlady. It sounded more like a dance hall name. Surely, Mrs. Bock had never been one of those women. She was too motherly.

And, as usual, she was baking. She slapped dough back and forth in her hands and then pounded it on the countertop. "What does that mean?"

"I'll be setting up some trays with chemicals in them and I'll need complete darkness, so I'll have to close off the door." When Mrs. Bock didn't answer, she hurried on. "I thought of my room, but I need water and the windows are too difficult to make light-tight."

"Oh, I don't mind if you use the bathroom, but the men didn't work today, so you can't close it off now. And old Henry drinks 'bout a gallon of coffee ever' afternoon. He'll be needing the facilities." Slap, punch. "Can you wait 'til ever'body's in bed?"

Nellie's shoulders sagged. "That will be fine. Thank you."

"Miss Burns, maybe you could do an errand for me while you're awaiting?" She didn't wait for Nell's answer. "Run over to the store and pick up a haunch of mutton? I'm stewing it for dinner tonight, and I didn't get away before I had to begin the rosemary and garlic bread here." After another slap, Mrs. Bock looked up. "You had me worried, Miss Burns. An easterner like you oughtn't to be out in snow at night. Suppose you froze to death!"

The market smelled of blood and fat and Nellie wasn't sure how long she'd last before she threw up her lunch. She tried breathing through her mouth and holding her handkerchief to her nose. "I'm here to pick up the mutton for Mrs. Bock," she told an aproned man behind the high counter. Dark spatters on his soiled apron reminded her of the sock on her dresser.

"You're that girl staying there," the man said. "Picture-taker, I heard. What kind of pictures do you take?"

"I take portraits, mostly, but here, I'm taking scenic photos." In her own ears, she sounded self-conscious and amateur.

"Do you now?" He took a huge piece of meat out of the case and began wrapping it in white paper. "The wife's been after me to get a picture took. Says we need something for pros-ter-i—the kids to have. No time to waste driving down to Twin Falls. Could you do it here?"

The request surprised Nellie. Portraits were part of the past she'd left. On the other hand, maybe she could make some money to replenish her nest egg. "I might be able to."

The man hefted the wrapped haunch and Nell nearly dropped it, it was so much heavier than she expected. "I'd need the proper film and lights," she said, trying to balance the package and at the same time think how she might accommodate the butcher, "and a place and more customers so I could cover the cost—." This potential customer certainly wouldn't want to hear her business uncertainties.

"The train comes here three times a week, Miss. You could call down to Twin and see that what you need gets put on the train. And I bet I could rustle up some more pictures for you."

"Thank you." She meant it. This opened up new avenues.

"I'm Nell Burns from Chicago." She balanced the meat with one hand against her hip and stretched out the other, then realized his were covered with blood. He wiped them on his apron and enclosed her hand in two slabs of flesh.

"I'm just Bert the Butcher. You come 'round again about your order and I'll tell the station agent to put it with mine for delivery here." The warmth of his paws and his words made Nellie feel good all the way back to the boarding house. "Here's your haunch, Mrs. Bock. My heavens, it's heavy." The kitchen smelled of baking bread. She could sit there and sniff until dinnertime.

"The sheriff was here," Mrs. Bock said. "He wants to talk to you?" The question in her statement bespoke her curiosity. "Wanted to see your room, so I sent him up to wait, but he left not more'n two shakes ago. And the dog's been howling outside. You'll have to do something about that. Can't be disturbing my roomers."

Nell was appalled that Mrs. Bock would let anyone in her room. Then, Moonshine howled and snuffled at the door. "I'll take Moonie to my room. He'll be quiet there."

"I'm not having that animal traipsing through here with his dirty feet."

The floor was marked with as many footprints as usual, from the men's boots, from everyone traipsing in and out. "If I wipe them off, would that be all right? He won't wake anyone up if he has a place to be. I'm sure of it."

Mrs. Bock grumped a bit. "I'll think about it."

Before the landlady could grump anymore, Nell took a rag to the back porch, wiped Moonshine's paws clean, and he followed her upstairs. In the room, she folded the rug up in a corner by the bed, so the dog would have a place to sleep. He padded around, his toenails clicking, put his feet up on the dresser and sniffed, dropped down, turned in three circles on

47

the rug, and then lay down on the bare floor.

"Here, Moonie. I have your toy for you." Nell went back to the dresser. Her film case was there. The rock-sock was gone. First a body and now a dog toy. Was that why the sheriff left in a hurry?

CHAPTER 5

Nellie locked herself in the boarding house bathroom after everyone else had gone to bed. A single electric bulb over the mirror provided light for her tasks. Her first order of business was to develop negatives. The bathroom was sizable with claw-footed tub, pedestal sink, toilet, and space for a huge old bureau with drawers marked by room numbers, one for each of the eight bedrooms in the house. Her number was five. The top of the bureau was large enough to hold her trays, and she used a step stool to comfortably reach it.

The rag rug plugged the gap under the door. Her black cloth served as a curtain over the door frame so that no light leaked in at the edges. The bathroom had no windows. The film itself was flammable and its smoke poisonous. The usual procedure during developing was to have a bucket of sand ready in case of fire to douse any flames, which of course, would ruin the film, too. She intended to be careful. As she pounded small nails into the door frame to hold up the cloth, she was startled by a voice on the other side.

"What are you doing, Miss Burns?" A woman's voice was low and intense. It couldn't be Mrs. Bock.

"Did I wake you?" Nell asked back, keeping her own voice quiet. "Mrs. Bock said I could use the bathroom to develop negatives." It must be the boarder whose name Nell did not know. No answer from the other side. "Do you want me to stop? Do you need to use the facilities?"

"She didn't tell me." A whine colored the woman's voice.

Nell sighed and raised the hammer to pull out the nails. "I'll open the door. Then you can use the bathroom and I'll do this later."

"No. No, I wouldn't think of bothering you, especially if Mrs. Bock said you could use it. I'll find her and use her bathroom." Her footsteps moved down the hall.

Nell returned to her task. As she secured the black cloth at four corners, she wondered about the woman roomer. What did she do all day?

In order to work in absolute darkness with sure hands, Nell readied all of her equipment. The three trays fit across the bureau top, one with developer solution, one with water to stop the development, and one with fixer. Her boss in Chicago would have laughed, but she did a dry run with a blank piece of paper first. With her eyes closed, she placed the paper in the developer tray and tilted it up and down for half a minute, counting out the seconds aloud, then letting it sit quietly with only a few agitations for another half-minute. With film, she would have to repeat this process for eight minutes. From there she picked up the paper—that was the tricky part, picking it up by edges in the dark—and placed it in the plain water in the middle, again with constant tilting, then moving the paper to the fixer tray. After four minutes in that tray, she opened her eyes. Using the real film, she could turn on the light after two minutes, and decide when to move the film back to the water. She was ready.

Developing three negatives took much longer than Nell expected, and by the time she was ready to turn on the light for the last time, she was tired, her mouth was dry from counting, and her back ached. The late hour, around midnight, and the altitude probably contributed to her weariness. And likely her fear that the negatives would not develop properly. Whether she had failed or not, though, she intended to return to Last Chance Ranch.

One by one, she held each negative up to the light. First, the wheatgrass and aspen trees. The picture in the negative was a dark gray, the opposite of what it would be in a print. She could make out the white lines of grass and tree bones. Not quite the definition she wanted, and she would have to work with the snow surface to make it brighter than it appeared.

The second negative showed a black circle for the moon, with too much light on the cabin and meadow. In the print, they would be too dark. Only the river rock on the fireplace would appear whitened by the moonlight in a print. And there were arcing streaks that almost looked like scratches on the film. Failure, or almost failure.

With trepidation, she picked up the third negative. If the man had indeed been a figment of her imagination, the celluloid strip would show only a couch. Then she would know she was out of her mind, as Rosy had implied.

No, the firelight did catch a figure.

The door to the bathroom rattled and a hand pounded. "Who the hell's in there? I been waiting hours! Let me in!"

Startled, Nell dropped the negative, still wet, on the floor. "Just a minute!"

Afraid it was ruined, she picked it up by the sides and looked once again. How detailed the person was, she could not see, but the strip of celluloid had been dry enough that no harm seemed to have been done. "I'll open the door as soon as I can." No chance to print that night.

Working backwards, Nell poured her trays down the toilet and flushed, responding politely to the continued hammering on the door, then pulled out her drawer to store the trays and chemicals. A gun lay on top of linens. She realized she had the wrong one and closed it again. Indeed it was drawer six. She opened her own drawer and finished stowing things away. Odd place for a weapon. Maybe it was a toy gun. She pulled out the nails on the cloth, scooted the rug back into position, and swung the door wide. "Here you are."

No one stood there. Whoever it was, probably a miner judging by his various blasphemies, had gone. Nell gathered up her cloth and the negatives and headed for her room. A door opened and a shadow fell across the carpeted hallway. From instinct, she hid the negatives behind the cloth, then looked toward the door across from her own. A tall woman with a round face and rosebud mouth, like a kewpie doll at a carnival, stared at her. No words, only the stare. Then the door shut.

Back in her bedroom, Nell studied her moon negatives again. Maybe the photos weren't as bad as she first thought, but her dreams of fame and fortune would certainly have to wait. Like George Eliot and George Sand, she considered adopting a man's name. Times were better for Nell than they were for those women writers in the 1800s, but they hadn't improved all that much. No major newspaper would consider her for a job as a photojournalist. Could she succeed as an artist?

The third negative was the best. It must have had to do with her timing and the ability to wait. She studied what the film had captured. The ice mask had melted more than she supposed; the man's features were almost discernible. She had more of his body in the negative than she remembered, including most of his torso and his arms and one hand. His hair was a tangled mess, as long as the sheriff's had been, but not as kempt, and much lighter in color, perhaps a light brown. He might be identifiable from a print.

The next morning, sunlight streamed through the window into her room. Today, she could scout again. At breakfast, she broached the subject with her landlady. "Is there a taxi service?

I want to go north again and I don't want to use Rosy."

"Now what do you want to do that for? Haven't you caught enough trouble yet?" She turned from the stove with spatula in hand, a pancake on it.

Moonshine sat by Nell's chair. Mrs. Bock wouldn't let Nell keep the dog in at night, so he'd been tied again to the back porch, looking miserable. When he howled again after the household was up, the landlady relented and permitted the dog into the kitchen, but only so long as Nell was there, too.

"I want to take more photos. Rosy gripes so much, I can't work. Late afternoon or early morning is best, and he's either drunk or not around." She left out that she wanted to return to Last Chance Ranch. The memory of the coyotes howling was daunting, but she wanted to prove that she could be as brave and smart as a man. Someone moved that body and she wanted to find out who and why.

"Can you drive?"

"Not well," Nell said, deciding a half-lie was better than a whole one. Hardly anyone drove in Chicago. Taxis or trolleys were always available.

Mrs. Bock plunked the pancake on Nell's plate. "Mrs. Smith has a car. She doesn't use it most days. Maybe she'd let you borrow it if you put gasoline in it."

"Who is Mrs. Smith?"

"You know, Gladys Smith. Room 6, across from yours."

Drawer six was the one with the gun in it, the gun Nell had seen lying on top of a black silk something. She had forgotten about it.

"Oh, I didn't know her name. Did she wake you to use your bathroom last night? I'm sorry I caused inconvenience for the other roomers."

"Wake me? No one woke me." Another pancake plunked down. "Now eat up. I'll ring her and see if you can use it. She usually takes a ride with young Robbie to the mining office and don't get back 'til long after supper. It's no wonder she's such a skinny thing." Mrs. Bock studied Nell. "Now you, you're nice and healthy looking."

Nell immediately dropped her fork. "Fat" and "healthy looking" were probably synonymous in Mrs. Bock's opinion. Next time, no butter on her pancakes. On the other hand, she would need lots of energy to tromp around again on snowshoes. Maybe she could drive. It didn't look that hard.

"Tell you what, Miss Burns. I'll ask Henry to drive you if Mrs. Smith will lend her car."

What was her choice? "Thank you." Henry was the old-timer who liked to talk.

Moonshine filled the foot well by Nellie's legs in the roadster owned by Mrs. Smith, and rested his head on her lap.

"Now, in the old days, these roads was filled with ore trucks and horses from dawn 'til dusk," Henry said, "traveling to and from the mines, pulling lead and silver out and bringing supplies back up. Men, why there was so many men, you couldn't count 'em. Not like these days. Puny lot compared to the big hulks back then. 'Course not much work was done then in the winters—too much snow closed the roads." They passed a Model-T parked alongside the road. "A few die-hards come up, camp out. Go out on boards—skiing, they call it—and hunt or fish." He shook his head. "Crazy is what I call it."

Nellie made appropriate noises. Most of Henry's talk was interesting, but she was trying to concentrate on the scenery. Animal photos were out of the question; it took much too long to set up her field camera. The Eastman Kodak cameras weren't suitable either. The negatives were too small. If she could only earn enough money to buy modern equipment, she'd make her way so much better.

Mrs. Smith's automobile was fairly new, so she was obviously making money at whatever she did at the mine offices. "Now take this here Willis-Knight," Henry said, rolling the name out. "It's new-fangled and always something wrong with it. Those old Model-Ts were the thing. That's what I learned to drive on. Lot better than a horse, I swear, but then a horse could go most anywhere and cars can only go on these damn roads. That's why you need snowshoes and boards these days." His voice vibrated and jumped as the car jounced around on the many ruts. Nell hung onto the door handle. Moonie lifted his head.

"I'm surprised that no one has claimed this dog," Nell said, hoping to turn the comparisons to something else. "He's such a lovely animal. What did you call it?"

"Labrador Retriever. Best hunting dog there is. And loyal? Can't get no better dog than a black Labrador." He turned his grizzled face in her direction. "Looks like you been adopted, don't it?" Envy tinged his words, but his kindly face with its gap-toothed smile and soft blue eyes seemed to approve. "Rosy don't want it, not since . . ."

"Rosy? It's Rosy's dog? Why didn't he say something?"

"Dog likes wimmen." Henry almost leered. "Rosy, well, he can't take care of a dog. Still carts him around some days, though."

Moonie looked from Henry to Nell and again laid his head on Nell's knee.

"This is where I want to stop, please, Henry." The pile of snow on the roof of the old ranch house glistened in the distance. Because the air was cold, nothing had melted. Last night's additional brushing of snow rested lightly on fir branches and bare aspen limbs alike. Nell was struck by the purity of the winter scenes and the crystal sharpness of the days in central Idaho.

The dog climbed out, then Nell, and she retrieved her equipment and sled from the boot. All the while, Henry hovered. "What's that?" He pointed to her field camera. "Looks like a box."

Anxious to begin scouting, Nell briefly explained how the hidden latches worked and then showed him when he persisted. The doors of the "box" opened and revealed her Premo camera, polished wood and bright brass fittings, like a fancy piece of furniture. She didn't take time to show how the bellows slid on rails or how the shutter opened or how the film holders slid in and out. Fully opened, it was the size of a large breadbox.

"I'll be back just like we talked," Henry said. He had openly disapproved of leaving her for the rest of the day and returning at sunset. "You'll be right here?"

Nell nodded and looked around for a landmark. "Right here by this broken fence post."

Henry waited while she donned her snowshoes and tied her sled to her waist.

"Bye, Henry. Thank you!"

Nell moved off in her snowshoes, feeling like a maimed baby elephant with her extra clothes on top to keep her warm. The automobile putt-putted in a U-turn, smelly smoke puffing from its exhaust. *Beep, beep.* He had been looking for an excuse to honk the horn, such a silly high-pitched sound. Nell waved her hand without looking back. Today she had walking sticks with her, which helped with her balance, a Jack Lane contribution.

At Last Chance Ranch, everything looked different. From the outside, the square-cut log house appeared trim, waiting for its family to return and light a fire. The trough she and the others had made with their snowshoes and her sled showed up as an indentation in the new fall. Under the mid-morning sun, a photo of the cabin would look like a stack of pancakes plunked on a white plate. By late afternoon, though, light and shadows might create an artistic photo. She looked at angles and tramped back and forth a bit, then removed her snowshoes. Photos were secondary today anyway. She wanted to solve the mystery first. She stepped through the doorway. The dog hung back until Nell pushed the door forward.

Inside, Nell could hardly believe she had spent a night there with a dead man on the floor. Besides her own neatening of the bed, it appeared the place had been swept out and cleaned up. Who had been there? No additional tracks marked another's presence. Maybe the night and candlelight had made it feel more sinister and dirty than it had been. Moonshine rediscovered his dish and licked at it, scraping it along the floor, making a racket.

"Stop, Moonie. I'll open another can for you." She selected more beans and then noticed the earlier can still sat in the sink. If anyone had cleaned up, surely he would have tidied the can away. The house was the same—abandoned. The raw smell, whatever it had been, was replaced by the burned wood odor in the fireplace. The dog's water dish was in the corner; Nell filled it.

First, she inspected the floor near the door where she had fallen in on the dead man. There were dark spots, but they could have been anything—oil, spilled jam, dog stains. The scrape in the dust where she'd pulled him around to prop him against the couch remained. She opened the door between the bunks to the stairs leading up. Moonie leaped ahead, barking. This was just an ordinary abandoned house with ordinary doors and stairs. Children had lived here and probably laughed and cried and called and played and dreamed. Nell ceased tiptoeing when she realized that was what she'd been doing. The stairs opened into a large room with a door at one end. The room contained a full bed, empty of bedding, with rusted springs tilted half onto the floor between bedposts. A stuffed chair sat by the window and in front of it; half a dozen cigarettes were crushed out on the floor. She moved one with her toe, saw a dark mark, and let them lay. The sheriff might be back for them.

Nell strode to the other door, clunking in her boots on the wood just as the men had the morning before, and looked through. A bunk bed, with a faded teddy bear–patterned blanket spread across the lower bunk, pressed forlornly against the opposite wall. Curtains printed with the same pattern hung limp at the window. Tears gathered behind her eyes, stinging. Once, this house had been a happy place. Tragedy and death had shoved laughter out. Goosebumps crept up her backbone. "Someone's walking on your grave," her mother would have said. She closed the door, sorry to have disturbed the heavy atmosphere in the room.

Back at the upstairs window, she sat and looked out. Several birds flitted from tree to tree, magpies again. Their blue and black feathers, outlined by white, seemed cheery, and her mood lifted. At first, the short snowfield in back appeared empty, dropping gradually down to the Big Wood River. Light shone off the ripples and gleamed on ice at the edges where the water froze in plates. Another scene to photograph when the sun dropped lower. The field was empty, but across it, just as in front, a shallow trough marked a path. She stood and looked in the direction the trough led and could see perhaps a quarter mile up the river.

"Let's go look, Moonie." The dog had been sniffing around the edges of the chair, at the springs on the bed, at the bureau against the wall. He pushed at one of the drawers and made a funny sound.

Arp. He waited. Arp, arp.

"All right, let's see what you've found." The top drawer groaned open when she pulled. Inside were small leather pouches, the kind that were supposed to hold gold nuggets, if the moving picture shows could be believed. She picked up one.

Empty. All the others were empty, too. She turned one inside out and flecks of dirt dropped out. The bags were soft and well-used as if many hands had rubbed them, and they smelled of leather and—what?—something metallic, like coins.

In a second drawer, Nell found more pouches, all empty.

At the third drawer, a smell drifted out before she had it fully open, as if this were Pandora's box. Lavender scent flooded into the room. Four or five sachets, delicately embroidered with purple flowers and pine branches, were stuffed with the herb and lined one end. Two more rested on top of a black Chinese silk robe, sewn with rich gold and silver threads into a figure. She lifted it out. "Oh, my!" It was the most elegant piece of clothing she'd ever seen. The robe was large enough for a man and could wrap almost twice around a woman. On the back the stitching revealed a twisted dragon with a long red tongue. Sachets filled each pocket in front.

Moonshine cried. There was no other word for it—a long, mournful sound, followed by a series of small yips, while he nosed the sachets. Yes, this was the drawer he had wanted her to open. The robe looked as if it might have belonged to the master of the house given the size, but more likely the mistress, given all the lavender in and around it. The wife who died.

Once again, silence wrapped around Nell and she felt like a trespasser. This was not her business, either. She should move outside and see what there was to see, so when she gave the photo to the sheriff, she could also tell him what else she knew about the place. Then she could be rid of the mystery and return to why she came to Idaho in the first place. She re-folded the silk and replaced it, shutting the drawer. Moonie arped twice, but stepped away, waiting for Nell to leave.

At the top of the stairs, Nell decided she couldn't leave the robe. This house was abandoned, and therefore, the robe was abandoned too. She clumped back, opened the drawer, took out the silk and several of the sachets, folded them all together, and carried her prize downstairs. Before she could regret what she was doing—stealing in all probability—she emptied her pack and placed the robe and lavender in the bottom. By now, she was used to the heavy scent, but suspected that it probably filled the downstairs too.

Before she left, she removed her extra coat and sweater. The sun had warmed the day and she wouldn't need them. Without her sled and because the snow had settled slightly, the walking was easier.

"Moonshine, why didn't you wake up?"

Moonie cocked his head, his ears flopping slightly at the ends, and looked around. He marked a spot by the house, spied a piece of kindling that was well-mouthed, ran to it, brought it back, and dropped it at her feet. Bark.

"No, I'm not going to throw it. I don't want you mucking up whatever tracks we can find."

He lay down, his tongue hanging out, and barked again, then put his head on his paws.

The trough led to the river. If Nell stepped in it, *she* could muck it up. She decided to move to the right edge of the snow-field and follow it from there. At the edge of the river the track ended. Now what? On the other side, she could see another indentation that continued toward a grove of aspens. If someone had crossed the river carrying a body, surely she could cross too. Then she spied a snow bridge. She hesitated, wondering whether to retrieve her camera. No. As long as the sun was still too high to take good photos, she would carry out her self-assigned task.

The snow bridge creaked as she hurried over. In the grove the track widened and became a large circle, as if someone had tramped around, looking for something. She rested against one of the trees and carefully studied the white ground. Just as she decided there was nothing to see and therefore nothing to report to the sheriff—let him destroy the track—the sun moved enough to cast a shadow from a mound of snow. Moonie stepped away from her leg, where he had been patiently waiting. He lifted his nose and sniffed and took two steps in the direction of the hump.

Nell weaved around several aspens. The dog nosed into the snow, then arped and pawed at the edge. When she, too, leaned over to scrape snow away where Moonie pawed, she saw the snow had been packed hard by a shovel or some other instrument. Other paws had been digging at one end, without much success. The coyotes! Was this what they had been yipping over?

With one of her walking sticks, Nell dug through the snow pack, then reached in with her hand. Her fingers touched cloth and under it, something hard and frozen. The body. She jerked her hand out. This was different than moving the ice-faced man in the dark of the cabin. Then, she had assumed the man had frozen to death, a grim ending, but not all that unusual in winter. Now, what she touched, buried out of sight of the cabin, the road, and men's eyes, was sinister. The grove was quiet. Shadows extended on the snow. Time to return to the cabin.

"Come on, Moonie. Let's leave." She re-packed the snow around the hole she'd dug, hoping the coyotes wouldn't find the body before the sheriff did. The dog began to cross the snow bridge, then stopped, barked, and returned to Nell. "Come on!" Nell tramped onto the narrow bridge. In the middle, she understood why Moonie had stopped. The snow groaned. She stood still. Now what? Go forward or go back? One more step. Ice under the snow rasped like a saw on wood. The bridge broke. Nell dropped and heavy blocks hit her back, her leg, and then her head as she fell sideways. Snow brushed against her face. The river swirled around her. *Water does rush,* she thought, before it covered her head.

CHAPTER 6

The river filled Nell's mouth as the current bumped her against the rocks. She choked and scrambled for air. She still clutched one walking stick and shoved it down to stop herself. Her head poked above the river and while she gasped for breath and labored to bring one snowshoe under her, she leaned on the stick to push up, discovering she had almost drowned in water hardly deeper than her knees! Her clothes were drenched, and clumps of ice splashed around her. The icy shock dizzied her. Moonie leaped up to grab her arm, almost tipping her over again.

"I'm all right. Stop!"

He barked and butted against her, pushing her toward the snowbank. Wading in snowshoes was easier than she expected. They and her stick lent stability in the rushing river. Getting out and up the bank was more difficult, but finally she succeeded. Already, her clothing felt stiff, and she shivered so much, she could hardly walk.

Sunshine still flooded the field, adding a touch of warmth to her hands when she removed her gloves. Not again, she thought. If she had to be rescued a second time, she'd give up and return to Chicago. Moonie huddled next to her and she warmed her hands on his belly, and then slogged back to the house. There, she stripped off her clothes, hung them on the rock fireplace, and wrapped the Chinese robe around herself—twice—as she had guessed. Still trembling and hardly able to function, Nell slumped down to the couch. What next? Moonie barked, and she jumped, startled. Wood. Paper. In a dazed slow motion, she crumpled paper, and stacked three pieces of wood. Then what? Oh, light it. Matches. In her pocket. Wet.

Tears gathered and spilled, warm on her cheek. "Need matches. Fire." So tired.

Moonshine nosed around his dish, pushing it out of sight under the counter. Was he thirsty again? Nell stood. She had to move. He had helped her; she could help him. The sideboard was plywood with linoleum tacked to the top. Underneath were shelves behind a dirty curtain of sorts. On one of the shelves was a jar of wood matches.

"Fire. Then water." The floor was so cold, her feet turned numb. Once the fire started, she pumped water for the dog and then lay down as close to the flames as was safe. Moonie trotted over, his toenails clicking, and sidled up to her back, making a fire-Nell-dog sandwich.

She couldn't sleep, but she did.

Beep, beep. Beeeeeeep. Beep.

Nell came to, shoved out of a dream where coyotes yipped and chased her, gnashing at her heels with jagged teeth, while she struggled on snowshoes. Moonie still slept.

She crawled to her feet and went to the door. On the porch, she saw that it was still afternoon, almost gone, but not quite. Henry had returned early. Waving her hand, she shouted, "I'm not ready yet." In the distance, she could see him wave, too. His bass voice carried better than hers, but all she could gather was that he would wait.

Back inside, Nell discovered her clothing was dry, except for her socks. She dug in her pack and found the extra pair Jack Lane had given her, and dressed in a hurry, adding the sweater and coat she'd left there earlier. The light was perfect. While she was waving and shouting, she'd noticed that pillars of cloud, textured gun-metal gray and white against the blue, had marched into the sky south of the house. This photo would be exactly what she wanted.

"Moonshine, wake up!" He lay as if dead. She shook him. He roused and licked her hand. How strange, but she couldn't worry about it now. "Come on. We're leaving."

The dog scrambled to his feet and watched her gather her camera and then followed her out the door. This time as Nell left, she felt as if she were leaving something she owned, and strangely, leaving something behind. She paused at the doorway and studied the room. What was it? This cabin had sheltered her twice and saved her life the second time.

Close to the location where she had taken the moon photo, Nell again stood her tripod and camera. A rosy glow suffused the meadow and the mountains behind. She waited a few minutes more. The light turned almost blue, chilling her again, but she knew the photo would be worth the wait. At the edge of her vision, she saw Henry watching from the road. From no men in her life except a boss who treated her like a cipher, she now had Rosy, Sheriff Azgo, Bert the Butcher, and Henry. All were curious about what she did. Once she printed the negative of the body, she could tell the sheriff the full story.

Nell set the aperture and shutter and exposed the film, pleased at how the light again changed the cabin. This time, it appeared sinister, although perhaps her guilt colored it. She turned to face the opposite direction and saw another scene—a sky filled with cloud patterns like fish scales and a single sunbeam pointed toward the Boulder Mountains. As quickly as she could, she turned her camera, re-focused, and slid in another film holder. The beam grew larger rather than disappearing and she thought this photo might be the *one*. Even if it was sentimental.

The sky changed yet again, but it was too late to try for

another. Something moved close to the river, catching her eye. She saw a dark figure, but couldn't tell if it were man or animal, the way it hunched over. Bears were in their winter caves, so if it were an animal it would have to be wolf or coyote or maybe a deer. "Moonie, do you see what I see?" She pointed the dog's nose toward it, but he wasn't interested. Soon, the scene was empty and growing dark. Henry no longer stood waiting for her.

Fifteen minutes it took to dismantle camera, tripod, and pack everything onto the sled. The effects of her earlier dunking had worn off, although she shivered from time to time, and the elation she felt over the newest photographs buoyed her spirits. Pulling the sled no longer seemed such a chore and she joined Henry in the car and they bumped back to town, this time with Nellie talking about the light, her photograph, the beauty of the area, how the snow sparkled, the silence in the trees, the difference between this scene and the noise, smell, and dankness out her window in Chicago. Henry could hardly tell a single story.

Her mood was as changeable as the clouds. In the boarding house, Nell climbed the stairs reluctantly, her pack too heavy, her boots still a little squishy and leaving marks. Mrs. Bock had scolded her for missing dinner and ordered her to return for something to eat. Nell wasn't hungry. She had to talk with Sheriff Azgo, tell him what she'd done. Her tale sounded like a flight of fancy. And she still didn't have a print to confirm the first part. The negative would have to do, for now.

When she passed the bathroom, she spied the tub. A hot bath—that was what she needed, not food. She turned on the spigots and scurried to her room to retrieve her exotic robe and some bath salts. Against all the rules, Nell filled the tub to within six inches of the top and let herself down until she was immersed to her neck. Her eyes drooped and a nap threatened when she heard a commotion.

"What are you doing?" A woman's voice shouted. "Stop, thief!"

Clunkety-clunk. Boots pounded down the stairway, along the hall. A door slammed. The boots ran out the back way.

"Oh, noooooo!" The wail died away, and then Moonie howled from the back porch.

Hands pounded on the bathroom door. "Miss Burns! Miss Burns! Better come out!" The voice belonged to Mrs. Bock.

Nell pulled the plug to let the water out. She didn't want her landlady to scold her again. She stepped carefully out onto the rug, glimpsed herself in the mirror, pink and "healthy looking," grabbed her new robe, smelling again the lavender from the sachets she hadn't yet removed from the pockets, unlocked the door, and poked her head out.

"What is it? What happened?"

Mrs. Smith, the woman with the kewpie-doll face, stood at Nellie's door, turning one way and then another. "I tried! Stop him!" She moaned like an old lady, which she was not.

Fear stabbed at Nellie. "Stop who? What happened?"

"Your door. It was open." Mrs. Smith spoke in jerky phrases. "That man. He had—things. The drawer." She faced the stairway. "He ran."

Nellie dashed out of the bathroom. The door to her room was open, and inside, everything was tumbled. The bedclothes had been pulled off, the mattress spilled to one side. Every drawer in the dresser was open with clothes and personal possessions hanging out or scattered on the floor.

Her pack! When Nellie saw the pack was still there, she was so relieved, she almost cried. Nothing else mattered. The camera was irreplaceable. Then she realized the pack, too, had been rifled and the contents perhaps dumped on the floor. She sidestepped the mess to assess the damage. Her camera was behind the pack, one box panel cracked, but the lens was intact.

The tripod she found on the floor next to the bed. The film holders from her day's work were beside the tripod, thankfully not broken, and the film case, although open, still had its contents intact.

"Who did this?" she demanded of Mrs. Bock and Mrs. Smith, both wringing their hands in the doorway. "Why did someone ruin my things?" Moonie howled again from the porch. Nell turned on her landlady. "If you'd let Moonie stay here, this wouldn't have happened!" Shouting wouldn't help. She tried to calm herself.

"Who was it?" Nell asked Mrs. Smith. Although upset, Nell's indignation was not as keen as if her camera had been truly broken and her film stolen.

"I don't know! His face. Bandanna around his nose." Mrs. Smith's mouth opened in O's before each phrase and her black bun of hair slid sideways each time she turned her head. Unlike the night the woman wanted in the bathroom, her voice was breathy and soprano with excitement. She pointed to the room, to the stairs, and then she mimicked someone limping, clutching her breast. "Carried things." The woman's long skirt was a remnant of pre-war fashions, and she nearly caught her foot in the hem. The hallway was dim with only one light at the top of the stairs, but Mrs. Smith's cheeks glowed red, as if she'd lavished rouge on them.

"But what—?" Nell scanned her room quickly. Was anything missing?

Only then did Mrs. Bock realize what Nell wore. "Where did you get that Chink robe?"

"I—I brought it—" Nell stumbled on her words and jammed her hands in the pockets, rubbing against the sachets.

"Figured as much. Ain't no one here would wear such as that, except those two Chinese in Hailey. Damn Chinamen. Them and their opium. Burned theirselves down near Hailey.

67

Most of 'em left where they ain't wanted." Mrs. Bock sniffed. "Smells like 'em." Then she took Mrs. Smith's elbow. "Come on, Gladys. I'll call the sheriff and warm up some dinner for you and Miss Burns."

Gladys Smith, too, looked at the robe, as if noticing it for the first time. The O of her mouth widened and drooped. Then the two women slipped down the stairs.

Nell was thankful they left, but surprised they didn't offer to help clean the mess. The venom in Mrs. Bock's voice shocked Nell. And what was missing? The first place she checked was beneath the paper lining in her underwear drawer. When she felt the little store of bills, all of her money, she breathed easier, although her camisoles and personal things had been pulled forward and most were on the floor.

One by one, Nell sorted her belongings, folded her clothes, replaced her belts and scarves, all the while thinking she knew what was gone, but couldn't place it. Then she did know. The negatives on the dresser top. Her moon shots. Who would want them? And the body. Then, she too wailed. Her proof! She dropped to her hands and knees and felt all along the floor, under the carpet. Nothing. She sprawled on the floor. Maybe they flipped under the bed. The sachets balled up against her stomach and she sat back on her feet. That was it! The extra sachets she had taken from the drawer at Last Chance Ranch were gone, too. The man must have been after them and maybe the robe.

How would anyone know she had both the robe and the sachets? She felt violated. And frightened. The sheriff and Rosy knew she had a photograph of the man she mentioned, but they hadn't believed her. Nausea threatened her. Maybe she did need some tea. She began to take off her robe but decided to wear it to keep it safe.

"Mrs. Bock," she called down the stairs. The landlady appeared at the bottom.

"Dinner's ready. You come down here and we'll help you clean up later." Her voice was back to normal, even though Nell still wore the robe.

"Would you send Moonie up, please? I won't leave my room unguarded again."

Without an argument, Mrs. Bock turned back to the kitchen. A few minutes later, Moonie bounded up the stairs, tongue hanging out, and yipping with pleasure. He rubbed against the robe, sniffed at the pockets, tramped out a circle in front of the dresser, and then lay down near the door.

"Good dog." Nell patted his head, then leaned over and hugged him. She closed the door and went down for tea and something to eat. She was famished. Just let the thief try again.

In the kitchen, Mrs. Smith and Mrs. Bock stopped talking when she arrived. Mrs. Smith sat at the table with one foot in a pan of water. Her landlady brought them pieces of warmed shepherd's pie. "I called the sheriff, not that he'll do much good."

"Thank you, Mrs. Smith, for trying to stop the man," Nell said. "Are you all right? Did you hurt your foot chasing him?" She moved to Mrs. Smith and touched her shoulder. It felt like a bird wing.

The woman shook her head and stirred her foot around. "Blisters."

"Did you see who it was?"

Her mouth full, Mrs. Smith shook her head and gestured with a fork, pointing toward the ceiling. Finally, she said, "Tall, he was. He knocked into me and I tried to grab him." She was an ordinary woman of thirty-five or so with gray streaks in her black hair, vertical lines framing her mouth—not laughter marks, Nell surmised—and eyebrows so faint, she carried a look of surprise.

"I hope he didn't hurt you. You were so brave to try and stop him."

Mrs. Smith nodded, ate rapidly, and shoved her plate away. She dried her foot off in a towel, poured the liquid into the sink, and donned a pointed toe shoe. She drummed the table with her fingers, groped in her pocket, found nothing, and stood. "I need sleep—long day tomorrow." The lines in her face deepened. Her cheeks no longer glowed.

Rosy stomped in the back door.

Mrs. Smith lifted her shoulders and smiled. "Why, Rosy. You missed all the excitement. I almost caught a thief!" She leaned toward him and raised her hand as if to touch him. "If you'd been here, you could have saved us."

Rosy snorted and sidestepped. "Wondered why that no-good hound was howlin'." He turned to Mrs. Bock. "Got anythin' for a feller to wet his whistle?" Then he glanced at Nell, a glance that turned into a stare. "What in the devil—?"

"I got coffee," Mrs. Bock interrupted.

Rosy rolled his eyes. Mrs. Smith hurried to pour him a cup of the black brew, which he took. She sat down again, as if she'd never complained about sleep and work.

"Lettin' thieves in now, are you? What got stole?" He continued to look at Nell.

Before she could frame an answer, more boots clumped on the back porch and everyone turned to Sheriff Azgo as he entered. "What is this? A town meeting?"

He took off his hat and nodded at Nellie. She noticed the hat was practically brand-new, not dusty and sweat-stained around the band, like Henry's. Watching the sheriff fuss with the brim gave Nell a minute to study his face. She was struck by the many planes, defined cheekbones, almost gaunt cheeks, high forehead. She added Basques to her mental list of photographic subjects.

Then he looked up and studied Nell, for too long in her opinion. Tit for tat, she supposed. "I'm glad you came, Sheriff. A thief has stolen some of my things. I want them back!" Nell only wanted her negatives back, and she was afraid they were gone for good. She wondered if the thief would know what he had or could do anything with them in this town. The sheriff's silence caused her a ripple of unease, and she sounded more defiant than she felt. "Do you want to see what he did to my room?"

Mrs. Smith, who had been so effusive with Rosy, said nothing.

"Yes," the sheriff said.

Nell turned to lead him upstairs. "Mrs. Smith tried to stop the thief, but could not." She glanced at the woman, who lowered her face. Her ears changed from the bone white of her face to blush pink, but the sheriff was already climbing the stairs. Nell hurried after him, afraid Moonshine would growl or maybe even snap at the man.

Although Nell had cleaned up part of the mess, the ransacked room still assaulted her sense of self and order. She hated to walk back into it and hovered near the door for a moment. Moonie stood when the sheriff entered, but made no sound.

"What are you missing?" the sheriff asked. He went to the window and opened it, looking up and down the street and then across at the schoolhouse, a brick monolith of a building.

A little late to see the thief, Nell thought. "He ran out the back door, not the front."

"I think about how the thief learned you weren't here." Cold air entered the opening like a dank dream. He closed the window. "Rain tomorrow." He faced Nell. "What are you missing?"

Nell stepped into the middle of the room. There was a stillness about the sheriff she hadn't noticed before, probably

71

because she'd been the focus of attention, both at the cabin and in the kitchen. And in each place, her mind had been groping, struggling to make sense of events.

"The negatives for the photos I took the other night."

"Why would a thief want your pictures?" He stepped to the dresser. "They were here, yes?" He smoothed the embroidered dresser cloth with hands that were brown and rugged, as if they were used to heavy work—lifting, hauling, pounding, gripping. And yet his nails were short and clean, unlike those of the miners who lived in the boarding house, and unlike Rosy, or even Henry.

"They were shadows cast by the moon, but also the man I told you and Rosy about. You didn't believe me. He wasn't a ghost." Alone in a room with a man, he fully dressed and she covered only by silk, Nellie felt her nakedness. She hugged the robe tighter around her. This man was an officer of the law, not a man who could affect her future as a photographer. Not a man who would withhold a job. From Rosy's words in the car, she thought the sheriff and she might have something in common: differentness.

"The dog toy," Nell said. "You took it, didn't you?"

He nodded.

"When I was out, you came into my room and took something of mine. How is that any different from the thief who scuttled out of here with my negatives? And they were negatives, not prints." Nell wished she had on her clothes, especially her pants and jacket.

"Was it yours? The dog brought it to you, yes, but—." He shrugged, leaning against the dresser.

Nell couldn't outlast his silence. "Not mine, then, but Moonie's. And what did you want with it? I thought police couldn't go into someone's house and steal things. The constitution says something about that. This is my home. These are my things.

72

"Sheriff Azgo," she continued, "someone stole my negatives and several sachets from this room." She sat on her bed, and then stood up. "The reason has to be that one of the negatives shows the dead body."

He remained silent.

"At Last Chance Ranch the other night, when I fell into the room—the moon was almost—the dog was—." Act like someone with presence of mind, she told herself, and took a deep breath. "It was the dog I'd seen at the window. A dead man lay on the floor. He had a mask of ice on his face. I assumed he'd frozen to death in an abandoned house. I moved him closer to the fireplace, lit a fire, and took his photograph."

The sheriff's eyebrows finally moved, lifting in a question.

"I took photos of dead people in caskets in Chicago. I thought maybe a photo of a man with an ice mask might bring some money from a newspaper." Her reason for taking the picture sounded mercenary and a little grotesque. "Something unusual, like this photo, might open—." Let him say something. She leaned over and petted Moonshine, who rolled on his back.

"The rock in the sock was not a toy. Dried blood and a small piece of hair make it a possible murder weapon. What I needed was a body."

"And you have one," Nellie said. Her stomach shrunk as she remembered the rigid form under the snow.

"You are cold? You will change. Then downstairs, we talk." He left and closed the door.

His absence made the room feel empty, messy, and crude. A little like Nell felt herself. Moonshine barked, and sat up, touching her leg with his paw. His nose was cold and wet and his muzzle slightly pointed. His black coat was smooth and silky to her touch. Sadness for him flooded her. Rosy apparently didn't want him. What could Nellie give him? Food and water, but no home and little love. She didn't have time. She had so many things she wanted to do. A dog would be a burden. "If Rosy was your master, I don't think he wants you anymore. Maybe you can belong to me. Finders, keepers."

This time the kitchen was empty except for Sheriff Azgo and a piece of peach pie and a cup of hot tea. Mrs. Bock must have forgiven Nell.

Between bites and an offer to share with the sheriff, Nell re-told the story of falling into the cabin, discovering the man, tak-ing the photo, and going to sleep with the dog. "You know the rest," she said. "No man in the morning, the chair and the cigarettes. I don't understand how someone got the body out past us. Especially past the dog."

The sheriff sat, thinking, waiting.

"We found it today." Nell busied herself with the pie.

"Who is 'we'?" No accusation in his voice.

"The dog and I. Before I told you about the whole thing—I thought—you didn't believe me—" Nell stopped. A strange look passed over the sheriff's face, like the one she'd seen in the cabin. Did he think she had killed the man? She would not like to be his target. The planes in his face would not only be interesting to photograph, they also gave him a merciless aspect.

She began again. "I followed the trail from the back of the house and across the river. In the aspens, there was a hump of snow. In the snow was a body."

"How do you know? Did you dig it up?"

"Heavens no! Moonie dug at it and I felt where he dug." She couldn't restrain a grimace. "I touched an arm or a leg. It was frozen hard."

In the silence that followed, Nell tried to take another bite, but couldn't. She heated more water and poured it into her cup. Minutes passed. Finally, she said, "Is someone missing? Maybe it's the man who owned Last Chance Ranch and drank himself to death after his wife died and boys left. No, that wouldn't make sense, would it? He's dead."

The last question brought the sheriff out of his reverie. "He's not dead. He's Rosy."

"What do you mean, 'He's Rosy'? It was Rosy who told me about him."

"Rosy's wife died—a growth in her chest. He sent the boys back East to family, I think. He *is* drinking himself to death, but hasn't yet finished the job." The sheriff picked up his hat and worked at softening the brim again. "Anything more you have to tell?"

Nell was still absorbing the information about Rosy. How callous of her to make him take her there twice. No wonder he was grouchy, and still, he came back to help her. "No, that's all." But was it? Whatever else she knew eluded her. The sheriff's studied reaction bothered her. She would have preferred a scolding to clear the air. Instead, she felt guilty.

"I want you to take me to the aspens tomorrow."

Nell took her plate to the sink and rinsed it off. Another snowshoe trip? "I thought you said it was going to rain."

He shrugged.

"I told you how to find it," Nell said. Now that the story was told, she wanted nothing more to do with the dead body or Last Chance Ranch. Poor Rosy.

"Miss Burns, I do not understand why you are here or what you are doing. No city woman I know or have ever heard of travels alone, takes such risks going into the woods by herself at night, or could sleep next to a dead body. I believe you should show me what you found. Maybe your story is true. Maybe not. But at least then I know where you will be." He jammed his hat on his head and left the kitchen by the back door.

"I'll be here," she called to the door. Did he think she would lie about finding a body? She flung open the door and yelled after him. "Find my thief!"

CHAPTER 7

When Nell told Mrs. Bock at breakfast about Bert the Butcher's interest in a family photo, Mrs. Bock said she wanted one of herself. Then Henry piped in, asking for one, too. Nellie would have sworn they were all poor as rendering-plant workers based on the ramshackle buildings in town, all except the schoolhouse, and the deserted streets and former saloons. Hailey, ten miles down the valley, appeared much more prosperous.

"I'll have to charge you," Nellie said. "And purchase some equipment and supplies."

"You think we can't pay? I don't ask for nothing for free."

"I—I didn't mean that. It's just . . ." How could Nellie comment on the shabbiness of the boarding house? "There are so many empty buildings on Main Street, and you said the mines were mostly closed."

"*Some* people," Mrs. Bock said, "save their money. If you took my picture, I could send it to my family in Indiana. They ain't seen me in twenty years." She tucked some stray hairs into her bun and sat straighter.

Mrs. Smith poked her head through the doorway, ignored Nellie, and said to Mrs. Bock, "I'm taking my automobile today. I have an errand in Hailey." She had drawn in black eyebrows, changing her face entirely. A large black hat with a crepe veil tucked up on the wide brim caused her face to look pale as a ghost's. She glanced at Nellie, flashed a quick, shy smile, and left.

"Oh dear. Was she angry that Henry used her auto the other day?"

"No. She lets me know if she's gonna drive so I won't worry if it's gone."

Henry piped up as if there had been no interruption. "I want one for my funeral. That's what my people did in Ioway." He picked up his hat, set it carefully on his head, and turned so his profile was to Nellie. "How's that look?"

"Your hat might shade your face too much. But I can make certain you look western."

"Hat?" Henry clicked his tongue. "Rosy's right. You don't know much. This here's a true Stetson. Just like the cowboys and sheepmen wear." He took it off again and rolled the brim. "You need one of these for the sun around here. Without it, you chance blindness, if you go out. Hunting and skiing and like that. If you do much more tromping around in the snow, you'll need something, too. Snow can blind your eyes, even more than just sun. Why, in the old days, I can remember—"

"All right," Nellie interrupted. "If I'm going to take portraits, I must travel to Twin Falls and find what I need."

"Train goes down today," Mrs. Bock announced. "I heard it come in this morning. You get ready, and I'll fix you up a packet of food. You can stay at the Clarion Inn—it's not so expensive as other places—and ride back day after tomorrow." She rummaged in a drawer to find a pencil and piece of paper. "Here's the address and I'll ring to tell Franklin you're coming."

Nellie felt as if she'd been almost pushed out the door. Before she left, she extracted a promise from Mrs. Bock to watch Moonshine, and to feed and water him, and she obtained a skeleton key to lock the door to her room. To be safe, she brought the exposed film holders in her pack, nesting them along with the mutton sandwiches and her little stash of money next to her Chinese robe and sachets. A warm coat—she still

77

felt chilled—and a traveling bag completed her ensemble. She was ready for a stay in a real town. Even if Twin Falls were small, there was a photography studio; she might find a darkroom to rent for a short time. And then she remembered: The sheriff wanted her. In all the excitement of planning a portrait studio and the hustle of catching the train, she had forgotten about him.

Photography brought her to Ketchum. Photography was also what took her to Twin Falls. Nell needed more chemicals and she wanted to inquire about lights for portraits, although if they were too expensive, she could use natural light. If truth be told, she didn't want to accompany the sheriff on his fact-finding tour. The half-iced face of the dead man haunted her. Freezing to death was one thing; a disappearing body was another, the implication of which frightened her. Nellie hoped Mrs. Bock would explain what happened.

When Nell was fired by Sebastian Scotto, her anger sparked her to examine her life. She haunted the library for days, reading about photographers—Edward Curtis, Alfred Stieglitz. She would show Scotto. She'd find her own niche, take photos he could never claim as his own. Her search led her to a book on Idaho, published by a railroad company. Buried in all the fine descriptions and information about tourist camps and hot springs was the detail that Idaho was one of the first states to give women the vote. Surely, a woman could be independent in Idaho. She didn't tell her mother all of her plans and let her believe that California was her destination after touring several of the western states.

Before Nell left home, her mother had tried to dissuade her: She didn't know where she was going. She didn't know anyone. A plus in Nell's mind. People were dangerous in the West. They'd never see each other again. It was too far away. Nellie knew she would miss her mother. To her mother's credit, she had never said Nell couldn't leave because she was a woman. On the day of her departure, her mother hugged her off at the train station. "Stay away from wild horses and Indians."

On her way west, Nell had liked the clackety-clack of train wheels on steel rails, the passing view of small towns and neat red barns and white houses, the scrubbed look of harvested fields, the suspension of time. Her first ticket purchase out of Chicago had been to Omaha. In the large, echoing station there, she transferred to the train to Pocatello, Idaho. The empty spaces as the train rushed into western geography hypnotized her, and she felt her mind and heart open as if they had been closed in among the streets and buildings of Chicago.

At her hotel, the restaurant manager told about the state's splendorous mountains, thick forests, and gemlike lakes. The station master at Pocatello had rhapsodized about Ketchum, Idaho, and the mountains surrounding it: Sawtooths, Boulders, Pioneers, White Clouds, Smoky, Lost River. She was a flat-lander and wanted to see mountains close up, not just from a train window. He also mentioned the hot springs. The idea of soaking in hot pools had sounded European and appealing. The fact that it was January hadn't deterred her. Nothing could be as cold as Chicago and the wind off Lake Michigan in winter. Taking the spur line to Ketchum was a natural next step in her quest.

In Hailey, a Chinese man and woman entered the railroad car. They must be the two Mrs. Bock referred to—strong people to stay after a fire and all others left. Few Chinese people had lived or worked near Nell in Chicago, so she watched them curiously. Their faces, when they turned and talked to each other, were the color of old parchment. The man wore a braid down his back and shapeless blue pants and coat. The woman was quite fashionable in a long dark silk skirt that stopped several inches above her ankles, a gold-colored coat, and a black hat that fit her head closely. Nellie thought they argued, although she couldn't understand what they said. Their words were a singsong of vowels unlike any she had ever heard. Once, the woman caught Nellie staring. Nell quickly turned her face toward the window.

On the trip south, the snow disappeared to be replaced by desert—miles and miles of sagebrush and black rock. The countryside was desolate, lowering Nellie's mood. She hadn't realized how cheerful she felt around snow. So far, she'd taken five photos and three were missing. Not much of a beginning for a new career. Clearly, Ketchum was not going to work as a place of business. Hailey was a possibility, but she really needed a thriving area where people earned money and wanted to spend it. She was certain her sense of photographing the West sprang from an artistic intuition, even if it didn't include cowboys and Indians. Everyone in Chicago had been convinced she was going to end up as toast in an Indian raid, and she'd not even seen one. The real West—that was her goal. The Indians were no more. White men had wiped them out. The real West meant mining, logging, sheepherding, and, she was beginning to realize, desert.

At the train station in Shoshone, a small town between Hailey and Twin Falls, the passengers loaded onto a bus for the final leg of the trip. Nellie noticed the Chinese couple retreated to the back and no one sat near them. The ride into Twin Falls took little time, and Nell again watched the scenery, thrilled at crossing the high bridge over the Snake River gorge.

To her surprise, the same Chinese couple were asking for a room at the Clarion when she arrived. Nellie, wishing she looked as exotic and svelte, smiled and nodded at the woman. Perhaps the man was a servant. Up close, he was younger than she had earlier guessed, and, in contrast to the woman, seemed clumsy and stupid, like the caricatures of Chinese men.

Franklin Olsen, the proprietor of the Inn, peered down at Nellie from his lofty height. He was thin as a broom and dressed in black. When she announced herself, he nodded and handed her a card to complete and then a room key with a metal fob in the shape of a silver ingot. Still without words, he pointed to the stairs at the side of the lobby and she turned to climb them. On the stairs was a woman who made Nellie feel smaller still.

"I'm Mabel Olsen. You must be Nellie Burns. Do you want help up the stairs? You look too small to heft that pack and bag." The speaker must have weighed two hundred pounds and she wasn't any taller than Nellie herself.

"No, thank you. I can carry them."

Mrs. Olsen immediately turned to the other two guests. "Mrs. Ah Kee. This is a surprise. You'll be happy to hear your usual room on the second floor in back is empty." The woman's triple chins jiggled as she chattered. "Will Sammy take your bags up? Franklin will if you like. All right, Sammy will. He can stay in his usual place." She flopped her hand toward a door off the lobby. "Breakfast is at 8 a.m. sharp. Do you wish a reservation for dinner?"

Without losing a breath, she turned again to Nell. "Goldie said you were coming. You're on the second floor, too. Two nights she said, and dinner and breakfast both. Dinner is at 6 p.m. sharp. You'll find the photograph place at the corner of Main and Elder, just a two-block walk. Now, Goldie thought you might need to work in the bathroom on your pictures, but I called the photographer and arranged a darkroom for you, 10 a.m. sharp tomorrow. Don't be late.

"Tonight, we have a special treat, a Chautauqua all the way from Kansas City. We'll take two cars. You too, Mrs. Ah Kee.

You won't have the same trouble as last time. Franklin will see to that!"

As Mrs. Olsen took Nell to her room, she continued to talk, this time in a whispery voice. "A woman from Ketchum went into a tirade about the Chinese and struck at Mrs. Ah Kee. It was most uncomfortable for all of us." She opened the door. "Not that you would do any such thing, of course. You're respectable. Goldie said."

Once alone in the room, clean and bright with a window looking down on a wide street lined with shivering trees, Nellie lowered her bag to the floor and began to close her door. Sammy was just leaving Mrs. Ah Kee's room. His face looked lively and intelligent. He saw her, and his mask, a servant's mask, slipped back in place and the look of recognition in his dark eyes glazed and slid away from her.

From her window, Nellie watched motor cars puttering back and forth, people walking, and an occasional horse clopping by. Twin Falls felt like a city after Ketchum. She donned her robe over her slip to go to the bathroom to freshen up before venturing out to explore. The lavender sachets had become such an integral part of the robe, she hardly noticed their scent anymore, but in this small room, it spread across the floor and rose to the ceiling, filling the space like smoke.

As if they had coordinated timepieces, Mrs. Ah Kee stepped from her room at the same time. They stared at each other in blank surprise. They wore identical robes: black silk, silver and gold dragons, red tongues. Except Mrs. Ah Kee's robe fit her perfectly.

Before Nell could say anything, Mrs. Ah Kee's expression turned malevolent. The venom in her dark eyes was as startling as the discovery of twin robes. Without uttering a sound, Mrs. Ah Kee stepped back into her room and closed the door. Nellie trembled, as if the hatred she had just encountered were a palpable force. When she finished her ablutions, she listened for noises in the hallway, then poked her head out and scampered back to her room, her slippers beating a muffled tattoo on the wood floor.

While she dressed, Nell puzzled. Perhaps only Chinese were allowed to wear a robe like this. Maybe Mrs. Ah Kee knew the robe was stolen. Maybe Sammy made the robe for Rosy's wife and—had Rosy's wife been Chinese? Such a possibility had not occurred to Nell, not even when she found the robe and assumed it belonged to the dead woman.

Leaving the robe in the room troubled Nell. Anyone could take the key off the board behind the front desk in the lobby. She folded the robe carefully and placed it at the bottom of her carrying case. No, if someone wanted it that would be the first place to look. She emptied her photography pack, placed the silk in the bottom, re-packed, and walked out to look around downtown Twin Falls, taking the key with her. Her warm Chicago beaver coat—her one extravagance—enveloped her in short dark fur. In it, she felt rich, capable, and lovely, a feeling wealthy people probably carried without thinking. Money exuded its own self-confidence. She could only pretend.

At the corner of Main and Elder, she spied the photography studio, a converted house, and decided to visit before it closed for the evening. Already at four in the afternoon, darkness was almost upon the town and even Nell, with only a month-old sensibility, could sense rain or snow would fall soon. Before she could cross the street, the front door opened and Sammy stepped out from the brick structure. "This is really too much," Nell said to herself. She hoped Mrs. Ah Kee was not in the place.

Sammy turned to walk up the street without looking across. He disappeared into another business and she entered the studio. A man with a neat, carefully trimmed beard, dressed in suit pants, white shirt, and no collar, sat at a table in what was probably once the living room, studying proofs through silver-rimmed glasses. He took her in, beaver coat and all, stood, and smiled. "May I help you?" His voice was pleasant. He looked more like a man of the city than anyone she'd met since she left Chicago, even if his dress was less than businesslike. A receding hairline emphasized his high, intellectual-looking forehead.

"Yes," Nellie said, trying to match his pleasant tone. "I'm Nellie Burns. I think Mrs. Olsen may have called you about the possibility of my using your darkroom."

The man laughed heartily. "I thought she was leading up to that point, but I could hardly tell." He motioned to a chair. "Would you like to sit, Miss Burns? Could I hang up your coat?"

Nellie sat, not intending to stay long. She felt as if she were back in Chicago. Framed portraits of men, brides and grooms, family groupings and baptisms, filled the walls.

"I could not get a word in edgewise with Mabel to tell her that I do not let anyone use my darkroom." He sat again after Nellie took the chair and began assembling the proofs he had been studying into a stack. "Was there anything else I could help you with?"

Nell could see that the photos were portraits of a man and a woman—not Chinese, so Sammy had not been there to select a proof. She picked one up by the edges and held it close to the light he had been using.

"I see you are using artificial lights. Do you prefer that to natural light?" She motioned to the photos on the walls. "Your portrait work is impressive. It reminds me of Stieglitz." She stepped over to a photo of an ancient Chinese woman. "This appears to be natural light, and you've captured what looks like five centuries of age in her face, yet also a youthful cast to her eyes."

The man's expression changed from that of a helpful but

"steer clear" professional speaking to a mere woman who couldn't possibly be permitted to use a darkroom to play in, to one of curiosity. "You are familiar with portrait work?"

"I worked at the Scotto Studios in Chicago and received my training there."

He cleared his throat. "My name is Jacob Levine. I know of Sebastian Scotto, of course."

One would hope so, Nell thought. "Do you? Yes, he is, of course, famous in Chicago and points east but I didn't know if his reputation was also known out here." It was difficult not to imply that "out here" meant in cow- or sheep-town, U.S.A. She decided to take a stab in the dark. "Have you also photographed Mrs. Ah Kee? The angles of her face and the exotic tilt of her eyes would be extraordinary, I think, in a study."

"You know Mrs. Ah Kee?" If anything, the level of impression in Mr. Levine's voice deepened and broadened.

"Not well, of course. I live in Ketchum at the moment, and we rode the train together from Hailey. In fact," Nell said, as if it were an afterthought, "I thought I saw Sammy leaving here just as I arrived." She moved from her position by the Chinese woman's photo back to the table, and noticed then a small envelope at the edge of the table.

"He brought in several negatives to be printed. Landscapes I gather from a cursory look. These are not the typical work I undertake."

"What a coincidence!" Nellie exclaimed, hoping he did not detect how phony she sounded to herself. "I *am* doing landscapes at the moment as a change from portraiture. I've absolutely fallen in love with the area north of Ketchum. In fact, I have several I had hoped to print in your darkroom. There are no facilities in Ketchum, although I plan to establish a small darkroom and continue doing some portraits. Sebastian asked me to send prints of anything I think worthy." "Sebastian" would have had a screaming tantrum to be referred to by anything other than "Mr." in a breathless and adoring tone, and he certainly had not asked for samples. "I do understand, though. One's darkroom is so personal." She decided a pensive look was best.

"Mr. Scotto wants prints? Of your work?"

"He seemed quite pleased with my progress." Nell didn't want to simper. "But he was also interested in work from the West." In fact, he probably had no idea there was even a state by the name of Idaho. "He's always felt that Chicago had a rare opportunity to help open the West to true art." She closed her coat, which she had opened but not relinquished. "I'm sorry to keep you so late. Perhaps I could come back tomorrow and look at more of your work? I'm always eager to learn what I can . . ." She let her voice drift, almost disgusted at herself for acting so much like a woman, although she knew her mother would approve.

"Indeed! Please come back. Perhaps, uh, you could come into the darkroom with me and we could do these landscapes and then you might watch while I take the portrait of one of the sheep ranchers. He is an irascible old man, but his face! Wait until you see his face. I rather doubt if the Scotto Studios have anything like him in their files." Mr. Levine's excitement extended to his fingertips, which he tapped on the envelope. "If you think Mrs. Win Kee—senior over there, the mother-in-law of Mrs. Ah Kee—looks old and young at the same time, you will be startled at Gwynn Campbell. His Scottish forebears stretch almost as far back as the Chinese."

"I would love to, Mr. Levine, but I do need to find a darkroom for the work I've done. I want to see if I'm on the right track. A photographer in Pocatello might be able to provide what I need." This was really a gamble. Nell did not want to return to Pocatello. It would have felt like going backwards.

"And I do need supplies. I'm not certain I can find what I want here in Twin Falls."

The man stood up and took Nell's hand. "Miss Burns, of course you can use my darkroom. I thought you were an amateur—." He stopped, dropped her hand, and began again. "Anyone trained by Scotto Studios is welcome here. And I could perhaps sell you some of my supplies. It is much easier for me to re-supply than for you to do so from Ketchum." A telephone burred in the back. "Don't leave," he pleaded, as he left the room, pulled by the rings.

Nell had never been in a truer "saved by the bell" situation. She picked up the envelope with a Chinese character written on it and pulled out the negatives, three of them. And they were hers. The moonshadow photos were problematical, but she needed the one of the body back. Without stopping to think how Sammy came to have them, she slipped that one into her pack and replaced the envelope. She doubted if Mr. Levine would notice until he went to print them. Maybe he didn't realize there were three, if he had only seen landscapes.

She moved to the door, hoping to depart before he returned, but he caught her.

"Ten o'clock, then? I will expect you." Once again, he caught up her hand, as if he were going to kiss it. His hand was sweaty from holding the telephone, but his rather old-fashioned manner of speaking gave him a courtly air.

"Tomorrow. Ten o'clock sharp!" Nell heard herself echo Mrs. Olsen. Clearly, the name Scotto had more cachet than she had realized. That was something to think about, as were the photos in the possession of the Chinese. Mrs. Bock certainly would not have told Mrs. Ah Kee or Sammy of Nell's presence at the boarding house, but someone else might have. Someone who knew she used the bathroom as a darkroom and had an incriminating photograph.

CHAPTER 8

"He's gone!" Gladys Smith grabbed Rosy's arm, her fingers digging in, as if she would pull him onto her bony lap.

"Who's gone, woman?"

"My brother. What am I going to do? My own heart, the last of my family." Her words were barely understandable because Gladys broke into quiet weeping. "We were orphans and now I'm alone."

"For god's sake, everyone's an orphan when they're old." Rosy looked toward the dining room door at Mrs. Bock's.

Gladys, who had been crouched over herself on a chair by the fireplace, straightened up. "Speak for yourself, you old cuss. I'm not old." She tucked a stray gray lock behind her ear. "At least not as old as you are."

"Did you tell anyone else he's gone?"

"Who else would I tell? Who else would care?" She stood. "No one cares about my brother and no one cares about me." Her back was to Rosy, but she turned her head with a sideways glance. "It's your fault. I know what you did."

Rosy flinched. "Damned right I don't care about your brother, not after what *he* did." When Gladys's face crumpled, he added, "Didn't I see you found a place to live? After that devil's mate clobbered the living daylights out of you. Why do you care if he's gone?"

"He's my flesh and blood. Blood is thicker than water. And you—"

"What's going on in here?" Mrs. Bock bustled in. "Rosy, are you making her cry, again?" She rounded on Gladys. "For heaven's sake, Gladys. You're like a pump that needs a raindrop of priming and then you pour out water all over the place. Get hold of yourself. Now what's wrong?"

Gladys flushed. "My brother has disappeared."

"Well, thank your stars for that! If he's not on a binge, or worse, he's roughing up someone. You moved here to be quit of him. Now isn't that the truth? Good riddance, I say."

"But he didn't even say goodbye." Gladys's wail marched up a chromatic scale of hysteria.

Mrs. Bock circled Gladys with her arm and pulled her toward the kitchen. "That's enough, Gladys. You can tell the sheriff and post a notice on Bert's board. Maybe someone knows where he is. Land sakes. You've lived here nigh on to a year and I doubt you've known where he was the whole time. Nor cared, either."

Rosy watched them go. He had to admire Gladys. He'd known some cold-hearted women in his time, but ice clanked in her veins. Orphan, his foot. She had broken all ties with that black-hearted brother of hers and laughed about it besides.

"Can't a fellow get some sleep around here?" Henry's voice trailed down the stairs.

"Not unless you're dead," Rosy called back. He'd had enough and stomped out, only to be met by driving snow. Sometimes when the weather was bad, he slept in a back room at Bert's, who had a heart big enough for ten people. It didn't suit him that night. He found an empty stool at the Casino Club and nursed a whiskey for an hour or two, thinking about summer and when life was better. Four Basques played *mus* around a table, winking and scratching and shouting over their cards. All they did was drink, gamble, and hang around, waiting for spring when they would take the sheep back up into the mountains and be alone. What good would summer do him?

Fields of lavender swayed in his memory with the kind of summer breeze that ran along the mountains like a flute trilling. Long, dirty days with a sledgehammer and pick in the flickering light of candles in the mine were the price he paid to give Lily a home.

In the spring, bands of sheep traveled along the road in front of the small ranch, herded by dogs and Basque horsemen. Lily knew them all. Rosy mostly ignored them and watched her wave. The sheep hooves clicked on rocks in the dirt road and the hordes of animals filled the air with the smell of lanolin. One horseman stopped to hand her two leather pouches. Seeds, he said.

"Look." She spilled the seeds into her hand.

"What are they? This soil won't grow much but sage, grasses, and wildflowers." He turned around, wishing he could make things grow for Lily. Ground squirrels skittered back and forth like comic creatures, standing to sniff the air, then dropping down to pick at seeds and chomp at green sprouts.

"I don't know." Lily took a finger and stirred the seeds in her palm. "I'll plant them. They'll grow along with me." She grinned at Rosy and he couldn't help but laugh back. "We'll see what comes first." Then she rested on her haunches and absorbed the sweet aroma of white and yellow lupine.

From the wellhead in the cabin, she pumped water into cans and carried them to the patch under the kitchen window to tend her raked rows. Rosy built a wire fence to keep out deer and elk, and tied red cloth strips to wave in the wind and scare away smaller creatures. They both waited and watched.

Before long, green heads peeked into the early summer. Soon, buds hung from green stems; pale lavender nodules appeared above dusty leaves. By mid-summer, poppy heads and lavender buds dotted her patch. The strong lavender scent drifted across the sage and into her kitchen. Red and purple flowers colored their lives.

And gold. Rosy's summer sojourn into the mountains where the sheep grazed and the sheepherders spent long, lonely weeks, yielded hidden treasures. He filled pouches and brought them to her.

The other seed grew. Lily placed Rosy's hand on her own mound when movement began. With gold and sweat, they built onto the ranch. As late October snows returned, he descended into the mine again, while the kitchen garden paled and died. One day when Rosy returned from work, Lily lay in the bed upstairs, lathered in sweat and moaning.

"The baby won't come," she panted. "I don't know what to do. He wants out." She cried "Help me, Rosy," then shoved the quilt into her mouth to stifle her screams.

He held her and brought cold cloths to place on her forehead. He'd seen animals born, but what could he do to help Lily? He burned his knife to make it clean and cut where the head pushed against the birthing canal. The baby whooshed out into his hands. Lily screamed and lost consciousness and blood poured out, thick and red. Rosy cut the cord and swaddled the baby and placed him next to Lily. He wadded up an old blanket and pushed it between her legs, tying it around her hips and legs with one of his belts and one of hers. Then he left, walking to Ketchum to seek help, knowing mother and baby might both be dead when he returned.

Mrs. Bock and the Celestial, who had just finished tending a man in Ketchum who lost his leg in the mine, returned with Rosy in a borrowed automobile. They heard the baby bawling from the road. "Hurry," Mrs. Bock cried. As if he needed her to make him run across the field, slipping and sliding in an early snow. He hadn't left a fire in the fireplace or cookstove. Lily might be frozen.

Rosy dashed upstairs. Mother and child were as he left them in the double bed, swaddled and packed. The babe snuffled and his mouth trembled. Lily was white as death, but she turned her head to Rosy. "It's a boy."

The next summer, the baby boy crawled in the poppies and lavender, spreading in a colored arc from the kitchen garden toward the aspen grove.

Those were the summers he remembered. The one bad winter, followed by summers steeped in flowers and Lily. Rosy wasn't a fool. She didn't love him, but what they had came close to happiness, love or no love. Respect for each other and laughter made up for what wasn't there. Rosy almost gagged. He was getting to be a sentimental fool, an old man carting around a flibbertigibbet easterner. Time to turn in, but he called for another drink.

Rosy liked to watch Nell Burns sass the sheriff. She wasn't much bigger than a bug, but she had spirit. He didn't believe she really had a photo of the dead man in that camera of hers. Even someone with spirit would have a hard time spending that much time and effort on a dead body. Still, the body had been moved. She must have done something. And she did sleep right there, with it next to her. The dog wasn't any help. Lily had called it Moonshadow. She wouldn't care if the girl took him over. Rosy wasn't doing much of a job taking care of him. He couldn't stand to lose another living being so he'd like to be shut of the dog. Just like Gladys was shut of her brother. Too much responsibility.

Just as Rosy was close to his goal—drunk enough to forget but sober enough to walk—the sheriff swung up on the stool next to him.

"Care if I sit here?"

"Free country. Don't matter to me. Long as you pay for your

own hooch."

"Care to tell me about anything you know?"

Rosy mulled that one over. "Like what?"

"About cabins and dead bodies, for one."

"I don't know nothing 'bout that." Rosy lifted his glass but it was empty. He wondered if the barkeep would give him another splash. He could use one, but he needed gasoline worse than he needed whiskey, if that were possible. Keep his head tied on straight. Maybe he was a fool, but this sheriff wasn't, at least, not anymore.

"About Three-Fingered Jack and opium, for another."

Rosy scratched his head. "Well, I know the two went together like a horse and carriage." He giggled to himself. "If you found Three-Fingered Jack, you'd likely find opium, and if you run across opium, you'd likely run across that good-for-nothing on its trail."

"That's what I heard." Sheriff Azgo had ordered a glass of soda, and he swirled it around like a real drink. He asked for ice, plentiful now that it was winter, so it clinked now and again.

"Who you hear that from?" Everyone in town knew, but who would talk to the sheriff?

"Oh, around. Henry, over at the boarding house. Others."

"What do you think of that little photographer?" Rosy chuckled. "Quite some girl, don't you think? 'Course she was probably dreaming up Wild West tales in her sleep. Cute little thing."

"How long did Jack stay with you?"

"Which time?"

"He stayed more than once?"

Rosy found one more drop in his glass. "A long time ago. Before me and Lily got hitched." That was something he could have gone all year and never said to the sheriff.

"I mean this last week. I dropped the Celestial Ah Kee out

93

there to help a sick man. Jack was gone when you took me to the ranch the other morning. Did he up and recover?"

While he tried to think what to say, Rosy dug in his pocket for another coin. He needed another jigger. The sheriff tossed two bits on the bar and gestured to the bartender.

"Thanks, Charlie. I got a powerful thirst. I like my own liquor better, but I run out." Rosy lifted his glass. "Here's to Prohibition." He drank it down in one gulp. "Jack never was one to hold his own with liquor or dope. Or his temper. He got mad and skipped." He stood up. "Gotta go see a man about a horse."

"Rosy, this whole deal is strange. I think you'd be better off if you told me about it. You've had a rough few years, what with your eye . . . and all. I'd hate to see you get yourself mixed up in murder and mayhem. Once, you were a solid citizen."

Rosy looked back, then away. If he weren't so drunk, he might take a swing at the sheriff, except the sheriff was a lot younger and stronger. In his haze, Rosy knew the man was just trying to do his job. Everyone thought he'd fail at it anyway.

"This eye, here," Rosy said and leaned up close to the sheriff, almost touching his forehead, "it sees things. Like having a leg cut off and feeling it itch and want to run. My eye might look blind, but I can see some things well as a two-eyed bugger." He steadied himself by gripping the sheriff's shoulder. "Better maybe, 'cause I can see things in the dark. Things *you* might not see at all." He almost fell over.

The sheriff helped him stay upright. "Go sleep it off, Rosy. But think about it. Right now, I would say you are in a whole ore load of trouble."

Rosy swayed, wishing he had something smart to say back. Better to just leave. He carefully placed one foot in front of the other, and returned to the snow.

The silent snowfall covered the streets and ramshackle buildings. It almost looked like a real town again. The hustle and bustle of ore wagons, miners and townspeople out and about—he missed all that. A couple million sheep might pass through come summer, but it wasn't the same.

Rosy wished he could cry, like Gladys. No, she was phony as a three-dollar bill. His bad eye itched sometimes. Maybe he *was* blind, in both eyes.

CHAPTER 9

Franklin and Mabel Olsen were a true Jack Sprat and wife duo. He was also much quieter than she, and said little when Mrs. Olsen hurried her charges through dinner so they wouldn't be late for the Chautauqua. At first, Nell thought she would not attend, but Mrs. Olsen insisted. "You've been stuck in Ketchum for weeks now. You should see some city life here in Twin, and the goings-on at the Chautauqua are just the thing." She turned to Franklin. "Isn't that right?" He nodded, probably having learned that edgewise words had to be as skinny as he was.

"But aren't Chautauquas summer entertainment? In tents?" Nell did not relish sitting in a tent in mid-winter.

Frown lines etched Mrs. Olsen's face. "A *real* Chautauqua is in the summer. But we've got to calling all traveling entertainments and revues by that name. Just seems easier. The high school gymnasium is decorated with bunting and crepe paper, just like the park would be in summer. You'll feel just like you been to a real Chautauqua, won't she, Franklin?"

She didn't wait for his nod. "And the best thing is the speaker tonight. He's talking about high moral principles and how the drink tests them and undermines them. Now that we have the demon-rum under control, we need to control how we think about drinkers and their sad failings. My land, there's been more than one man's life, and woman's too, ruined by the drink."

"All right," Nell said. "I would like to hear the speaker." Her mother's life had been ruined by "the drink." Nellie's father's drinking led directly to his early death and to the debts that her mother tried to pay off by selling everything nice that she had ever owned—a small house, a set of silver goblets, two pieces of jewelry, including her engagement ring and the pearl necklace she'd worn at her wedding. All Nellie could remember of her father were his rages and then his brief charms and finally, his face in the casket, white and not the choleric red when he was angry. Only his watch escaped the creditors because Nellie's mother had hid it.

Six of the hotel guests squeezed into Mrs. Olsen's Ford, which she drove. Franklin hired a car to take himself, Mrs. Ah Kee, and Sammy. One of the other guests explained in a low voice to Nellie how in 1905 the men of Twin Falls had put all the Chinamen out of town and told them never to return. Two finally did and opened a restaurant and then more came. When Nellie inquired of her informant about Mrs. Ah Kee and Sammy, she was told that the woman was fabulously wealthy from the sale of opium at a den in Hailey, and that Sammy was her servant and supplier both. The fire that burned out Chinatown had been set by an opium-eater to destroy a moonshine still. And that wasn't all, the informant breathlessly continued, Mrs. Ah Kee was said to have four husbands in China and one in Hailey.

By the time Nellie sat through the magician who made several mistakes but no one seemed to care, the Indian who danced a ceremony called Mating of the Eagle, and the Hawaiian who crooned to the ukulele he played, singing about the beaches of Waikiki and the tropical moon on water—a scene Nell thought might photograph much like the moon on snow—she was ready to sleep. The inspirational speaker announced there were sixteen moonshine operations within one hundred miles of Twin Falls and it was up to his audience to destroy them by refusing to drink the product. If they did not, the evil that might befall the good citizens of Twin Falls, Jerome, Bellevue, Hailey, Ketchum, Carey, Shoshone—he sounded like a train conductor—was their own fault. When he likened the evils of rum and the evils of opium-eating, staring directly at Mrs. Ah Kee, who sat with Sammy in a row in which no one else sat, to the evils of giving women the vote, Nellie stood and walked out. Her action was spontaneous, but several other women followed, including Mrs. Ah Kee.

"Fool!" The Chinese woman's voice contained the venom Nellie had seen in her eyes. "A town of fools."

Several women congregated by the outside door of the school, chattering and exclaiming about the speaker. Most were matrons dressed in long skirts and button shoes, but they talked like suffragettes. Their expressions were determined, as Nellie and her mother had been when they marched in parades in Chicago, carrying signs and chanting, the one independent action her mother had ever shared with her. Pride filled Nellie again, for her mother, for herself, and for these women. They had gained the vote, and women like Nellie would see that it wasn't lost.

"But can you vote?" Nellie asked Mrs. Ah Kee, instantly regretting it.

Mrs. Ah Kee turned on Nellie with an expression that said, "you stupid toad." "That man is a fool and will never know it. You are a fool but can learn." She spoke in unaccented English, but with a cadence that reminded Nellie of the singsong words she had heard in the train. "Whether one can vote or not does not matter. No votes count. The highbrows ignore the will of the people, the lowbrows. Always that has been true. It is no different in this country."

"But this is a democracy. We fought a terrible war to remain a democracy. Every single vote does count. And now that women can vote, we will be able to change the direction of the country, to help those in need."

Although Mrs. Ah Kee did not say "Fool!" again, Nellie felt it as surely as if she had. She blushed, embarrassed for her childish speech. She had seen politics in Chicago long enough to know that the men in control before the 19th Amendment were still in control.

Mrs. Ah Kee looked toward the other women before she dropped her voice and asked, "Why do you interfere? You do not know anything of Hailey and Ketchum. Leave. It will not be safe for you if you stay."

"I don't know what you mean. I am trying to make a living." She didn't owe this Chinese woman any explanations. "I'm a photographer," she said. "I'm a good photographer. Everyone said the West was the land of opportunity. I plan to open a portrait studio—"

"Go away. Go to San Francisco." At that moment, Sammy scurried out of the meeting, and plucked at Mrs. Ah Kee's sleeve.

"We go now." He took her arm and hustled her out the door.

The crowd began to emerge in twos and threes. "Damn Chinamen. Selling opium to children!"

"We'll get up a posse to break them stills apart!"

"Leave it to the gov'ment. That's why we pay taxes."

"It's them foreigners' fault. Think they can steal our minds from us."

"And women too with their white slavery."

A tide of ill-feeling threatened to bowl Nellie over. She stood her ground, though, as did the other women. In fact, they blocked the door briefly after the Chinese woman and her servant departed.

"Ladies," one of the women said. "Stand and sing!" They launched into a suffragette anthem, to the surprise of nearly everyone. Nellie didn't know the words, but she clapped her hands, and many of the women coming out of the gymnasium began clapping in rhythm too. Soon, the rancor evident at the front of the throng dissipated and turned to weather as people departed the school. Outside, snow fell in flakes the size of goose feathers.

By the time Nellie joined her group in the motor car, everyone was in high spirits. As they pulled up to the Clarion, Mrs. Olsen said, "Home again, home again, jiggety jig." Nellie climbed out and entered the house, deciding that women could accomplish more than she had suspected, in out-of-the-way places, in small ways. She didn't give another thought to Mrs. Ah Kee's warnings.

The next morning Nellie arrived at the Levine Portrait Studio eager to use the darkroom. In her pack were her camera, her film holders, print paper in its dark covering, several empty bottles to be filled with developer, and her robe. Inside the studio, another scene was in progress: Sammy confronted Mr. Levine. "My photos ready," he said, a demand that was obviously untrue. Unlike Mrs. Ah Kee, his accent was quite heavy.

"No, Sammy. *You* said they would be ready this morning, but I did not. I have not had time. If you will come by later today, after your noon meal, I will have them."

"Need now!" Sammy was not a large man, but the menace in his voice made him seem dangerous. Always before, he had appeared hunched over, but today, he stood tall, on a level with Mr. Levine. The expression on his usually flat face was warlike, a la Genghis Khan.

The photographer was not intimidated. "They are not ready now. You can have the negatives back, but no one else will be able to develop them before I can." He shrugged and began to turn to Nellie, who stood with the doorknob still in her hand.

She motioned with her finger to her lips not to say anything and then quickly backed out of the doorway, hoping Sammy would not see her. What if Mr. Levine handed over the negatives to Sammy and he discovered one was missing! She should return and demand them herself. After all, they were hers. But instinct warned her not to, so she scampered around the corner. Soon, Sammy crossed the street and stormed back toward Mrs. Olsen's. He carried nothing.

"What was that all about?" Mr. Levine still held the envelope with the negatives. Relief surged through Nellie, but she would have to tell him something. All night she had thought through the motions of trying to develop a print as fast as possible in his darkroom, assuming she could make him leave on some pretext. It all worked, in theory, until it came time to dry the print. That took time. So did making a second negative from the first.

"Those negatives are mine," she said. Honesty was the best policy, although she hoped partial honesty would suffice. If he didn't know there were three, so much the better. "The ones Sammy brought to you. I don't know how he got them, but they were stolen from my room in Ketchum."

"Yours?" Mr. Levine looked at the envelope in his hand. "But—"

"One is wheatgrass and aspen in the snow at night, and the second is a full moon and a tumbled-down cabin. I took them." Nellie stepped toward him. "I'll show you. They're not very good, unfortunately." It was difficult to keep discouragement from her voice, when she knew she needed to exude confidence and expertise. "Maybe you could help me analyze where I made mistakes."

Mr. Levine did not put the envelope into Nellie's outstretched hand, but he did open the flap and bring out the negatives. He held each one to the light. "They are certainly different. Who would have thought to capture moonlight on snow?"

"The moonshadows intrigued me the most," Nellie said. "Look at the shadow of the grass." She moved next to him and used her fingernail to point. He smelled soapy. "That shadow was almost as dark on the white as it would be in daylight, perhaps darker. But I think my exposure time was off. Do you think I could intensify the negative?" So far, he hadn't said anything about a third negative.

"Let us go to work and see. I told Sammy I would have contact prints ready for him around noon, not that he knows what a contact print is. We can do the test prints first and see what we can learn." He led the way from the studio front, past a space already set up for portrait work with electric lights, a chair, and two backdrops—one dark and one light gray—to a door marked DO NOT OPEN—PHOTOGRAPHER AT WORK.

Inside the darkroom, lit by a central white light in the ceiling with two porcelain holders on each of two walls holding red lights, Nellie saw that it was well-equipped: a sink for rinsing prints and negatives; a counter for trays for developer, stop bath, and fixer; a "dry" counter with enlarger; and, under it, blotters for drying prints. On shelves were bottles with chemicals and packs of dry hypo to make fixer, glass beakers for measuring liquids, a metronome, and a breadbox look-alike that presumably held paper, protecting it from light. At the end of one counter, a metal cabinet with wheels held negatives. She was impressed with Mr. Levine's cleanliness and organization.

"First things first, hmmm? I will mix the chemicals. I have several sets of portrait proofs to do. If you will help me with those, you can use the same chemicals to develop the contact prints and do test prints on these landscapes."

"I'll need an apron," Nellie said. She had hung her coat in a closet at Mr. Levine's direction. Already anticipating her request, he held out an apron, clean but with stains from chemicals, and too large. He even helped her with the ties so it would cover her dress without dipping into the trays when she began the print process. She felt awkward as he asked her to lift her arms so he could circle her waist and tie the ends in back.

They worked side by side, Mr. Levine mixing the developer, Nellie mixing the hypo with water to make the fixer. She was so happy to be in a darkroom again, she hummed a quiet ditty, "Over There," not realizing it until he commented, "Not something you had to do, was it?"

She looked up, not understanding.

"Go to the war," he added. "You were humming 'Over There.' I did go. And ever since, I have been limited in the amount of time I can stay in my darkroom." Regret etched his voice, although he continued to measure and pour. "I did not think I was gassed. I never had trouble until I returned to the darkroom." He wound the metronome and set it near the enlarger.

"Then you are generous to help me with my photographs."

"Not at all. I like the darkroom work best of all. You give me an opportunity to do something other than portraits."

Nell was careful not to hum anymore.

"The print paper is in the box." He had pulled from a lower shelf a flat board with a glass top, which he cleaned. Then he brushed the first negative to remove any pieces of lint or dust. "Ready?" he asked. Nell nodded. With a light touch, he set the metronome tocking so they could time the processes, then pulled the string on the white light and they in were absolute dark. He turned another switch and red light filled the room.

From the paper box, Nell removed a piece, slightly larger than the 4×5 negative itself, and handed it to Mr. Levine. He placed the paper, emulsion side up, on the board after lifting up the glass, then positioned the negative, emulsion side down, on the paper and closed the glass. He placed the whole thing on the counter, under where the light in the enlarger would aim, and turned on the enlarger light. It lit the contact board and glass. With a separate piece of paper, he covered three-quarters of the negative; after ten tocks, he moved the paper back to cover only half; after another ten tocks, he moved the paper so three-quarters of the negative was lit, and then after a final ten tocks removed the paper all together and turned off the enlarger light. The result was a test print, so they could gauge how long to leave the light on the combined negative and paper to get the best straight print. He opened the glass and handed Nellie the paper. She turned and placed it in the developer tray and used her hands to agitate the liquid.

"Those of us at home during the war didn't know how much you suffered in Europe. We could do so little." Nell's only war effort had been knitting socks and scarves once a week at Mrs. Scotto's house.

"I am much better," he said. "Look! The magic is working once again."

The first time she had seen an image appear on paper, the process did seem magical to her. The first time and every time. She watched as she soaked the blank paper in developer, pressing the sheet back and forth. Soon, the image began to appear and grew recognizable even though the print had stripes of different shades of development: the full moon, the dark line of trees, the flat log structure of the Last Chance Ranch, the lighter river rock on the chimney, and the streaks. They were stars moving, not bad film. Nellie held her breath.

Over her shoulder, Mr. Levine, too, watched as if mesmerized by the phenomenon of silver particles absorbing chemicals to reflect a picture. They both seemed touched by how a world emerged from blank paper. "Most unusual, Miss Burns."

From the developing tray, Nellie picked up the print with tongs and dipped it in the stop bath. Then she moved it to the fixer and again agitated the liquid, this time lifting the tray up and down by a corner so the liquid sloshed back and forth.

When she moved the photo to the water bath, she turned to the photographer. "Let's do the other test print. This is better than I expected." As he turned on the white light, she took a deep breath and said, "And I have a third negative, taken the same night. It's a portrait . . . of sorts." She didn't look at Mr. Levine, but turned to her pack near the door, slipping the third negative from a side pocket. "I took it from the envelope yesterday when you answered the telephone. This one, I think, is the reason the negatives were stolen."

"Well," he said. She handed the negative to him and he held it up to the light. His eyes widened, but he said, "Let us do the other landscape first." With Nellie's assistance, he began the process all over again.

When all three test prints were hanging from clothespins on a string, Nellie helped develop one set of proofs of a man standing with his foot on the running board of a shiny new Stutz Bearcat roadster. With the white light on, they studied the test prints of Nell's negatives and decided the time for the final contact on each would be thirty seconds.

Mr. Levine sighed and began removing his own apron. "I must return to fresher air. Mr. Campbell is due any moment, too. When you finish the contact prints on your three negatives, do you want to assist me with his portrait? He is a crusty old son-of-a-gun."

Nellie was honored he would ask, particularly after her subterfuge, but she truly wanted to stay in the darkroom, making larger prints of the moonshadows and the dead man for her own use, along with developing the negatives of her daylight efforts. Even working on a proof set for Mr. Levine sounded more exciting than taking another portrait. She had grown weary of shuttling fifteen or more people a day through the studios in Chicago like cattle through chutes into the meat plants. Working with Mr. Levine had also been a nice change from the factory mentality in the Scotto Studios. Although this photographer in Twin Falls had been impressed with the name, Nellie no longer was. Proximity had bred contempt after a while, along with low pay and long hours. Still, her boss had given her a profession. She sighed too.

"Come out and rest a bit," Mr. Levine said. "We can do more work after he leaves." A bell rang in the front reception area. "That'll be him."

But it wasn't. It was Sammy, demanding his photos. Nell could hear the Chinese singsong all the way into the darkroom. The test prints were dry enough to handle, so she took them down. She did not want to turn over the print of the dead man, or any of them, and the prints themselves weren't ready anyway. Under no circumstances would she release the negatives again. Loud voices came from beyond the door. Footsteps trod on the wood floor, nearing the room.

"You cannot go in there or you will ruin the negatives. Then you will have nothing." Mr. Levine's voice rang loudly. "And the door is locked." Nellie turned the lock immediately.

For a few minutes, nothing happened. Then the handle jiggled and a shoe kicked at the lower panel so hard, she was afraid it would splinter. More loud voices and then silence. She decided to stay where she was. While she worked on the second contact print, she was startled by bumps and a loud thud that shook the floor, followed by a crash and glass shattering. Then the handle of the darkroom twisted, followed by a slow hammer on the door, almost like the metronome tocks. Nellie had an urge to pound back, but did not. She could feel her heart beat like a tom-tom and hoped the man on the other side couldn't hear it. Her presence in the darkroom was not known by Sammy. But what if Mr. Levine had been hurt trying to protect her?

CHAPTER 10

The hammering stopped. Nellie held her breath and placed her ear to the door. Nothing. Was Sammy on the other side doing the same thing, their heads separated only by the quarter-inch panel? She waited and waited some more. Which of them had more patience? She had to breathe, so she turned her head and faced the contact prints.

The moonshadows on the landscape calmed her and her heart slowed. With the photos no more than four inches from her nose, she studied them, willing herself to look at each detail—the gradations of black and white and gray, the rock pattern of the chimney, the trees beyond, the shadow that obscured two white tree trunks. Perplexed, she loosened the clothespin and held the photo in her hand. She didn't remember a shadow on the trees.

The bell rang again. And again. What in the world was happening?

"Hullo? Where are you, dagnabbit?" *Brring, brring.* "I reckon I'm late, but you were supposed to be here. Hullo!!"

Nellie unlocked the door, stepped outside the darkroom to an empty room, closed the door behind her, and hurried to the front. On her way, she almost fell over a bundle on the floor. Only it wasn't a bundle, it was Mr. Levine. "Oh no!" She knelt and turned him toward her. One of the lights had fallen and the bulb was smashed. Mr. Levine had landed on the glass and his face was covered with blood, blood that dripped and congealed

107

on her hands as it had on the floor. "Mr. Levine!" Her cry elicited no response.

"Where did you come from? What did you do to him?" A man as large as any she had ever seen stooped down to her level. His hair was white and bushy, his mustache thick with gray, and his eyes, almost buried in wrinkles, were periwinkle blue in a face tanned like leather. Their bright color stunned her for a moment.

"I didn't do—"

"Is he dead?" The man's Scot accent identified him to Nellie. "Did you kill him?"

"I don't—"

Mr. Campbell grabbed her hand. She was still aghast at all the blood. With fingers as thick as ropes on a boat, the man felt at Mr. Levine's neck. "Still alive." He pulled a large white handkerchief from his back pocket and began wiping off the blood. "Pick up the telephone, Lassie, and tell the operator we need a doctor. Pronto."

"But my hands—"

"Do it!" Mr. Campbell roared at her.

While Nellie searched for the telephone, finally finding it in a hall between the portrait studio and what might have been another studio, Mr. Campbell took two cushions from the chairs in the reception area and placed them under Mr. Levine's feet and legs, raising them higher than the photographer's head, and then he leaned over the body. She watched his back as she cranked the handle and an operator came on. "Jacob, honey, what can I do for you today?" A distinct southern accent spoke words as slowly as the proverbial molasses in winter.

"Mr. Levine is hurt. We need a doctor right away!" Nellie could hardly keep a shake out of her voice. "His face is cut all over. There's blood everywhere." She wiped her hand on her apron. Blood had even caught under her fingernails, which she kept purposely short so chemicals wouldn't rest there. "Hurry!" She rang off, opened the door to the darkroom, pulled a towel off a hook, and sped to help Mr. Campbell.

"Goddamn mess," he scowled. "That glass cut his lip, his nose." Red lines seeped in a dozen places and she turned her head. He grabbed the towel from Nellie and applied it to Mr. Levine's face. "You do this, Lassie?"

"No! No—" Nellie sank to her knees beside the two. She leaned over Mr. Levine, thinking she should touch him, smooth the red lines away.

"Get me some ice. See if there's a box in the kitchen back thataway." He jerked his head in the direction Nellie had come from. "Gotta stop this blood."

A kitchen—maybe that was the other door. Nellie ran back and found a kitchen that appeared as neat and tidy as the darkroom. She opened the icebox, then needed a pick to chop off some ice. One drawer after another, she jerked open, scattering utensils and dishcloths and hot pads all over the floor. She found a pick and jabbed at the ice until several chunks fell off. She gathered them in her bloody apron and scurried back to drop them by Mr. Campbell's hands. One, scarred and battered, held Mr. Levine's head and with the other he grabbed a chunk of ice and applied it to the bleeding lips.

The front door slammed open against the wall and another man hurried in, carrying a leather bag. He, too, knelt by the unconscious man on the floor and pulled gauze pads out of his bag. "Here, hold these—one to his nose and one to his lips," he instructed Mr. Campbell. The doctor took a bottle labeled "Alcohol" from his bag and poured it over the cuts, as Mr. Campbell slowly moved the pads away.

"My gawd, he lost so much blood," Mr. Campbell said. "More blood'n a sheep, I'd say. Look at this towel and that girl's apron!"

The doctor gave quiet orders, including a call to the operator again to summon an ambulance from the hospital. The slow southern voice said she had already asked for one and wanted to know how Mr. Levine was. Nellie wasn't certain she should tell what happened, so just hung up. When the ambulance came, the doctor accompanied Mr. Levine on a stretcher out to it and wouldn't let Nellie or Mr. Campbell climb in. The emergency auto wheeled away, its siren wailing, echoing the sound in Nellie's head.

Mr. Campbell and she entered the studio again. "All right, Lassie, what went on here?"

Nellie sat down by the table where just yesterday she had first seen Mr. Levine. Again, she wiped her hands on her apron, but the blood was dried and burgundy red now. Flecks dropped onto the carpet. For the first time, she felt dizzy.

"Could I have some water?" She leaned over to rest her head on the table. It must have scared Mr. Campbell, as he hurried off, calling back, "Don't faint now. Don't faint. Can't handle a fainting woman."

What did happen? There they'd been, working together in the darkroom. An argument in the reception area and then Mr. Levine was lying on the floor. Did the loud voices happen before or after all the pounding on the darkroom door? She couldn't remember the sequence of sounds. Nellie stood up and tiptoed to the door of the portrait room. She heard Mr. Campbell banging cupboards. With luck, she could get the negatives into her pack and hide the prints in the drying blotters, pushed as far back as she could get them, for later retrieval. She hurried into the darkroom.

When Mr. Campbell returned with a glass full of water, she was in place again at the table, and felt much better. He plopped down and looked as if he might expire on the spot. "You'd better drink this instead of me," she said, offering him the glass.

"I sure as hell need something stronger than that!" He closed his eyes and she felt as if two blue spotlights had been turned off. After a minute, he said, "Any alcohol in those chemicals of his?" It might have been a different man entirely asking that question. The voice was low and tired and old. She realized for the first time that he was probably sixty years or more, and that his tanned leather look had washed out to a gaunt beige. "Never could stand it when the lambs were slaughtered," he added. "Now wool, that's another thing. Undressing those sheep with shears and sending them out naked as jays to grow another crop felt good." He seemed to be seeing all this activity behind his closed lids, lids that were veined and white. A smile hovered on his lips. "Too bad the bottom dropped out of the wool market when it did." He opened his eyes. Nellie felt as if she were pinned to her chair by their intensity.

"Do you want me to look for—"

"Where were you when Jake there got slammed down on the glass?" He took his index finger and mimicked a knife across his own throat. "May as well answer me. The police are going to want to know where you fit into this deal."

"I was in the darkroom—"

"Hiding from Jake or from the man that caused that mess?"

"No, I was—" This time, she was interrupted by the door opening and three policemen rushing into the room.

"Jake'll be glad to know he merited the whole damn Twin Falls Police Department," Mr. Campbell said, "about an hour too late."

The tallest one reported Jake was conscious and bandaged and in bed with ice packs on his face. He had sent them over to make sure Miss Burns was all right. He hadn't seen his assailant, had no idea what happened, but worried that someone was lurking outside and waiting for his guest to come out of the darkroom. Then he turned to Nellie, "Did you see what happened?"

"She was crouched over the man when I come into the room," Mr. Campbell said. "But I didn't see a bludgeon."

Nellie looked at Mr. Campbell. Was he implying that she had hurt Mr. Levine? Her expression must have conveyed her shock at such a suggestion.

"I didn't mean you done it, Lassie, but you damn well could have!"

"I was in the darkroom," she said to the tall policeman. He looked like a cowboy dressed up in someone's idea of what a police uniform should be. So did the others. Their shirts were dark blue, and so were their pants, but any uniformity ended there. Two wore sheepskin coats and the tall one standing by her wore a canvas coat that reached to the tops of his boots. All three wore hats—no, Stetsons, she remembered. "Mr. Levine had left the darkroom to meet Mr. Campbell, and I thought I heard him arrive and some bumping around in the portrait room there." She pointed to the room and saw that the position of the remaining light had changed. It had been raised to focus light on the face of a tall person. She turned back to Mr. Campbell.

"You could have done it, too. Maybe you did it while he was adjusting the light." Her first thought had been to retaliate for suggesting she had hurt Mr. Levine, but as she pointed out the height of the lamp, she realized it might be true. And judging from the fury that dashed across his face, she was afraid it was and a cold chill grabbed her.

"Ha, ha, ha!" Mr. Campbell's laugh filled the room. "Sure, Lassie, and then I came back in and helped him while you dithered like a stupid ewe!"

The policeman looked from one to the other and then spoke to the other two men. "Take a look around and see what you see." And back to Nellie. "Who else was here this morning?"

Nellie did not want to answer the question. It could have been an accident. If she mentioned Sammy, judging by the reaction of the night before, he would be blamed. But what would be the reason? Late prints surely weren't enough to cause mayhem, and if they were, she indeed would be in danger. Sammy and Mrs. Ah Kee both knew she had an appointment with Mr. Levine at "ten sharp," thanks to Mrs. Olsen. Whether they knew the negatives belonged to her, she didn't know. "Sammy was here," she said. She didn't know his last name. "Mrs. Ah Kee's companion."

"I knew those Chinamen would be trouble," Mr. Campbell said. "Now they've beat up a white man. When we threw 'em out of town last time, we should have strung 'em up instead. Damned foreigners."

"Sheriff Azgo in Ketchum is looking for you," the policeman said. When she said nothing, he continued. "Why were you in the darkroom?"

The other two policemen returned. All four men looked at Nellie, assessing her. At that moment, she felt as if she were the foreigner—a woman surrounded by men who apparently thought she was in league with Sammy.

Nellie stood, and immediately felt less intimidated. The Ketchum sheriff must have been angry, but she had explained where the body was. He didn't need her. Sheriff Azgo may have told this policeman about the dead man at Last Chance, that Nellie had found him. She wanted her coat, her negatives, her prints, and her camera pack. She wanted to leave. "I was helping Mr. Levine develop proofs. I am a photographer from Chicago and I have extensive experience with portraits." All true. "I'm cold and I want to go back to the Clarion Inn. Can I see Mr. Levine?"

She felt faint from the blood and no food since the early

breakfast. No one stopped her as she moved to the closet and donned her coat. Steady, she told herself.

"Do you want to see the darkroom before I go?" She led all four men to the door, opened it, and pointed to the proofs hanging on the clothesline. "We worked on those." Then she stepped closer to the first one. "Oh, dear, look at the spot on this one. Mr. Levine will be most unhappy. Maybe it was on the film." She stooped to a cupboard filled with negative sleeves and pulled out the top strip, then turned to the men.

"I'm sorry, you can't stay in here. You'll get dust on everything and possibly ruin all the work we did this morning. As you can see, no one is here. I'll need to re-do this proof. Now, more than ever, Mr. Levine will need my help." She took off her coat, walked back to the portrait room, sidestepping the broken glass, draped her coat over the chair, returned to the darkroom, and gently closed the door on the men, keeping as apologetic a look on her face as she could muster.

Nellie turned the lock and sat on the stool in the dark, totally spent. One dead man and one disfigured man in less than a week. What kind of world had she rushed into? Chicago and safety were a million miles away. Even Moonshine was seventy miles to the north. Tears threatened.

There were things to do and no time to cry. Someone knocked and she said, "Go away! I'm working." Men's voices murmured. She took the negatives from her pack, turned on the metronome, feeling as if the *tock, tock, tock* could restore her balance, turned off the white light, and switched on the red ones. For a moment, she felt bathed in blood and her throat caught. She opened the glass plate, slid in paper and negative, and went to work.

CHAPTER 11

At the doorway to Mr. Levine's room in the hospital, Nellie stopped. Would he even want to see her? He lay in a white iron bed in a room by himself, his face almost covered with bandages. Only his eyes, nostrils, and mouth showed. He looked so much like a mummy, Nellie smiled and controlled a giggle. This was not a laughing matter.

"Do I look that funny?" Mr. Levine asked. "I do not feel funny." Swollen lips made his words fuzzy, but he didn't abandon his careful grammar.

"I'm sorry. This is my fault." She hurried to his side and took his hand. Antiseptic smells hovered in the green-painted room, making her feel queasy.

"Besides," he said, "if I laugh, it is very painful for my lips." He squeezed her hand. "Do not blame yourself." His fingers felt warm to her skin.

"Sammy did this, didn't he? If I hadn't come to Twin Falls, I would never have known he had my negatives. You would have made his prints and nothing would have happened to you."

"Sammy? Yes, he was in the studio, demanding his prints, but . . ." Mr. Levine looked puzzled. Because Mr. Levine did not have his glasses on, Nellie noted, for the first time, the unusual gray of his eyes. The bandages emphasized his dark lashes as well. "I cannot remember what happened. I would not think that Sammy did this. Mrs. Ah Kee would . . ." His voice trailed away. "Sammy would hardly dare cause trouble for a white

115

man, not with all the strong feeling in town against the Chinese." He shook his head. "But were you hurt? I told the police that you were there."

"No one touched me. Mr. Campbell thought I did this to you." She withdrew her hand, as it was getting hot. She could hardly keep an offended tone out of her words.

"Gwynn was there?" Mr. Levine moved his hand away, as if embarrassed by her grabbing it. "I did see—. No, that is not right." He stopped talking when a nurse, crisply starched from hat to hem, came into the room, but he seemed troubled.

"I finished your second set of proofs," Nellie reported. "The ones of the baptism. That baby was beautiful. How did you get her to smile so broadly?" Business might be a better subject with a stranger in the room, fussing with Mr. Levine's bedclothes and removing a dinner tray. "Keeping her still long enough for the photo must have been difficult."

"Babies like me. My beard tickles them and usually calms them down." He touched the bandage that covered up his chin. "The doctor shaved my face. I will not miss the hair. It is a nuisance to keep free of food." The nurse left.

"I have to return to Ketchum tomorrow. I hate to leave you like this. I could do some more of your work tonight or early tomorrow, but I leave for the train around 10 o'clock I gather." Mrs. Olsen had said "10 sharp!" and then amended it to "10:15 sharp!" "I'd like to help as much as possible, and I need to buy some supplies from you and find a metronome and more film. And I need to order lights. Is there any place in town to buy these things?"

"The music store will have a metronome. What kind of film do you want?"

The two of them discussed film speeds and quality and finally settled on film Nellie could buy from Mr. Levine. He pulled a key ring from a side table drawer and handed her one so she could work that evening in his darkroom. She felt she should leave, that he was getting tired, but she had one more request.

"Could I show you the prints I made of the negatives that caused all this trouble?" She didn't wait for an answer, but took them from a folder in her pack. All were 8×10s, large enough to see detail better than the contact print size. Before he could say no, she lined them up against the bed railing beyond his feet.

In the first one, to her eyes, the wheatgrass almost trembled, its shadow was intense, and the aspen branches cast trailing skeletons on the snow. The Last Chance Ranch in the second appeared desolate in the moonlight, while the moon itself looked like a paper cutout suspended in the heavens and the star streaks gave it an unworldly feel. Sadness permeated the photo, and she didn't know why. But the last photo was the strangest. The dead man's face was distorted by the ice, so that he was a mask of Tragedy, sorely needing a Comedy face for balance. The firelight had been sufficient to give only the broad impression of the rest of him, except for gray matted hair on his head and one hand shown in minute detail—the fingers grasping as if trying to snatch life back from the edge. In place of the last two fingers was a smooth, shiny, very short stump. Even the bitten fingernails on the remaining digits showed their ragged edges, and small scars and scratches marked his skin like spider webs. She hoped Mr. Levine's face was not going to look so terrible.

"Who is that?"

"I don't know. He's a dead man that I stumbled over when I entered that house." Nellie tapped the cabin. "I have to return to Ketchum because the sheriff thinks I'm involved in his death somehow." She looked directly at Mr. Levine. "I wasn't. But the next day, I went back to scout around and I found the pile of snow where he was buried after he—" She bit her lip. How could she possibly explain?

"It's too complicated. What I need help with is enhancing the

image of his face. I want to make it as clear as his hand. Can
I?"

Mr. Levine lifted his hand for the photo and Nellie handed it
to him. He studied it a moment. "I am not certain. Without my
glasses I have difficulty seeing clearly. But his face is blurred.
Given how clear the hand is, that is puzzling."

"It was covered with ice."

"Ice?" Mr. Levine closed his eyes. "I don't understand."

Clearly, he was too tired to have this discussion. "Never
mind." Nellie took the photo and placed it and the other two
back in her pack. "I'll stop by tomorrow before I leave. What
shall I do with the proofs?"

He explained that one of the customers would come by in
the morning—the Stutz Bearcat fellow—and that the others
would be picked up the following day. By then, he fully expected
to be back at work, but if she could print proofs of a bride and
groom, he would appreciate the help. Nellie gathered up her
things to leave.

When she was at the doorway, he said, "Miss Burns."

She turned.

"The moonshadows are stunning."

Nellie studied him a moment, seeking assurance that he
believed what he said, nodded to him, and left the room. Joy
gripped her heart.

Speculation about the attack on Mr. Levine swirled around the
dinner table at the Clarion Inn. No one mentioned the Chinese
who sat by a table near the window, although a few pointed
glances left no doubt one or both were suspected. Nell reported
that Mr. Levine was able to talk but couldn't remember the
events. Otherwise, she said little and excused herself early. She
went up to her room and waited until she heard the other guests
disperse. Then she slipped downstairs, found Franklin, and told

him what she planned.

Entering the studio at night made Nellie nervous. Each shadowed corner could hide a man, each door opened could reveal someone waiting to steal her negatives, destroy her camera, harm her. But no one was there. She re-locked the front door after she was in and switched on lights as she made her way to the darkroom. It, too, was empty, although the mess she had left still awaited her. She talked out loud so she wouldn't seem so alone.

"Proofs. Mr. Levine wants proofs. The negatives are in the negative cabinet. Makes sense. He is so organized." She retrieved several sleeves, finding a series of photos of a woman in a wedding dress and then a man and woman together. "Young bride, handsome groom. I doubt if I'll ever be in a series such as this."

Was that a noise?

She listened and heard nothing. But she locked herself in.

Whispering seemed in order, so she could hear any strange sounds. "First, I'll develop the film of my day shots. Can't have any light for those." She mixed developer and fixer and poured them into trays, then retrieved her film holders and lined them up on the counter so she could do all the rest of the work in complete dark. She started the metronome—so much easier to count tocks than rely on counting to herself—extracted her film out of the holders, placed them one at a time in the tray, agitated, then dipped each into the stop bath, then fixer, and hung them up to dry. The tocking of the metronome soothed her and kept her moving at the same time.

When both negatives were fixed and in trays of water, she turned on the lights again. The photograph with clouds looked good; the other seemed busy and without a balanced composition. She'd see. While they dried, she set about printing the proofs of the wedding couple, humming the march from *Lohen-*

grin and imagining them walking up an aisle to commit themselves to each other for life. Would they have children and raise them in Twin Falls? It seemed a nice town. Would she keep house? Was he a farmer, growing sugar beets for the sugar company? It sounded like a quiet existence and held no appeal for Nell. She mulled several ideas while she worked her magic on celluloid negatives.

Why not photograph the miners at work? Light might be a problem, but not if they worked outside. Photographing them inside the mine, which is what she really wanted to do, the flash powder would be difficult to work with, creating smoke and a smell that a miner might not appreciate. Perhaps electricity would be available. And what about loggers and sheepherders? None of the books she studied in Chicago showed people working. The crux, though, was who would buy photographs of such subjects? The public wanted movie stars—Valentino, Douglas Fairbanks, Lillian Gish. They wanted their art to reflect Egyptian motifs and Greek columns. And so many people took their own photographs now with those Eastman Kodak cameras. Newspapers wanted photos, but only to reflect the news.

The telephone rang as Nell turned the white light back on. The sound surprised her. Who would be calling Mr. Levine at this time of night? Her timepiece showed almost eleven. Goodness, it was late! Perhaps she should answer the telephone. Then the ringing stopped.

What was the safest place for her negatives and prints? She had made duplicate negatives and prints of her moonshadows and the dead man, and decided to leave one set with Mr. Levine, just in case he had to respond to Mrs. Ah Kee. She put them in paper sleeves and added them to his negative store. Her 8×10 final prints she placed in with her paper supply in the camera pack. After some thought, she decided to place her original negatives into film holders. The contact prints would accompany her, too, and they went into a side pocket. Those, she would give to the sheriff.

The new negatives she had hung to dry tempted her. After such a full day, she was tired and aching, but having a darkroom to use was a treat. It wouldn't take long to develop a print of each. Again, she made certain all was in readiness, then turned off the white light and turned on the red lights and the metronome. Within twenty minutes, she had two test prints in the water bath and she turned off the metronome. Except she could still hear a quiet tick-tock sound. With the white light back on, she listened. The sound came from outside her door, almost as if a clock were being held up against the door panel. Her insides squeezed. Was someone listening?

"Who's there?"

No answer. She placed her ear against the door. She thought she could hear someone breathing. Then the ticking stopped. After a moment, she heard a thick scratching sound. She grabbed her negatives and shoved her camera pack down behind the negative cabinet, dropped to her hands and knees, and scrunched as small as possible, pulling the cabinet in front of her.

The door exploded in white light, blue fumes, and a series of loud shots like a gun firing. Nellie was pushed back against the dry counter so hard she thought her heart would stop. Then, the impact released her. She gasped for breath and choked with the sulfur in it. She had to get out and into the fresh air beyond or she'd suffocate. All the chemicals might explode and the film would surely fuel a fire.

Fire! She couldn't let Mr. Levine's hard work go up in flames. Before she could think, she grabbed the stop bath and poured it on a few licks of flame that had begun around the door frame and then dumped the developer down the sink, along with the fixer. The proof sets, all neatly waiting to be delivered to customers, she stashed in the negative cabinet. She pushed the cabinet in front of her as a partial shield, and shoved through the broken door, dragging the camera pack behind. Pounding filled her head. She held the apron up as a mask and lowered her face to stay as much as possible underneath the smoke of the outer room. She feared a hand would grab her, or a weapon would slam against her head. She scuttled like a crab, pushing and pulling. When pieces of glass crunched under her shoes, she knew she was in the portrait room.

The pounding intensified and then the front door crashed open.

Voices shouted. "Fire!" "Bring water." "Get away!" and last "Nellie! Where are you?"

"I'm here." She tried to shout but coughed instead. And then arms pulled her up, tried to pry her hands from her pack, and then carried her and it out of the building. "The negatives—!" She struggled to free herself to run back for the metal cabinet. Someone stopped her.

"We'll get them. Don't worry. The building won't burn."

Much later, she was in her nightgown and in bed, her hand still grasping the camera pack on the floor beside her.

"For goodness' sake, Miss Burns. You'd think you carried gold nuggets around in that bag of yours." Mrs. Olsen's voice scolded but Nellie felt comforted at the same time.

"Mr. Levine's negatives? Did the cabinet get pulled out in time?"

"Nothing burned. When you didn't answer the telephone, Franklin decided it was high time to see what you were up to. You musta stopped any flames after that explosion. We saw it from the windows and Franklin, he ran down to the fire station. Lucky thing it was so close."

The horror that she was responsible for the possible destruction of the studio left her. Thank heavens for snoopy older women.

"Was anyone hurt?" Nellie hoped whoever set off the explosion was damaged in some way, but she was glad that person had left before she got out of the darkroom.

"No, and they can't figure out what caused the explosion. Now you get some sleep."

"Don't leave me!" How could she have said such a thing? "I mean, when you leave, could you lock the door?"

Mrs. Olsen patted Nellie's cheek. "I'll lock it, but Franklin is going to sleep on a pallet right outside. We figured you didn't set that bomb. Someone else knew you were working late. When I take a person in, I'm going to send them out again all in one piece. Mrs. Bock would have my hide if something happened to you."

Next morning, Nellie was up, dressed, packed, and ready by 8 a.m. When she entered the dining room, she stopped in shock. There were Mrs. Ah Kee and Sammy. Why wasn't that man in jail? If not for assaulting Mr. Levine, then surely for causing the explosion last night. But then, no one else knew what she knew—that they had stolen her negatives, which she had stolen back, and they wanted them back again. Why, she had not yet figured out, but it surely must have something to do with the dead man. The police knew Sammy had been in the studio yesterday, but here he was, eating eggs and ham and biscuits and gravy as if he had no worries. He glanced up at Nellie with a triumphant gleam in his eyes.

Mr. Olsen guarded the door. "Your breakfast is in the kitchen, Miss Burns." His attitude suggested he had misgivings about the Chinese couple.

Nellie was wrong. The same policeman who questioned her the day before waited at the kitchen table. When she entered, he stood, but sat down again when she did. An empty breakfast plate showed he had been waiting awhile.

"I wouldn't let him up there to bother you before you was good and ready," Mrs. Olsen said, slapping a plate down in front of Nellie. "You eat first. You've had a bad shock."

The man looked more than ever like a cowboy, even without his Stetson, which sat on the cupboard by the door. His handlebar mustache had obviously been groomed that morning, and curled wickedly on either side of his mouth. "Can you tell me what happened last night, Miss Burns? Maybe begin with why you were in there so late."

His tone was insolent, angering Nellie. "I was working, which is perhaps something you should have been doing. Why is that man out there in the dining room, scot-free, when he assaulted Mr. Levine yesterday?"

"As it happens, he didn't. What were you working at?" He shoved his plate away and took out a cigarette from a pack and laid it on the table. The scratch of his match on his boot brought back the sound from the night before. She flinched and almost ducked. To cover her confusion, she reached for the pack.

"Do you mind?" She shook out a cigarette before he could answer and waited for him to light it. Now he was confused, but he accommodated her.

"How do you know he didn't? I heard his voice in the reception area and the portrait room. I told you all that yesterday. How could it not have been him?"

"Because Mr. Campbell said it wasn't."

Then Mrs. Olsen chimed in. "But Gwynn hates all Chinamen, ever since—"

"That's how I know Sammy didn't do it," the policeman interrupted. "If Mr. Campbell says so, we couldn't get it from a better source, under the circumstances."

Both Mrs. Olsen and the policeman knew something Nellie

did not. It underlay all their words. "What do you mean? I may not be an eyewitness, but I'm an ear witness."

"Gwynn's daughter was killed by a Chinaman. She died of opium poisoning." Mrs. Olsen's voice had dropped almost to a whisper and she glanced toward the dining room door. "There's folks that say Mrs. Ah Kee was responsible, her being the opium queen hereabouts, but I say, nobody forced Lily to take the vile stuff."

"Mrs. Olsen, I'd like to talk to Miss Burns alone, please." The man shoved his chair back and stood. He was two heads taller than the big woman.

"All right, Tommy. But you be nice to her. I knew you in knickers, you know. You don't scare me." She turned to Nellie. "And don't let him browbeat you none neither. His record ain't so spotless as he might make it sound." She sniffed and went out the door.

"I'm gonna get straight to the point. Did you set off that bomb last night?"

Nellie was dumbstruck.

"You seem to be on the scene whenever something happens, Miss Burns. You say you 'found' a dead man north of Ketchum and then you hightail it down here on the next train out of town. Jake Levine gets bonked on the head when supposedly you're in his darkroom. And then a bomb goes off when you're back there in the middle of the night."

Words failed her. Nellie took a draught from her cigarette, blew it toward the policeman's face—Tommy?—and then crushed it out in the congealing remainder of the food on his plate. What could she do but laugh at such stupidity? And she did. Being alone in the West gave her more courage than brains.

Tommy's face burned red. "Is that your answer?"

"Mr. Policeman, or can I call you Tommy? Let's see. I'm perhaps five feet, four inches, weigh 112 pounds. I can carry my

125

camera pack, which weighs around twenty pounds, with ease. I guess I could use it to kill the man in the cabin, freeze water on his face, then drag him across the river in the middle of the night and bury him in the snow. After that, I came to Twin Falls to meet a photographer I've never seen before in my life, but because of professional jealousy, I bonk him on the head, and then try to blow up his studio while I'm in it. Yes, I guess that makes sense. I am from Chicago, after all." She scowled at Tommy. "Don't I look mean?"

Her mother had told her many times that a smart mouth would get her in trouble.

"I'm just doing my job, Miss Burns. Mr. Campbell said he found you leaning over Jake with blood on your hands. And no one else was in that studio last night."

"Someone was. But you certainly weren't there searching for clues as to the assault on Mr. Levine." Nellie stood up too. "If you think I did all this, arrest me. Otherwise, I'm returning to Ketchum after I visit with Mr. Levine. Where is the negative case? There are proof sets I promised to deliver for him. He, after all, has to earn a living and isn't on the public payroll." She bit her tongue. That perhaps was going too far.

"No wonder you're still a 'Miss,' " he said. His arrow stung. "Can't imagine anybody that'd want to marry a bitch like you." He grabbed his Stetson. "The negative case is in the studio."

"Unguarded?" Her shock made her squeak.

"Who would want a cabinet full of negatives? We covered the door last night, so weather couldn't get in. Good luck getting at it." With that, he turned and slammed out the back door.

Nellie's anger rose and fell. She deserved the stab, she guessed, but how could he be so stupid as to leave the negatives sitting in plain view in the studio where she'd left them? Maybe someone had the presence of mind to put them in the portrait room. But then, only she knew what was in the cabinet besides portrait negatives. And she knew, without a doubt, that the duplicates would be gone. If only everything else were intact so Mr. Levine wouldn't suffer more damage.

Back in the dining room, she told Mr. Olsen that she was going to pick up the proofs to deliver to Mr. Levine. He could figure out how to deliver them to his customers, but at least they would be in safe hands and he wouldn't lose the business. She asked Franklin if he would go along with her to the studio, the hospital, the music store, and then the bus for the train, making certain Mrs. Ah Kee and Sammy heard her.

At the studio, she did indeed have difficulty entering. Wood covered the doorway, but Franklin had no qualms about levering it away. The negative cabinet sat in the portrait room, which was sooty with smoke, but otherwise not damaged. She peeked into the darkroom, and it, too, was intact. Only the door was splintered. She took two bottles of chemicals, several packs of hypo, and some film, saying to Franklin, "I'm buying these from Mr. Levine." He shrugged.

In the cabinet, she drew out the proofs and then checked for her moonshadow negatives and prints. They were gone. No surprise that, but nothing else was harmed. Her news to Mr. Levine wouldn't be as terrible as she thought. She would pay to replace the darkroom door.

"Franklin, did Mr. Campbell's daughter really die of opium poisoning?" She asked her question hesitantly. The Clarion Inn proprietor had hardly said two words to her in the time she stayed at the hotel.

"Some say so," he said, and seemed not inclined to add anything else.

At the hospital, Franklin said he'd wait for her and reminded her of the time so she wouldn't miss her connection to the train. And then he added, "Maybe she had her reasons." It took Nellie the walk up the stairs and down the hall to Mr. Levine's room before she connected those words to Lily Campbell.

Nell stopped in the open doorway. The bandages had been unwrapped, his chin was bare, but several plasters still covered his lower lip, his nose, his left temple. She began to comment, then saw a visitor. Standing at the end of Mr. Levine's bed was a willowy young woman wearing a hat, gloves, and a dress that covered her ankles. She looked like a poster out of time, perhaps 1915 or so. When Mr. Levine introduced her as Emmaline Sherman, she nodded her head and ignored Nellie's out-stretched hand. Nellie felt almost risqué in her much shorter dress, hatless head, bare hands, loose hair. In the confusion of the night before, she'd lost the barrette she used to tie her hair back in a more ladylike fashion. Until she met this picture perfect lady, she'd forgotten how she must have looked to Tommy the Policeman: wanton as well as brash. Emmaline's lips were a perfect cupid's bow and she looked at the floor while she murmured her sympathy for the difficulties Nellie was having in Twin Falls. No recriminations for causing distress to what was obviously her man friend.

Nellie maintained as businesslike a tone as possible, placing the proof sets on the table, returning the key to the drawer, telling Mr. Levine what had happened and that little damage had been done. "I did take the chemicals and film we agreed upon." She extracted several bills from her purse. "Here is the payment. I owe you for the door as well."

Emmaline spoke directly to Mr. Levine. "Jacob, I'll take the money to the bank for you."

Nellie handed the bills to Emmaline. "The last set of negatives, the ones we discussed," Nellie said, "are missing. I have the originals. I doubt if you'll be bothered by that customer."

Emmaline filled a glass for Mr. Levine, moving to the other side of the bed, and holding it to his lips as if he were helpless. Nellie watched for a minute, and then said, "Thank you for the use of your darkroom, Mr. Levine. If you don't mind, I'll call next time I'm coming to town. Perhaps we could work together again. And any time you wish to consult regarding anything, please telephone me at Mrs. Bock's in Ketchum." Emmaline turned toward her, daggers in her eyes.

On the train ride back to Ketchum, Nellie gradually relaxed and succumbed to the stark desert beauty. The train scooted around Timmerman Hill, and when it neared Silver Creek, the partially snow-covered hills looked like chocolate with a heavy sprinkling of powdered sugar. She felt as if she'd been gone for eons. Two days away, and already she longed for deep winter, although she had awakened sneezing.

Mrs. Bock and Moonshine met her at the train station, several blocks from the boarding house. The dog barked and wriggled in pleasure as Nellie knelt and hugged him. She should have taken him with her. He followed at her heels as the two women walked along the cleared boardwalk. Sun sparkled on ice crystals in the air, and the bracing cold invigorated Nellie and chilled her too. She half-listened to Mrs. Bock's concern about the news from Twin Falls and the half-questions at every turn in her chatter. Well-being filled Nellie's lungs. Her incipient congestion had disappeared. She absorbed the clean crisp smell tinged with a faint remnant of motor oil and she stopped and hugged Mrs. Bock. "It's nice to be back!"

At the boarding house, Moonshine held back from the front door and barked. "I'm home, Moonie. What's wrong?"

A shiny motorcar sat out in front, with a printed label on the door: Blaine County Sheriff.

All of Nellie's spirits deflated. Now she would pay for her brash escape to Twin Falls. She remembered Sheriff Azgo's cool air of competence, nothing like Tommy the policeman's innuendos. Moonshine growled in a half-hearted manner.

The door opened and the sheriff, also shiny in a new dark

blue uniform, stepped out.

"Good heavens, Sheriff. You and your auto look like brand-new pennies. Did the county fathers strike gold and fill your coffers?" Nellie asked, laughing. Mrs. Bock gave her a warning jab.

He scowled.

Nellie stopped laughing. "I'm sorry. I didn't mean to insult you. I was joking."

"Miss Burns, you have some explaining to do, running off like that."

"Run off? Not really. I went to Twin Falls to do some developing, and I now have what I promised to give you."

Several people on the boardwalk had stopped to listen. Nellie could see Henry behind the sheriff and Rosy walked around the corner just then. "Hi, Rosy," she said. "I even missed you!" She surprised herself by grabbing his arm, and he surprised her by planting a beery kiss on her cheek.

"We heard you had yourself a spot of trouble, girl. Glad you're back where it's safe!" He chuckled and was obviously pleased she had singled him out.

Sheriff Azgo came down the steps. "Miss Burns, you will accompany me to the city hall. I have some questions for you." Moonie growled at him as he neared her. The lawman grabbed her pack and she had no recourse but to follow him to his auto. The male voices behind her buzzed.

"Hey, Sheriff," Rosy called. "Go easy on that big bad criminal." Everyone laughed.

The sheriff's ears turned red. Nellie waved at Rosy, thankful he at least was on her side. Moonie leaped into the motorcar when the sheriff opened the door for Nellie. He frowned, but let the dog stay.

"Did you go across the river and get the body?" Nellie asked when both doors were closed.

Sheriff Azgo ignored her while he turned on the ignition, choked the gas, pressed the starter, and prepared to drive away. "Yes, no thanks to you."

"I told you where it was," she said.

At the city hall, he ushered her into a small office marked Blaine County Sheriff. The dog accompanied her and then sat down, nosing at the pack.

"Why not put me in jail? The police in Twin were going to do that, I think."

"Miss Burns, I am not the police in Twin." His voice was low and dignified.

"I know you aren't, Sheriff. But I have been subjected to more incompetence than I care to think about. Being met by the law upon my return upset me. I'm sorry if I've been disrespectful." She lowered her gaze and folded her hands. "How can I help?"

"Do you have the photo you took at the cabin?" He sat down behind the scarred desk. She wondered if he had a choice, new desk or new auto, and chose the latter. The room was hardly large enough for the desk, two chairs, and two people. Moonie would have to move to let anyone else in.

Nellie opened her pack and pulled the photo of the dead man from her paper package as carefully as possible, so as not to expose the blank paper to light. "Here it is. Do you know him?"

He studied the photo, and then looked up at Nellie. "Is this a joke?"

"What do you mean?"

"The body across the river was Chinese. This man is not."

CHAPTER 12

Nellie reached for the photo. As she studied it again, she could smell the burning wood, feel the emptiness of that house. She patted Moonshine. "No, of course, he wasn't Chinese. I would have mentioned that." Then the sheriff's words sank in. "I don't understand."

"The man I found across the river, buried in snow just like you said, is Ah Kee, a man well-known in Hailey."

"*Mrs.* Ah Kee—"

The sheriff had been searching for something in a drawer and glanced up, giving Nellie a sharp look. "That's his wife. You know of her?"

"She was on the train to Twin Falls and stayed at the Clarion Inn, where I did. They said she sold opium." She supposed she would have to tell him the whole story about Sammy and the fiasco with the negatives, Mr. Levine's injuries, and the bomb in the darkroom. "It was her servant, Sammy, who stole my negatives—the one you're looking at now. He left them at the photographic studio where I went to do some work. It was pure chance I found them, and then he stole the duplicate negatives as well."

"Sammy is her son, not a servant." He brought out a photograph of a dozen Chinese men standing in front of a Chinese restaurant. "This is what's known as a Tong—a sort of rotary group of Chinamen, but much tighter. They control the businesses and hierarchy and have much power. Ah Kee was head of this Tong." He pointed at a figure. "Tong wars are murderous. Fights between tongs result in butchery."

Nellie shuddered. She could believe Sammy might butcher someone, but then she realized that was unfair. She didn't know him and all the xenophobia she'd been around in the last week might be causing her reaction. "Was Ah Kee . . . butchered?"

"No, that's what's strange. He was killed by a hard blow to his head—no fingers chopped and his throat wasn't cut. Remember that 'toy' the dog there brought to you?"

"The one you stole from my room?"

A glimmer of a smile played on the sheriff's face. "That one."

"Was it the murder weapon?"

"It might have been. It was heavy enough and the sock had blood and maybe hair on it."

"But sheriff—" Nellie didn't want to think of the strength it would take to kill someone with a rock, and the death of a Chinese man seemed removed from her. "What about the dead man I found?" She motioned to the photo. "Where is he?"

The pack fell sideways from Moonshine's nosing, and he stuck his snout under the flap, barking and whining.

"What do you want?" She tried to grab her pack and move it, but he wouldn't let her. "I'm sorry. So far, this dog has been well behaved." Again, she tugged at the pack, but now he had a strap in his mouth and pulled back. "Moonie. Let go!"

Sheriff Azgo stepped from behind his desk and grabbed the dog and held him. "Open the pack, Miss Burns."

"But it's just my camera and chemicals, film and gear." But she did as instructed, releasing the straps and opening the mouth. "Oh, and the bathrobe." She removed the camera box and slid her hand to the bottom, then pulled out the Chinese robe. Moonshine almost had a fit trying to free himself. His barking in the small room was deafening. The sheriff released him and the dog jumped on the robe and moved his nose from

133

side to side until he got it into one of the pockets and pulled out a sachet with his teeth. He looked at Nellie, the sheriff, the door, and then crawled behind Nellie's chair, circled around twice, and lay down with the lavender packet between his paws. Then he growled.

"Good heavens! He's never done that before."

"What's in there?"

"Just a lavender sachet—to make things smell good." She handed over the sachet from the second pocket. "Moonie didn't do this when we found a dozen of them in the cabin. I don't know what's wrong." From a squatting position, she reached in to rub Moonie on the ear, and he growled at her, seemed to think better of it, and nosed her hand.

The scent of lavender intensified as Sheriff Azgo opened the packet on his desk and then changed to a bitter smell when the lavender leaves spilled aside to reveal a half-dozen dark chunks the size of wrapped taffy candy. "What is it?" She reached for a piece and brought it to her nose. "Oh, dear." She dropped it back on the desk. "That smells terrible."

"It's opium."

"That's opium? How could anyone stand to eat that stuff?" She knelt back to Moonie, and he licked her hand, the one in which she'd held the opium.

For the first time, Sheriff Azgo laughed. It was a full, deep sound, and Nellie found herself smiling with him. "It's hideous smelling. And here I thought Moonie liked the lavender. This robe and sachets came from the Last Chance. It must not smell as bad to him."

The laugh ceased abruptly. "You took them?"

"I shouldn't have," Nellie said, shame flushing in her cheeks. "But they seemed abandoned. Like the dog."

The sheriff stared at her. "He belongs to Rosy. Didn't he tell you?"

134

"Henry did. Rosy either ignores the dog or swears at him." She sat down, feeling overwhelmed.

With a shrug, the sheriff rolled up the sachet, scooping the lavender leaves into his wastebasket with the edge of a piece of paper. "I think you and I should take a ride out to Last Chance Ranch. Seems like there's unfinished business."

"Now? I'm too tired. You forget I've had an unsettling couple of days." The thought of the rest of the day with this serious, almost grim, man exhausted her. Now there were two dead men. She wanted to untangle herself from the whole mess and return to photography. Unbidden and unwelcome, the thought that someone might have been after her in the darkroom flared in her head. She looked at her lap, not willing for the sheriff to see any sign of fright. He would surely misread it.

"Be prepared to be unsettled again. We'll load your snowshoes and you may change. We have to make this trip before it snows." He waited for her to stand. "Do you have any more photographs?"

Nell was tempted to say no. So far, her photography seemed to get her in trouble. This was not what she imagined when she left Chicago. The West had sounded adventurous and romantic. New enterprises demanded new thinking, she had argued to her mother. Staying in Chicago was not an option. She must support herself as she had no man to do it, and she would not be reduced to groveling and simpering for a man in order to marry and be imprisoned in a house, reading the *Ladies' Home Journal* and cooking and cleaning and serving lunches and teas to other women. She must find her own path.

"I have two more artistic photographs. I doubt if you'd be interested in them." Nellie folded the robe and stowed it away in her pack and placed her camera on top. "Are you bringing that photo? And you didn't say if you knew the person."

At first, she thought he wasn't going to answer, but he might have been thinking. "I'm not sure, so I won't say. With this injury," he said, pointing to the hand, "probably a miner."

"He must have frozen to death. There wasn't any blood around." Surely the spots she saw were something else, not fresh dried blood. Of course, that begged the question of why he had been removed while she was sleeping.

"Maybe. Maybe not. That's why I want to look again. You can show me exactly where you found him and we can check around the outside. Your exploring there alone was a foolish thing to do, although the Ah Kees should be grateful. Maybe you will remember something else when we are at the ranch." He waited for her to gather her pack and then looked directly at her. "You are the only person who saw a dead body. This photo is the only proof that you saw what you say you did. Without you and without this photograph, a murder and possibly two murders might never have been detected." He placed his Stetson on his dark hair. "Be careful, Miss Burns. I believe you could be in great danger."

With that sobering thought planted in Nellie's head, they walked out the door. This time, Nellie noticed his name painted on the cloudy window: Charles Asteguigoiri, Blaine County Sheriff. No wonder people called him Azgo.

Fear disappeared outside on a sunny day. Although the sheriff was on skis and had less trouble than she did with sinking down into the snow, Nell could keep pace with him, pulling her sled and using her walking sticks to balance herself. She felt like an accomplished snowshoer. She had insisted on bringing her camera. The sheriff had insisted the dog not come. Along the way to the cabin, she pointed out where she had taken her photos of the moonshadows. He inspected the scene carefully, and then motioned for her to lead the way to the cabin.

Nell showed him where the body had been, where she moved

it, and then wandered to the pump and cranked up enough water to fill her hand for a sip. Then she found a cup, and pumped a little more. It tasted earthy, as it had before.

"After you took the picture, then what did you do?" The sheriff shook his head at her offer of a sip from the cup.

Nellie tried to remember. "I heard Rosy yell and I called out to him that my snowshoe broke and I would stay all night. He went home then, I guess, and brought you back."

"Did you tell him you'd found a body?"

"N-no, I don't think so. Maybe. I didn't think he could hear me very well. And I was exhausted by then. I pumped some water for the dog and for me." She drank a little more and set the cup on the counter, wrinkling her nose at the aftertaste. "I crawled onto the bed and pulled the blanket around me. I was sure I wouldn't sleep with . . . the body in the room. The dog climbed up and slept beside me. I lay awake a long time listening to creaks and the wind howl, but I was asleep when you and Rosy arrived."

"And the body was gone."

"I couldn't believe it when I looked over there. You two made me doubt I'd really seen anything and that I did dream the whole thing. Then I remembered my photo. I mentioned it to you and Rosy, but—" She shrugged. She still couldn't understand why she didn't hear a body being moved, or why Moonie slept through it.

Just being in the cabin made Nellie feel sleepy. She sat on the broken-down couch, wishing she could take a nap.

"What else?"

The sheriff stood over her. His voice seemed soft and far away. She closed her eyes, resting them, and forced them open again. He had moved behind her. "How about when you returned the next day?" he asked, as if from the other end of a long tunnel.

137

"I looked for photo possibilities outside, then came in here. I looked upstairs, like you and Rosy did." She closed her eyes again and wished she could lie down on the bed. "I'm so sleepy, Sheriff. Could we come back another day?"

No answer. She looked around for him. He stood at the sink, pumping water for himself. Afternoon sunbeams filtered in through a dirty window. A bird croaked outside, and Nellie closed her eyes again.

"Wake up, Miss Burns! Wake up!" The sheriff's voice broke through Nell's dream of Moonie leaping at her with his jaws open wide and his teeth dripping with saliva. He held her cup out. "Drink this—all of it."

"N-no, it tastes awful." She tried to push him away, but he insisted.

"This is snowmelt. It won't taste awful. Drink." Then he held it to her lips and began to tip water into her mouth. She had to drink, and even then, some of the water spilled down her front. "We're going outside again. Stand up."

"I can't," she wailed. "I'm too tired." He pulled her off the couch and stood her up and circled her back with his arm. It felt like an iron rail that she couldn't dislodge. He walked her to the door, opened it, and thrust her onto the porch. She caught at an upright stanchion and held on, feeling sick, but awake. How dare he treat her like this?

"What do you think you're doing?"

The sheriff brought out her coat and put it around her shoulders. "That's better." His wide, white grin made her angry, but when he laughed, her anger dissipated. "What's so funny?"

"Remember you asked how someone could eat opium? Mostly, people smoke it, but someone stashed opium buttons in the pump. When you drank that water, you got a taste of it yourself." He handed her the snowshoes and motioned for her to fasten them up.

"No wonder the water tasted strange." She leaned over to pull the straps into place on her boot. Wooziness hit her and she straightened up. Her mouth still tasted like rust and dirt. "Is that why I got so sleepy?"

"Must be. Opium has different effects on different people, but that's one of them. And the longer a man takes it, the less he can function in the world. That I've seen. Makes him lose all desire—for anything."

"Both Moonie and I drank the water. We slept so hard, although I dreamed terrible dreams. So the opium was in the pump then. Maybe that's why we didn't hear someone take the body."

Sheriff Azgo nodded. "Are you all right now?"

"Yes." She forced herself to tighten the snowshoe straps. When she stood up, he motioned toward the trees on the south side of the cabin.

"Let's look over there. Stay in my track."

The sun-warmed air still held enough chill to clear Nellie's head. Without her sled, she moved easily, following the sheriff to the stand of aspens, white and gray-trunked. Their branches tangled like bony hands entwined against the blue sky. The snow was deep enough to cover any undergrowth and she studied the clean lines with an eye to a photograph. In another hour, their shadows would mark the snow where they stood. The sheriff looked down at the snow, then back at the cabin, toward the road, and then beyond to the river. In the afternoon silence, Nellie heard water running and chattering under ice and out into the open. A tiny movement seen from the corner of her eye caused her to turn.

"Oh, look. It's the ermine!" The creature dashed across the snow with a mouse in its jaws. The mouse wriggled and squirmed. The ermine hid behind a tree, then peeked out to watch the humans. When they didn't give chase, he dashed to another tree, aiming for a pile of snow and red willows near the water's edge. His black-tipped tail swung from side to side. Nellie wished she could catch the whimsy of the animal on film.

Sheriff Azgo motioned to Nellie, then put his finger to his lips and pointed down the river. At first, she couldn't see what he wanted her to see. Then, as she studied the aspen branches, the thick cottonwood trunks, and the willows, she drew in her breath. Gray and white branches moved—a bull elk with as large a rack of horns as she'd ever seen in any picture—no, larger. His massive head and chest posed for her as he studied them. Beyond him, several cows stood and two or three lay in a sun-filled glen.

"Can I set up to take a photo? Will they stay there for a while?" Her whisper seemed loud and she was afraid she would spook the animals.

The sheriff whispered back, his voice a low rumble. "They're far enough away from us so our presence doesn't cause worry."

"Will they attack?"

His low rumble broke into a chuckle. "No. A moose might, but the elk won't unless you approach too closely."

Then Nellie realized her camera was still at the cabin. "Damn!"

Sheriff Azgo waved her on. "Maybe later. Let's go toward the river. I'm following an interesting dip in the snow."

"What dip?" Nell had nearly forgotten what they were do-ing—searching for a dead man. Uneasiness filled her as they approached the Big Wood River. She wasn't certain why she felt fear when she was with a sheriff, while her exploration several days ago with only herself and Moonshine had been much more lighthearted, even though she had touched a dead man under the snow and then fallen into the river.

The sheriff slid forward again and didn't stop until he reached the willows where the ermine had dodged. When Nellie caught up, she peeked around the branches to see if she could find the small animal, thinking it would take dozens to make a coat. Connecting the beauty of the live creature with the beauty of a white ermine wrap caused her to wince. Something unwillow-like caught her eye.

"There's a piece of blue in the willows—down there." She leaned over to see what else she could find.

The sheriff took off his skis, long narrow wood pieces turned up at the front end, and sank to his knees. He waded below the willows, splashing water as he did so. Nellie began undoing her own snowshoes, but the sheriff spoke sharply to her. "Stay there."

"What is it?" She glanced up from the rawhide thongs to see him pulling at the blue. It was blue denim, wrapped around a leg. She almost tipped over. She didn't want to help and clambered back toward the trees.

"Don't go too far," Sheriff Azgo called. He labored to get the body onto the snowbank. It flopped over and Nellie could hear the squish of water. A bloated monstrous face rolled on a swollen neck toward her. "Go get your sled. I can pull him back to the road with it."

Nellie felt distinctly queasy with the bread and cheese she had eaten in the automobile sitting heavily in her stomach. Before she could lose lunch, she followed the track back to the trees and then to the cabin, glad to be heading away from their discovery. Her exertions settled her down. At the cabin, she again tied the sled to her waist and pulled it to the trees, where she off-loaded her camera. The elk rested in the snow and the bull still grazed along the stream in the bend away from where the sheriff worked. They ignored the humans.

"Here's the sled. I don't think I can help with the . . ." She untied the rope. Setting up for a photo would take her mind off what he was doing. "I'll be over by the trees."

As with the night photography, positioning the tripod on a firm footing took some effort. Nellie was aware of the activity at the stream and heard the body plunk onto the sled. "Elk," she mumbled to herself. "Stay right there." The play of the sunlight through the branches turned one side of the bull's rack silvery in color while he nosed the bark of a branch overhanging the river and then tore off a strip. As he munched, she covered her head and camera with the black cloth and focused, hoping the sun would stay bright. She pulled a film holder from her pack, inserted it in the camera, pulled out the slide, and opened the shutter. Perfect. She'd take one more with a red filter to emphasize the rack even more.

"How are you going to get your camera back to the cabin?"

Nellie jumped and almost fell into the pack. "Don't do that." She stood and nearly bumped into the sheriff. The sled trailed right behind him. "I'll carry it."

"How much longer will you be? I want to get this body to town. You'll have to identify it, you know, as the one you saw in the cabin, if that's who it is."

"Do you know who he is yet?" Her quick glimpse of the face told her it would be difficult for anyone to place a name on the man.

"His arm's been cut off at the elbow and I couldn't find the piece." He pointed to where the shirt had been raggedly cut. Missing was the lower left arm, the one with fingers missing. The axe under the pillow. Someone must have used it to cut off the arm. She would look for the axe back at the cabin. Nellie scanned the area around her after the sheriff moved off. If she could find the arm, maybe she could help solve the crime. It was beginning to be personal to her: her photo, her axe, her mystery.

Flat tracks, like those the sheriff made with his skis, marred the snow near the trees. She hoped they didn't show up in her photo and at the same time realized he had not tracked in that direction. Who did? And when? She followed the tracks to the edge of the trees facing the cabin, where they stopped, covered by fresh snow.

A somber light filled the aspen grove and, as she watched, the bull elk stepped with stately grace away from her. Two of the cows scrambled to their feet and clumsily followed him. She struggled to re-pack her camera, heft the pack onto her back with the straps around her shoulders, prop the tripod on her shoulder, and slowly pick her way in snowshoes back to the cabin. The deep trough cut by the sled weighted with a body smoothed her progress.

At the house, Nellie removed her snowshoes and went inside while the sheriff secured the body more tightly on the sled. Her hand slipped under the pillow and came up empty. So, it had been used, if not to kill someone, then to chop off the arm. The sheriff called her to come out.

The man lay face up, his bloated features sheathed in ice. Sheriff Azgo stood beside the sled, watching her.

"It's the same man. I'm sure of it." With a deep breath, she wrenched her stare away from the sled and back to the sheriff. "The ice was almost the same. Did you do that?"

"I wanted to see if I could get the same effect. I piled snow, wetted it down, and the freezing temperature turned it into a mask. And it was colder the night you were here." He gestured to the sky, which had changed from blue to cloudy gray in the space of half an hour. "Clear night then. No clouds to warm."

A tremble began in Nellie's breast and crept to her limbs and throat.

"He may have drowned, been carried to the cabin, then away again." Sheriff Azgo shook his head. "Or he may have been murdered, dropped into the stream, and retrieved. I am puzzled."

Tears began to stream from Nellie's eyes and she couldn't stop them. They froze on her cheek and her shaking grew. A sob threatened to choke her as she fought to stay still. The terrible deeds around this cabin smothered the joy she had felt the night she took the photographs, replacing it with a sorrow so profound, she too could drown in it.

The sheriff took the pack off her shoulders. He wrapped his own coat around her, then placed the pack on the sled between the man's legs, went back into the house, and clomped onto the porch again, pulling the door to. "Let's return to the auto. Activity will help you. Go first."

Nellie put one snowshoe in front of her, then the next. The coat smelled of used leather and sheep and man and smoke. It comforted her. With only the tripod, she could step faster. Her throat opened and her tears stopped. A pale star flickered in a break in the clouds, even though night had not yet descended, and the creak of snow as the man behind her pulled his heavy load became a winter sound. A lazy flake floated down, followed by another and another. Two men were dead and a woman as well, but a star still hung in the sky, and the earth turned and winter covered the land with a luminous light.

CHAPTER 13

Rosy knew he had a job to do, but he'd rather be back in the mines planting powder and setting it off than visit Mrs. Ah Kee. He wasn't exactly afraid of her, although he'd seen her mad—at him and Ah Kee both. Mean as six snakes. He figured she'd as soon stab a body with a butcher knife as look at it. Tongs were supposed to be bloodthirsty. It must be the women in the background who thought up ways to let more blood and trundle up bodies in more ways than Genghis Khan ever thought of doing. Or maybe, she was a direct descendant.

After a late night washing up Bert's butcher shop in exchange for his bed and some meals here and there, Rosy practiced what he'd say to Ah Kee's widow. If she had her own name, he didn't know it.

"Mrs. Ah Kee, you may not remember me . . ." No, she'd remember him all right. After the first scare with Lily, Rosy bought himself an automobile. He'd never walk again if he could help it. And then when Lily took sick, Rosy showed up at the Ah Kees at any time, day or night, to take the doc out to Last Chance Ranch. The town doc already said there wasn't a thing he could do for Lily. He didn't even try.

After Ah Kee sewed Lily back together again when the boy was born, Rosy was willing to lay her life in the Celestial's hands. He'd saved her once already and it worked. Maybe the doc could eke out another miracle.

"Mrs. Ah Kee, I have bad news . . ." Why start there?

"Mrs. Ah Kee, the doc came out to the ranch to help out an old friend of mine . . ." Friend. Rosy spit on the floor he mopped. Well, he was once, wasn't he?

Those were the days, though, back when the only war was across the seas and lead and silver prices jumped to the moon. All the old mines up and down the Wood River Valley had played out decades earlier. The two remaining—the Triumph and the Independence—couldn't shove the ore out fast enough. Two, sometimes three shifts a day, stoked up the Idaho mountains, north and south.

Jack showed up in Hailey, said the Bunker Hill Mine up north was on strike. The miners were just butting their heads against a lead wall. He wanted work and someone sent him up to the Triumph where he joined Rosy's crew that winter. Which winter? It was 1915, before the first boy, when Rosy fell for Lily.

He and Jack worked like dogs, then headed for a saloon. When they could, they caught a ride out to the ranch and bunked there. Otherwise, they found a pallet at one of the miners' boarding houses. Jack played his horn, sometimes in the saloon, most often on Sundays in the town band. In those days, there were still enough people to attend concerts—a mix of miners and sheep people and their families. Rosy hung around Bock's Boarding House after he met Lily at one of the big dinners Mrs. Bock prepared for boarders. When they married and moved to the ranch, he didn't see Jack so much. Jack wanted to go to the war, see the world, but the avalanche up at the North Star Mine, a penny-ante operation, ended those plans. He was laid up a long time.

"Mrs. Ah Kee, I loved my wife more than life itself. Doc Kee saved her once . . ." How was that going to make it any easier? She didn't like Lily at all, or any other woman near as Rosy could tell. Especially a woman who got to keep her kids with

146

her, unlike Mrs. Ah Kee. Once, just once, he'd seen the old bat soften.

Lily had insisted Rosy bring the Ah Kees out to dinner. "Bring Jack, too," she said. "Maybe Dr. Ah Kee"—she always called him doctor—"can help him with his bad back." Rosy didn't tell her what Jack thought about Chinamen, pretty much the same way all miners thought of them—as Chinks—but Rosy had been converted.

Lily served Mrs. Ah Kee a Basque dinner of salted cod and home-canned peaches and beans and carefully prepared tea made from dried lavender. The doc's wife had probably never been waited on in her life and she sent Lily a fabulous Chinese robe afterwards. Too big for Lily, but when she was sick, she hardly ever took it off.

Gawd, he missed Lily. The boys too, but Lily . . . What could he say to Mrs. Ah Kee? She'd had a whole life with her husband. Was that better or worse? He'd give anything to have Lily back.

Rosy knew the route to the Ah Kee house in the woods. Near the Big Wood River, the snow was wetter, harder to drive through. He carried a shovel in the boot in case he got stuck. By now, it had served all sorts of purposes. If a tool could hold memory, this one had too many. Maybe he'd toss it in the Wood.

The dead cottonwoods loomed over him, their bare branches clacking against each other in a late afternoon breeze. He'd take the bare open hills any day, even if they were dry as spit. Clouds scudded past the sun, creating moving shadows on the lands. Spooky in a way, like the shades of the once living, coming back to haunt him.

Rosy sat so long in his automobile, someone came out the door of the little house onto the front stoop and stared at him. Sammy. Rosy had forgotten about Sammy, a big strapping Chinaman. He might be more than Rosy bargained for. Mrs. Ah Kee was one thing—but two. Rosy shrugged, took a draught

147

from his bottle, set it on the floorboard, and climbed out.

" 'Lo Sammy. Is your mother to home?"

Sammy folded his hands at his waist and bowed so slightly, Rosy might have missed it if he weren't watching every move.

Rosy waited, the two of them looking at each other. Another shadow passed by.

"I need to talk with her."

"What about?" Sammy made no move to step aside or open the door.

"I'll tell you both, but I won't tell you first."

After another silent moment, Sammy disappeared inside and the door closed.

"Well, hell." Rosy waited. When nothing happened he headed toward the boot of his auto. Might as well not make it a wasted trip.

"Mr. Kipling. You wish to speak with me?" Mrs. Ah Kee stood where Sammy had stood. A shaft of sunlight struck her and Rosy realized she was beautiful. Pearl skin, almond-shaped eyes, black hair in a roll around her face framing its perfection. She looked old and young at the same time, like an Oriental cameo. He had never really noticed her face before and found himself making a slight bow of assent.

"Please come in." She entered the house, leaving the door ajar.

Inside, Rosy wasn't sure what to do. There was little furniture, only a table with chairs, and a small side cupboard with herbs on top. The air was thick with the smell of incense and something else, a memory. Sammy was nowhere to be seen. Mrs. Ah Kee motioned to one of the chairs. "I will give you tea." She moved toward an electric burner—the whole valley had electricity because of the mines. Still he was surprised to see a burner back in the woods at a Chinese house.

A smile played around Mrs. Ah Kee's mouth. "We are

modern, too." Her eyes, like black pebbles in a pool, did not smile.

"Wait, Mrs. Ah Kee. I have bad news." He stood just inside the door, holding his hat in his hand, not the way he planned it. "Your husband . . . Doc . . . Ah Kee. He's dead."

Her expression froze in a half-smile.

"I buried him. Next to Lily. In the aspens." Still nothing. "I'm sorry."

Sammy came in from a side door, his face like broken rock, his hand around a huge knife. He glanced at his mother, who continued to stare at Rosy.

"You kill him." Sammy's words carried as much menace as his weapon.

"Nope. I didn't." Rosy felt his breath leave him, as if he'd been hit. Sammy's face came together again. "But I might as well have." He sat in the chair. He wouldn't have so far to fall if Sammy stabbed him, and his legs wouldn't hold him up any longer anyway. Saying it out loud made it more true than all the carrying and digging and sweating and swearing had done.

Mrs. Ah Kee moved to another chair and sat down. "A woman killed him."

"No. No, a woman didn't kill him." Rosy had seen the blow to Ah Kee's head. No woman could hit with that kind of force.

Sammy raised his knife. Rosy waited for the blow. He wouldn't fight it. He could almost feel the blade cross his throat, see blood gushing. He remembered the scent: lavender.

Mrs. Ah Kee raised her hand. "No."

The word stopped Sammy. He turned to his mother.

"Not yet." She stood again, filled a tea kettle with water, set it on the burner, and turned it on. She brought out three handleless cups and a brown package from the wood cupboard. When the kettle whistled, she poured steaming water into a rounded tea pot. After a moment, she emptied the pot of its water, placed loose tea leaves into it, and then added hot water again.

No one spoke. Rosy heard the wind rising outside. Through a window at the back of the house, he saw the shadows darken. The silence didn't threaten him, and Sammy stood still, a statue in coolie clothes.

When Mrs. Ah Kee had placed tea cups in three places, she sat down and motioned for Sammy to do the same. "A young woman, a photographer, killed him. A Tong in Chicago hired her to come. My husband would not suspect her. He is a man who loves women. Many women."

Rosy sat up straight. He touched his tea cup and felt its warmth. Then he laughed out loud.

Sammy half stood up, reaching for the knife he had laid beside his place. "You laugh at my honored mother?"

Rosy raised his cup, so small in his hands he was afraid he'd crush it. He could pretend it was whiskey, he guessed, and slugged it down. He scratched his head. "I don't know where you come by such a fool idea. That bit of a girl wouldn't harm a flea."

"She fooled you, too." Mrs. Ah Kee lifted her own tea and Sammy sat back down.

CHAPTER 14

Nellie slept sixteen hours, disturbed by dreams. She forced herself awake in a dimly lit room. Beyond the window, snow fell in a dense curtain. Her half-formed plan to find the arm wasn't possible now. This time, all traces of the macabre events at Last Chance Ranch would be obliterated. She hoped Moonie was on the porch or in the kitchen with Mrs. Bock.

Equal parts of relief and frustration battled within her. Her presence had neither caused death nor could she have saved anyone. The fate of the two men—Ah Kee and John Doe—hung on passions far removed from a Chicago refugee.

Her photographs made the mystery part hers. If she could solve it, then she would lose the jitters that caused her to grind her teeth at night, lose the dark circles under her eyes when she woke up in the morning, and lose the sense of unfinished work to be done. Most of all, taking some action might reduce her rising level of fright. Sheriff Azgo's warning hadn't helped. A spider dropped on a gossamer strand from the ceiling almost onto Nell's bed. She watched it, thinking it was high time for her to move as well. But in what direction?

How could she hope to solve a crime in Idaho when she knew so few of the people and the relationships leading to murder? Hate, revenge, love, drugs—these were motives. Mrs. Ah Kee looked at Nellie with hate. Gwynn Campbell was said to want revenge for his daughter's death—a connection to the Ah Kees. Nellie wanted revenge against Scotto, but she wouldn't murder for it. All she lost was a job and her pride. Rosy must have loved his wife. Opium fairly hung in the air—yet another connection to the Chinese.

Sammy and his mother would not let the murder of father and husband remain unsolved nor would his death go un-avenged. Nellie hoped they realized she had nothing to do with it other than to find the body. And until John Doe had a real name, whoever killed him might want Nellie out of the way. She had seen and photographed him.

Nellie dressed slowly. She took her copy of the photo of the dead man to the window, where the light was better, to study it again. There was the arm; the ice had begun to melt from the fire. There was the belt she had moved to hide the reflection. There was his messy hair. Wait. The belt. The man on the sled wore no belt. Nellie closed her eyes and pictured the sheriff's "re-enactment" of ice. She only looked at the face. When the sheriff pointed out the missing arm, Nellie had seen no belt. She would tell the sheriff when she saw him next.

In the meantime, she had to take care of herself. If she didn't begin to replenish her nest egg—part inheritance from her grandmother, part savings from her job, and part gift from her mother, who could ill-afford it—she would have to return to Chicago a failure. She could not let that happen. She liked be-ing independent, and her only source of a relatively steady income to keep her independence was portrait photography.

Mrs. Bock, as usual, stood in her kitchen, this time rolling out pie crust as delicate as fine linen. A half-made red cherry pie waited on the counter, the empty preserve jar standing near as evidence of summer labors for winter rewards. "Miss Burns, I was beginning to worry. Thought maybe you died in your sleep." Her fingers flew to her face. "I should never have said that."

So, word of dead bodies must have surfaced, even if their

names weren't known. "Never mind. I'm alive and much too full of sleep." Nellie filled the kettle, placed it on a stove burner, and switched it on. "I'm ready to photograph portraits. I need your advice." She did not want to talk about the dead.

"I don't know nothing about taking pictures." Mrs. Bock held the pie plate above the rolled crust to measure the size. "Now, cooking—I could advise you all day long and into the night, too." With practiced ease, she rolled the fine crust onto the rolling pin and then unrolled it on the pie. A look of sweet pleasure crossed her face.

"I need that, too, but not today. Today I want to find the best place to set up my camera and open for business—some place with as much natural light as possible, with electrical outlets and enough room for extra lights and my tripod, preferably with a small waiting room and a room with a sink attached where I could at least develop negatives and make contact prints. Several sizes of chairs would be helpful, too. I thought Hailey would—"

Mrs. Bock's chuckle turned into a full-blown laugh. "You don't want much, do you, as Rosy would say." A strip of dough fell neatly around the pie as she cut the lap-over with a paring knife. Her laugh quieted to a chuckle again while she crimped the pie edges.

"I'm just trying to list the best of all possible places," Nellie said, a little abashed. She could catch the train to Hailey, but the only souls she knew there were Mrs. Ah Kee and Sammy. Remembering the woman's warning, Nellie cringed.

The tea kettle whistled. Mrs. Bock removed it from the stove as she opened the oven door to the side of the hot burner. She had already heated the oven by setting the levers for the oven at 400 degrees. In went the pie. For a moment she fussed with two cups of tea, then sat with Nellie at the kitchen table.

"Maybe this won't work," Nellie said. Disappointment welled up, surprising her. "Are there any jobs to be had here in winter?"

She couldn't cook or sew or type. Maybe a waitress job in Hailey or even Twin Falls. How embarrassing if Mr. Levine saw her.

"Don't backslide before you start," Mrs. Bock admonished. "Can't never did anything." She folded her hand and placed it on her mouth with her thumb rubbing a small mole on the side of her face. "Let's think."

Nellie's mother would have agreed with Nell and sunk into discouragement. A list of reasons not to do something would have splashed out and spread wide. Nellie didn't want to fall into the same habit. She kept her mouth closed so the negative inclinations wouldn't leak out.

"My parlor might work, but it's cold in there, being on the north side of the house. Light is good, and on sunny days, it warms up for a few hours. Doesn't no one use it on account of the fireplace in the dining room."

"Oh, I couldn't—" Nellie wanted her portrait studio to be an official one, like Mr. Levine's. Otherwise, people might think she was just dabbling at a profession.

"Hang on now. You and me could agree on certain times for you to use my bathroom so the roomers wouldn't be upset like last time. What you need more'n anything is customers. You got me, Bert, Bert's sister, their passel of young ones—you'd have to give them a special price—and Henry, maybe Robbie and Mrs. Smith. The schoolteacher. Maybe even a—" Mrs. Bock hesitated, and settled upon a euphemism that made Nell smile "—fancy lady. I doubt Rosy would want his picture taken. That eye of his bothers him—how it looks. He hates himself as it is. There's Jack Lane and a few others. But you'd need folks to come up from Hailey."

A gleam shone in Mrs. Bock's eyes and she rubbed her hands and wiped them on her apron. "Why, I could set up for nice dinners two or three days a week—same days as the train—at a fair price of course, and we could take pictures, serve tasty food, maybe rent a room or two—"

"These ideas sound wonderful." The ideas sounded like pie in the sky instead of on the table. "But who could afford all this—train fare, photos, meals, and even a room? Won't that be too much?" Still, her landlady's enthusiasm was catching.

The older woman stopped, thought again, and began more slowly. "There's the sheep ranchers—they're mostly down in Twin and Jerome but some come to Hailey and Ketchum regular. And other business owners, new babies, teamsters, and a few miners with money to burn. We get Sammy Kee up here— you might have to do him for free—and maybe he'd bring up them Chinamen from Twin. Still a few opium dens there, I hear. Every one of them has a chest of money hid out." Apparently Mrs. Bock's prejudice didn't extend to money.

"I met Mrs. Ah Kee and Sammy in Twin Falls. I don't think they would come to have their photos taken by me." And maybe Sammy would be in jail soon.

"So Mabel said. It's a wonder anyone else will stay at her place—"

"And maybe the sheriff?" Nell interrupted.

Mrs. Bock shifted in her chair and continued her list. "Then there's brides and such in the spring." She patted Nellie's knee. "People up here hate to go all the way to Twin. It'll make our little town a nice place to be with pictures in everyone's parlor." The gleam returned. "And Goldie's Pies in their stomachs and larders. And don't forget all the tourists in the summer." She grinned and held out her rough hand.

Nellie took it and they shook. Nellie didn't raise more doubts about Sammy Kee nor ask why he would come to Ketchum. She would cross that Rubicon later. First, she would tackle the parlor.

When Nell opened the door, a series of odors wafted out: old brocade, ancient incense, camphor from mothballs, and an overlay of tobacco from a pipe, long unused. Such a combination of smells conjured in her mind social evenings of another time when men sang harmony, women displayed themselves in whalebone-corseted dresses, foursomes played games of pinochle, and cordials were served in small crystal glasses with cut cherries on the sides. A wave of nostalgia for an era she had never known filled her.

How ridiculous, she thought. The room was dark, smelly, overcrowded with heavy furniture, freezing cold, and totally unsuitable for a studio. She began to close the door to her "new" profession, but noticed a sliver of light from the opposite side of the room—a window covered over with heavy drapes. It wouldn't hurt to pull them and see more of the parlor.

Any room closed up for a while would smell. Her own room in her mother's apartment in Chicago would smell of paper, glue, the slightly acid odor of celluloid film, the chintz of curtains and bedspread she had sewn during a high school home-skills class, hating every stitch but proud of the end product. Perhaps even the faded roses from a corsage souvenir of a long-ago dance where she fell in love with someone else's husband. She couldn't even remember who took her, but she could never forget the attractive, saturnine features of the man who whispered words in her ears while they danced to the "Tennessee Waltz," telling her he felt the same strong emotion toward her. And then he was killed at Verdun.

Her heel caught on the heavy rug, but she kept herself from falling by grabbing at a lamp with a fringed shade. She pulled the string hanging down and was pleased that light sprang on, muted by pink velvet. On the table under the lamp was a blush-toned wedding photo revealing a slender bride, lovely in a satin dress with a train gathered around her feet, and a rather plain-looking man with a square, determined-looking jaw and carefully slicked-back dark hair, parted in the middle, and gray sideburns. He was quite a bit older than the bride. She replaced the photo, thinking both the man and the woman seemed somewhat familiar, but the woman didn't look like Goldie.

At the window, Nell pulled back the draperies and light spilled in, even though the snow continued to fall. There were two wide windows rather than a narrow single one as in her room upstairs. This room was not large, but not small either, and completely square except for an alcove where an upright piano stood. She was right about evening singing. Maybe Goldie played. Another lamp stood on the piano, which meant a second electrical outlet. Good. The alcove should work well for photos of two or three people, like a bride and groom or a small family grouping.

The furniture might have come from a Victorian castle, it was so ornate and dour appearing. All of it would have to go and the walls painted white or at least ivory to reflect more light. The carpet should go too, depending on what was underneath it. Nell lifted up one corner and saw a parquet pattern exactly like the wood floor of the house where she grew up, her grandparents' home in Chicago. She sat down, fighting off the desire to be back at her dull job at the Scotto Studios, to enjoy the quiet evenings with her mother when one sewed and the other read and a grandfather clock ticked and chimed away the days, to be safe.

And yet, working for Scotto had not been safe.

"What do you think?" Mrs. Bock rushed in. "The furniture has to go—I'll get Rosy to help move it out and store it somewhere—and you and me can paint the walls, liven 'em up a bit." She turned in a circle. "Take down those moth-eaten drapes—good riddance to them, I say. Maybe keep the piano. Might work as a prop. Henry can rig up some wheels or a dolly so's you can move it around without breaking your back."

The older woman's enthusiasm brought Nell to her feet. "I

thought the alcove might work for wedding photos, and what a good idea about the piano. The rug is too dark and this floor is beautifully crafted."

"Ain't it? Reason I bought the place as I remember. Can't think why I covered it up, but I had all these odds and ends of furniture, including that old Oriental rug, so I stuck it all in here."

There went Nell's imaginings of a more graceful era than the one in which she lived. She laughed. "But someone must have used this furniture and room. I could even smell pipe smoke when I opened the door."

"Before my time," Mrs. Bock said. "Nobody I know ever smoked a pipe in here unless maybe it had opium in it. Never know who's took up that filthy habit." She picked up the wedding photo from the table, touched the front gently. "You'd never think Rosy was handsome once, would you?"

"That's Rosy?"

A commotion at the front door interrupted them and Mrs. Bock ran to stop someone from tracking water into her front hall. The telephone rang and rang until Nell answered it.

"Hello. This is Mrs. Bock's boarding house."

"I wish to speak with Miss Nellie Burns, please."

Only Mr. Levine spoke so formally. "This is Nellie Burns. How are you feeling?" She felt guilty all over again for his injuries and the damage to his studio.

"I am quite well, thank you. It is kind of you to inquire." He paused and Nell wondered if she should ask whether the darkroom door had been repaired.

"You must think it unusual of me to telephone you in Ketchum," he finally said.

Until then, she hadn't.

"The reason I am making this telephone call to you rests upon the photographs you kindly showed to me in the hospital.

They were so distinctive and, I think, unusual, that I have returned to them frequently in my mind while recovering. Not that my recovery was prolonged."

Having another photographer's good opinion of her work was important to Nellie. She had been unable to assess objectively her own abilities, and Mr. Levine's words gave her some corroboration upon which to hang her determination. "Thank you, Mr. Levine. I appreciate your kind words." She kicked herself for adopting his speech patterns. He might think she was making fun of him.

"You are probably much more aware than I of a photography magazine published in New York City by Mr. Alfred Stieglitz, himself a famous photographer, as well as a supporter of the arts." Mr. Levine's voice, modulated but distant traveling through the wires, reminded Nellie of their ease working together in the darkroom.

"I'm familiar with Mr. Stieglitz's work, and in Chicago I recall seeing several issues of the magazine, but I believe it was discontinued. *Camera Work* was the name." She remembered how expensive the magazine had been. One photo in particular had spurred her to seek her own artistic avenues for photography after she was forced to leave the Scotto Studios. It was a photograph of New York City at night with a brightly lit skyscraper in the background and in the dark foreground, white wash hanging on a line and two lit windows. His portrait photography, too, showed real people, not posed mannequins, as she herself came to think of her subjects.

"It was discontinued," Mr. Levine said, "but several photographers in San Francisco, among them a woman, are doing photo work not dissimilar to Mr. Stieglitz, art photography. You should send your photographs to this group for critique and possible showing."

This sudden presentation of an opportunity, however far-fetched it might be, sent shocks through Nellie. Could she? Would she? Dare she?

"Miss Burns, are you there?"

She took a huge breath. "Yes, I'm here. I'm just floored by your suggestion that I should send those photographs to such a group. I—I had no thought myself that they were good enough even to consider showing them." She gripped the telephone earpiece so hard, her hand ached. "They need so much work."

"Yes, that is another reason I called. I know you will need a darkroom and that you have none available there. I wished to offer mine to you and also to suggest that I could offer you some work from time to time with my developing if you were able to come to Twin Falls."

"Mr. Levine, thank you so much for your suggestion and your offer. I'll have to think about what I could do with my photos, but yes, I would appreciate doing some work for you." Now was a good time to test her new project. "I hesitate to be bold with this counterproposal." She heard the telephone lines softly zing. "I am going to do some portrait work here and could trade work for you in exchange for using your darkroom after hours for some development time for myself." Again *zing*. "I've been asked by several people to take portraits, and I need to begin earning a living. I wouldn't want to compete with you, of course, but I don't think these people would come to Twin Falls for portraits . . ."

"I would be delighted to work out such an arrangement with you, Miss Burns. When can you come again so we can discuss a mutually agreeable working relationship?"

Nellie was so relieved, she barely heard an argument developing at the front door between Mrs. Bock and a man's voice. "I could come early next week, if that would work." She would check into the train schedule, if there was one. "I'll call and let you know."

"I will expect to see you, then. Goodbye, Miss Burns." He rang off.

"You can't come through this door like you owned the place!" Mrs. Bock's anger was evident. Her voice was shrill as she guarded the door with her body.

"Me see Missee Picture-Taker," another voice answered, almost as shrill. The door wavered, pushed on one side by Sammy and pushed back by Mrs. Bock.

No one was in the house but the two women. Nellie worried that the Chinese man might hurt Mrs. Bock, so she headed for the door. "I'm here, Mr. Kee. What do you want?"

Mrs. Bock ceased her push-push war with Sammy and opened the door wider. "You be polite to Miss Burns, or I'll tear out that pigtail of yours." She looked as if she could do it.

Sammy no longer wore his servile expression. He was angry and his dark eyes swept Mrs. Bock with contempt. Nevertheless, he bowed slightly to Nellie, who found herself bowing in return. From a bag, the strap of which circled his neck and right shoulder, he brought forth three contact prints—Nell's photos. "You take these pictures."

"You know that I did. You stole the negatives from my room."

"You mean this Chinaman was in my house?" Mrs. Bock turned from one to the other, her mouth slightly open. "I knew they were all thieves."

Sammy ignored her. He bowed again to Nellie. "You took photo of dead man. My mother wants picture of my father." He sorted out the photo of the iceman. "This not my father. Where my father?" He showed the other two photos of the moonshadows. "Father not here." His voice rose again. "You hiding picture!"

Nellie turned to her landlady, knowing that Mr. Kee should have some explanation because she knew where his father was, or at least, who had him. "Could I take Mr. Kee into the parlor and talk with him?"

"Humph. Don't let no one see him." She glared at Sammy and stomped to the kitchen.

In the parlor, Nellie did not sit down, nor did Sammy. The standing lamp was still lit and the draperies pulled back. In the snow-filled light, his face reflected some of the same character of his grandmother's photo in Mr. Levine's studio.

"I think I found your father buried under snow across the Big Wood River from the Last Chance Ranch." Bluntly told, but she didn't know how else to begin.

"We know he dead," Sammy said. "Body in cold room in Hailey."

His eyes seemed teary to Nellie, but she couldn't be sure. With relief, Nellie sat down. The sheriff had expressly warned Nellie not to tell anyone she had found the Chinese man. If his family already knew, then it didn't matter if she told Sammy.

"You found him at Ranch. You covered with snow. Where picture?"

"Indeed I did not find him at the Ranch and I did not cover him with snow. Thank heavens someone did, though, or the coyotes would have eaten him." Few people had ever accused her of lying. "And I did not take his photograph. I don't even know what he looks like."

Sammy struck a menacing pose. "My father like me. Warriors." He dropped the pose and melancholy invaded his features, dampening them in the waning afternoon light. The lamp shone on one side of his face and Nellie regretted she had left her camera in her room. Could such sorrow be captured? She could hardly say "Wait here while I get my camera."

"Mr. Kee, I am very sorry about your father's death. You must have loved him very much. I did not take his photograph. I thought this man—" she pointed to the photo in his hand "—was the person buried in the snow. Look at me. I'm too small to carry a man across a river by myself." She held out her hands in a pleading fashion. "But if you look so much like your father, I could take your photograph. Perhaps that would be some consolation to your mother." She was almost afraid to suggest another idea, the one that had generated the photo of the iceman. "In Chicago, where I came from, the Midwest, a huge city—"

"I know Chicago," he said.

Nellie regretted her assumption that he was somehow not knowledgeable about the world. "I often took photographs of the deceased for their bereft kin. Would your mother consider . . ." She let the idea drift between them. Perhaps such a suggestion was total anathema to the religion of Sammy and his mother. And she had no idea what Mr. Ah Kee might look like, although if he had been in snow for days he might be well preserved. Still, a macabre suggestion. A photo of a murdered man. She corrected herself: a photo of a second murdered man.

"You no have picture of father?"

"No, I don't." Nellie made her face as resolute and open as she could. He peered at her.

"You take picture of dead men?" The idea seemed to intrigue Sammy.

"I have in the past. And I took that photo—the one you stole from me." She couldn't let it go. "How did you know I had it?"

"Honored mother want picture of dead father."

"Do you know this man?"

Sammy held up the photo. "Three-Fingered Jack. Opium-eater. Dead at ranch?"

If Sammy knew, then the sheriff must know too. "I thought he froze to death. His face was covered with ice. That is why his features aren't clear."

"Ice?" Sammy, too, studied the photo. A soft "ahhhhh" escaped him; a look of understanding filled his eyes when he glanced again at Nellie, puzzling her.

"I ask mother." He brushed past Nell and opened the door.

"Wait, I want my photos back. Those are not yours to keep!"

Sammy ignored her, trotting to the front door where he slipped out.

"*Damn* that man."

"No lady talks like that."

Nell spun around. "How would you know?" she snapped at Rosy, who stood in the dim hall. How much had he heard? The grief she'd just seen in Sammy's face filled Rosy's. "I'm sorry," she said. "I had no call to say that to you. What do you want?"

"Goldie says you're gonna take pictures. I want one. I'll be your first customer, girlie."

CHAPTER 15

"Take that greenish-yellow chair up to Room Four. It'll fit next to the bureau." Mrs. Bock ordered and Rosy obeyed. They'd all begun work early in the morning. "That plushy lamp will work fine in the dining room."

"There ain't no room for it." Rosy picked it up, nevertheless, and wrapped the cord around the stand. "And no plug either." He leaned it on his shoulder as if it were a baseball bat.

Gladys Smith appeared in the doorway. "So this will be your portrait studio. How nice." She pinned her black hat to her hair. "Rosy, dear. I'll take the lamp." She touched his sleeve.

He thrust it toward her without a word.

"Oh, could you please bring it up to my room? I don't want to get my skirt dusty." She turned, and he followed her.

Nellie wondered if Mrs. Smith had set her sights on Rosy. She was always so . . . what was the word? . . . flirty around him. Nell waited until the two were out of sight and then whispered to Mrs. Bock. "Do you think Mrs. Smith and Rosy might get together?"

"The parson's table there might fit in the entry. Give us a place to rest bundles and such." Mrs. Bock glanced over at Nellie. "And no, I don't think Gladys and Rosy will get together. Gladys had her fill of men, taking care of her brother. He wasn't so nice to her. And who'd want an old drunk when there's scads of men around and hardly any women? You, now, you could take your pick, if'n you felt like pickin'."

Nellie moved the table. The end pulled out as an unmarked drawer; the opening motion caused something inside to roll back and forth. She scooped it up and noticed it seemed to be a child's toy. Mrs. Bock snatched it from her. "Don't let Rosy see that." As if in explanation, she said, "No place for children's things." Her face lost its moving-day animation. "No one around here wants children." She tucked the toy in her pocket. "No one but me."

Mrs. Bock pointed to the davenport. "Rosy'll need help with that. See if you can scare up Henry. He ain't so broken down he can't lift one end."

When Nell walked back from calling Henry in the dining room, she saw Rosy and Gladys deep in conversation at the top of the stairs. Rosy emphasized something with a strong arm gesture. Gladys placed her hand on the arm. He shook it off, saying something. Her response was not audible either, but Gladys stepped back and raised her own arm, as if to fend off an attack, then moved out of sight. Rosy scurried down the stairs to where Nellie stood. Henry joined Rosy and Nellie and the three walked into the parlor.

"Where's the couch go?" Rosy asked.

Mrs. Bock pondered the question. "Telephone Missus Reedy. Maybe the dentist can use it in his waiting room. The carpet, too."

"Them moths and carpet worms might give his patients fits," Rosy said. "Then again, his patients might 'preciate a softer wait than those hard old chairs of his. Enough to break your butt." He and Henry carried the heavy piece out the door.

Nellie rolled the rug gingerly, watching for worms that might crawl out, then brought in a bucket and mop and rags and vinegar and cleaned the rapidly emptying room. Even Henry helped scrub walls, standing on a stepladder for the corners, coming down with cobwebs caught on his hat. His cradle for

166

the piano rocked a bit but permitted Nellie to move the heavy instrument around. The two men carried the carpet to the basement, and Nellie heard the landlady joking and the three of them laughing together as they descended rickety stairs. Moonie, apparently in Mrs. Bock's good graces, followed down and up and back and forth, but finally settled in the parlor, watching Nell.

Everyone knew each other well in this town. Nellie envied the sense of belonging that must inspire. She couldn't help comparing it to the cold relations most people had in the city. Or maybe she was the one who was the outsider everywhere.

While she worked, Nellie pondered what to do next. She could call the sheriff. Enlarge the photographs of the iceman, who now had a name, and the night. That would give her more information to work with. The shadow on the trees that she had seen in the studio on the contact print might be important. Or it might just be a shadow.

Her mind turned back to photographing and how to take Rosy's photo. Not technique, but the sensitivity of it. What she wanted, she was certain he would not: A full-face picture, stubble and all, of both eyes and scar to show what mining and life in the West had done to him. Not to make a sideshow of his failings or physical defects, but to reflect this particular man and how he was or wasn't handling the lot passed to him. With her landscape photos, she struggled with how to transform a pretty postcard scene to reflect the depth of feeling she herself had felt. Here it would be how to make an ugly scar reflect the depth of the man.

Mrs. Bock found extension cords for the lights the butcher had brought over upon their arrival from Twin. From the jumble of furniture, Nellie retained the piano and its bench, a curious three-seated chair in the shape of a pinwheel and upholstered in red velveteen—a "gossip chair" Mrs. Bock called it—two upright wood chairs, an end table, and the parson's table for a desk.

In order to move the gossip chair to the alcove, she needed to shift the piano bench. To avoid scraping the parquet, she lifted one end and set it down at a forty-five-degree angle. Moonie stood and nosed the lid. When Nellie went to the other end to shift it, he barked. "What is it?" He nosed the lid again. She raised it, expecting to see music. And inside was a stack of sheet music but also a belt with a large buckle. It was as if her earlier thoughts had conjured up the object. She inspected it, feeling the bumps on the buckle. This must be the belt from the iceman. Now, she had something. But how did it get there?

Boots in the hallway caused her to drop the belt and close the bench with a crash.

The smell of alcohol preceded Rosy into the room. Nell could have sworn he had no bottle with him while he worked. He must have stopped at his car or nipped into one of the saloon-cum-cafes at the south end of Main Street. His familiar sullen look had returned, a marked contrast to the aiming-to-please expression of most of the morning.

"I earned my picture, girlie. Take it now." His words almost slurred together.

"All right, Rosy. You have definitely earned a photo." Certainly his disheveled appearance worked into her plans to reflect his life, but Nellie felt awkward taking advantage of Rosy's state. "But wouldn't you rather wait until morning when you're all slicked up?"

"You don't want no picture looking like you do now," Mrs. Bock declared as she walked back into the room.

"Mine your own business, Goldie. Want my picture." He sprawled in the three-seater, mumbling to himself.

Mrs. Bock harumphed and left, muttering, "Go to hell your own way you old . . ."

Nellie busied herself setting up her camera on its tripod, fixing the lights to shine on the alcove. The words ". . . boys . . ." and ". . . resting place . . ." and ". . . damned liar . . ." sifted out from the low grumble. " 'Course I'm old as dirt," was clearer. She placed one of the wood chairs where the most light shone. "Sit here, Rosy."

"I ain't sittin'." He walked unsteadily to the chair and placed his foot on it. "Women sit. Men stand." He leaned on his knee with his forearm, dropped his hat on the floor by the chair, and leered at Nellie. "This here is how I want it."

She wondered if he knew his bad eye was closest to the camera. "It will take me a few minutes to get focused. Do you want to sit while I finish setting up?"

"Nope." He continued to stare at her while she covered herself with the black cloth and studied him through the lens.

"I'm excited about this studio you helped with. Still, taking outdoor photographs is my longing. And I'd like to visit a mine, say, and take photos of the miners."

"Can't be done."

"Why not?" She removed the cloth and made some adjustments to the lights, re-focused, and slipped in the film.

"No women allowed. Bad luck."

Nellie removed the dark shade and used a shutter release to trip the shutter. At the sound, Rosy stood and gathered his hat and began to move toward the door.

"Come back here, Rosy. I'm not finished."

"Yep you are. Only want one." He disappeared out the door with Moonie tagging along.

Such a strange man. He hadn't noticed the wedding photograph on the piano where she'd moved it. Probably a good thing. Nellie thought she would feel elated at getting her "studio" organized for business. Instead, a sense of loss filled her.

She peered around the doorway to make certain Rosy was

gone and then retrieved the belt. Under the electric photo light, she examined it more carefully. The buckle had a musical instrument, she thought, outlined on it—a horn of some kind—and an engraving: something Band, 19 . . . 1918, maybe. On the reverse side were engraved initials difficult to read. By tilting the belt, she could make out "To J.B. with love forever." The final initials were almost rubbed off, but looked like "I.K." or "I.H."

Nellie glanced up when she heard a soft sigh from the doorway. There stood Moonie with Rosy right behind him. "Thought you'd want your dog."

"It's your dog, isn't it?"

"Not no more. You can have him. He likes a lady." Although the light around Rosy was dim, Nellie saw a tear track down his face.

"Do you know a man named Three-Fingered Jack?" she asked.

A shade pulled down over Rosy's good eye. "Did."

"What is his last name?" She looked again at the belt. Surely Rosy saw it, too.

"Smith." Rosy snorted. "Everyone's name is Smith in these parts."

He slipped back into the shadows and was gone. Moonie trotted over to her and mouthed the belt. What to do with it? Hide it, but not in her room. People walked in and out of there as if it were a department store—Marshall Field's. She looked at the back of the belt again. "J.B." This man was a Jack. Who killed him and Ah Kee? The deaths must be related. Find whoever hid this belt and she would know who removed the body from the cabin, and, in all likelihood, the murderer. Someone had gone to a lot of trouble to hide the identity of the body. Who else but the murderer?

More footsteps in the hall. She shoved the belt deep behind the cushions of the gossip chair. That seemed safer than back in the piano bench.

Over the next two days, Nellie had little time to call the sheriff. She decided to do more investigation herself. The sheriff was one of the people who had been in and out of the ranch, walking around on his own. He was not free of suspicion.

Friends of Mrs. Bock's trooped in to have their photographs taken. Bert the Butcher brought his wife and children and wanted a single photo of each, then a photo of Bert and his wife, and then one of them all together. Nell explained she usually took two to four photos of each subject in order to get the best pose of everyone.

Bert's sister-in-law, the local schoolteacher, came next, a woman who seemed much too timid to control a roomful of children. Then Bert's brother, who ran what used to be a livery station and now sold gas to the dozen or so cars in town and the hundreds who came through in summer on their way to the Stanley Basin so their owners could fish and camp and enjoy the great outdoors. His sheepskin vest, Levis, six-shooter slung around his waist, Stetson, boots, spurs, and chaps would thrill a magazine in the East. He was a nonstop talker and before she finished with his photos, Nellie figured she knew all the best spots for any kind of outdoor activity in the area.

"Is there a band in town?" she asked him.

"You mean a music group? Used to be. Got dis-banded a while back." He chuckled. "Miners who played in it mostly left town." He pursed his lips and whistled two notes.

Nellie asked him if she could send his photo to a magazine, assuring him she would pay him something if she sold it.

"I'll say so!" His smile broadened and he curled the end of his mustache. His customers surely told stories about him long after their vacations were finished.

Two elderly sisters, one who ran a small library from the back of the grocery store and the other a local seamstress, came early the second day, asking if they could have their photographs taken even though they didn't have an appointment. They could have been twins, and perhaps they were, dressed alike in the latest Salvation Army fashion, their hair twisted into gray buns on top of their heads, and each with a touch of lipstick and rouge.

"We don't have anyone who would want our photo—" began the librarian, adjusting her rimless glasses.

"—except ourselves. That's all right, isn't it?" The seamstress took off her glasses and peered myopically at Nellie.

"Of course." Nellie arranged them in the three-seated chair so that they seemed to be mirror images. Only a close study of the photo, when printed, would reveal these were two different people. She liked the idea of an optical illusion that wasn't. Neither used the third seat where the belt was hidden.

All the people who sat for photos thanked her and paid her a deposit. Nearly all of them said they would send in another relative or friend, mostly from Hailey. Mrs. Bock sold four pies. While Nell began to put away her camera and plan how she would develop the film—wait until she went to Twin Falls or use Mrs. Bock's bathroom—a sharp knock sounded at the front door. Moonie, who had lain quietly near the tripod the second day, stood and barked.

Nellie walked to the door to forestall Mrs. Bock.

Sammy stood there, wearing a heavy coat, a coolie hat on his head. She should have known. Only this Chinese man knocked. Everyone else just entered. "Come, come." He gestured for Nellie to come outside.

She stepped back. "No. What do you want?"

"Come. Take picture." He wore his servile expression. Then he pointed inside. "Get picture-taker." He motioned putting a camera between his hands and said, "Click click."

Nellie sighed. Eastman Kodak cameras were everywhere. By then, Moonie had followed her and begun to growl. When

Sammy reached to pull on Nellie's sleeves, the dog barked and would have jumped on Sammy if Nellie hadn't caught him. "No, Moonshine."

The Chinese man leaned toward the dog, bared his teeth in a huge grimace, and said, "Chinee eat dog!"

Nellie slammed the door in his face as Mrs. Bock scooted down the hallway toward her. "What's all the ruckus?" The smell of rosemary and garlic accompanied her.

"Sammy threatened to eat Moonie!" Nellie kneeled and put her arms around the dog, who continued to growl. "He wants me to go somewhere with him and bring my camera." Moonie had never reacted that way to anyone, even with all the strangers trooping in and out. He hadn't even minded the children trying to climb on him, and all day, he hadn't growled or even barked.

Bang, bang. A hand pounded on the door. Mrs. Bock opened it. "Get outta here, you . . . you . . . foreigner!" She began to close it once more, but Sammy stuck his foot in the door. "Want Missee. Take picture honored father." He prevented Mrs. Bock, who was not slight, from closing the door.

"Wait." Nellie inserted herself between the landlady and Sammy. "I suggested to Sammy that I could take a photograph of his father, even though he's, um, not alive." Afraid Mrs. Bock would think she was entirely crazy, she added, "We used to do this in Chicago. The bereaved often want photos of their deceased loved ones." It was easy to slip into the mortician-like phrases she had once used in funeral homes and in gloomy parlors of the survivors.

"Disgusting is all I say. People ought to be ashamed of theirselves. Pictures of dead people." She followed up her disgust with a slap of her hands, from which flour fell in sprinkles. "You shouldn't go anywhere with that Chinaman." With that warning, she left.

Moonie growled, a long low rumble of sound, but he stayed by Nellie's feet.

"Have you asked the sheriff about this?" She couldn't imagine that Sheriff Azgo would give his permission for such a bizarre request.

Sammy bowed. "Come. Come."

Nellie hesitated. She knew Mrs. Ah Kee hated her but she didn't know why. If she went, perhaps the Ah Kees would understand that Nellie had nothing to do with the Chinese man's death. She wanted to know more. The Chinese pair knew some of the answers, she was sure, but a squiggle of caution told her they might know because they were directly involved. "All right, but my dog is coming too. Wait here. I'll get my things."

The man slipped into the hall, now seeming a mere shadow, and followed Nellie into her studio. She was surprised he was so much taller than she was and tried to think if she had stood beside him before. It was almost as if he were a shape-changer.

She pointed to one of the lights. "Bring that, too. Where are we going?"

"Cold room." He gestured to the out of doors. "Mother wait auto."

The presence of Mrs. Ah Kee offered more danger than Sammy, Nellie thought. She decided to go anyway. The sheriff presumably would be at hand. She couldn't forget, either, that she had been certain it was Sammy who attacked Jacob Levine, despite the sheep rancher's word to the contrary. Nellie found more film and loaded up her gear. "Don't touch this until I return."

"Come, Moonie. I'm getting my coat." In her room, she thought hurriedly what to do with the Chinese robe. If she left it alone, someone might take it, although she would be with the person she suspected. Finally, she decided to leave the dog instead of taking him. He would guard her room. This whole thing might be a ruse to lure her out of the house. She also left her moonshadow photos but brought the negatives, placing them in a small purse that she tied around her waist under her dress. They were too valuable to leave. Then she decided to change into her long pants. At the last minute, she placed the robe under her mattress, just in case. "Bye, Moonie. I'll be back later."

Before Nellie returned to the studio, she found Mrs. Bock and told her she was leaving to take a photo. Mrs. Bock frowned at her. She must have known that Nellie was going with the Chinese man. Nellie was not sure why she herself had agreed to go, given her dread of Mrs. Ah Kee. Still, she knew what it felt like to lose a father. When Nellie returned to the studio, she studied the equipment and decided that nothing had been moved. Sammy stood exactly where she'd left him.

"Where dog?"

"He is guarding my room and will bite anyone who tries to enter it." Nellie lifted the pack with her camera and motioned to Sammy to bring the tripod and the lights. "Mrs. Bock knows where I'm going."

Outside, snow fell again, draping the town with a soft mantle. Lights shone from a window or two, but otherwise the street was the dreamlike combination of black and white that snow lent every scene. Once again, Nellie felt the urge to photograph, to continue her experiments in transmitting light and dark onto celluloid. She stopped to study a composition from the boarding house porch across to the schoolhouse and on up the street, taking in two Model-T Fords that seemed, at that moment, to be sorry substitutes for fringed carriages pulled by horses. Nothing marred the blanket. When she turned to look in the other direction, Sammy urged, "Come. Come." The door of one of the Model-Ts opened and Mrs. Ah Kee peered out.

Cold Smoke, Nellie had heard one of the miners call powder snow, repeating an Indian term, he said. Each step she took raised a white cloud, as if she were walking along a sky lane. Even the object of her journey could not erase her delight. Mrs. Ah Kee did that.

CHAPTER 16

Rosy studied Nellie while he helped move and tote, load and store. She reminded him too much of Lily, who seemed so close to him now. They didn't look a bit alike. It was their "I'll show the world" attitude, even if the world didn't give a damn.

Maybe she did fool him, just like Mrs. Ah Kee said, but he knew it wasn't about murder and mayhem. Maybe he invested too much in her spirit because he needed to. He wanted her business to succeed. He wanted her to show the world. He couldn't say why. He was probably just an old man in his cups.

All morning, he and Henry and Goldie helped Nellie. Rosy felt like they were in a booster club, like the one that used to hold dances in the school gym and get the band together to play, raising money for some poor sod who was on the verge of ruin. A new business in town raised all their spirits.

Running into Gladys spoiled some of the fun. He hefted the fancy lamp onto his shoulder and she followed him up the stairs.

"What did you do with it?" She stopped him at the top of the stairs. Her voice was low and harsh.

"What you talking about woman? I got the lamp right here." He set it down. The fringe swayed. "You can carry it yourself."

"You know what I'm talking about, you—" Gladys pressed her lips together, looked around and leaned closer, grabbing his arm, her head about even with his. The strength of her grip surprised him. "I told you . . ." She let him go and pressed her hand against her forehead. "If they find it, they'll know."

"Hell's bells. You think no one knows now?" He wanted to strike her for being such a dunderhead.

Gladys cowered. "Don't you hit me!" She grabbed the lamp and hurried to her room, where she turned at the door. "It's you they'll want. Not me. I am just trying to save your skin. You dirty old man." These words, she yelled, and then closed the door behind her.

Rosy was thirsty, but Henry waited and so did Nell and Goldie. There was more work to be done. He looked back up the stairs, hoping Gladys wouldn't reappear. How he disliked that woman. He and Henry hefted the davenport, not easily. Goldie held the door open so they could squeeze the heavy piece of furniture through. As they tramped by on their way to the dentist's waiting room, Charlie Azgo stepped out of his box of an office there in Ketchum.

"Rosy, we need to talk."

"Can't you see I'm busy?" He felt his age at his end of the davenport. "Want me to drop my end and break Henry's back?" They kept on walking.

The sheriff caught up and hefted the end Rosy held away from him. Rosy would have turned and walked away, but the sheriff took one arm from the couch and plucked at Rosy's sleeve, gesturing for him to come along.

After the couch was delivered, Henry gave the other two a deadpan look and hightailed it back to Goldie's, even though Rosy offered to buy him a drink. "Now that you've ruined my morning and scared away my fellow worker, what do you want?"

"I've got Doc Kee on ice in Hailey. He was killed with a blow to the head."

Rosy nodded.

"Do you want to tell me what happened?"

They stood in the slush on the boardwalk. Along with the damp, Rosy could feel his thirst rising and his stomach hurting, like he was crawling in the desert with his insides turned out. It happened more and more lately and gave him a better understanding of his friend Jack. Rosy closed his eyes, wishing the Basque away, but when he opened them, there the sheriff stood, solid as a pillar.

"I didn't kill him, if that's what you want to know."

Once, Rosy was like the sheriff, tall and broad and not so bad-looking himself. *Wasn't I, Lily?* Once, he didn't shake with palsy in the morning and he had a clear head and clear eyes. He worked hard, he looked forward to his time at Last Chance Ranch, even to looking for gold in the mountains. The world showed him what for anyway.

"I've got Three-Fingered Jack there too, or what's left of him. Part of his arm is gone and he's been in water for a while." The sheriff waited for a response. Rosy didn't give him any. A wagon drawn by two horses splashed by in the street, followed by two motorcars.

"He didn't drown," the sheriff said. "So far, I haven't figured out how he died."

Rosy looked down so as not to give away his knowledge. Finally, talking to the ground, he said, "He got what he deserved."

"What?"

"Maybe they killed each other," Rosy said. He lifted his head to look the sheriff in the eye. "The ghost saved him. Maybe she—it changed its mind." He stepped back. "I got work to do, Charlie." He almost slipped, caught himself before the other man could, and headed back to Goldie's. No one stopped him.

The bottle in his auto looked better than usual. He sat in the front seat, sipping slowly, trying to empty his mind of scenes and words and recriminations. He was so tired. Maybe if he took a short nap, he'd feel better.

Jack had showed up at Last Chance Ranch late at night when

Rosy was sitting quietly, hoping her ghost would come back while he was sober. The dog slept by the fire, sometimes making sounds and moving his legs, as if he were dreaming, too.

"You gotta help me, Rosy. Look at my hands. They're crawling with worms." Jack held them out, gone soft after years of hard work, the usual shiny place where two fingers were missing wrinkled like prunes. They trembled so hard, he wouldn't even be able to hold a drink, all Rosy would offer. His face suffered a tic—one eye, half-closing, opening, half-closing, then closed. It was as if he had the bad eye. "I need some stuff."

"I ain't got any. What you need is to get off it. It's killin' you." Rosy resented the interruption and was sorry Jack knew the back road into the cabin.

"Help me, Rosy. I hurt all over. I need some stuff. I can't play my horn. I can't work. I'm good for nothin'. I know you got some dope here. You gave it to Lily." Tears smeared on his face and his eyes were red as hot coals. "Food won't stay down." He gagged and a thin string of what might have been gruel dropped from his mouth.

Rosy, disgusted and angry that Jack would even bring up Lily's name, pulled Jack inside. "I'll help you, but only if you promise to quit takin' dope. I'll get a doctor out here."

"Get that Chink." Jack tumbled in and fell on the floor.

Feeling as if he had no choice, Rosy pushed and pulled Jack to the couch and settled him in front of the cheerful fire. Rosy left him to heat up the coffee. His erstwhile friend stank of vomit, whiskey, and opium. No cheer in that man. His face was so gaunt and gray, he might have been a ghost himself. Still, Jack had listened to Rosy many a night when Lily was ill, and he stood by when Rosy buried his wife in the grove across the river.

Holding Jack's head, Rosy coaxed coffee into him, then some warmed pork and beans. The man's skin livened up some and he slept, covered with Rosy's coat and groaning from time to time. Rosy had to feed the fire all night to keep the place warm enough for Jack, who shuddered and shook. The dog kept Rosy warm.

In the morning, Rosy headed out, his auto bucking and belching smoke. He wouldn't get to Hailey, so he stopped at Goldie's. "Call the sheriff," she said. "He'll pick up the doc or take him out. Lord knows Doc can find his own way, but I don't know if he has a vehicle."

"Why would Azgo help me, or Jack? He ain't got no use for either one of us."

Goldie poured Rosy more coffee. "It's his job. I'll call if'n you want. A man deserves a chance, even if he's a good-for-nothin'. Remember, Jack wasn't always like that. The way he played that horn." She shook her head. " 'Ballin' the Jack,' 'Alexander's Ragtime Band.' You couldn't not dance. And ending every evening with 'Melancholy Baby.' Like to broke your heart." Then she put her finger to her lips and whispered, "Here comes Gladys."

With a snort, Rosy drained his cup and went to the telephone in the hall. He roused the operator to find the sheriff for him. Before long, he was explaining the circumstances, sounding like someone groveling for a favor and getting mad at himself all over again. He stepped back into the kitchen, nodded at Goldie and Gladys, grabbed his hat, and left to see about fixing up his own auto. Probably just needed some oil.

When someone tapped on the window of his automobile, Rosy raised himself from his slump, ready to blister the sheriff with swear words. It wasn't the sheriff. It was Sammy. God, what now? Maybe the Chinaman had come to slit his throat. His mother's leash didn't seem to be around. Rosy motioned for him to come around and get in. Sammy opened the door, looked in first, then climbed in. A whoosh of cold air entered with him. He kept his hand on the door handle and sat as far from Rosy as he could on the bench seat. No knife was evident.

"You want a ride somewhere?"

"No. Need help."

"You and every other miscreant in town." Rosy offered up his bottle. Sammy looked at it, but finally shrugged his shoulders and shook his head.

"What doin'?"

"Honored father lies in Hailey. My mother wants him." Sammy's lower lip stuck out. In the afternoon light, his face tinged into gray.

I want Lily, too, Rosy thought. "He's dead."

Sammy flinched, then bowed his head.

"All right. I owe you that much, anyway."

After a moment, Sammy opened the door and climbed out. "Tomorrow night, after dark. I borrow truck. Please to come to our abode."

Rosy sighed. He must look like a sucker to the whole damned town. "One condition, Sam."

The Chinese man hesitated and waited.

"Don't nobody, not you, not your honored mother, not nobody, touch a hair of that girl's head."

Sammy's face was inscrutable. Finally, he nodded. Rosy reached for the door and slammed it shut. He finished his bottle. The work ought to be done by now. He already told Nellie he wanted his picture taken. Guess he would go and get it now. He might send the picture to his sister. No, given his current state, she'd think he was close to death. Well, maybe he was. He'd figure out later who might want the photo. Or maybe he just wanted it for himself.

CHAPTER 17

"Get into the back seat." Mrs. Ah Kee spoke in a low but firm voice, as though Nellie were merely a servant. There was no peace offering either in her words or demeanor. Sammy placed the lights across Nellie's feet while she held the camera pack in her lap. It was colder in the auto than outside. After Sammy returned with the tripod, he started the automobile, pulled out into the snow, and began the drive toward Hailey. Neither he nor his mother spoke.

"Do you have Sheriff Azgo's permission for me to take this photo?" Her voice shook.

Neither answered. Worry sprouted. She did not want more trouble with the sheriff. If these people really believed she was a murderess, they might take their revenge on her, maybe torture her for information she didn't have. Maybe they were taking her to appear before the Tong. She hugged herself, remembering the sheriff's words about butchery. The axe was missing. John Doe's arm—Three-Fingered Jack's arm—had been chopped off. Maybe Sammy did it for the Tong.

The seats squeaked and the motor rumbled. Through the small back window, Nellie could see two narrow tire tracks behind. Through the front windshield, although she had to lean forward to see, there was nothing to give any indication where the road was. All was dark inside the car and only two headlights lit their world as they moved through it. She was beginning to feel as if this were one of her nightmares. To ground herself, she decided to talk. Even if the two Oriental people did not answer her, she would know that she was awake.

"I'm sorry about your husband, Mrs. Ah Kee." Her funeral words escaped her. What would her mother say? "This must be terrible for you both." Still no response. "Do you have relatives here?" Did Chinese people have funerals? "Will there be a funeral?"

Nellie sat back. The black "horseless" carriage reminded her of a real nightmare and prompted her to continue. "My father died in Chicago. He was killed in a street fight. It was terrible to see him in the morgue. My mother could not bring herself to view his body so I identified him. His attacker broke his nose and jaw with a baseball bat and huge dark bruises turned his skin almost purple. He should not have been beaten that way, although he often insulted people when he was drunk." As the cold wormed its way to Nellie's center, she realized she was being tasteless and probably offensive, but it felt as if she were alone in the auto and speaking only to herself.

"I had seen him only occasionally on his visits to my mother, when he asked her for money. Always, I was sent to my room, even as an adult. His smell preceded him, hanging like a distiller's advertisement in a bubble around his head and his clothes." Nellie felt queasy with the memories. "My mother aired out the house when he left. And then we lost the house and moved to my grandparents' home and still later to apartment after apartment. He still found her." Even Nellie could hear the bitterness in her voice. Stop this, she told herself. "I can't say I was sorry he was dead, but seeing him like that, I was sorry he had been beaten. And I was relieved he wouldn't hound my mother anymore for money to drink."

The auto traveled along the road. "I didn't take his photograph." She concentrated on the snow reflected in the headlights. For a long stretch, it was driven by the wind directly toward the windshield, hypnotic and dizzying. Then it slowed and stopped. No other autos drove toward them, and they met none going their way.

"Who would kill Mr. Ah Kee?" Nellie didn't know she was going to ask the question until it came out of her mouth.

"My husband was a good man." Mrs. Ah Kee's voice had almost no inflection. "He smoked opium, it is true, but he pressed no opium on anyone else. His talents lay in treating maladies and always he took special care of women. He boiled and dried herbs to ease women in their particular troubles. They came to him. Their men did not like this. Someone struck him down like a dog. He did not deserve this. Now, their women will moan and suffer. They will have babies they do not want. Their insides will torment them." Mrs. Ah Kee's voice had lost its indifference, and her slide into singsong carried a tone of pleasure. "Their men will be sorriest of all. The women will be witches and grow warts like toads, ugly growths. They will die."

The interior of the auto felt warm compared to the cold menace of Mrs. Ah Kee's voice, disembodied and humming. When the lights of Hailey began to glow in the night, Nellie was relieved. However would she ride back to Ketchum with this strange couple, if, indeed, they intended taking her home again? At the courthouse, she decided she would get help, telephone the sheriff if he wasn't there.

Instead of turning the auto toward the county building where the body must lie, Sammy turned toward the river and followed a winding road that took them into even darker territory.

"Where are we going? The courthouse is the other way." Nellie hoped she managed to keep her rising panic out of her voice.

The town lights disappeared, but a small lantern lit the front of a shanty-like dwelling over which loomed several evergreen trees and a black mountain. Sammy stopped the auto, jumped out, and opened the door opposite Nellie, retrieving the lights.

He motioned to her: "Come. Come."

Little snow had penetrated to the ground. Clumps of dead leaves and tree branches littered the area along with empty broken bottles and smashed tin cans. Blackened fence posts and the burned edge of the door stoop were mute evidence of an old fire. At the front door, Mrs. Ah Kee wielded a large key, turning the lock with a clunk. The door opened to a dark room that again seemed colder than outside. She lit a candle. "He is in here." She opened another door and led the way.

Mrs. Ah Kee lit two candles on a table at the foot of a four-poster bed, and Nellie found herself in another world. She felt the stare of both mother and son as she absorbed her surroundings. Elaborate silk hangings draped the walls and served as a canopy over the bed; incense, thick and spice-laden, almost choked her. On the bed in the center of the room, a body dressed as elaborately as the room's decor lay in state. His head had been shaved or he was bald already, and its moon color was like a large egg lying on purple pillows. A wispy beard, gray and white and limp, lay on a black Chinese tunic with dragons embroidered in silver and gold, each with a long red tongue. His bloodless hands rested one on top of the other at his waist. On the floor, rich and intricately patterned Oriental carpets covered every square inch, muting any footsteps and cushioning Nellie's feet. The candles flickered and shadows danced on the ceiling. The light cast a long cylindrical shadow behind Ah Kee's head. Another moonshadow, Nellie thought, trying desperately to remain calm. Bodies in caskets, even the strange body at Last Chance Ranch, had never bothered her. This one frightened her to her bones.

"You see my husband at Last Chance Ranch." Mrs. Ah Kee's dark eyes, her sallow skin, her narrow face, stitched mouth, and cruel voice accused Nellie.

Maybe she had seen him, thought Nellie. Maybe under that

ice was this man. But it couldn't be so. "I did not." She stepped close to this Ah Kee's head. "I've never seen him before." Except in bad dreams. Nellie stared back at the woman, hoping her fear did not reach her eyes.

Mother and son, who waited in the doorway, glanced at each other.

"Missee take click-click." Sammy lugged in the lights and Nellie's tripod. She still held a death grip on her camera pack.

"I can't." She turned to leave. Mrs. Ah Kee barred her way. The strong incense threatened to bring Nellie to her knees. She was dizzy and felt as if she floated near the ceiling watching this scene, while her brain absorbed words and smells slowly. "I'm too cold. My hands are frozen." She held them out as proof and perhaps for Mrs. Ah Kee to touch, but when the Chinese woman moved toward her, Nellie stepped back.

Mrs. Ah Kee grabbed her arm with fingers like talons and pulled her into the outer room, closing the death bed away. "I'll make you tea. The auto was cold. The house is cold. The incense . . . is . . . difficult." Mrs. Ah Kee's voice sounded normal. She lit two lamps. "We must keep the house cold," she said, and motioned toward the closed door. "The snow preserved my husband for many days, but now, he must be buried soon. When my son said you offered to take his photograph, I knew we could keep him only a little longer. Then he must return to his ancestors, and his bones will be sent back to China."

While she talked, she placed a tea kettle on an electric plate. Nellie welcomed its everydayness. A cord ran to an outlet near the front door. No other electrical appliances were in evidence. A large black pot rested on a wood stove, but no fire warmed the room. Yet it smelled medicinal, away from the incense. She lost her fright, and when the woman handed her a small cup with green liquid, Nellie sneezed, took the hot cup, and sipped, feeling strength return to her hands as well as her heart.

187

Furnishings were sparse in the tiny house. On one table, pushed to a pile beside a kerosene lamp, was a stack of pouches. Three polished chairs stood around a low table, and in the corner, three mattresses had been rolled, tied, and stacked. Dried herbs hung upside down along a side wall above a cupboard, explaining the intense smell. When she finished drinking, Mrs. Ah Kee took the cup. Nellie's chest was beginning to feel tight, as if caught in a vise, but her dizziness was gone.

"Now, will you photograph my husband?" Her face had lost its cruel expression and her eyes, hooded and dull, reflected only defeat.

"Yes." Nellie stood. "Now, I can do it."

Back in the room with the body, Nellie placed lights and asked Sammy to prop his father's body closer to a sitting position. Only then did Nellie see what looked like a deep gouge at the back of his head. If there had been blood, it was gone now. She wanted a photo of the cleaned wound, without making it obvious she was taking it, because his head looked as if it had been hit with much force. She moved her camera around, trying different angles, taking long enough that Mrs. Ah Kee left the room. After a full frontal photo, she suggested a side view. Sammy shrugged. Nellie set up the camera, deciding to trust her judgment that she had the right angle, removed the dark slide and took the photo, then moved to a full side view. She doubted Sammy noticed the extra click of the shutter lever and reversal of the film holder.

Touching the dead man brought back his humanity to Nell, and she keened inside for this victim of hate, something she had never done for her own father. The Chinese man was much older than her father had been; wrinkles laddered up both of his cheeks, sunken now with his skin shrinking back to reveal his skull. The impression of a Buddha had disappeared while she worked, causing her to wonder what religion these Chinese in

America practiced. Sending bones to China reminded her that at least these two people considered China home, not Idaho, not America. Or perhaps the wife and son did, but the ancient traditions still applied to old men.

In the automobile on the return trip to Ketchum, Nellie coughed, trying to relieve the tightness in her chest. It didn't help. "Mrs. Ah Kee, did your husband treat the woman who died at Last Chance Ranch? Was she Rosy's wife?"

"My husband treated Lily. Without him, she would have died sooner and in excruciating pain." With the last two words, Mrs. Ah Kee's voice again held the singsong timbre.

"But surely Rosy didn't—wouldn't—" Nellie didn't even want to mouth the words that Rosy might be the person who killed Ah Kee. The man was a drunk and a loafer, but surely not a murderer.

"Who knows what men do in sorrow or in rage? Sheriff Asteguigoiri took Ah Kee away from here." She pronounced the Basque name carefully. "The sheriff said Mr. Kipling needed a doctor. Which man suffered rage? Which one sorrow? Enough to lie? To kill?" Indifference had recaptured Mrs. Ah Kee. "But someone will repent in burning fire and agony."

Nellie said nothing more, afraid once again of attracting Mrs. Ah Kee's hatred, but now she had more information to ponder. Heat suffused her head, clouding logic. Maybe the sheriff was the murderer and even warned Nellie. No wonder he told her not to tell anyone anything. He knew who the iceman was. But others knew too: Sammy and maybe Rosy. Or Rosy knew because he did it.

The time was past midnight when Sammy and Mrs. Ah Kee delivered Nellie to the boarding house. The porch light was a beacon in the night. Tire tracks marred the streets and the wind swirled the "cold smoke" around Nellie's legs as she climbed onto the porch and opened the door. Her earlier delight in the

189

winter scene had disappeared hours ago. Sammy carried the lights and tripod into her studio and left without a word. As the door closed, Nellie trembled, cold again, but she remembered other questions she should have asked.

Wasn't Lily the name of Gwynn Campbell's daughter? Could it have been the old sheep rancher who murdered Ah Kee? And why did Rosy need a doctor?

The boarding house was silent as a cemetery until Nellie began coughing on the stairway. Too much night air, she concluded. She tried to hold the coughs in until she unlocked and scooted into her room, closing the door behind her. Moonie greeted her with his tongue and she hugged him for a while, absorbing his warmth and murmuring her questions to him. He probably knew all the answers.

"You need to go out, I'm sure, and you must sleep on the porch. If you don't, I'll get kicked out of here. Maybe there's some syrup in the kitchen for my cough. Let's look." Nellie padded around the kitchen after she let the dog out, and found a bottle of bright red tonic labeled "coughs." A smell of the contents revealed something that was mostly alcohol, but she took two big tablespoons anyway.

A noise, maybe a sensation, woke Nellie several hours later. She lay still, at first thinking she was back at Last Chance Ranch and she had an axe to hand. When she couldn't find it by groping around, she awoke even more and knew she was in her room. She waited for a repeat of the noise, a sliding sound like a sled runner. Although she tried to make her breathing sound like a person still sleeping, she wanted to hold her breath. There was the same breathless quality hovering somewhere near her. Should she cry out? Would a knife plunge into her? She didn't have to decide.

Her cough began again, a deep, harsh grating in her chest.

Under cover of her hacking, she felt as much as heard the sound again and knew it was a drawer sliding. A strong smell of an evil unguent pervaded the air.

The overhead light flashed on, blinding Nellie. She screamed and tried to leap up, covering her head with her arms. "Stay away from me!"

"Miss Burns! Miss Burns. It's just me, Gladys Smith!" The apparition near the door was indeed her neighbor from across the hall, dressed in black silk pajamas. Around her neck was wrapped a flannel cloth and on her head she wore a black nightcap. She might have been an Arab assassin. She carried a wrapped towel, reeking of the smell.

"What do you want? What are you doing in here?"

"Now, now, dear. You coughed loud enough to wake the dead. I went to the kitchen and Goldie and I made up this mustard plaster for your chest. You've come down with the ague, it sounds like." Her voice changed from placating to irritation. "No one can sleep."

"What time is it? It's the middle of the night." Nellie pulled her feet back under the covers, still coughing. "You opened the drawers. What are you looking for?"

Gladys's shocked expression set Nellie back. "I did not. How could you say such a thing?" She bustled to the bed. "You were dreaming. Lie down now, and I'll just place this on your chest." Up close, Gladys smelled like mothballs, as bad a smell as the mustard. "It's almost six in the morning. I don't know how I'll work all day, what with listening to you cough out your lungs for hours." She slipped into a whine easily. "It was hard enough to convince them to hire me. I must be bright and cheerful at all times."

"I heard the drawers open and close." Nellie pulled her legs in close to her body.

The bedroom door opened and Goldie hurried in. "What in

the world is going on in here? Land sakes, Nellie. We're just trying to help. Here, Gladys, give me that. You go back to bed. Now shoo!"

Gladys almost threw the concoction to Goldie and scurried out of the room. Nellie stretched out again and let Mrs. Bock administer to her. Her head felt stuffed with cotton and her chest hurt. Even so, she knew Gladys had never been bright and cheerful in her life, and beyond a doubt, that woman had been in her room for some time. What was she looking for in the dark?

CHAPTER 18

"Every time I think I'm shut of you, you're somehow involved again," Sheriff Azgo said.

"I'd like to think I'm finally 'shut' of you as well. I have work to do." Nellie had been pulled from the darkened bathroom where an intense day of developing negatives was proceeding with time out every several hours for more cough medicine. Fortunately, no undeveloped film had been exposed to the unexpected light. Her landlady had ignored all of the signs and warnings. "I'm extremely busy, Sheriff. What do you want this time?"

Nellie stood in the kitchen, feeling lightheaded. To stay warm in the unheated bathroom, she had donned her wool pants and a sweater. Her work apron was stained with developer, her legs were weary from standing, and her shoulders ached.

"The dead Chinese doctor has disappeared. Mrs. Bock told me you went out with the Ah Kees last night and came back late." The sheriff took off his Stetson and pushed his black hair back. "Did you three steal the body?"

"I did not steal any body." She turned to Mrs. Bock so that her knowledge of Ah Kee dressed so elegantly and so lovingly would not show. This man always seemed to know what she was thinking. "Is there any hot tea or coffee available? Your bathroom is cold as a tomb."

"Then what were you doing with them?"

"I was taking photographs. Something nearly everyone in

town wants, with the possible exception of you." Nellie was disappointed he had not made an appointment.

The sheriff blushed. He probably did read minds. Nellie felt her own face grow hot. Mrs. Bock looked at him and then at Nellie and laughed. "Here's your coffee. You better set a minute. This lawman has you in his sights. I'll just leave you two to wrangle it all out." She chuckled as she left the room.

"Miss Burns, you have withheld information from me in the past. Are you doing so now?"

"You didn't tell me that you took Ah Kee out to Last Chance Ranch. How do I know *you* didn't kill him?" As soon as the words were out, she regretted them.

The sheriff's eyes narrowed, and if brown skin couldn't turn white, his did a fair imitation. He replaced his Stetson. "You are like the others in this town." His voice shook. Was it rage?

Nellie felt contrite. Whatever loyalty she felt for the Ah Kees or for the dead Chinese man, she should ignore. Loyalty to her was probably not in their lexicon, although the kindness of tea last night when she was frightened and cold had softened her view of Mrs. Ah Kee.

"I did not steal Ah Kee. I did photograph him." Nellie dropped into a chair at the table. If an argument was forthcoming, she wanted to rest her feet at least. "I assumed you had released the body to his wife. Apparently, that was not so."

When the sheriff continued to stand, saying nothing, Nellie looked up. "That is the truth."

"I don't doubt it's the truth." Some of his color returned. "Why do you want to photograph dead men? Isn't this a strange way to earn money?"

Nellie took a deep breath. "I apologize, Sheriff Azgo, about what I just said. But you have no right to make judgments about me, either. Men can have a job for the asking. The only jobs available to me are someone else's maid, or cook, or seamstress, or secretary, and forever to be treated as someone's chattel, incapable of thinking, only recently able to vote in my own right. I earn money how and where I can, at a calling that is honored in some places. Your disapproval means nothing to me." Her ire expanded along with the level of her voice and she stood up to face him. "And you kept a dead man away from his wife and family who needed to mourn and bury him with the solemnness his tradition demands. How could you be so insensitive?"

Her anger left almost as abruptly as it arrived. This was one of the few men she'd met who probably understood what she was talking about. She'd heard what some people thought of the Basque. And she knew she was being hypocritical about the Ah Kees. They wanted to find the murderer more than the sheriff did.

"I don't understand you," the sheriff said, again removing his hat. "Women should be at home and men should take care of them. That is always what I have been taught and what I see of the world." He raised his hand to stop Nellie from responding. "If you had told me of the body in the snow as soon as you found it, he would not have lain there several days. I am responsible for finding the murderer—not you and not the Chinese, whatever they may think. I am sheriff because no one else wanted to be sheriff. Many times, I am sorry I fought against those who said a Basque cannot do such a job. They are only fit for sheepherding. But I say to myself, I will be a good sheriff. To prove a murder, I must have the body. Now it is gone."

And if there is no man to take care of the woman? Nellie wanted to ask, caught by the first of his statements. Then, the woman must take care of herself. This was an argument she could not win. She hadn't persuaded her mother. How could she persuade a stranger? Even one who had contrary evidence staring at him every day: Mrs. Bock, Mrs. Ah Kee, the elderly twins, Mrs. Smith, the schoolteacher, any number of unmarried women and widows.

"I know how Ah Kee was murdered—with an axe," she said instead. "I'll have a photo to show you. I think I know who murdered Ah Kee, too. He was treating Rosy's wife, Lily, for some sickness. Lily's father was Gwynn Campbell, a sheep rancher who hates Chinese, because he thinks opium killed his daughter. I believe Mr. Campbell tried to steal my negatives in the photo studio in Twin Falls. He somehow learned I'd been in the cabin and took pictures, but he made the same mistake Sammy did. Both thought I had a picture of Ah Kee and that it would show something." She folded her arms. "That's all I know." No, she knew the name of the dead man. But the sheriff knew the name if Sammy did. "I'm going back to work."

Sheriff Azgo stepped back to let Nellie pass, his stare hard as stones. Just as she was going through the door to the hallway, he said, in a low voice, "And the iceman? And the dog toy?" His face contained a primitive look that made her think of masks she'd seen in a Chicago museum, masks used for killing rituals. There was less emotion in his features than in Mrs. Ah Kee's, but a similar dislike was mapped there. Moonie barked and then growled, a low muttering warning, as he strode out the back way. Poor dog, Nell thought, distracted. Maybe Rosy would take him back and love him. Someone once did. Only then did she remember the belt, but she was too tired to chase after the sheriff.

"Little Nell."

Nellie jumped and turned. "What?" Rosy stood behind where she sorted negatives in her newly made studio the next day. Mrs. Bock had gone out. "Don't call me that."

He grinned. She couldn't tell if he'd been drinking or not,

but he had a black patch over his eye, something she'd never seen before.

"What say I take you out to the Triumph Mine. Show you where my face got bunged up." His grin held in place, stretching his whole countenance.

"Now? Today?" Nell wanted to see a mine. This might be her one chance to photograph miners. Her camera was packed for her trip to Twin Falls, so she needed little more to get ready. The negative sorting she could finish that evening.

"Yup. Gotta take a package to Miz Smith. Goldie said you'd like to get out."

Nell couldn't imagine Goldie saying any such thing, but it was a good idea. Also, it was a way to avoid the sheriff before she left town for a couple of days. "Yes, I'll come. Should I take my snowshoes? I might want to take a photograph of the mine buildings."

"I ain't no damned beast of burden. And you won't need no snowshoes in the mine."

Nellie grabbed her pack and tripod, picking up her coat and boots along the way, and followed Rosy to his auto before he could change his mind. The whiskey and tobacco smells hadn't changed much.

"I thought you said no one would permit a woman in . . ."

"I'll tell 'em you ain't no woman. You're a professional photographer." He drew out the last two words. Was he making fun of her?

"Your negative looks good, Rosy. I think you'll like the picture. I'm going to Twin Falls tomorrow to work on developing prints for everyone." Rosy might not like the picture at all. He looked mean and somehow beaten down, but still, there was a touch of the noble in his scarred face. "Why are you wearing that patch?"

"Can't stand my bad eye. Looks white."

"Do you want another photograph with the eye patch?" If she could get more photos, she would.

"Nope. You got my picture there?"

"No. The portraits are in the house. I just have . . . older negatives with me." Now why did she tell him that? At least she hadn't spouted out that she carried the negatives of the iceman and the moonshadows with her. They were too valuable to leave unguarded. On the other hand, were they? The Ah Kees had the photo of Three-Fingered Jack. So did the sheriff. Since people knew who the dead man was, no one should care about the negatives anymore. Not everyone knew, though. Maybe not the murderer. She could hardly shout out the news from the porch. The murderer still might not hear. And Rosy? Was he safe to travel with?

The trip to the mine, up a narrow road alongside the East Fork of the Wood River, took over an hour. For the first half, Rosy didn't talk, but Nellie was relieved he'd dropped the dreadful grin and was more his usual half-surly self. When she asked him about the mines, he explained that those near Hailey had closed down years before when the silver ran out. The valley had fallen on hard times before the war, and the population that had once been over 2,000 people in Ketchum had dwindled to the bunch of die-hards she saw now. "There's maybe three hundred on a good day. Times is gettin' better, though, what with all the sheep that go through town and out to the world. Summers is busy around there. But you'll probably be gone by then, don't you think?" He flashed his sham smile.

"Why no. I want to photograph the sheepherders and their sheep and dogs. Maybe travel over the Galena Pass and see the Sawtooth Mountains with all the other tourers." She saw visions of herself riding a horse, hiking in wildflowers, taking landscapes unlike those of any other photographer. "Maybe you'd take me, Rosy. You're getting used to my photography aren't you?"

He snorted. Then he mumbled a few words, groped under the seat, and brought out the ever-present liquor.

"I wish you wouldn't drink while you're driving."

"I'll do what I like, girlie." He took a huge swig, but screwed the lid back on and shoved the bottle back between his feet.

"You knew Three-Fingered Jack, didn't you? He was the body at Last Chance Ranch. The sheriff knows. So do the Ah Kees." The more people who knew, the less danger she should be in.

If Rosy knew about the body, then that confirmed he was the person who moved it. Or maybe he was the murderer, and she was in the wrong place, in the auto alone with him. A chilly memory struck her. When she'd asked Rosy this question once before, he used the word "did." Then, she assumed he had known Jack sometime in the past.

"A drunk. Like me." The auto wandered on the road and Nellie worried Rosy was indeed drunk. "Not always a drunk. Neither one of us. He used to play trumpet with the band in Hailey. Wasn't no one who knew more songs than Jack. Then he got hurt in the North Star avalanche, back in '17. Army wouldn't take him then. He'd been all set to go and fight the Hun." He shook his head. "Then he got into the opium. Ruined a good man."

"Did you play an instrument too?" She tried to imagine Rosy blowing on a trumpet or playing a drum. She couldn't imagine him killing someone. But she didn't really know him. Instead of a sometimes good-natured, sometimes bad-natured drunk, he could be evil.

"Nope, I worked."

"Did you go to the war?" He certainly didn't sound evil.

"Too old. Bigger worries than some foreigners across the ocean shootin' each other to bits." He reached for the bottle but changed his mind midway. "Sick wife. Two kids."

"Was Jack married to Gladys Smith? I know it's a common name . . ."

"Not married. She acted like they was." He snorted and slapped the wheel. "Some people don't know how lucky they is. I'm one of them." His hand twitched on the wheel and he clamped his mouth shut. A few minutes later, they drove up to the building at the mine entrance.

It was a cold, clear day and Nellie breathed deeply. Her cough had subsided. She did need to get out. The steep mountains on either side of the pinched valley hardly left room for the town of Triumph, a mine office, a building that stair-stepped up the blackened north slope, a tall wooden derrick-like structure, and a large metal building with an arched brick entrance. Sounds of machines whirring filled the air. There were several other autos parked beside the office, and metal cars creaked and swayed overhead as they moved along a cable stretched from one wood trestle to another up the gulch and over the mountain to the north. Rosy pointed up and shouted, "Ore. Headed over to Independence Mine and down to the railroad tracks."

In the office, several men and Mrs. Smith worked at desks. A haze of cigarette smoke hovered. Nellie was interested to see that her fellow boarder also smoked and no one seemed to care. Rosy handed her a long package. Mrs. Smith seemed an entirely different person than the woman Nell had seen at Mrs. Bock's boarding house. Although her eyes wore dark circles, the rest of her was brisk and businesslike. Even her rosebud mouth no longer looked frivolous. Nor was she surprised that Nellie was with Rosy. When he left Nellie's side to talk to a man in an outer office about entering the mine with the "lady photographer," Mrs. Smith watched him with a strange expression, her eyes flat, her mouth working, although she said nothing. The coquettish attitude she'd shown at the boarding house was gone. She ground out her cigarette in an ashtray on the counter without looking down.

"Mrs. Smith, is this where you spend your days?" Nellie wanted to distract the woman.

"Nearly every day. I schedule ore trains and help prepare the reports for the borings and samples and type up assay reports. It is quite interesting work. Men don't seem to want to type, do they?" She simpered, the package still in one hand.

"You're speaking a language foreign to me," Nellie said. "You must know so much about the whole process." She admired Mrs. Smith for her steadfast work. Even on the worst days, she left early with her ride to the mines.

"I do. Samples are taken from every ore car sent out of the mine, numbered, and posted to the laboratory in Twin. Borings go to Salt Lake City. All by train, of course. We have a small assay office here to test the silver and lead content in selected samples. This is a promising mine, but we need to dig much deeper. That could take years and the prices of heavy metals have to improve." She sighed and leaned forward to whisper to Nellie. "When you enter the mine with Rosy, watch yourself. I don't trust him." Then she moved back to her desk, opened the front drawer, and tried to stuff the package in. It wouldn't fit, but she continued in a normal voice. "Would you like to see one of the reports?"

"How did you learn everything?"

"I've been around mines all my life. My da worked for a big mining company up north in Kellogg. After he was killed, I worked there too and took care of my brother." Mrs. Smith's face softened for a moment. "I moved here to be with him when he got work at a local mine, and then . . ." She tried a drawer in a filing cabinet. The package fit. She dropped it in and slammed the drawer shut. "When I needed work, I came up to the Triumph and they hired me." Mrs. Smith's voice broke and she lowered her head for a moment. She seemed close to tears. "This is what I do all day." She offered up some sheets of paper.

Nellie stepped behind the counter. She didn't know whether to ask about the brother or Rosy, but decided on the latter. "Why don't you trust Rosy?" she whispered.

"He was fussing around your door one day when you were gone and I found him. I didn't know if he was coming or going. He might be the one who stole your things the day you were in the bathroom." She looked over Nellie's head, and again raised her voice. "Approximately 40 tons of ore go out of here every day."

"C'mon, Little Nell," Rosy said. "We got permission to hike in a ways. There's electricity along the drift they're minin', so's you can see to take a picture. I told the man if you could use moonlight, you oughta be able to do it with an electric bulb. Here, let me heft that pack for you."

Rosy had never offered to lighten her load in the past.

"I'll carry it. How about taking my tripod?"

He reached for the pack, but Nellie avoided him. Then the man came out of the office. "We've got a car you can ride in. It's hooked up to a trolley that'll take you in 'bout half a mile. You can see some men workin' a drill. No deeper now, mind you. We've had an unstable condition back farther. Rosy, you know what that can do to you." The man laughed and stepped back into his office.

Mrs. Smith picked up a paper from her desk. "If you can be finished in an hour-and-a-half, I'll schedule the trolley to pick you up again."

Nellie thanked Mrs. Smith, who walked out to the mine entrance with them, pointing out ore cars on the track. "My assay samples tell how valuable these loads are. What I do is important."

Nellie, glad she had worn her wool pants, climbed after Rosy into a car behind a trolley engine. "Take care now," Mrs. Smith called as the car moved forward.

The car rumbled along with its two passengers facing in the direction in which it traveled, not quite touching each other. When they entered the mine itself, darkness swallowed them. A weak light at the front of the trolley engine didn't lessen the darkness more than a whisper. It blinked off, on, and off again. Nellie couldn't see her hand in front of her face. She wanted to tear open the black. It felt thick, as if it would seal her nose and mouth forever.

"Rosy?" Her voice trembled.

"Right here, girlie. Black, ain't it? We'll get to some light in a jiffy."

With his words, the air seemed lighter, but smelled of creosote, a brown, almost sour odor. Her pack sat in her lap, her arms around it. She was afraid her arm would be snapped off if she reached out. The car swayed as the trolley rounded a curve and Nellie almost lost her balance. At the same time, something jerked on her pack, but she gripped hard as ever. "Rosy, leave my pack alone," Nellie said, her voice low but as firm as she could make it.

From the bench opposite her, he answered. "What're you jabberin' about? I just changed my seat."

Then she wanted to drop the pack. Maybe a . . . a thing was crawling on her. Get a handle on yourself. It could only be Rosy. She better watch out. Mrs. Smith might not be imagining things.

One more jolt and the black turned gray and then to dim light under bulbs that stretched into a distance off to their left. The car stopped and Rosy helped Nellie out. Nothing crawled on her pack. The engineer saluted and the trolley rattled and rolled away. She noticed Rosy's eye patch was gone. "Where's your patch?"

"Tossed it. Hate that bugger."

Maybe that was what she had felt, Rosy knocking against her pack.

"Follow me. We're headin' down this drift." A deep humming echoed from far away and grew louder as the two of them walked toward it. The tunnel was tall enough to stand in comfortably, but not wide. Damp earth smells mixed with an acidic one that tickled Nellie's nose and became danker as the walk sloped downward, not steeply, but enough that Nell grabbed for Rosy's arm so she wouldn't trip. He didn't shake her off. Every hundred feet or so was a bare bulb, providing enough light to guide them forward.

The hum turned to a whirring so loud Nellie wanted to close her ears. The light bulbs ended and Rosy lit a candle he pulled from his jacket pocket. Along another short tunnel, they entered what felt like a large cave where three men worked. One held a machine at one end, another guided it into the rock wall above their heads, grinding out dust and bits of rock. Candles in sconces on the walls illuminated their labors. The third man stood with an iron bar in one hand. None of the men wore a shirt, and indeed, the temperature felt much warmer than outside and the air moist. Sweat slickened their bare chests. Their hair, where it wasn't wet, was dusty. Black streaked their faces almost as dark as players in a minstrel show. Mighty knotted arms rippled in and out of the shadows their bodies cast. They looked like demons in one of Dante's rings. She wanted a photograph of this tableau.

"Hey!" Rosy's shout attracted the men's attention and the drill stopped. The sudden silence was almost shocking. "This here girl wants to take your picture." He pushed Nell forward. "See that drill? I was operating one of them and a piece of rock flew out and hit my eye. Had to walk back to the adit, blood spurtin' all the way. Thought my eyeball was gonna drop out. I bet if them lights were better, you could still see the trail."

Nell winced at the image and the pain Rosy must have felt. She touched his arm, but he shook her off. The men all grabbed shirts and crowded together, already posing for her. But she didn't want a pose; she wanted the scene.

"Hey, Rosy, want to get in it too? That eye of yours would make us look handsome!"

"Can I get one to give my wife? She don't think I work for a living. Says I take naps in here all day."

The candlelight wasn't going to work. These men could not hold still as long as she would need for the light to accumulate. Nell went about setting up her tripod for the camera anyway. She would have to use a flash pack, something she didn't want to do in this cave space, and she only had one. They had left in such a hurry, she didn't think of bringing more. She fiddled with her camera, trying to think where she would set the f-stop.

Nell handed the flash pack to Rosy and explained where he was to light it and how to hold it. While she went through her usual steps—covering her head to focus, adjusting how the men stood, and getting them to hold the drill between them, fine-tuning the focus—all four men talked back and forth about the ore being mined and the chances the Triumph too would close down, just like the Minnie Moore and the Croesus outside Hailey.

"Okay, I'm ready. When I say so, Rosy, light the fuse. Get a match ready first." He pulled a small box from his pocket, rasped one, and a flame leaped up.

"One, two, three, light!" Nell opened the shutter while she counted, and after the flash exploded, shut it again. The illumination was so strong it hurt Nell's eyes, like a lightning strike up close. Smoke billowed and the rancid smell of sulfur and gunpowder choked her.

"That's the only flash pack I have." A coughing fit stopped

her for a moment. "I'd like to come back again, better equipped. I thought there would be electric lights." The air in the tunnel through which Nell and Rosy had walked drew the smoke out, and the space around them cleared. "The best thing would be light bulbs in here or a less enclosed space for my flash packs. Would either be possible?"

The guffaws told her it wasn't. "We could all go outside, lady."

"I won't know for a few days whether the flash pack worked. I'll tell Rosy and he can tell you." Her exposure had been only a guess. "Thank you so much. I'd love to come back and take photos of you working."

"Don't count on it," Rosy said, glaring at her with his one good eye.

"Sure, come back any time," the beardless young man said. "Leave old Rosy home, though. He's ugly enough to break a mirror." The men laughed, including Rosy. He passed a few insults, commenting on the speaker's lack of beard because he was so young, another's bushy chest, calling him "ape-man." The men situated the drill and the iron stick and began work again.

"Let's go," Rosy said. He stood on one foot and then the other and small drops of sweat rolled off his temple near his blind eye. "Hot in here."

To the contrary, Nell was feeling cold, but she hefted her pack, letting Rosy take the tripod, and they walked back to where they'd been left off. No trolley or car waited for them.

CHAPTER 19

"Guess we gotta hike from here. Ain't too far." Rosy pointed to a cable running above their heads. Nell looked up, lifting her hand toward it.

"Don't touch that! You'll fry." He slapped her arm down.

"What do you mean?" Her eyes grew big.

"That's the electric cable. Juices the trolley along the rails here." He kicked the track.

"Then why aren't there lights in the tunnel?"

"Blamed if I know. Probably ain't working or all the juice goes to pull the ore out." Rosy was sorry now he'd brought her. He didn't feel like hiking. He was thirsty. He couldn't remember why he thought it was important to bring her into the mine. He'd wanted to prove something, but whether it was to her or to him, had escaped him.

"But it's coal black up that tunnel. How will we find our way?" Her voice shook, then firmed up.

"Only goes in one direction. And I've got my candle." Rosy struck a match from the box and lit the wick again. He began walking. She scurried after him. He stopped and motioned for her to go first so the candle would give her some light. They moved along slowly, not talking. Nellie picked her way over the slats between the rails. The walls were rock and dirt, sometimes with water dripping along them, sometimes with timbers holding up the hanging wall, sometimes with pieces of lagging along the sides. He felt at home.

After the first bend, except for the flickering candle, there was no light. Even the smallest sound was amplified: the girl's half stumbles, the creaking of the pack on her back, his own heavy breathing. It felt like they could be at the center of the earth, walking along, with time no longer an ingredient of living and light unknown.

"Scary in here, ain't it?" She turned to him and he pulled his face into a Halloween grin, thinking he'd frighten her some. Maybe she wouldn't be so cocky. Then he stumbled and dropped the candle. Crimey, he thought. He'd forgotten how Stygian the dark was.

"Rosy? Are you all right?"

He heard her take a step, then two, while he dropped down to find the candle. Getting clumsy in his old age.

"Rosy?" The girl's voice was edged with panic.

His knees soaked up mud. Hell. He groped around, felt the track, felt the rough wood where it met the ground, then felt something give. It was the girl's foot. She jerked it away. "Rosy!"

A distant grumbling gathered force. The ore train, not the trolley, Rosy knew. The sound grew to a roar, filling the tunnel like a huge animal, and the rail near his hand vibrated. An engine light rounded the corner and bore down on them. Then the light blinked off.

Thunder filled the chamber, threatening to split Rosy's eardrums. He moved as swiftly as he could—grabbed Nellie, pushed her hard toward the wall. She stumbled and fell to her knees. He pulled her up again, grabbing some of her hair because it came to hand, shoved her against the wall, pressing her and the pack against it with his own body. He felt rather than heard her scream. At the same time a searing pain burned his ankle. The mass boomed by and its slipstream threatened to suck them into it. Thick dust sifted into his mouth, choking him. As soon as the train barreled past, he let go of Nellie and sagged down. She fell with him. He gagged and coughed, trying to clear his mouth.

"Rosy?" Her voice exploded in the fading clatter of wheels on rails, so close he could have bitten her.

"Goddammit, girl," he answered. "Twisted my ankle." He searched his pockets and found the matchbox. He fumbled and almost dropped it too. "Hang on."

He scratched the match, twice. "Can't find the goddam candle."

The bright flame filled the tunnel, briefly. The girl was almost behind him, on her knees. He tried to raise himself on one leg, but lost his balance. "There it is. Hand it to me."

When she didn't, he shouted. "You gonna stand there like a flea plastered against the rock all day?" The flame reached his fingers and he yelled. Again, they were steeped in tarry night.

"No. No, I was . . ."

Rosy lit another match. Nell picked up the candle and handed it to him, her hand trembling. Then she rubbed her head.

"What was that?" she asked. "You saved my life."

"Goddam ore cars. Coulda squashed us like bugs. Someone's gonna pay hell." He handed the candle back and managed to stand on one foot.

"What do you mean? Someone did that on purpose?" In the light, her eyes looked big as dinner plates. "If you hadn't grabbed me, I'd be dead. So would you."

Rosy stumbled, catching himself on the wall, swearing.

"Can you lean on me and walk?"

"I can lean all right, but you're too bitty to hold me up." Still, he put his arm around the girl's shoulders and took a hesitant hop. His weight nearly shoved her to her knees.

"Wait. How about the tripod? I'll carry the candle and you lean on the tripod and me together. Just don't pull my hair again." She gave a shaky laugh.

209

Candle in one hand and an arm around Rosy's waist, the girl took small steps forward and Rosy tried to hop and walk at the same time. Her arm was strong, but he could feel how heavy he was compared to her. She felt like a child. Even so, she straightened her shoulders under his arm and tightened her grip. He was afraid he'd hurt her, but they hobbled in this fashion down the tunnel for a ways.

"This ain't gonna work."

"Yes it is. Keep moving." Her breath was as labored as his. "Unless it hurts too much?"

They moved once again, stopping frequently to let Rosy rest and then to let Nellie rest. The candlelight wavered and they stopped to let it steady itself. "Been awhile since I been in here," Rosy said. "Seems like the tunnel got longer." He stopped again. "Lookee here. Let me carry the pack."

Nellie shook her head.

"I promise I won't do anything to it or let your precious camera get hurt. That would lighten your load some."

The girl looked at him. He could imagine what she saw—a grizzled old man with a white eye, coated with dust, looking meaner than the devil. "Are you sure?"

He nodded. Nellie handed the candle to him and then slipped off her pack. She wiggled her shoulders back and forth and took the candle back, then helped Rosy get his arms through the straps. After that, they made better progress. Neither one had much breath to talk with. Rosy did his best not to groan with pain.

By the time they exited the mine, he hurt like hell. He supposed the girl did too, but she was a trooper, he decided, and a lot stronger than she looked. He handed the pack back to her. "Thanks, Nell."

Inside, Rosy plunked down on a chair to rest. Light never looked so good. Gladys fussed over Nell, glaring at him. She whispered something to the girl.

"No, no. He saved me. Without Rosy, I would have been . . ." She shuddered and bit her lip.

"Without Rosy, you wouldn't have been in the mine."

With the help of the tripod, Rosy stood up. He ignored Gladys. He'd done what she wanted and now he wouldn't bother to spend the energy to spit on her. "Let's get the hell outta here. Goddamned criminals."

"You can't drive in that state," Gladys said. "I'll take you both back to Ketchum."

"Your auto ain't here and you ain't drivin' mine. Get me a length of bandage and I'll fix up this damned ankle. I'm drivin' back."

As soon as he reached his automobile, Rosy pulled out his bottle and drank. He felt like the river of life was flowing through him. That was a closer call than the time he lost his eye. Gladys was right about one thing. It was his fault for taking Nell into the mine. His hand trembled and he didn't want her to see it, so he took another long draught. He glanced at Nell, figuring she wouldn't object, and she didn't.

Nell chattered. "It must have been an accident, don't you think? An ore train instead of the trolley? The driver must not have seen us. I've never heard anything so loud in my life."

He let her think what she wanted. Probably better that way. He grunted.

Nell coughed, a deep one that came up from her lungs. She pulled out a hankie and covered her mouth. "I'm going to Twin Falls tomorrow. There, I can print up all the portraits I took. Yours will be the first." Her hacking started up again.

Rosy held his bottle out to her. "Best medicine there is." She surprised him by taking it and sipping some. She swallowed and shuddered, but her cough stopped and she handed it back.

"Why did you bring me out here?" There was a different tone

in her voice this time; the chattiness had disappeared.

Rosy readjusted his seat, took the bottle from between his legs, emptied it, and sat up straight. "You said you wanted a picture of the miners. Seemed like you was tryin' awful hard to make a go of it. You ought to get somethin' of what you want." He was getting to be such an old fool, his eyes watered. "Some women do and some don't."

Rosy clamped his mouth shut. He sure as hell wasn't going to cry in front of an easterner. Neither said a word the rest of the trip back to Ketchum. At Goldie's, he stopped the car. Nell leaned over and kissed his cheek. "Thank you." She helped herself, her pack, and her tripod out of the auto and closed the door. Rosy waited until she was clear and drove off, tossing the empty bottle out his window over the top of the auto and into the snow. The bit of water filling his eyelid dropped down his cheek.

CHAPTER 20

Next morning, as Nellie left to catch the train, laden with her camera pack and all of her negatives, Mrs. Bock handed her an envelope. "This was slipped under the door last night. Came from those Chinamen." She sniffed and dropped it in Nellie's outstretched hand as if the paper were on fire. Nellie stuck it in her bag and dashed out, leaving the stuffy house behind her. The fumes of another mustard plaster still clung to her pores, but the fresh, blue morning revived her spirits. Even the air sparkled.

The clackety-clack brought back the stark fear of the day before. Was Rosy or Mrs. Smith after her? Who killed Ah Kee? And why? Exasperated with herself, she took out the negatives and studied them by the light of the train window. Portraits, portraits, portraits. Here she was, working at what she swore she had left. Still, she now had miners on a piece of film. That was a start, along with her landscapes. Enlarging her moon-shadow photos might also advance her endeavor to find out what happened at Last Chance Ranch. Indeed, she was beginning to equate solving the mystery with success in photography. One would lead to the other. That wasn't logical, but there it was.

Jacob Levine grinned when Nellie arrived. He showed her the new door on the darkroom, a new negative holder, a more substantial lock. Even his face looked all right—slightly more used, perhaps, but the scratch marks were disappearing. They spent an hour discussing photographic news and new techniques that Mr. Levine had learned while in the hospital and at home, recuperating by reading magazines and newspapers. Then they talked about what work Nellie could do for Jacob, and the times she could use his darkroom. And last, he brought up her moon-shadow prints and asked her to accompany him to supper, bringing the prints with her, when they finished their schedule for the day.

Having an opportunity to discuss photography was so rare. Even though she had tried to sound like an expert at their first meeting, he had more experience and she could learn from him, especially about running a business.

While her new colleague took portraits of customers, Nell printed a small stack of negatives for him. She slipped in a few of her own, beginning work on Bert the Butcher's children. At closing time, she and Mr. Levine followed his plan, stopping to tell Mrs. Olsen, who treated them like two chicks.

After supper, while the two of them drank coffee, they studied Nellie's prints. "If I do send these to San Francisco, then you must send your portrait of the Chinese woman."

"Thank you for the compliment, Miss Burns. I will consider it." Then he pointed to the photo of the cabin with the moon overhead. "You could lighten the rock chimney, could you not? Is this smoke rising against the background?" He leaned forward and took a magnifying glass from his chest pocket. "If that small detail, there, could be brought forth, it would be quite effective."

Using the glass, Nellie studied the pale wisp. She remembered smoke when he mentioned it, but had forgotten about it since. Certainly, something white and wispy seemed to hover over the house. She had conjured up a ghost at the time, but that was silly.

"I can try by dodging that part of the photo." Dodging meant covering over the section of the print while the remainder was exposed to more light. The result would be to make the dodged section lighter than the rest. Nellie's technical thoughts were interrupted by a puzzle. If it were smoke, wouldn't the stove have had some warmth?

Mr. Levine was talking and Nellie pulled her attention back to him. "—covered up the rest of the negative, then it might work."

She didn't want to admit her distraction, so she nodded her head.

"And this photo of the grass and trees in the snow. I wonder if you could lighten up the background to capture more detail. I'd like to know what this is." He pointed to the dark place that Nellie intended to study with an enlargement. "It almost looks like someone standing and watching."

"I planned to enlarge it and take a closer look. I doubt if it's a person. I was alone in the meadow. Rosy was back in the car and I heard no one else." She looked up at the photographer. "Do you suppose it might have been a wolf or a bear?"

"Not a wolf. I am afraid the wolves have been destroyed by the sheepmen, cattle men, and bounty hunters." His half-smile reflected regret. "A bear? They're hibernating. Perhaps an elk or a deer, although . . ." He too used the glass to study the photo. "No, now I see nothing but a dark shape. If it were an animal, the photo might be even more striking. It would be a discovery for the viewer that was not immediately apparent—a mystery."

With a last sip from his cup, Mr. Levine said, "Shall we return to the studio? We could finish my proofs tonight if we worked together for an hour or two." Concern wrinkled his forehead. "But, forgive me, you may wish to wait until tomorrow?"

"Oh, no, let's begin." Nellie pumped as much enthusiasm as she could, although she didn't feel it. She wanted to enlarge and dodge both photos to see what she had missed. And her chest was feeling tight again.

They walked back to the studio, streetlamps lighting their way. After Ketchum, Twin Falls felt like a metropolis. Automobiles passed on the avenues and several store windows contained displays to attract shoppers. Maybe a store here would carry trousers made for women, the long loose-legged kind that were just beginning to appear in Sears catalogs along with much shorter skirts as she left Chicago. If she wore one of those short skirts in Ketchum, or even in Twin Falls, people would be scandalized, especially if she smoked a cigarette in a long holder at the same time. She smiled. And why not? If she ever had her own photography show, that is exactly what she would do.

They worked together, finishing his prints. Nellie wanted to stay and work on her photos, but Mr. Levine insisted she leave with him. Her crestfallen expression was probably the reason he agreed to return early the next day to let her work alone, while he caught up on paperwork.

The morning was still dark when Nellie left the boarding house. Snow fell lightly, but the air was warm enough to melt it, creating slush along the street and slicking the sidewalk. A temporary lull in autos passing by gave her an isolated feeling, the only life in a deserted town. She trod carefully, watching each step and only half-noticed a large man hurrying across the street toward her. When he grabbed her arm, she gasped and nearly fell.

"You little harpie! Comin' into my town and tellin' lies about me! Who do you think you are?" His fingers were strong enough to pull Nellie off her feet.

"Let go! What are you talking about?" She tried to pull back. "Who are you?" The man wore a thick sheepskin coat and a cowboy hat. "Let go, or I'll scream."

He tightened his grip. Nellie thrashed, trying to release herself. The darkness and trees in the planting strip hid them from the view of anyone on the road. The man pulled her close and clapped a gloved hand over her mouth. "Scream, you goddamn hussy!"

Fear strengthened Nellie. She stomped on the man's instep as hard as she could. "Let go!"

"Owww!" The man loosened his grip, but not entirely. He lost his footing and they both went down in a heap. Nellie's dress caught on her heel and ripped, and she landed chest-first so hard on the man's knee that the wind was knocked out of her. She couldn't move for a minute, but then rolled away, choking for breath and clutching at her breasts.

Nellie, groaning, crawled to her knees and pulled herself up by the trunk of a tree, feeling bruised in body and mind. She was on the point of kicking her assailant as he lay on the sidewalk, when she thought better of it. One whole side of her was sopped and she wanted to run to the studio. But who was this? She edged closer and grabbed the hat from his head. At first, she had no idea who this big shaggy, white-haired man could be, until he opened his eyes. Even in the dim morning light, their blueness surprised her. Gwynn Campbell, the sheepman.

"How dare you!" Nellie swatted the man's head with his own hat, once, twice, and again. Each swipe compounded her anger. He raised his arms to shield himself.

"Stop!" He rolled to his knees, and she kept hitting him. "Stop, please." The last word sounded so weak and broken, Nellie caught herself. He was an old man.

She glanced up and down the street. Day hinted at its presence by a subtle decrease in the gloom hanging over the trees, although globby flakes continued to fall. One auto passed, then another. Up the street, a bench marked the entrance to a small park.

With an effort, Nellie helped Gwynn stand and aimed him

there. When he dropped to the seat, he motioned for her to sit beside him. She had no moral obligation to help him further, but his bedraggled appearance and woebegone expression tugged at her.

"What do you want?"

"Tommy said you called me a goddamn murderer." She handed him his hat and he placed it on his head, a shame because his hair gave him a dignified demeanor. Otherwise, he could have passed as a bum on Chicago's south side.

Nellie couldn't decide whether to quibble with the policeman's term. She had suggested he had killed Ah Kee, but she had not used the word "murderer." "When did he say that?"

He shifted on the bench and it creaked under both their weights. It was meant for strolling ladies who wished to rest. "Said I was gonna be charged with the murder of that goddam Chinaman, the one who killed my Lily." He mumbled on, but Nellie couldn't hear what he said.

"What? You'll have to speak up." Cold slats were beginning to turn Nellie's backside numb. She gathered herself to leave.

"I wished I'd a done it."

"And you didn't?" She slumped back.

"I woulda, but he was already dead."

New news. "Do you mean you saw him dead?"

But Gwynn was off on a tangent. "That goddamn Kipling. That's who I shoulda killed. Old enough to be her father. He never shoulda married her. She'd be alive today. But no, first she wanted to marry that sheepherder. I stopped that one. No daughter of mine was goin' to make me a laughin' stock." He made a queer grating sound. "Then she married a goddamn miner. Told her no miner was gonna inherit my sheep ranch!"

Nellie wasn't certain what Gwynn meant, but clearly, he had dictated a course of action that his daughter had rebelled against. "Maybe, then, it was your fault she died."

The stricken look he gave her confirmed that he, too, had blamed himself at least once, even if he was casting the net of guilt everywhere else. Another thought occurred to Nellie. "Did you knock Mr. Levine down in his studio?"

A crafty expression replaced the stricken one. "What're you talkin' about?"

"Were you after my photographs?"

"My Lily was like you. Smarty mouth and thought she knew it all."

"You and Sammy?" Nellie persisted, not certain if he heard anything she was saying, but he understood her then.

"That goddamn Chinaman. I told him a thing or two."

Mr. Levine walked hurriedly up to them. "Miss Burns, are you all right? You were late, so I decided to look for you." He reached for her hand and she used his to pull herself to her feet. "What happened?"

"Mr. Campbell fell in the snow. I tried to help him." No sense in accusing him again. The short, soggy rest had done little to restore Nellie. She was freezing cold and her chest hurt; she could hardly breathe without wheezing. Mr. Levine looked so concerned and inviting with his carefully cropped beard back again, warm overcoat, and broad shoulders that she stepped close to him, giving him little choice but to wrap an arm around her.

With only a moment's hesitation, Mr. Levine led her away. Then he stopped and called back, "You better go home, Gwynn. You will catch pneumonia if you do not."

"Catch pneumonia and die is how it goes," Nellie whispered. "Serve him right."

The studio was bright and toasty. Mr. Levine led Nellie into the kitchen, sat her down, and filled a coffee pot. Soon its perking, the tocking of the clock, the burnt toast smell of strong coffee, and finally, the *brring* of the telephone brought Nellie back to normal. She stopped trembling, but a coughing fit hit her. When she stopped, she said, "Thank you, Mr. Levine."

As he entered the hallway to answer the telephone, he said, "Could you call me Jacob? I am tired of 'Mr. Levine.' "

Upon his return, she answered. "Only if you call me Nell. Everyone has been so formal here in the West, I thought I should be, too."

"Nell, then. Is that a shortened version of Eleanor?"

"No, it's just Nell. My mother named me Cora Nell, but my father always called me 'Little Nell.' Thanks heavens 'Cora' was left by the wayside." She looked down at herself. "Which is where I might have been left. Look at me. My dress is torn, my hands are dirty, and my coat is soaked. I can only imagine what's happened to my hair."

Jacob smiled at her. "You could return to the inn, or if you do not mind men's clothing, and I understand some women have adopted such a fashion as men's trousers, I have a spare pair and a shirt in the bathroom on the linen shelf. They are old, but clean. And your hair—well, I have nothing to stop it from curling. You should change or you, too, will catch pneumonia and die." He placed the creamer back in the refrigerator. "I have some other work. You can use the darkroom when you are ready." He studied her a moment longer and left.

A plethora of men, Nellie thought. Is that like a covey of quail? A gaggle of geese? Or a band of sheep? She thought of Gwynn Campbell. Having no father seemed not such a bad thing anymore. Were she and Lily alike? She removed her dress and slip, glad to be rid of them, and pulled on the trousers and shirt, then turned up the cuffs and sleeves so that she wasn't wading in extra material. The belt from her dress pulled the pants tight around her waist.

Her hair frizzed in every direction, but re-fastening it in back would smooth it out. From her bag, she pulled a brush, and the envelope Mrs. Bock had handed her dropped out. Inside, Nellie found bills, twenty ones. Money from the Ah Kees, but why? For the photos? These must be payment—far too much. Still, she could order trousers from Sears, purchase more film and paper, save part of the money for an enlarger, and still have enough to buy an Ever-Ready flashlight for another venture out at night. She planned to return to the cabin one more time. Some clue was missing and she needed to find it. It might lead her to the murderer and to safety. More photographs at twilight were part of her plan, too.

The morning felt used up by the time she entered the darkroom with her negative pouch in hand, but it was still quite early. Just as she knocked on the door, heeding the Do Not Enter sign in case Jacob was in the middle of printing a photo, she heard voices inside.

"Where is she?" A woman's voice.

"In the bathroom changing. Ah, there she is." The door opened.

Inside, Jacob and his fiancée stood very close together and, judging by the deep flush that came to Emmaline's face, Nellie was certain they had been in each other's arms. So much for the plethora of men.

"You two met at the hospital, did you not?"

Nellie nodded. "It is nice to see you again." she said. There was clearly no room for three people in the darkroom, so she stood in the doorway, not knowing what else to say or do.

"You look like a man," Emmaline said. "How odd."

"We have work to do, so you must leave us to it, Emmaline," Jacob said. "I will see you for supper at your parents' home. Thank you for coming by. It is always so sweet of you to be concerned about me." He walked her to the front door, while Nellie closed the darkroom door, shutting them out. She did not want to watch them kissing goodbye. The feel of Jacob's arm around her shoulders was still strong.

The moonshadow photos were her first order of business. Her paying business be damned. The portraits would keep. Enlarging the art photos required new test strips and the manipulation she had discussed with Jacob challenged her. Then she printed the negatives from her portrait sessions, including the photo of Ah Kee's wound, and developed the film of the miners and the elk seen at Last Chance Ranch. While her own work dried, she turned to the exposed film from Jacob's portrait sessions of the day before.

"Here are your prints and negatives, Jacob." Nellie wanted to please him. "And I have my enlargements, too. Would you like to see them?"

"Already?" He checked his pocket watch. "Yes, let us look and then find some dinner. Do you think the innkeeper would begrudge me a noon meal?"

If she did, Nellie would pay her separately. "Why don't I telephone and let her know we're coming?"

On the large front desk, Nellie and Jacob studied the photos. The white smoke, if that's what it was, still was not clearly coming from the chimney, but it hovered over the house. "Maybe it is a small cloud or a string of fog," Jacob suggested. "There is an otherwordly feel to this photograph, Nell. The movement of the stars emphasizes the strangeness. It should become the first of your Idaho portfolio. And sending it to that group in San Francisco for their gallery is worth the effort and even the possible rejection. Now let us see the second one."

In full daylight, the dark blob in the trees behind the wheatgrass took a definite form. It was no wild animal, and Nell knew instantly it was a man and who it was.

"I think the dark form is a man," Jacob said. His well-kept index finger outlined the blob. "See? Here is a head wearing a hat, two arms, and two legs. They're all akimbo it seems, but it's a man. I wonder what he was doing out there?" He frowned. "I wonder if you were wise to explore in the wilderness by yourself at night."

"I was safe, although I certainly didn't know he—anyone— was in those trees." She picked up the magnifying glass and peered again at the figure. Only one man walked as if he were a puppet on a string, and that was Rosy Kipling. Her heart sank. She'd suspected for some time that it was probably Rosy who moved the iceman. He was out there; it was his cabin. But she still could not believe Rosy had killed Three-Fingered Jack, then moved him, cut off his arm, and stripped him of his belt. Why would Rosy get a doctor to help him and then do him in? There must be another answer.

Chapter 21

Before she left Twin Falls, Nellie wanted to talk to the sheep rancher. His words continued to nag her. Maybe he could help her find out what happened. And she'd tell the sheriff, of course. It was early evening and Nellie and Jacob had called it a day, he because he was meeting his fiancée, and she because she had finished what she had wanted to, including another set of negatives of the moonshadows, which she left with Jacob. She could pack up to catch the connection for the train in the morning. One day a week, it left at eight a.m. Sharp.

Mrs. Olsen told Nellie that Gwynn Campbell lived near the falls. She offered up her husband as driver. "He's not doing a thing. Just reading. Want to go now?"

Nellie and Franklin set off in the dark, dry evening along a paved road, he as quiet as usual. A light shone on the wide front veranda of a graceful mansion. Several windows were lit upstairs and down. Would he welcome her or try to bash her head in? "Do you want to wait, Franklin, or maybe you'd come in with me?" She had told neither Mrs. Olsen nor Franklin about the morning's set-to.

He pulled out his flashlight and a book, *The Call of the Wild* by Jack London, and smiled. "I'll wait, Miss Burns, if you don't mind. I'm at a good spot. If you need me, just holler or flash the lights or something."

A Mexican maid answered the doorbell and said the old man was in bed, not feeling well, but nevertheless led Nellie across a

224

marbled entry hall, up a sweeping staircase, along a carpeted hallway to a closed door. The maid tapped, went in, announced "Señorita Burns" in a soft, sweet voice, then left Nellie to manage by herself.

Even without his sheepskin coat and cowboy hat, Gwynn Campbell hardly seemed diminished, sitting against three pillows in a large canopied bed in a room with a row of windows black with night. His skin no longer looked leathered, just wrinkled and worn out above a couple days' growth of salt and pepper beard.

"Won't say I'm sorry if that's what you're here for, Lassie." He coughed and covered his mouth with a white handkerchief with lace embroidery, such a non-cowboy, non-farmer scrap of material that Nellie wondered where a Mrs. Campbell was. No one ever mentioned her.

Nellie took the chair beside the old Scot's head. She ached all over. "What did you mean when you said Ah Kee was already dead? Did you see him?"

A stubborn expression and a slight tinge of color improved Gwynn's face. "None of your business. You and your damned pictures."

"It is my business. I found a dead man in the cabin and I found a dead man in the snow. The second one was Ah Kee. I've photographed both. I want to know what happened. If I'm wrong about your killing the Chinese doctor, I'm sorry." Accusing this weakened old man of murder didn't faze Nellie. He'd attacked her. "You led me to believe you might have."

"How'd I do that?"

"After Jacob was hurt. You swore at all Chinese and said one killed your daughter. Maybe you wanted to get even." When he still looked mulish, she added in a low tone, "And maybe you were entitled to."

Grief replaced truculence. "Entitled I was. I went out to that hellhole because I knew he kept his drugs upstairs . . . in her bedroom." Tears slid from the outer corners of each eye. "Saw him dose her myself. Figured he'd want his opium some time. I got word he was going out to the ranch. I followed. Dead already. Some damn fool cheated me." His voice strengthened and the sag in his cheeks lifted. Then he laid back and wiped his eyes.

"Dead how? Where?"

"Conked on his head in the snow and dead as a squashed bug." He mumbled a few more words, ending with ". . . damned sheepherder." He pulled the sheet up to his neck, his strength wilting in front of her. Nellie's remembered image of Ah Kee was of a gentle-faced Buddha, swathed in brilliant silk clothes, lying like a statue. Who else was he referring to?

"Didn't seem so evil then," Gwynn said. "Red blood just like the rest of us." He seemed to plead with Nellie. "Couldn't do a thing, could I? I puked up my lunch in the snow there—back of his head was bashed in—and left."

"Blood? I didn't see any blood." Thank heavens for that. Would the snow have wiped off the blood?

"Snowed since then. Good thing about snow is it covers all sorts of sins."

What other sins was the old man thinking of? Maybe not murder, but could she truly believe him? She knew so little about Mr. Campbell, except his own nattering about revenge and his attack on her. The sheriff would have to put it all together.

"Who killed Three-Fingered Jack?"

Gwynn either didn't hear her or chose to ignore her. "That Chinaman was as dead as my Lily." Some of the anger returned to his eyes. "Hope he hurt as much as she did."

"I suspect his wife and son hurt as much as you do."

"What do you mean?" But he knew, she saw. "Jack Smith,

that three-fingered jackanapes, was a good for nothing, lying, cheating, son-of-a-whore. Killed my sheep and that's same as stealing money. Left a band in a corral up in the Boulders with no water and no food. Stole god knows what-all from the mine up at Triumph. Then smoked it all up." His lip curled. "Deserved whatever he got."

"You didn't kill him?"

"Got murder on your mind, don't you?" He closed his eyes. The ordeal earlier in the day had weakened him, and her anger seeped away.

Nellie pushed herself out of her chair and to the door, then turned back because he was mumbling again or perhaps he was dreaming and talking to the shades. "Maybe I did cause the whole sorry shebang."

Back in the automobile, Nellie turned to Franklin. "What happened to Lily, Mr. Campbell's daughter?"

For the space of a mile, he said nothing. Then he pulled the auto to the side of the road and faced Nellie. "Which time?"

"There was more than one 'time'?"

"Lily loved everybody and everybody loved Lily. Got lots of people in trouble, including her. Like the time she ran away with Gwynn's sheepherder, Charlie Asteguigoiri. Gwynn caught up with them in Yellowstone Park where they were camping out. Mad, I've never seen anybody so mad as—"

"Sheriff Azgo? He worked for the Campbells? She ran away with him?" It was hard to believe that taciturn man would have done something so adventurous. And yet, she, too, had been drawn to him. "No wonder Gwynn was angry."

"Not Gwynn. Lily. She swore she'd get her revenge on her father, and in a way, she did. Married a dirt-poor, twice-her-age miner and wouldn't talk to her father again. Not even when she nearly died having that first boy of theirs." Franklin's voice was soft in the darkness, almost as if he, too, had loved Lily.

227

Mr. Campbell's mumblings came back to her. Did he think the sheriff killed Ah Kee? If he thought her photos would prove the sheriff's guilt, that would explain why Mr. Campbell might have been anxious to get into the darkroom.

"That's the irony. The sheepherder rose in the community. Lily's husband, Ross something-or-other, worked the mines, became a drinker, although I understand for a while he did all right." Franklin shifted back around to face the steering wheel. "That cancer ate him up as surely as it ate up Lily. He's just been doing it slower, I hear—pickling himself."

The night wrapped itself around the auto. Nellie wanted it to protect her and Rosy, but she guessed it was too late for that. "Why does Gwynn insist that the Chinese killed Lily? I don't understand."

Franklin uttered a huge sigh. "When Lily nearly died the first time, that old Celestial, Ah Kee, was called in and he dosed her up with laudanum and some other Chinese remedy is what we heard. Gwynn thought she was being poisoned. Then when she got sick again, she wouldn't let anyone see her, except her children, her husband, the Celestial, and Goldie Bock. Goldie never told anybody either, until after Lily died. According to her, Ah Kee kept Lily alive as long as he could, kept her from going mad with pain, until he finally eased her out of her agony. Who's to know?" He started the motor going, shifted gears, and pulled back into the street.

The auto rumbled along and Nellie felt tears gather. She hadn't known Lily, but she did know Rosy and Goldie.

"Where was the sheriff when all this was happening?"

"Doing his job, I suppose. Goldie told Mabel that he cracked once. Said his God would wreak vengeance in His own good time. That he didn't have to. We didn't know who he thought should be revenged upon. Rosy, maybe? Gwynn? The Chinese doctor? You know, those Catholics have some strange ideas sometimes."

Nellie knew nothing about organized religion. She thought most religions had some strange ideas, but she wasn't going to pursue it with Franklin. "And the boys?"

"Lily's husband took them East and came back without them. Goldie knows where they are. She gets letters." He slowed the auto as they approached the Clarion Inn.

"Thank you for taking me to see Mr. Campbell. I wished I'd known all of this before I went into the house." Maybe it was better she hadn't known. She might not have been as blunt as she had been. The stories whirled in her head during the night and she rose in the morning low in spirits and feeling unwell. Heavy clouds and rain mixed with snow didn't help.

Satisfied with her work in the darkroom and armed with prints of her new customers, as well as prints of the daylight photos at Last Chance Ranch and the miners, Nellie caught the train in the morning. Jacob Levine had been more than helpful, even to the point of suggesting another way to sell photos: make contact prints on postcard stock, a fairly quick and easy process. Then her customers could send their photographs to relatives and friends outside the area. She once again studied the photo of the wheatgrass, the aspens, and the dark shadow of Rosy in the trees. He seemed such a simple man, and it was hard to think of him skulking along through the trees in the dark while she was working away. Still, the moon had been so bright, any number of activities could have been carried on in its light.

She remembered something the day when she had talked Henry into taking her back to Last Chance Ranch. As she met him after her misadventures, she'd seen a figure among the trees to the north. A crouched figure.

Another image: Mrs. Smith crouching low and scuttling along the hallway of the boarding house, imitating the man who stole her negatives. Always, she had associated Sammy with that theft, and if it were he, then he might have been the person in the trees. What a leap, she thought, from Mrs. Smith imitating someone to making that thief the person north of town. Empty landscapes no longer were what they seemed. Was that also true of all the people she'd met? The sheriff. Rosy. Gwynn Campbell. Three-Fingered Jack Smith. Was Mrs. Smith related? Everyone seemed to have a secret.

Who had been at the cabin in the day or two before Nellie went? Sheriff Azgo, Gwynn Campbell, Ah Kee, Three-Fingered Jack, Rosy Kipling. It sounded like a convention. How did they manage not to bump into each other? Or, more to the point, which man was a murderer? Two of those names were dead. Of the other three, Gwynn said he was not. She could hardly believe the sheriff would murder someone. And Rosy—it didn't fit. Her head ached with true and false names and shadows.

Photography held no secrets one couldn't learn. It showed a world and people in black and white. And yet, there could be secrets. Her photo of the moon over the ranch was a double exposure. The light color of the river rock stones came from manipulating the enlarged image. Timing, too, had an impact on what the viewer would see in the photos: more or less light, blurred or crisp lines. She would need to know much better all the people involved in this mystery to gain insight into their secrets, to shed light where some might not want it shed.

The train slowed on its entry into Hailey. Why not deliver the photos to the Ah Kees now? Nell separated them, her enlargements, and her negative sleeves from the rest of her prints. Before she could change her mind, she arranged with the porter to off-load her supplies in Ketchum and then disembarked onto the snowy pavement with no idea how she would get herself from Hailey to Ketchum by nightfall. She looped the strap of her camera pack over her shoulder, and walked the three blocks to Main Street, a longer trek than she had expected.

Hailey's main thoroughfare, the highway that headed north to Ketchum and south to Shoshone and Twin Falls, was wide enough for a horse and buggy to make a U-turn. Now that few horses and buggies populated any town, the street width diminished the size of the automobiles that motored along it. The clink of tire grippers and the exhaust smell of oil and gasoline sharpened her impression of busy commerce. A pang of regret rose and fell over her decision to stay in Ketchum. Never mind, she could always change her mind. A move ten miles south would be considerably easier to contemplate than the move from Chicago to Idaho, although going through a process of finding a place to live, meeting more new people, perhaps finding, too, greater resistance to setting herself up in business, loomed as obstacles.

But first she had to find the Ah Kees. Hailey during a dazzling sunny day looked nothing like Hailey on a dark and stormy night.

At the Clarion Inn in Twin Falls, Nellie had handwritten several medium-sized cards announcing:

C. N. Burns, Photographer
Appointments available on Thursdays and Fridays
222 Leadville Avenue (Bock's Boarding House)
Ketchum, Idaho

In smaller print at the bottom, she had added "Goldie's Pies Available." She had intended placing these cards in Ketchum, but decided to enter one or two businesses along Hailey's main street to see if she could post her card in the window, with an offer of a discounted photograph. At the same time, she could ask how to get to the Ah Kee residence. But where to begin?

Nellie walked the two main blocks of business, crossed the street, and walked down the other side. All residents probably shopped at the Golden Rule Grocers. Schilling's Hardware was a possibility but its windows held only dusty mining implements and agricultural small tools, reflecting mostly male customers. Many residents would stop at North's Dry Goods. Silver Star Furniture with its gold-scripted sign on the door looked like it would appeal to the kind of customer she needed—monied or propertied or both. Someone in the Greenley Shoe Repair, the local bank office, or the pharmacy with a soda fountain might have the information she sought, and she wanted to sit down. Her knees trembled.

A thin man in a black suit, white shirt, and string tie greeted Nell from behind a polished, large oak desk as she stepped into the bank. Although clean-shaven, his face still carried a heavy shadow around his jaw.

"Can I help you?"

"I wondered if I might place this card in your window." She showed it to him.

He looked through thick glasses at her, his eyes appearing double the normal size. "I see the business is in a boarding house." He sniffed and his nose wiggled. "Does your husband want to set up business here in Hailey? Ketchum is falling apart. Won't be long before it's a ghost town, if the people there don't use the remaining boards for bonfires."

Should she tell him she had no husband? She decided not. "We want to begin small, but certainly in the future, we would consider the move."

"Then I could let you put the card in the window for a while. You won't last long in Ketchum. And we could work with you on a loan."

The man probably expected a curtsy for his generosity. "I wondered, too, if you could direct me to the Ah Kee residence?"

The eyes became slits. "Why do you want to see them?" Then he waved his hand. "Of course that's none of my business." Still, his tone indicated he wanted an answer. "I always wondered why they stayed when the rest of Chinatown burned down. You'd think they'd go back to their own kind."

"I want to deliver their photographs to them," Nellie said, keeping a rein on her tongue. "They were one of my—our first customers."

"Oh." The man studied his hand, much plumper than the rest of him. "I don't think it's a good idea to have Chinese as customers of your studio. It'll put off everyone else." When Nellie said nothing to his advice, he added, "They live near the river along Della Avenue. If I were you, I'd mail the pictures. It's dangerous in those woods. Who knows what other thieves, kidnappers, and opium-smokers hide out there?"

Nellie nodded and was almost out the door before the man called after her. "Don't you want to display the card?"

"I've changed my mind."

A bell tinkled with the opening door at the repair shop, and the tangy aroma of shoe polish and leather warmed the air. Here, a man peered at her over his glasses and blinked twice. His bulky chest and the nut brown solemnity of his eyes resembled storybook drawings of dwarves, although he was not short. His hands, holding a battered boot, were stained a dark burnt umber and moved surely over the leather. He placed a small nail along the sole and seated it with taps of a hammer. Nellie dropped into the one chair available for waiting customers, relieved to rest. Her chest once again felt tight and full, and she coughed several times.

Three calendars hung on the walls—behind him near a door to the back, next to the cash register, and by a bulletin board to the right of the front door. She looked around for a clock but saw none. Days rather than hours were important to the shoemaker.

"Do you know where I can find the Ah Kees?" She might as well discover immediately if everyone in town hated the Chinese.

"The Ah Kees live near the river." His voice was much younger than his long gray hair, wire-rimmed glasses, and used hands suggested. He pointed with the boot. "If you walk down Bullion Street two blocks, turn left, and walk south for three blocks, you'll run into a path through the trees. Theirs is the only house remaining in the woods." He placed another nail. "Do you know the Ah Kees?" The question was softly spoken.

"I have photographs to deliver." She paused. When he said nothing, she continued. "I opened a photography business in Ketchum and they were one of my first customers." He tapped the nail into place. "Would it be possible to post one of my placards on your bulletin board?" She placed a card next to the boot he was working on. "My name is Nellie Burns."

"If you will wait—" the shoemaker said, and turned to go through the doorway and out of sight. The walk to the Ah Kees sounded a bit of a distance. Discouragement bent her shoulders, which were stiff from working in the darkroom. The rest of her body felt ill-used from Gwynn Campbell's attack. She wondered if a huge bruise were growing on her chest because it felt so tender. Even the soft camisole she wore felt like too much weight.

Sammy Ah Kee stepped into the shop from the interior doorway, followed by the shoemaker. "Missee." He bowed, folding his hands together at his waist.

Nellie stood and bowed as well. She didn't know whether to pull out the photos because of their private nature. "Hello, Sammy. I have the prints for you. I was going to deliver them to your house. Now, I can deliver them to you." She proffered the envelope and sat back down, in part because her legs gave way. "I need a ride back to Ketchum. Do you know anyone going that way?" The light in the ceiling seemed to swim from side to side.

"Do you work here?" The shop grew dimmer, and she began

to worry if it was going to snow again and how she would return to Ketchum. Asking Sammy to drive her didn't seem appropriate. He had his job. She could pay him, then remembered that most of the money in her bag came from him or his mother or both, and she giggled. Maybe she could telephone Mrs. Bock and ask if Rosy could come for her. He would probably charge $2.00 each way and be pie-eyed as well. Her mind dithered as she waited for Sammy to answer her question. Both he and the shoemaker continued to stare at her, the one with his hands still folded and the other blinking like a firefly. Her thoughts fluttered. Come summer, she hoped fireflies would light up the Ketchum nights the way they had done in the backyard of her grandparents' house before it was sold to pay debts. Here, though, the stars were brighter than fireflies.

When the two men hurried to either side of her, lifted her from the chair, and carried her through the doorway into the back of the shop, Nellie could only watch herself from afar. What were they doing? The shoemaker wrapped a blanket around her, binding her arms to her sides, making her feel like a mummy trapped in its threads. What are you doing? she asked, not once, but many times. Neither answered. When they bundled her into a strange automobile with a bed in the back, the brilliant sunlight hurt her eyes and she closed them. The blanket wasn't enough to warm her nor was the sun. The shoemaker held her so she wouldn't get loose or call out to passersby while someone drove. It must be Sammy.

Her camera! Nellie struggled to sit up, fight off the sixteen arms holding her tight. Already, the thieves had stolen her camera. Thank god the negatives were safe. Or were they? She couldn't remember where they were.

"The camera." A strange voice asked for her camera. Why would anyone else want it? Then she realized it was her own voice. Would opium-smokers be next? So this was how white slavery began.

CHAPTER 22

When Nellie awoke she didn't know where she was. She lay on her back with a weight on her chest. She smelled of Mentholatum. After her eyes adjusted to the darkness, she picked out two posts at the end of the bed. Her limbs felt heavy as death and she couldn't lift either an arm or a hand and wondered for a while if she had arms and hands. Gradually, the heaviness left her and she felt as if she were suspended in a dark place where soft breezes blew and rocked her cradle.

Her mind wandered from image to image: the brilliant blue of Lake Michigan covered with white sailboats that changed to seagulls and flew into the sun; the cozy red muff she'd owned as a child that was lost in one of the moves from place to place; the forest green pinafore she'd sewn and worn to work at Scotto's, then ruined by spilling developer fluid on it; and, finally, the crags of mountain peaks that transformed into the sharp teeth of a devil. She must escape, she told herself, but nothing in her body responded.

"Are you feeling any better, Miss Burns?" The devil, a woman with hooded eyes, stood beside her.

"Better?" Nellie's voice croaked. "Where . . . ?"

"You lie in our house."

A cool, dry hand touched Nellie's forehead. Only then did she understand that her bed was a pyre, her body a torch. "Hot," she managed to say, and struggled to grasp the hand to place it on her cheeks or her neck, but no part of her moved.

The presence left and reappeared and something cold covered her face, then slid along her neck, and, after the weight was lifted, it slid along her chest and stomach and down her legs and then her arms. Her dreams changed and she slogged through snow in bare feet, fell over again into icy river water, and stood naked in a snowstorm, shivering so hard she couldn't seek shelter. Hell was like this. Hot, then cold, then hot again.

The next time Nellie awoke, darkness had lessened and a gray light sifted through a drawn curtain. She rested on the same bed where the corpse of Ah Kee had lain, and a memory of incense mixed with Mentholatum and a deeper remnant of smell that caused her a moment's twinge. Whatever bonds had held her were gone and she sat up, shifting her legs to the edge of the bed. A long silk shift covered her nakedness. The remembrance of heat and something cool stroking her stirred forgotten feelings, and then she stood on the stack of Oriental carpets, walked carefully to the door so that the spinning quality of the air would not topple her. She opened it and stepped into an empty room.

On the table, where earlier she had noticed three settings, sat her photographs of Ah Kee, as well as the moonshadow enlargements. Her camera pack rested on the floor. A chair was placed in front of the enlargements and a magnifying glass lay alongside. For no particular reason, Nellie had also enlarged the photo of Three-Fingered Jack and it lay there too. She felt detached from it, as though this were someone else's work. The left hand, with its missing fingers, lay stump side toward the camera. The face, although partially hidden by the ice across the nose and all of one eye, was even more recognizable as Caucasian. At the corner of the photo was the business end of the axe that the hand grasped when Nellie stumbled into the body. The same axe she had gripped later that night. How had someone killed Jack if he had an axe in hand to defend himself?

The overturned table . . . There must have been a fight.

The sound of voices accompanied footsteps outside the small house. Nellie looked for a way to escape and saw the back door, but she was dressed only in a shift. Already, she was feeling the chill of the room. She hurried back to bed, leaving the door slightly ajar so she could hear whoever was coming.

"I don't understand why you didn't take her to the clinic or the doctor," a voice said. Nellie's heart lifted: it was Mrs. Bock.

"She die there." Sammy's statement contained no question in it. "Doctors kill."

"Don't be ridiculous," Mrs. Bock said. "Everybody died during the flu epidemic. The clinic and doctors didn't kill them." Her firm tread stopped by the table. "Where is she?"

Mrs. Ah Kee showed the much larger and taller woman into the room where Nellie had crept back into bed, glad to have blankets around her shoulders again.

"I'm here, Mrs. Bock." Nellie was so glad to see her landlady, she thought she'd cry, but she willed herself not to burst into tears.

"Did these China—people—hurt you?" Mrs. Bock sat on the edge of the bed and wrapped her arms around Nellie, who rested her head on the older woman's shoulder and tried to think what had happened. All she remembered was being held tight, traveling in a motorcar, being handled like a doll, and waking up once, no, twice.

"I don't think so. I don't know what happened."

Mrs. Ah Kee, still standing by the door, snorted. "Miss Burns collapsed in the store where Sammy works. He and Mr. Greenley brought her here and I treated her. If they had not done so, she would have died of pneumonia. She is better." She began to back out of the room.

"Wait, Mrs. Ah Kee. I was ill?" Nellie's aches and pains and coughs and her strange dizziness in the shoe repair shop finally made sense. "Did you give me opium?"

"I gave you my husband's nostrum for high fever and pain. You are improving, but you should not be moved." She looked pointedly at Mrs. Bock and then withdrew.

Nellie lay back against her pillow. Weariness invaded her limbs. "How did you know I was here?"

"When your stuff showed up at the house and you wasn't with it, I telephoned Mrs. Olsen. She said you'd been to see old Gwynn, then left the next morning without a word. The old reprobate himself is in the hospital all stove up and maybe dying. Land sakes, we've been worried. Conductor said you got off the train in Hailey and walked down the road. Last he saw of you." She patted Nellie's arm and moved a hank of hair behind her ear. "I called the sheriff and said he had to find you. This was his fault, getting you all upset the other day. He found your trail at the bank where that sharpie said you'd been in looking pale as any ghost and he wouldn't be surprised if you'd been doped up and kidnapped. Charlie wasn't buying any of that. Then Mrs. Ah Kee called me up last night. Said you were sick and in her house. I come a running soon as I could. Gladys brought me. She's waiting outside and has to go to work. Wouldn't come in." She leaned close and whispered, "Ah Kee was no stranger to Gladys. Says Mrs. Ah Kee don't like her." Mrs. Bock studied Nellie. "Your eyes are still a little shadowy, so I guess it's right, you been sick. Stick out your tongue."

Nellie did as she was told.

"Looks a little white still, but getting its pink back. Do you feel safe here?"

Nellie thought about it, nodded her head, and closed her eyes for a moment. When she opened them again, Mrs. Bock wasn't there anymore and the room was dark, the door closed with a murmur of voices behind it—the Chinese language spoken by Mrs. Ah Kee and her son on the train. Where had

Mrs. Bock gone?

The door opened and Sammy came in with a tray. "Missee hungry?" He laid it on the floor beside the bed, helped Nellie sit up with pillows behind her, and placed the tray on her lap. A delicious meaty aroma floated from the covered dish on the tray and her mouth salivated. In the dish were noodles, broth, chunks of meat, and pale vegetable-like pieces, along with ginger. Two sticks rested beside the dish. Her puzzlement meant something to Sammy because he called in Chinese to his mother, who came in with a ceramic ladle and a fork. "You can use these."

Nellie accepted the ladle and fork, but then picked up the sticks. Sammy took them from her and showed her how to hold one like a pencil while resting the other one on her fourth finger. She managed to click them together like a bird's beak, laughing at how awkward her fingers felt.

"Where is Mrs. Bock?" she asked.

"Ketchum. Tomorrow you go home." Sammy guided her sticks to the piece of meat and helped her grab hold. The first piece plopped onto the tray, but eventually Nellie got one bite and then another into her mouth. The noodles were slippery and she splashed herself as she worked to get several into her mouth at once. The ginger tasted spicy.

Sammy waited patiently while Nellie concentrated on moving noodles from bowl to mouth. He helped her twice, but otherwise stood silently by, his hands folded at his waist.

"I didn't know I was sick," Nellie said and slurped a noodle. "I thought you were kidnapping me and had stolen my camera."

He bowed.

"I'm sorry. My mother raised me to be open-minded and generous to people. I was neither one to you and the cobbler." Slurrrp. "You don't know as much English as your mother." Nellie didn't know if this was an offensive thing to say or not.

"Mother live America many years. I live two."

"Oh." That was food for thought. Mrs. Ah Kee left her son in China while she came to America. How could she do that? Was she forced to leave him? Those questions were too personal. "Why were you out at Last Chance Ranch the day I was there? I saw you in the trees."

His smile disappeared. He bowed his head briefly and moved to leave the room.

"Don't leave, Sammy. Help me solve this mystery. Who killed your father? You must want to know."

And who killed Jack, unless it was Sammy or his mother? If they did it, they must have known Ah Kee was already dead and he wouldn't have been buried in the snow. Or maybe Ah Kee had been an evil man and mother and son had killed him, too. What better way to hide a crime? Pretend love for someone and then smash his head in when he least expected it. And who stole Jack from the cabin and threw him in the river? Where did his arm go? Maybe the Tong chopped it off. Full with noodles and meat, she leaned back, wondering what to do with the tray.

There, beyond the foot of the bed, stood Mrs. Ah Kee and Sammy. She hadn't heard them come in. Indeed, they could have stolen Jack from the cabin and she and Moonie would not have heard a sound.

"Miss Burns. Neither Sammy nor I killed Ah Kee." Mrs. Ah Kee had once again adopted the familiar lilt to her words. "You murdered two men is what Sammy says."

"I killed two men? Why in the world would I do that? I—I didn't even know them. The first I ever saw Jack and Dr. Ah Kee was when they were dead!"

"Sammy watched you at the cabin. He searched for his father, who disappeared two days before. You went there to meet Ah Kee, like other women."

"I went to take photographs of the moon and shadows on snow. You've seen them. They're on your table." The two faces, malevolent in the shadows, frightened her.

"Why did you photograph the cabin and the dead man if not to document your evil work? We have heard of people from Chicago. They shoot and kill and maim and steal. You steal my honored husband's soul. You photograph him." The pair stood like statues, their hands folded at their waists, their heads held stiffly upright, Sammy in his coolie clothes and Mrs. Ah Kee in her modern dress.

"You brought me here to take his photo!" Nellie's hackles rose. "He was dead then. How could I have stolen his soul? You almost forced me to photograph him."

"You take picture at cabin," Sammy said. "Where you hide it?"

Nellie gripped the side of the tray, thinking she would throw it at them and then run. But she had no clothes. "Where are my things? I am leaving. I've told you several times that I did not photograph Ah Kee at the house. He was not there. Only Three-Fingered Jack." Curse her desire for money. If only she hadn't gone to the Last Chance Ranch.

Again, the two studied her. She stared at them. If they took one step, she'd throw the dish and tray. If she hit one, maybe she could run from the other. She could not look away. It would be a sign of weakness. Her eyes burned.

Then, although neither moved, Nellie sensed communication between the two. Sammy bowed. Mrs. Ah Kee said, "We believe you." The lines of her face deepened and hardened, aging her by many years, as if a great mourning had descended on her. She left the room and returned with a hanger carrying Nellie's clothes. "Here are your dress and underclothes. You cannot leave tonight, but in the morning Sammy will take you to Mrs. Bock. You will not be harmed while you are in our care." She laid the clothes over the end of the bed, motioned for Sammy to take the tray, and left.

This Idaho and its people were, in many ways, more complex than the city and its denizens, or at least the part of Chicago in which Nellie had lived and worked. There, stations in life were assigned and rarely deviated from. Here, there seemed room for different roles, different sensibilities. She would have thought that the opposite was true. Now, she wasn't so certain. The journey she was on became more hazardous the further she ventured.

She handed the tray to Sammy. "You do believe me, don't you?"

He nodded, but did not look at her.

"What else did you see out there when you were spying on me through the trees?" Nellie asked, on a hunch.

This time, he glanced at her face and the keen intelligence was back in his.

"We could work on this together, Sammy. Find out what really happened." She spoke in a low voice, not wanting his mother to hear, perhaps because Mrs. Ah Kee was all sharp edges and steel shields. To his silence, she said, "I'm going back out there as soon as I feel better, perhaps day after tomorrow. I know the snow covered up most everything, but there might be something the sheriff missed, something I didn't see when I was there, something you saw but didn't understand."

A slight hesitation on Sammy's part in moving around the bed with the tray suggested what she said resonated with him. "I know more than I did before. I think you know more than you've told, even to your mother." She remembered Franklin talking about Goldie and all of her knowledge. "Many people seem to know more than you or I do. We're the strangers here, so maybe we can see more clearly than the others. But I'm not sharing unless you do."

At the door, he studied Nellie. She was certain she saw a nod, or maybe it was just a blink of his eyes, before he left.

Another night of rest and medicine and Nellie felt almost good as new. The Ah Kees helped her into the auto that Sammy had driven the night they brought her from Ketchum to Hailey. He carried her camera and photo case and placed them in the back seat. Mrs. Ah Kee gave Nellie a steadying hand. Although she felt all right, her legs quivered.

"Thank you for taking care of me." Nellie wanted to explain how her initial fright had turned to respect, how sorry she was about the death of Ah Kee even if she had never known him, how she realized his death meant the end of a good doctor to the community, but she didn't know how to express herself, and whatever she said might be unwelcome and misunderstood. She was too new, too young, and too white to understand the difficulties the Ah Kees had faced and would continue to face daily for the rest of their lives.

A silvery cold etched the snow along the road to Ketchum with frozen crystals. Long wheatgrass, tall dead weeds, and bare Aspen branches all shone a dazzling white, like an iced-over fairy land. Even the air was spun with shimmering threads. In this radiant world, Nellie wanted to think only of the light, not of death and darkness, blood and lost love. On such a day, surely redemption could be found.

"Sammy," Nellie said, "teach me to drive."

Surprise widened Sammy's eyes. He glanced at her and back at the road.

"I need to know how to drive. If you won't take me out to Last Chance Ranch, I will go by myself. Even if you will take me, I need to know."

After glancing behind him, Sammy pulled over, out of the ruts heading north. He shut off the motor and sat a few minutes, then patted the steering wheel. "Steering wheel." He moved it to the right and to the left. He pointed to a button near the steering column. "Starter," and to the right pedal on the floor.

"Go gasoline." To the middle pedal. "Stop brake." To the left pedal. "Shift—no, clutch." To the stick coming from the floor to his right. "Shift." To his right leg. "Right foot gas and brake." Then he demonstrated moving his foot from the right pedal to the middle. "Left foot clutch." He pressed the left pedal.

Nellie leaned over to see what each foot was doing and mumbled after him, gas, brake, no clutch, brake. Shift. "But what are the no clutch and shift for?" Again, Sammy sat, chewing on his lip, then going through several motions. "Gas push, go. Brake push, stop. Yes?"

"Yes. If I push on the gas pedal, the car goes. If I push on the brake pedal, the car stops."

He nodded and smiled. "Clutch." He pushed it down again with his left foot. "Shift. Same time." With his right hand, he moved the shift knob forward and back. Then he took his foot off the clutch and said. "No clutch, no shift." He waited for her to say something.

"All right. No clutch, no shift." What did it mean? They didn't sound like Chinese words.

Beeeeeep. "Horn." He grinned. "You do."

Beep.

Sammy frowned and pushed the hub in the middle of the steering wheel again. *Beeeeeeeeep*. Nellie pushed a second time. *Bee-beeeeeeeeeeeeep!* They both laughed out loud.

"You drive," Sammy said. "Remember, no clutch, no shift." He climbed out his side of the car and came around to her door.

Nellie saw she could not easily slide past the stick—the shift—and swung out her door and walked around, climbing in behind the wheel. She took a deep breath, grabbed the steering wheel with both hands, and pressed her right foot to the gas pedal. Nothing happened.

"Start motor," Sammy said, pointing to the key and then to

the button. "Push starter." Then he leaned back with an expectantly fearful expression on his face.

Nellie turned the key and pushed the button. The motor turned over, and the auto jerked ahead and quit. "Oops."

"No no no! Push clutch, then turn on motor." He jabbed his left foot at the floor and touched the button at the same time, and Nellie followed his directions. This time, the engine rumbled and the auto rocked slightly. So, it was going. Now for the gas pedal. She lifted her left foot off the clutch and pressed the gas pedal with her right. The auto jerked and stopped.

Sammy snorted and climbed out his side of the auto, walked around to Nellie, and motioned for her to slide over. This time, she lifted her legs and skirt and awkwardly scooted to the passenger side. "Watch." He pressed the clutch, saying "Clutch," pushed the button, saying "starter," moved the stick toward him, saying "shift." She watched what he did. "Press gas slow. Let go clutch." The auto eased forward and he steered onto the main ruts, then pulled over again. "You do."

This required far too much concentration for Nellie, but she needed to learn. They traded places again. "All right. Clutch in." She pressed her left foot. "Push starter." *Rumble, rumble.* Maybe they could just sit there for a while.

"Go. Go. Right foot on gas, let go clutch."

Again, Nellie did as Sammy said and the car leaped forward in a big jerk, but then kept going.

"Steer! Steer!" Panic raised his voice an octave.

The auto bumped over lumps of snow and she finally steered it into the track of the road. The ruts pulled at the steering wheel, so she grasped it tightly. When the road began to curve, she moved the wheel to the right and almost ran off the road into the snowbank. Clearly, the wheel only needed a slight move to the right. But the motor sounded like it was groaning.

"Shift," Sammy said. Nellie reached for the stick but didn't know which direction to push it in. "Clutch clutch! Push down clutch." She did, and Sammy moved the stick forward. "Let go clutch. *Eeeeasy.*" The motor labored less.

Sammy leaned back, visibly becoming more easy himself. "I go find father. You see me. Honored mother and I think you . . . ," he said and paused. Nell couldn't take her eyes off the road. She nodded her head. "We think you kill. Tong sent you. Mr. Kipling says no. You see? You know? Yes, we decide." Again, he stopped and watched her drive. "Woman called Mrs. Smith—she bring pictures to me."

Nellie looked at Sammy. "Gladys Smith?" The auto headed for the ditch.

"Lookee!" Panic raised Sammy's voice again.

Nellie concentrated on steering the auto in line again. "How do you know her? *She* brought you the negatives?"

"She my father's patient. She say father in photo. Get pictures. Give to her."

"Then *you* struck Mr. Levine!"

Sammy reached over and straightened the wheel. "Watch road."

"I told the policeman it was you."

"Not me." An emphatic denial. "Door I blow up. Me." He slapped his chest. "Not hurt anyone. Honored mother shake ladder. Photo man fall. Accident. We run. Sheepman know."

It would be so much easier to talk if she stopped the automobile. She slowed.

"Go. Go."

"If your mother shook the ladder and Jacob fell, why did Mr. Campbell say you didn't do it?"

"Sheepman come to inn. He said father dead. He want to know who killed. I promise him pictures."

The sheepman knew a lot more than Nellie had guessed. His denial of murder weakened considerably. And Gladys Smith!

She said Rosy stole the negatives. If so, he must have given them to Gladys. Nell felt as if everyone in Ketchum watched her, signaling what they knew to each other. Maybe the anonymity of the city was more desirable than she thought. The auto slipped and she tightened her grip on the wheel, feeling as if she were on a carnival ride.

By the time Nellie pulled up to the boarding house and pressed her foot to the brake, jerking them to a stop once more, she felt like a driver. Sammy's face was covered with perspiration and he had long since unbuttoned his jacket.

Mrs. Bock came out the front door and down the steps. "What took so long? You have trouble with the motor?" She didn't wait for an answer. "Why are you driving, Miss Burns? This man too lazy to do the work?"

"Sammy taught me how to drive, Mrs. Bock. He's been ever so patient."

Her landlady looked from one to the other, then laughed. "No wonder you looked like you been rode hard and put away wet," she said to Sammy. "You better come in and rest afore you head back to Hailey. Your auto may need a little rest, too." Mrs. Bock grabbed Nellie's camera pack and the small bag she had taken to Nellie at the Ah Kee house. "Get on in the both of you." As Nellie climbed the stairs, the older woman whispered to her. "You learned to drive just in time. Rosy's gone missing."

CHAPTER 23

Nellie persuaded Mrs. Bock not to stuff her into bed by promising to stay seated by the fire in the dining room with her feet up while her landlady brought in tea, coffee, and cherry pie for her and Sammy. "And I need Moonshine here. I miss him."

The look Mrs. Bock gave her was indecipherable. "Moonshine is gone. I think Rosy must have taken him. He was outside on the back porch and under foot in my kitchen until a day-and-a-half ago. I was feeding him regular, so he wasn't looking for food."

"Oh no!" Nellie pushed herself up and ran up the stairs to her room, unlocking it with the key she had kept with her the whole time. For a second time, drawers were pulled out and her things knocked around. She went straight for the mattress and lifted it up. The Chinese robe was gone. Then she hurried down the stairs and out to the back porch. "Moonie! Moonie!" Mrs. Bock and Sammy converged at the back door.

"You get in here right now, young lady. You wasn't saved from pneumonia just to catch it up again." Mrs. Bock rested hands on hips and glared at her.

Nellie's knees buckled and she sat down in the snow, too desolate to cry. She deserved being abandoned by the dog. "I have to find Moonshine, Mrs. Bock. It's my fault he's gone. If I'd been here and taken care of him properly—"

"Feathers. Get yourself back in here. You're not going nowhere today. I'll tie you in your bed if necessary. Tomorrow is soon enough to gallivant around, if you don't het yourself up so much you get a fever tonight."

Even Sammy's expression had turned dark, he who was usually expressionless. And, in truth, Nellie did feel tired. "All right. In the morning, then." She followed her landlady into the dining room. "I'll eat the pie and go to bed. I'll be strong enough in the morning." After several bites, she asked Sammy, "Will you take me out to Last Chance Ranch? I know that's where Rosy went."

"Missee, auto not mine. I . . . borrow." Such a look of sadness had never crossed his face before. "Maybe come. Maybe not."

"If you are not here by noon, I'll borrow Mrs. Smith's." She walked to the doorway and stopped. "Thank you for bringing me home. And thank you for teaching me how to drive." There was something else. She studied his face for clues. "And most of all, thank you for saving my life." Before she left the room, she turned to Mrs. Bock. "Someone searched my room again and took my robe. Please tell the sheriff. If he can't find a murderer, maybe he can find a thief, although his record to date is not good."

An afternoon nap strengthened Nellie. The house was quiet. She had awakened with the belt on her mind, having forgotten it since she stashed it in the triple chair. As quietly as possible, she dressed and scurried downstairs. There was no one around. In the studio, she felt behind the cushions in the chair and her fingers touched metal. Relieved, she pulled out the belt, hurried back upstairs, and hid it in her pack at the bottom. The initials, indeed the whole buckle, cried for inspection in broad daylight. Then she crossed the hall to enter Gladys Smith's room; she had been lying all along. Nellie wanted to find out why.

A crepe material served as drapes on the windows, darkening the room with its canopy bed. A dozen photos stood on the dresser and the bedside stand, along with a pot of face cream, one of powder, two lipsticks, a sewing kit, a jewelry box, and a full pin cushion. A hat hung off the top of the fringed lamp, which Nell turned on. A pink glow lit up the photos. Most of them were of a girl and a boy. Nellie picked up one to study. The girl was a young Gladys. The boy a handsome youth with a solemn expression. They held hands. Another photo of the two had been ripped in half and then repaired. On a third one with an older man and woman and the two young people were written the words "The Bradleys." Three others showed the boy as he grew older, playing baseball, playing the trumpet, in a suit.

Nellie scanned the room, which was larger than her own. Bed, dresser, armoire—all looked normal and she couldn't bring herself to search drawers. There, behind the door was a pair of long narrow skis. This was a surprise. Mrs. Smith looked like a hothouse flower. Nell lifted one ski and found it was fairly heavy. A sock roll fell to the floor. Beside the boards were two poles with baskets on one end and leather straps on the other. A scarf draped from one strap. Nell pulled it loose and held it out. Two holes marred the material. She could picture a woman in black hat, black coat, and long skirt, her eyes shielded with a black scarf, scooting across a snowfield like a wingless raven. The scarf didn't hold the promise of much protection from the glare of sun on snow. The whole outfit didn't fit the Gladys she knew. But there was a photo on the dresser—she went back to check—a young girl on skis.

Nellie remembered the night Gladys had been in her room, dressed in black, like an assassin. Sounds of movement below indicated the house occupants were returning. Then she saw a piece of paper stuck in the frame at the mirror's edge: "Gwynn Campbell" was written on it along with a telephone number. Below it, hidden by one of the taller photo frames, was a weathered piece of cardboard with Chinese characters and Ah

Kee's name. She reached for it and found that attached to the card with a long sturdy hatpin was an ancient ad for Palmer's Patent Medicine, a medicine for "women's problems." The back door slammed, and Nellie's heart flipped. She tried to stick the paper things back into the edge of the mirror, but they wouldn't stay. Steps on the stairs. Another jab at the frame and the card stayed. She slipped out the door and entered the bathroom. Behind her, light footsteps entered Room Six. Then Nellie remembered she had left on the fringed light.

Just as Nellie slipped into bed, Mrs. Bock brought up a tray with a steaming bowl of split pea soup with ham and hot cornbread with butter and honey. Nothing could have suited Nellie better and she ate with relish. While she ate, Mrs. Bock rattled on.

"I never would have expected to find you in the woods with the Ah Kees. Do you think they slipped you something to make you pass out like that? No, I don't suppose they did. You can't give a body pneumonia. Now isn't it a coincidence that you and Gwynn Campbell both got it at the same time. Nasty weather in Twin Falls. I'd not live there for all the tea in China."

Nellie tried to sip her soup, and nibble at the cornbread, but it was difficult not to eat quickly.

Her landlady plucked at her skirt. "Mabel tells me maybe you had a falling out with Gwynn and somehow you two got caught in the rain. She wasn't too clear on what happened, but she said you went to see him." A long sigh. "Lily was the sweetest, prettiest girl any father could want and he just drove her away."

Nellie tested some of her newfound knowledge. "Lily ran away with the sheriff."

"Who told you that? That old reprobate?" Another long sigh. "Gwynn wouldn't stand for his daughter marrying a sheepherder. He figured Charlie wanted his money. Too blind and willful to see that them two loved each other. Lily came to me, wanted me to talk to her father. There's no talking to that Gwynn. Figured he knew everything. He didn't know the half of it." She contemplated the empty dishes on Nellie's tray. "Men."

Men were certainly more complicated than Nellie had given them credit for. "And Charlie made sheriff. How did that sit with Mr. Campbell?"

"Liked to bust his boiler. The old-timers 'round here was pretty tired of Gwynn running everything from Twin Falls clear up to Stanley. Figured maybe they'd do him one in the eye. Turned out they got a good sheriff. Charlie'd got some schooling down in Boise. Nobody cared he was Basque, except a few miners and Gwynn and he shoulda knowed better. Got Basque working for him. They're honest and hardworking. Rosy and Charlie now—they had a set-to here and again, but that's just natural. Both of 'em loved Lily. Rosy didn't get over her dying. I don't know about Charlie. He hid his feelings so long, maybe forgot he had 'em."

"Where are the boys?"

For the first time, Mrs. Bock seemed not to want to talk. "Well, you're done and I got work to do. Better sleep more if you're going out tomorrow. You'll need your strength. Looks like another storm barging right in."

"Aren't you worried about Rosy?"

"Some. He's not gone missing this long before. Sometimes, he goes off on a toot and holes up somewhere. I'd guess at the ranch, too." She nodded to Nellie. "Something about you must remind him of Lily. He's taken a shine to you, which he don't often do with people."

Mrs. Bock picked up the tray and pushed the light switch on her way out of the room. "Don't you bother your head. He'll turn up. Bet he's got Moonie with him. Nice dog, that."

253

"Mrs. Bock, who is Mrs. Smith?" It was easier to ask the question in the dark.

The landlady stopped in the doorway. "Gladys? Why she's . . . Gladys Smith. Why?"

"She had my negatives and gave them to Sammy."

"Land sakes." Her tone of voice belied her words. This was not news to Mrs. Bock. "Jack was Gladys's brother. Her and Rosy cooked up how to get your photographs so she'd have something to remember him by. That's what she told me when we drove down to Hailey to see you. Maybe she thought Sammy would tell, which he must have done. Jack was no good. Wouldn't work. Then he got mixed up in that blasted opium. She had enough. Left him and moved in here."

"But why 'Smith'?" Nellie knew it was Bradley, but she didn't say anything to her landlady. Sneaking around Gladys's room would not be acceptable.

"People use different names here. Sometimes, they don't want to be followed from town to town or they don't want to be found. Hers started with a 'B' if I remember correct. Gladys said she never wanted to hear it again, so I just forgot it." She made a *tsk*ing sound. "Then that brother started callin' himself Smith. Enough to drive a good woman crazy." The landlady closed the door. Then it opened again.

"Forgot to tell you. Sammy wanted to know if the sheriff killed his father."

"What?" Nellie was instantly alert and sat up.

"That's what he said after you left saying that about the sheriff—to find a thief 'cause he couldn't find a murderer. Said, 'Maybe he be one.' I remember Rosy called the sheriff to bring Ah Kee out to take care of Jack. Don't sound good." She closed the door again.

Nell was almost asleep when a floorboard creaked outside her door. She turned on the lamp and thought she saw the handle of her door turn, then stop. She slipped quietly out of bed, tiptoed to the door, and whisked it open. No one was in the dark hall. All the doors along it were closed tight, even the bathroom door at the end. No light shone from under that door. Was someone waiting for her to enter? She listened, her heart pounding. The skeleton key lay on her dresser. If she locked herself in and the building burned down, she might burn with it. She decided to risk fire rather than confront someone with murder in mind. But someone had already entered her room when it was locked and taken the robe. She shoved a chair against the door, but she didn't sleep for a long while.

No storm.

Nellie paced her studio. It was several hours before noon. She decided to deliver photos to her customers. She again used the skeleton key to lock her door and hoped Rosy was the only one with a duplicate. Except for Mrs. Bock, everyone seemed to have left for the day. The sun was bright again, the sky blue, the snow beginning to look old with an iced-over sheen. Against her landlady's advice, she bundled up, donned her boots, grabbed her photo case, and began her rounds, starting with Bert the Butcher.

"Good morning, Bert. Here are your photographs. I still have the negatives. If you want additional prints, let me know. Your bill is in the envelope, less the deposit you left with me last week." She wanted to hand him the packet, but his hands were bloody. "I'll just leave them by the cash register."

He thanked her and said he'd take them home to show his wife and children.

On the way down the street to the hardware store, Sheriff Azgo fell in step with her on the snow-covered boardwalk. "I heard you were ill. Anything to do with Mr. Campbell falling sick at the same time?" He matched his pace to hers, which

255

made him look as if he were taking rather dainty steps for a tall man.

"Do you suspect all sick people of being in collusion with each other?"

They walked in silence for the space of three storefronts. When Nell finally glanced at him, he was studying the ground as he walked. "Everyone who's seen my photograph knows the dead man is Three-Fingered Jack Smith. Why didn't you say so?"

The sheriff shrugged. "I thought I'd see who wanted to hide his identity. You wouldn't have known his name anyway."

"Hide his identity . . . Oh, that is what you warned me about. I was in danger because only I knew there was a dead man." They walked along a few more steps. Then Nellie stopped. "You used me for bait." The sheriff stopped too and looked down on her. "What if I had been attacked?"

"You were," he said, his face like stone. "I'm sorry. I should have published his name. The severed arm persuaded me that someone would go to some lengths to hide his identity, particularly if that someone didn't know he was in a photograph. Or, if knowing, the photograph disappeared. Who would believe a young woman, new in town, and crazy enough to go out at night to take pictures in the dark?" His mouth twitched.

"How did he die?"

He studied her and resumed walking and looking down. "He'd been hit on the head. He'd also been underwater, but not drowned."

"How do you know that?"

"There was no water in his lungs. There was faded blood on the sleeve of the cut-off arm and across his chest, but no obvious wound. Dead bodies don't bleed."

"Couldn't the blood have come from the part of the arm that was—" Nellie stopped. The sheriff had already answered that question. "There was no blood on the floor that I could see, nor did I notice any when I moved . . ."

An image of that dead body with an arm cut off lying on a slab in a cold room sickened her. "Did he freeze to death?"

"No."

"You're not going to tell me what you think about how he died, are you?" She paused at the hardware store. "I'm going in here to deliver photos."

"I'll wait." He seemed subdued and distracted.

The store owner studied each photo of his wife and him, then drew cash out of a box and paid her the money still owing. "I do have the negatives," she said, "if you want copies. Perhaps you have family who might be interested?"

"Good idea," the man said. "Let me talk to Harriet and I'll get back to you. These are darned good pictures." Then he lowered his voice. "Harriet is pretty picky about her likeness. I'll have to wait and see if she likes 'em."

Nellie smiled. "All right. But if you like them, I'd appreciate it if you'd send others to me for portraits if you're so inclined."

"I'll just do that. Our commerce group meets tomorrow noon. I'll take mine and show 'em around. You might get some business work too."

Until she almost ran into the sheriff, she'd forgotten he was waiting outside. Nellie felt mildly pleased to walk beside him. Not many handsome men who were also dedicated to their work had graced her life. The sheriff must be older than she first thought, perhaps as much as ten years older than she. His black hair and his high cheekbones might never give away his age, not until the former turned gray and the latter grew wrinkled. Neither happanstance appeared imminent.

"I was wondering," she said, and paused, slipping on the snow and grabbing his arm to steady herself. He waited for her to continue. She realized she could not bring up Lily. His connection to Campbell's daughter was none of her business. His serious expression was tinged with something besides law business, though.

"What were you wondering?" A hint of a smile flickered.

Although Nellie let go his arm, she rather wished she could hold his hand. She wanted to feel his skin against hers and a hand would do, to start.

"Are you all right, Miss Burns? You're red. Maybe your fever has returned." He led her to a bench where the snow had melted off and the wood had dried. "Sit here."

"No, no. I'm all right. I wondered why you did what Rosy requested—took Ah Kee out to the ranch the same day he disappeared." She hadn't known she would say this, but the question continued to prick at her. It seemed to her this information was much more important to know about than any long-lost love relationship.

His face resumed a blank expression, his badge of office. "The details are none of your business, but an emergency situation arose where I thought a doctor was necessary."

"But he wasn't a real doctor. He was just a Chinese herbalist." Saying so made her feel like a traitor. His nostrum had saved her.

"If you want to think that. Fortunately, his skills weren't limited by your opinion." His cold stare left her in no doubt about what he thought of her opinion.

"Certainly, his herbs, or whatever it was, rid me of pneumonia. But maybe it was opium. Isn't that wrong? Or against the law?"

"There are many things against the law these days. I don't try to catch all of them. If I did, the jail would be full and the streets empty. Opium sold as laudanum is not illegal. It's a patent medicine for headaches, bellyaches, toothaches, muscle aches, night aches, day aches."

"I see your point. But where did you leave Ah Kee?"

"I left him at the trail to Last Chance Ranch. Rosy said his friend Jack needed help, but that Ah Kee wouldn't come if Rosy tried to get him. Too much water under that bridge. I suppose you know that since you've stayed with Goldie. Hard to keep secrets in these towns."

Nellie nodded. "Some of it." On the contrary, she thought. Secrets abounded.

"I didn't know Ah Kee disappeared until I found his body under the snow at your direction," he said. "The Chinese are tight-lipped for good reason."

He didn't sound as if he were lying. The two of them began to walk again, but this time back toward Mrs. Bock's. It was almost noon.

"But then, it must have been Rosy who—" She refused to say more. She wouldn't believe that Rosy would kill the man who helped his wife. Anger at fate, rage even, but not murder.

"It isn't Rosy." The sheriff sounded firm. "But I'm not sure who. Or why. If it had been old Campbell lying under the snow, I could have arrested four or five suspects."

"Including you?"

His expression warmed and the smile hovered again. "Including me."

"The Ah Kees thought I did it."

"So did I, for a minute or two."

"Me? But how could I? And why?" She hurried her pace. She wanted to be inside before Sammy drove up to the door, and she wanted the sheriff gone.

"You might have been someone other than who you said. Nobody believed you really could take pictures until you opened that studio. Common thought was you were escaping from something in Chicago. You might be a hardened criminal. Just after you arrived, at least one man was dead, and there you

259

were, right in the same house with him. Then there were two dead men. What's a busybody town to think?"

They laughed together. Then Nellie, wanting to get away, said, "What did you want with me, Sheriff? I have some work to finish in my studio."

"I wanted to know what you thought of Gwynn Campbell. If you thought he could have killed either Ah Kee or Jack." He stood at the door as she made to go in.

"But I thought you considered that possibility remote." Sammy's remark about the sheriff made her wonder if he was trying to throw suspicion on Mr. Campbell. "I don't know about either one. Mr. Campbell thinks you killed Ah Kee. So does Sammy." She stepped over the door jamb into the entry. "I must go now." Slowly but firmly, she closed the door in his surprised face.

Noon came and went. Nellie sat down with Mrs. Bock for a meal and asked her landlady to ring Mrs. Smith to borrow the automobile. This time, she could drive, and this time, she didn't want Henry.

"You ain't going out there alone. Not when you been as sick as you was."

"All right, then, I'll telephone her. You don't want me to go with Sammy. You don't want me to go alone. Aren't you worried about Rosy? I am, and I have a photograph for him." She pulled out one of the envelopes from her photo case. "And here are yours. They turned out very well. See if you like them." She held up a second packet. "But first please ask Mrs. Smith. Or give me the keys. We know she'll lend her auto to Henry, so if I just go, she'll be none the wiser. I'll be back before she gets home from the mine office." Nellie left the table to load her camera and sled and tripod. As long as she was returning to the cabin, she would try for another photograph for her snow collection.

She considered trying to get another night photo or at least a deeply shadowed one around dusk and still get back before too late. She was glad to don long pants again. She added an extra blanket and extra socks. Her hand touched the belt. She had forgotten again to tell the sheriff about it, but everyone knew who the dead man was, so it didn't matter anymore. And she wanted to keep it a little longer. She found one last sachet in her camera pack and stuffed it in her pocket. For luck, maybe.

Back in the kitchen, Mrs. Bock studied the photos and looked up as Nellie re-entered the room. "I look old in these here pictures."

"A camera reflects what's in front of it." The words sounded cruel, but Nellie had heard Mrs. Bock's complaint a thousand times before. "What it does show is a woman who has worked hard for a living taking care of other people, cooking meals, keeping a house, listening to sad stories, and sharing in some happy ones. In these pictures, you look as if you've lived, not vegetated."

"Humph. That's what a young girl would say to an old woman, a girl without wrinkles." She slapped the photos down. "I can't send these to family in Indiana. They'll think I'm as ancient as Methuselah."

"Do you suppose they quit aging when you left?" Nellie scooped the pictures up. "If you don't like them, you don't have to pay for them."

"Could we try again? I'd fix my hair better, put on some of that rouge stuff and lipstick. Wear a better dress."

Her desire to please family who hadn't seen her for years touched Nellie. She put her arm around Mrs. Bock's shoulders. "We can try again if you'd like. No charge. And maybe you would help take a photograph of me that I could send to my mother. I think it might be the number of years bothering you rather than the photo. Could that be true?"

The landlady mulled the suggestion, then held her hand out

for another look. "Maybe that's the trouble. Just too many years." She rubbed the lines in her cheeks.

"Let me photograph you in the kitchen baking a pie. You won't look old doing something you love so much. I promise. And you could send the flyer about our joint business here in the boarding house. They'll be impressed."

Mrs. Bock went to a kitchen drawer. "Keys aren't here. They're in her room then. I'll get them." The telephone *brrrr*ed and she went to answer it. Nellie mouthed that she would get the keys. Upstairs, she let herself into Room Six. The keys lay on the dresser. Nothing seemed changed until she turned around. The skis were gone.

Downstairs, Mrs. Bock gave instructions. "You be back before dark. I don't want to have to send for a doctor to pull you from the brink. They'd soon poison you as look at you."

This time, Nellie had a plan. The snowfield in front of Last Chance Ranch had lain smooth and flat both times she traversed it. If people were going in and out of the cabin at the rate she was beginning to figure, they must have used a trail off to one side or the other. She'd seen one person to the north who had not appeared to be wearing snowshoes.

After a false start or two with the auto jerking like a bucking bronco, Nellie finally settled the machine into a smooth forward movement. This dance with her feet on different pedals would take getting used to, and yet she already loved how fast she traveled over the snow-packed road. The steering wheel gave her a feeling of power. The farther north she traveled, the less obvious the berms on either side of the road, the more rutted the track. Along the river, near where it curled close to the road, she saw a bull elk with a huge rack nibbling on bushes.

As Nellie neared the ranch, she slowed, searching for tracks in the snow. There was no trough or dip that Rosy might have followed. He must have taken a side cut through the woods to show up where he did. Perhaps there had been too much snow since then.

Nothing moved in the snowfield. No ermine. No elk. No magpies flitted from tree to bush and back again. When she went too slowly, the auto jerked to a stop and she had to re-start it to get going again. After the second time, she figured she must push in the clutch if she slowed down. Rather than stopping where she had previously begun her trek across the field, she continued north a short way and around a bend. Rosy's vehicle was parked beside the road, its right front wheel buried up to the fender. Nellie drove up behind it, turned off the motor, and climbed out. Frost etched the windows. Snow was frozen hard around the right wheel.

"Rosy," she called. A faint echo called back. Wind ruffled her hair and the branches of the cottonwood trees rattled like bones. In the distance, she heard the rush of water, but otherwise, there was a hush, as if she'd walked into a room and everyone had quit talking.

Near the stuck auto, footprints led toward the river, so she followed them directly to a half-trampled path branching to the south into trees. Whoever last walked on it did not wear snowshoes, nor were they needed. It was as if half a dozen people had already forged a trail. A hard edge crusted the old snow. She stepped up to test it and didn't break through.

"Rosy!" *Rosy, Rosy, Rosy,* dwindled into nothing.

CHAPTER 24

Rosy tramped beside the Big Wood River. He ruminated on what his life had come down to: a derelict taxi driver comforted only by his jars of moonshine, sought out by dope addicts and misfits, spurned by gentle folk and roughnecks alike. Not that he cared, he told himself. He stepped around the jumbled snow. He didn't want to tread on blood. Unwanted, the images returned: Ah Kee, bleeding in the snow. His skin, stiff as parchment, not yet cold as the air. Ooze from the back of his head turning into thick muck. Dry blossoms and stems had littered the area. Crouched against a frozen white tree trunk was Jack, shivering and trembling. In three giant steps, Rosy had reached and grasped the pile of bones and slobber, jerking it up and over his head. He wanted to shake the man until his brain rattled and died. Instead, Rosy heaved, throwing the man into the river.

That pale image, like Lily's face, had shimmered on an ice floe. *Don't do this.* It faded into the silver and gray water.

Rosy once again saw himself sliding down the cut bank, splashing into the river, ignoring the soul-crushing cold, wading up to his knees to the slowly sinking mess of wet clothes. He had pulled Jack to shore, leaking water and snot, and dragged him to the ranch. Rosy wished then and wished now that he'd left the killer in the water. Instead, Rosy left him in the cabin with the dog, who napped in front of the fire. "Aagh, help me," Jack said, weeping and spitting. Rosy left him there and went to bury Ah Kee.

When the dog stopped to nose around, Rosy shook the nightmare out of his head. He called and clicked his tongue. At Last Chance Ranch, Rosy took the key from his pocket and unlocked the back door. Inside, he re-locked it. No more ghosts would come through that door. And again, he saw Jack on the floor, dead beside an overturned table. The eyes stared. Rosy had taken care of that with snow from the porch.

Which reminded him. The back door needed oiling. He puttered around, fixing it. No Jack. His place was silent, clean, empty.

His delaying tactics only worked for a while. Then he steeled himself to do what he had come out to do. Walking up the stairs to the second story brought too many memories to mind, but especially the sounds of small boys playing. They were growing up and he would never see them again. *Why not?* He had failed Lily and the boys. He was a useless drunk. It was time, he thought. He knew where the rest of the opium was, the stuff that Jack hadn't found.

The robe, carefully folded with the dragon's tongue on top, fit in the drawer, where it looked like a jewel in a box. He grabbed a dozen pouches hidden behind a board under the chest, emptied the buttons of dope into his hand, and sat back on the rug. A mistake. He recognized pieces of material from a boy's shorts, a man's shirt, a skirt that swayed.

Lily had lain in bed, her head turned toward the field, its fragrance lofting high and into the room. Her eyes, glazed like water, turned to their youngest son. The opium kept her alive in a world unrelated to anything else, but also one without pain.

"Picanick," the boy said. He jumped up and down but did not touch the bed. He was learning. He dropped to his knees and ran a Tin Lizzie around the rag circles, catching a wheel in a white loop, satin.

"Tomorrow," she said. Only her voice sounded the same.

"Not tomorrow," Rosy said. "It's going to rain." He wanted the rain. He wanted buckets and torrents and downpours and cats and dogs of rain.

On the floor, the boy jerked the wheel from the loop and turned to Rosy. "Hate you." There was no anger in the words. They were plain, ordinary words, with no more inflection than words on a blackboard. But as his small fist rose and flung the toy at his father's face, the son's eyes were chips of blue ice, as full of loathing as his mother's were empty. The scrap of metal hit the door frame and broke into three pieces—two sets of wheels and the body. Each made its own particular sound as it landed on the floor.

Time.

Rosy dissolved buttons in the last of his whiskey. He always kept a jar back. In case he needed it. He hummed and fixed dishes of food and water for the dog. Someone would come. Maybe even that girl, the one he was supposed to protect. From what, he couldn't remember. Maybe she'd go back to the East, run into his boys there in Chicago. Funny about life's co-incidences.

He made up little stories in his mind, about her taking photographs of his boys, not knowing who they were. About his boys showing her the photo she took of Rosy. He watched the opium dissolve. He drank and hummed a little. The taste was acrid, like drinking dirt.

When he could hardly function, he let himself out the front door and stumbled back along the path. No dog where he was going. He remembered the dead Ah Kee and cried. Soon, his legs gave out and he crawled, across the snow bridge, along the trail. He pulled himself to the aspen grove and leaned against a tree. There he would see Lily again. He was so tired. And Ah Kee. No, he was gone.

Snow fell and he slumped over. He shivered and forced himself to sit up straight against the tree. He wouldn't die like that misbegotten fool, Jack. Instead, he dreamed warm days at the ranch, riding home from the mines in the Stanley Basin, hearing bees in the field. Two boys running out and jumping into his arms when he climbed off the freight wagon. Waving to the figure in the doorway, slender and lovely. And his.

Now the story would be all true: A family lived at Last Chance Ranch—wife, husband, and two boys. Wife died, boys went back East, man drank himself to death.

CHAPTER 25

Pulling her sled with the camera and tripod was easier on a trampled pathway without snowshoes, but she brought them, just in case. Little by little, the landscape came alive again: a bird song, a chickadee fluttering through the branches of an aspen, a flicker of movement near the river in a bush. Nellie looked around to see what she could see—a scene to photograph, an animal to watch. It was then she saw paw prints in windblown snow alongside the trail, prancing in and out, off to a bush, back to the path, sometimes deepening into thrashes and other times right on top.

"Moonie!" Her voice carried up against the hill again and back. She stopped and listened. "Moonshine!"

The trail aimed first for the river, then pointed south toward the Last Chance Ranch. Halfway to the cabin, she reached a section with dips and piles and spaces where the snow level was much lower than surrounding areas. Dog tracks circled each mound, but returned to one more than the others. Several patches of yellow snow reflected his mark. Nellie stopped and poked with her walking stick. Nothing there.

Then she heard a sound so eerie in its repetition that gooseflesh crawled up her back. *Tap, tap, tap.* She swung toward the cabin and this time could see Moonie scratching at the window. To rescue him as fast as possible, she untied the sled from around her waist and hurried along the path. It led to the back door. Inside, Moonie yipped and dashed from the door to the window. "Hang on, Moonie." She pushed and it opened easily. Moonie leaped up and licked her face.

"Moonshine! I'm so happy to see you." She knelt with him half in her arms and hugged and patted his bristly short hair. "What are you doing here?"

Two dishes held food and water, so he was cared for. She let him out the front door and he leaped off the porch to squat in the snow. "Oh, poor dog." He left a small pile, then sniffed around and marked a corner of the cabin. He came back, wagging his tail. He seemed as happy as she felt. "Where's Rosy?"

Moonie ran inside and to the stairway, taking two steps up, then waited for her. "Is he upstairs?" She had heard nothing, but remembered the cigarette butts. Was someone watching again? "Pooh." She was scaring herself. She had the dog to protect her, so she climbed the stairs and entered the room with the double bed. It was still abandoned, still empty. Even the butts were gone. Her footsteps to the bunkroom sounded hollow, but there too, nothing had changed, not even the melancholy. As bright as it was outdoors, these two rooms felt dank and gloomy. She opened the dresser drawer. And there was the robe, where it belonged. The empty leather pouches still half-filled each drawer, seeming more numerous than the first time she looked. A hint of lavender remained, but that was all. No more sachets. She touched the one in her pocket. That, at least, she would keep.

While she looked around, Moonie rolled on top of the braided rag rug, back and forth, making his strange arping sound. "Let's go. There's nothing more up here." The rug drew her attention. It was composed of many different materials and colors—pink crepe from a dress, dark silk with a pattern like a man's tie, flannel from pajamas or a shirt, white satin, red corduroy that reminded her of a child's playsuit. It was someone's life pieced together for comfort and memory, and gave her an idea of what

---

might be done with photography. The rug lumped on one end. When she stooped to straighten it, she found a sock under it, one like she carried in her pack. Moonie yipped and she tucked the sock in her pocket and tromped down the stairs.

"Where did Rosy go?" The dog tilted his head sideways, then straight, as if he understood and would answer if only he could. "Did he leave this morning? Is he hunting?"

Moonie dashed off toward the south, floundering from time to time. He nosed around the trees where Nellie had stood to photograph the elk. The dog barked, picked something out of the snow, and headed her way. A magpie flew over him and he dropped what he was carrying to give chase. "Moonie, come here!" He chased in circles, apparently delighted to be out of doors.

Nellie sat on her sled, waiting, then retrieved the belt she had hidden in the pack. In the daylight, the instrument on the buckle was clearly a trumpet. The band was the Kellogg Brass Band and the year 1908 rather than 1918. On the back side, the I.K. or I.H. became I.B. "To J.B. with love forever from I.B." Nellie licked spit on her thumb and rubbed the initials. This time she read G.B. To Jack Bradley from Gladys Bradley. Fourteen or so years ago, a sister gave a memento to a brother. That brother was Three-Fingered Jack, now dead.

Moonshine jumped on Nellie. When she patted him, he nuzzled her, then dashed toward the river. He barked again. Perhaps the miner was hunting and didn't take the dog for fear he'd scare away an elk or a deer.

"Not that snow bridge again. Let's find a better place to cross." While Nellie had been studying the belt, a high white haze had crept across the northern sky, diminishing the usual dazzling reflection of sun on snow to a dull matte, but the day still carried a winter brightness.

The dog finally gave up on his more direct route and joined

her. The trampled snow near her sled, for that's what it was underneath at least one layer of new snow, was more apparent because of afternoon shadows. It reminded her of how she had thrashed around at night, taking photos. Someone, or several someones, must have trod back and forth on this spot.

When the dog began pawing at a mound, she helped him. Her scoops were more effective than his scratching and she uncovered small stems and old buds or blossoms. The snow was tinged with pink, and in some places, a brownish red. Working much more carefully, she pushed snow aside to see how large an area the color covered, and, in one corner, how deep it was. Neither effort was successful. She was certain it was blood. This was something Sheriff Azgo should see. She marked it with a small snowman patted together, then decided she was hungry. She had taken a sandwich from Mrs. Bock along with a canteen of water in a canvas sling. Before embarking on a trek with Moonie, she decided to eat and drink a little and share with the dog.

At the sled, she noticed something flung off to one side and wondered if she had done it while digging. Only a corner showed, but when she pulled it out of the snow, she discovered it was a square of silk. "I know what this is," she said to Moonie. "It's a sachet bag. Here, smell." He sniffed and arped. "Those crumbled things were old lavender. What is this doing out here?" The dog was getting impatient. He ran off toward the river and barked.

"Opium. I'll bet that's what was in here. And this could be where Ah Kee was killed. That blood must have been his. Moonie, I should go get the sheriff right now." Instead, she planted the silk piece half in and half out of the snow next to her snowman, and then called to the dog. "Wait! I'm coming."

She left behind her snowshoes and took only the bag with part of the sandwich, the canteen, her newly purchased flashlight, and her walking sticks. The sling went easily around her neck and shoulder so the canteen hung at her side. By stepping lightly, she could stay on top of the snow and move faster. There wasn't all that much left of the afternoon, but enough.

A pathway, not as well marked, led toward the river. The going was easier on it than around the house, but Nellie still sank in from time to time, once up to her knee. They came to what looked like another bridge—a high heap of snow blocks—with tracks across. She knelt down and saw wide lines in the snow, as if someone crawled to the other side.

"What do you think? Is it safe?" Talking to Moonshine relieved her sense that she was so alone. He jumped on the blocks and sniffed his way across the snowy bridge, not breaking through. She took one step and then another, testing as she went. Even her stick wouldn't penetrate the icy top layer. On the other side of the Big Wood, the less defined trail continued. The cottonwoods were beginning to rattle again and the wind loosened the snow into miniature whirling dervishes.

The dog ran around, slipping here, sinking there, and barking. Their progress was uneven and the day was sliding toward dusk faster than Nellie had anticipated, especially with the sun obscured by a thicker haze. Where could Rosy be? She wasn't cold, but she also wasn't prepared to spend a lot of time outside at night and debated whether she should return to the cabin if not to the auto. The possible ire of Gladys Smith didn't concern her. Rosy was more important.

Nellie tried on the facts she did know. The sheriff had brought Ah Kee out to Last Chance Ranch because Rosy needed help with Three-Fingered Jack. Because there were no dips and tracks at the front of the ranch where she herself had hiked the first night she came out to photograph, she believed Ah Kee approached from the north. Had the sheriff been with him?

The two dead men were such disparate characters. What

linked their deaths? The doctor was well-known to those she had mentioned his name to, and with few exceptions, was admired as a person with medical knowledge. The patients she knew about were Lily and Mrs. Smith and now, obliquely, herself. As Nellie plodded along, trying to follow the track in the increasing gloom, she wondered what about him had led to his death.

Jack Smith. He was Gladys's brother, a former miner, someone who drank and took opium, who played a trumpet in a band, who was injured in an avalanche. Nellie had not seen Gladys grieve, but then she didn't know when Gladys found out about his death. There were miners in town who could have visited Last Chance Ranch, maybe to collect on a debt, maybe to find cocaine. Everyone in town apparently knew each other's business. It didn't have to be someone she knew.

The only link she knew of between Jack and Ah Kee was opium.

The snow where her sled waited had been roiled and there was surely blood there, along with a broken sachet bag. Someone had been hurt, if not killed, on that spot. The sheriff and Rosy both appeared uninjured, so it probably was either Three-Fingered Jack or Ah Kee. Because Jack eventually ended up at the ranch, she could guess it was Ah Kee. Jack might have attacked Ah Kee. With the dog sock? The sheriff said it had hair on it, and Ah Kee was bald, or maybe his head had been shaved as she first supposed. The axe made a better, sharper weapon.

If Ah Kee and Jack had a fight over opium, Ah Kee ended up dead. But so did Jack. Ah Kee was buried. Jack wasn't. He disappeared. If she hadn't stumbled on to his body, maybe no one would ever have discovered he was dead. She couldn't shrug off the idea that Rosy killed Jack, then took him away, cut off his arm and stole the belt so he wouldn't be identified.

And the arm. Was the arm in the box Rosy took to Gladys?

She could have stuffed the box into one of those ore cars and no one would ever see it again by the time the ore went through the mill. Her suspicions were much too gothic.

If not Rosy, then who? The sheriff? The sheriff had brought her out here alone. He could have murdered her. No, the whole town knew she was with him. Her feet crunched the snow. The path had taken her close to the grove of trees where she had stumbled upon the snow mound containing Ah Kee. Not too far distant and across the river was the ranch. She sipped some of her water. This grove of aspen from the perspective she now saw it assumed shape and form, as if someone had planted the trees in a double circle with an empty center. On her last trip, she had not seen what was clearly a rounded mound in the middle.

Light played tricks on her—there was a mound and then there wasn't—until she saw that snow had begun to fall, the small hard pellets closer to frozen rain than to lacy flakes. As she drew nearer to the grove, something dark moved away from the center. Quills of fear raced through her. Moonie growled deep in his throat. Then he leaped forward. When he reached the far side of the mound, he stopped and nosed at the snow. Nellie followed him, but away from the trees, the snow was thicker and she found herself wading.

"What is it?" The dark shadow had been low to the ground.

A bundle lay curled up in the snow. A deeper trench showed it had been dragged a few feet. It was Rosy. No face or skin showed, and coat and pants looked like a heap of cast-offs, but she recognized the greasy sheepskin coat, the intricate tooling of the boots. Moonshine whined and nosed at him. She shook the bundle and tried to unwrap the arms from around the legs. "Rosy, wake up." This was not a dead body. It wasn't stiff. The arms dropped. She took off a glove and found his face, placing her hand on his neck. It was warm and his beard scratchy. His eyes were closed, but even as she touched him, a moan broke from his lips.

He mumbled and Nellie put her ear close to his mouth. "Say it again. Wake up."

"Llllull." He pushed his face against her skin, like a dog nuzzling for pets.

Another low growl pulled her attention from Rosy. This time, Moonie's hackles rose straight up and he bared his teeth, facing in the direction the dark shadow had run. Nellie peered through the snow. Two dark shapes stood not five yards away.

Coyotes. They had dragged Rosy, trying to get through the clothes to the man. She couldn't leave to find help. What was wrong with him? She rubbed his arms and legs and hoped Moonie would stave off an attack. "Wake up. We have to get away from here."

"Lllle . . . lone." His voice was coming back.

Maybe light would scare them off. She dug in her bag, dragged out the flashlight, sent its beam toward the moving shapes. The two animals stopped pacing and stared back at her through the falling snow. They were scrawny with ragged coats and moth-eaten tails. Their eyes reflected orange and their teeth gleamed like fangs in a nightmare on either side of dripping tongues. One took a hesitant step forward. Moonshine growled, barked, and jumped toward them, his black coat shining in her light.

Rosy struggled, knocking the flashlight out of Nellie's hand. It landed in a hole where it illuminated only snow. Snarling and snapping told her where the dog and the coyotes were. She tried to wrap one arm around Rosy, press him to sit up, and at the same time protect her head and his in case the wild animals attacked. She thrust her feet toward the thrashing, thinking she could fend off at least one by kicking, but knew the light would make a better weapon. Rosy struggled to escape and she grabbed him. They rolled over and buried the flashlight. The twilight seemed like midnight until her eyes adjusted.

The semi-conscious man lay heavy on top of Nellie. She squirmed out from under him, still aware of the struggle between the dog and two coyotes, filled with growls, yips, gnashing of teeth. "Rosy, wake up!" With a strong push, she managed to flop him to one side and she wriggled onto her knees to dig out the flashlight. She directed the beam to the trees. The sudden light was enough to scare one of the coyotes back a few steps and out of focus, but Moonshine still writhed and twisted in the snow with the other.

"Stop it!" Nell grabbed a walking stick and threw it toward the animals. She missed. The coyote's teeth slashed at Moonie's neck, his short hair no protection. Something, anything. She aimed carefully and threw the flashlight. It hit the top animal, the coyote, and dropped onto the snow. The coyote jumped sideways off the dog and then he, too, scrambled back. Nell stood and waved her arms. "Get away!" Both coyotes turned and ran. Moonie made to follow.

"Stay." Rosy's deep voice, although weak, was strong enough to hold the dog in place, to face him back toward his master. "Come." With a glance after the coyotes, Moonie stepped forward, stopped, glanced back, stepped again, his breathing heavy and rasping, then walked over and sat down by Rosy. The dog licked his front paw and then tried to lick his hip. Nellie could not see whether he'd been wounded. She rubbed her hands around his neck. Extra folds of skin had protected him, although he flinched. She turned to the man.

"Oh, Rosy. You're all right." But he wasn't all right. He sagged back onto the snow, breathing with difficulty, and then he vomited. "Roll over! You'll choke to death!" She grabbed him, shouting, trying to get his mouth turned toward the snow. His body heaved again and again but after the first dribble of evil-smelling glop, nothing more came up. Exhaustion or unconsciousness claimed him and he lay still, his breathing a repeated wheeze and groan.

Nellie clambered over to where the flashlight still lit the fighting ground, picked it up, and staggered to her feet. If she left Rosy alone to retrieve the sled, the coyotes might come back. She and Moonie would have to drag him across the river and into the cabin.

Unconscious, he was easier to move. She turned him onto his back, removed first one arm and then the second from the sleeves of the coat, and buttoned the coat back over him, his arms to his sides. The sleeves would give her a handle for pulling him. Her belt was too small to wrap around Rosy to hold the coat in place. She unslung her canteen and jerked and shoved and managed to get the sling around him just above his waist and around the arms under the coat. She looped the strap on one of the bone buttons to hold it in place. Good thing he was thin.

Her makeshift travois was awkward. She stood up, face forward, and held the sleeves on either side of her and tried to walk. Her heels hit his head. "Help me, Moonie." She tried crawling backwards, pulling at the sleeves. The dog got the idea. He grabbed a sleeve near Rosy's head and inched backwards on his haunches. At first the body stuck, but with a jerk by Nellie, the coat began to slide across the icy surface. What they'd do at the old caved-in snow bridge, she had no idea. Get there first, she thought. The flashlight, under her arm against her side, teetered and bounced, reflecting snow falling, but also lighting their way.

At the bridge, Nellie missed her sticks. "Stay," she ordered the dog. She returned to the mound, found only one stick, and hurried back to the river, where she tested the snow on the bridge. The cold weather for the last few days had served one good purpose—freezing over the spot where she had fallen in. By shoving and then pulling, she managed to get Rosy across and almost to the house. She trembled from the exertion, her sweat beginning to freeze. Rosy hardly seemed alive. She leaned close again to check his breathing, but she couldn't tell if he breathed or not. "You stupid drunk!" They would not freeze ten steps from safety. She crawled up the step to the back door.

"He's more than a drunk." A voice growled from the doorway. "He's a murderer. He killed my brother."

CHAPTER 26

Nellie looked up, disbelieving, and faced Gladys Smith and the muzzle of a gun. She almost fell hurrying to Rosy, where she shielded him. Where was Moonshine? He'd been right with her. Then she saw the dog had entered the open doorway, where lamplight lit a path as gloomy dusk turned to night.

"What are you talking about? This is Rosy." The black hole of the barrel loomed large.

"You stupid girl. You mixed in where you don't belong. Acting like life is . . . is a . . . a song. What do you know about people like Rosy or my brother or me? You've been protected all your life." Mrs. Smith's mouth clamped shut and she stepped down from the porch carefully, still aiming her gun at Nellie and Rosy. "Now move. He must pay for what he did."

"What did he do?" Nellie was frozen by the gun. She'd seen it in the bureau, but it hadn't seemed real then. She backed up so her leg was resting against Rosy. He shivered either from the cold or his drug-induced sickness. "He's sick and needs help."

This Gladys Smith was different from the flirting woman in the boarding house and then the businesslike clerk in the mine office. Her face in the ambient light had melted into that of a haggard old woman, as if she had removed a mask, if not of youth, at least of middle age.

"He needs what he gave Jack—death." She took a step to the side, giving Nellie a breath of relief. From the expression on the woman's face, she just might shoot through Nellie.

"Wait! How can you know it was Rosy? Maybe it was—" she hesitated, searching for any name that might distract the woman, "—Sheriff Azgo. He brought the doctor out here. Maybe he killed Ah Kee and Jack, who saw it."

Moonshine came back out through the cabin door and stood, watching Mrs. Smith and Nellie. Mrs. Smith's mouth opened in a dreadful grimace. "I know it was Rosy. He told me so. Get away." Her last two words were spoken in such an intense tone that Nellie almost obeyed.

"But your brother was sick, you said. Maybe he froze here. He was frozen when I found him. There wasn't any blood." How could the sheriff be sure Jack hadn't drowned?

"My brother was addicted to opium. On account of that . . ." She motioned with the gun toward Rosy. A sob broke from Mrs. Smith. "He didn't play his trumpet. He couldn't work. He left me alone." So much pain and longing filled the word "alone." Moonie heard it, too, because he took a step forward.

Mrs. Smith dodged quickly to the side and pointed the gun at Rosy. Moonie, with a sound Nellie would ever after think of as a roar, leaped from the stairs onto Mrs. Smith. In the midst of the shattering explosion, Nellie, too, jumped toward her. The smell of gunpowder choked her. Their force knocked the woman to the ground with Nellie on top, but the gun was still clutched in the woman's hand. "Let me go!" She tried to roll away. "I'll shoot you, too. I hate you!"

Nellie could feel Gladys's strength under her, but held on. She shoved Moonie aside, pulled her leg up so she could press down on the woman's middle with a knee, and then stretched her arm out to grab the gun. As she did so, it exploded once again, reverberating with sound and smell. The shock forced Nellie sideways and she lost her balance, falling backwards. The gun dropped into the snow. Moonshine grabbed at it.

"Stay, Moonshadow."

Rosy's voice was so startling, Mrs. Smith and Nellie stopped wrestling in the snow. He was half-sitting where Nellie had dragged him. Moonshine moved over to him and butted him with his head, trying to push his master to his feet.

A tall figure blotted out some of the light in the doorway. "Who shoot gun?" A beam from a flashlight pinned them in a bizarre scene.

"Sammy! She tried to kill Rosy. Get the gun. It's over—" She pointed to where she thought it was, but night had covered all of them and the falling snow was like a curtain in the light. "Help me. Rosy might be wounded."

There was no motion behind the light for a moment, and then Sammy scurried over to the two women, who floundered, Nellie trying to stand, Mrs. Smith crawling to where Nellie had pointed. He beat her to it, but the dark thing in the snow was the axe. He threw it down and Nellie grabbed it, wanting any weapon she could find. "There it is," she said. Sammy leaped toward where she pointed, found the gun, and shoved it into his waistband. "No shoot. Want Rosy a-live." Mrs. Smith grabbed at his legs, but he loosely kicked her away.

Moonie growled at Sammy when he squatted near Rosy, but Nellie stumbled over to the dog. She dropped the axe on the step and ran her hands up and down his neck and body. He smelled of the gun blast, but seemed unhurt. "I was so afraid she shot you!"

Together, Sammy and Nellie brought Rosy into the cabin and placed him on the one good bed. The kerosene lamp lit the room, as did a fire in the fireplace. The lamp's light jumped and weaved without a chimney. She removed the canteen sling, unbuttoned his coat. "What are you doing here?" she asked Sammy, motioning for him to pull off the boots. Rosy's color was so pale, he looked dead, but he wasn't bleeding anywhere. With the bedclothes pulled up over his feet and legs and his coat wrapped around his upper body, he'd be warm. His face was slack, the scar near his bad eye white and puckered like a worm stuffed under his skin. His hair was more gray than brown and stringy with grease. He looked old as dirt.

"Give me back my gun," Mrs. Smith demanded as she entered the cabin. "I'll kill him." Her threat no longer frightened Nell. Gladys sat down in a chair and lowered her head.

Sammy pulled another chair over by the bed and guarded Rosy. He fingered the gun as if it were a familiar tool. His watchfulness disturbed Nellie as much as Mrs. Smith's keening pain. Why did Sammy want Rosy "a-live"? And for how long?

Moonie nosed under the counter for food, shoving cans and jars aside. He pushed his water dish across the floor, then lay down with his nose near it. He crawled forward on his haunches and swatted his paw under the cupboard. His actions reminded Nellie of the axe, which she retrieved from the step and placed on the wood by the stove.

Mrs. Smith's crying shook Nellie. She crossed to the table and knelt down. "I'm sorry about your brother," she began.

"No, you're not," Mrs. Smith said, lifting her face. The kewpie doll was cracked and all traces of color drained. "You took his picture when he was dead. You're like a ghoul, watching other people suffer." Although she had sounded as if she were crying, there were no tears on her cheeks. "You searched my room. What did you want?"

Nellie stood. Moonshine scraped something metal around on the floor and then brought his prize to her. She thought it was another broken toy, but it was not. All the information she'd learned in the past few weeks coalesced. The dog toy. The dark spot on the cigarette. The skis. The extra sock. Nellie, the answer in her hand, stared at Mrs. Smith, remembering her with her feet in a pan of water.

"I wanted to find the murderer of the man here in the cabin.

You were here, weren't you? You parked back on the road and skied to the cabin the day the sheriff brought Ah Kee to help your brother. You smoked cigarettes upstairs and waited for someone to kill Ah Kee."

"What do you mean, you twit?" Gladys's face contorted.

"You heard Rosy calling the sheriff to pick up Ah Kee. Then you called Gwynn Campbell to tell him Ah Kee was going to the cabin, hoping Gwynn would kill him, as he had always threatened."

Sammy started up from his guard post.

"Stay there, Sammy. There's more."

"It's none of your business that I came out here," Mrs. Smith said. "I wanted to nurse Jack. I found opium upstairs, hidden in the lavender bags. I dumped it in the well when Rosy and Jack were out. And then I left.

"Now Rosy won't even talk to me anymore. He follows you around like . . . like . . ." The hatred on her face was so physical, it knocked Nellie back on her heels. "I took his lavender. I came back later for the robe, but it was gone. You stole it!" She wailed a long, quivering cry.

"Jack killed your father, Sammy. The sheriff said he had faded blood all over his sleeve. I think Rosy came on the murder, after leaving Mrs. Smith here in the cabin. He banged Jack on the head, maybe, or tried to drown him. Rosy would do anything to protect Ah Kee, but he was too late. Then he brought Jack back here to Gladys so she could revive him. Rosy went back to bury Ah Kee in the most sacred place he knew—next to Lily."

Sammy and Mrs. Smith listened, as frozen as two cats in front of a mouse hole. Nellie edged toward the stove.

"You did revive Jack. Then you, Gladys Bradley, his sister, attacked him. You'd prepared yourself—tucked a rock in one of your ski socks. Maybe he attacked you, but you were ready. A horrendous fight overturned the table, broke the lantern chimney, knocked off these glasses." She held up the dog's discovery: a pair of ski goggles with dark glass in the eyeholes. Like a broken windshield, one purple lens was starred. "Sunglasses for bright snow. Skiers use them." Mrs. Smith raised her hand as if to grab, then tucked it back in her lap.

"You killed him. You swung that rock in the sock and bashed him on the head. Then you probably stuck him with one of your vicious hatpins. There were a few stains, but not many. I thought they were oil, not blood. *Then* you left and, without socks, blistered your foot." Nellie pulled the sock from her pocket and dangled it. Mrs. Smith looked ready to pounce. At the stove, Nellie grabbed the axe and felt safer. "Rosy came back, found a dead Jack, thought he'd been responsible, covered Jack's face with ice, maybe to avoid seeing the eyes, drank himself silly, and left. I'd guess he put the axe in Jack's hand. He told you he killed Jack but you knew that wasn't true. Maybe he said that Jack killed Ah Kee. You told him to cut off the arm, take the belt, hide the body. No one need ever know."

"You're crazy." Mrs. Smith glanced at Sammy and wiggled her chair back. "She's crazy, isn't she, Sammy? I wouldn't kill my own brother. And I certainly didn't want Ah Kee to die. He helped me. You know that."

Sammy remained silent, his face impassive. Nellie began to doubt herself. Was her theory built on pieces of a puzzle that didn't fit together? It was true she didn't know why Mrs. Smith would kill her brother, but Gladys herself admitted she had come to Last Chance Ranch. There had been a fight. Maybe Rosy did all the damage, as Mrs. Smith claimed. And yet . . .

"You went to Ah Kee for help, Mrs. Smith. Did he help you because you were pregnant and didn't want a baby? Maybe your brother thought you were a loose woman."

"Shut up!" The woman leaped at Nellie, her hands clawing toward Nellie's throat. Nellie raised her axe. Mrs. Smith shied, stumbled, and fell. This time, her sobs were real.

"It was my brother," she said. "*He* made me pregnant. I thought once or twice together wouldn't hurt anyone—we were so alone here. I loved him so much. But then he wanted it—me—again and again. Said he needed me. And I . . ." She sat up and stretched her legs out.

The meaning of her words stunned Nellie. Then she remembered Mrs. Bock's statements about how Gladys hated Jack—that he abused her—as well as Gwynn Campbell's lowdown opinion. A man like they described could do anything.

Mrs. Smith's voice dropped to a whisper. "I did go to Ah Kee. He ended that problem." She looked up at Sammy. "And he helped with Jack's . . . passion. Said if I fed him small doses of opium, he wouldn't bother me again. That's what they did with Chinese railroad workers."

Sammy nodded and looked at the gun in his hand.

"It worked. But Jack found out what I was doing. Said he'd kill Ah Kee. Then he said he'd kill me." A sly smile hovered on her lips. "So much for that." She stood up clumsily.

"But why would you want Ah Kee dead?" Nellie asked reluctantly. The story was already terrible.

"The inscrutable Celestial told my secret." Mrs. Smith spat the words. She lunged at Sammy this time, but he merely sidestepped her and she dropped to her hands and knees. She might have been a religious supplicant, groveling. "And he made my brother an opium-eater. Doomed him."

You did that, Nellie thought. What a tangled web. Quiet descended, disturbed only by Rosy's harsh breathing. Mrs. Smith on the floor, Nell with her axe in front of her, Sammy with his hand on the gun. Moonshine waiting.

What to do now? She couldn't hogtie Gladys Smith, nor grab the gun from Sammy. "We're stuck here until the storm abates," she said. She laid the axe close by, lit a match and started a fire in the stove, lifted the pump handle, and then remembered the pump was contaminated. From under the sink, she drew out a deep pan with her left hand, picked up the axe in her right, and headed for the door. "We need snow for water."

Gladys creaked to her feet. "I'll get it." Nellie decided it was safe to let her out. The storm still raged.

"How did you get here, Sammy? I waited for you as long as I could." The gun still worried her.

"I work. Then come. She say you steal auto. Pay me . . . drive. I wait." He shrugged. "She not come back, so I follow."

"Where is your mother?" Heat was beginning to radiate from the stove and Nellie sat down to wait for the snow. It was taking Mrs. Smith a long time to get a panful.

"At house." Sammy continued to watch Rosy, who lay still. Even his stertorous breathing had stopped, but he still wheezed.

"Did your father tell Mrs. Smith's secret?" Nellie asked.

"No," Sammy said. "Honored mother. She jealous of Mrs. Smith—told innkeeper."

"Oh dear." Mrs. Ah Kee may have realized her indiscretion cost her husband his life.

Where was that woman? Nellie went to the back door. Soft light from the windows lit squares in the snow, but Mrs. Smith was nowhere in sight. Damn!

"Sammy." The Chinese man was leaning close over Rosy, his ear to the prone man's mouth. "Oh no! Is he gone?"

"Shhh!" He listened, motionless. Then shook his head. "He breathes." He sat down again and took the gun from his waist and placed it on the bed.

"You have to find Mrs. Smith. I shouldn't have let her out. Now she's gone, and there are coyotes out there. We can't let her escape. I can't go. I'm too tired."

Still, Sammy sat on the chair.

"You must go."

He narrowed his eyes, pressed his lips together, and continued his vigil.

"Your mother would agree with me. You can't let this woman go. Maybe she didn't kill your father, but she surely killed her brother. Rosy got caught in the middle. I'm sure he didn't do it. I'll watch him. Please. Here, take the flashlight. Leave the gun. I might need it."

He stood up, pulled on his coat, and brought out gloves and a hat. "I go." The words sounded threatening, but Nellie just said, "Thank you." Then she picked up another pan to collect snow. "Be careful," she called into the darkness, as she watched a beam of light follow the trail north along the river. Snow continued to fall and the flakes were bigger. Inside, Nellie put the pot of snow on the stove and waited for water.

When the water was hot, she threw in coffee from a can that Rosy must have brought out, swirled it around, then filled a cup. She went to the bed, sat where she could hold Rosy's head up, and tried to get him to drink, saying his name over and over. Then she remembered that his real name was Ross. "Ross, wake up. Ross, don't die. Ross, wake up." Even Moonie helped, making long half-moaning, half-squealing noises.

Nellie, recalling what the sheriff had done for her, put down the coffee and pushed Rosy into a sitting position. She sat beside him and placed her arms around his chest, hoping to push him to a standing position. She wanted to get him up, make him walk, but could not do it. In the mine, he had been able to hobble. Here, his weight and sinking warmth made him feel so close to the edge of life.

"Tell me about Lily. What are your boys like? Do they look like you or like her?" She couldn't see his face, but his jaw began to move. "Tell me where you worked, Rosy, and how you came home at night. Tell me about summer here at Last Chance Ranch."

287

Julie Weston

A long sigh escaped Rosy. He shifted of his own accord and his eyes fluttered, his mouth worked. He wanted to talk.

"Matt. Dark, quiet. Like his Pa. He'll be . . . good'un. Black . . . ice."

Nellie wondered if she was understanding his words. She hugged Rosy tighter. "And the other one?" Moonie decided life was in order again. He curled around a circle and lay down.

"Mine. Like Lily. Ice like son . . . bitchin' Campbell."

"Now you sound more like the Rosy I know." She kept her arms around him, and placed her cheek on his whiskery face, trying to warm him even more. "And Lily, was she pretty?"

He nodded. His whiskers burned, but she wouldn't let go.

Another mournful sigh. "Docky. Tried to save her." A long shudder and Nellie grew aware of wetness on both their cheeks. Rosy was crying; perhaps she was too.

"Who is Docky?" Then she knew. Doc Kee.

"Goddam pain. Can't stop. Better . . . this way." The pitch of Rosy's voice moved higher. "Ancestors hold her. Comfort her." He turned slightly, his voice lower. "Who'll comfort boys?"

And who comforted Rosy? Drink and opium, she guessed. "And Doc Kee?"

"Son . . . bitch Jack killed him!" Disbelief and outrage colored his voice. "What'd you do that for you fuckin' . . . !" His eyes opened and he reached out. Nellie pulled her head back and looked up. He was awake. She tried to help him stand, but he wouldn't get up. He continued to rave. "Didn't know. My fault. Tried to help the fool. All he wanted—" Rosy grew so agitated, he broke Nellie's grip and almost stood up by himself.

"Fuckin' Jack. More dope. All he wanted." Rosy lay back against her and sobs shook his body. Nellie was afraid he was going into convulsions. She crawled around to hold him from behind, moving her legs up on either side of him. She managed to roll both of them down onto the bed and she lay next to him,

288

hoping to calm him, warm him.

After a while, he whispered, "Didn't mean to kill Jack. Knocked him into the drink. Fished him out. Took him to the ranch and left him." He shook his head. "Dead when I got back." He slumped hard against her. "And there you was. Lookin' like Lily. Brave and young. Headin' to the cabin. Didn't have my wits about me. Shoulda stopped you 'stead of followin' you. Shouldn't have told Gladys. She mucked everything up. Told Sammy."

They lay close together. "Don't marry no old man." The wind echoed his voice, rising around the chimney. Moonie jumped on the bunk and lay down at their feet.

"Tell Charlie. . . ."

The moan outside grew and the logs of the cabin groaned and creaked. Nellie hoped Sammy had caught up with Mrs. Smith and they had found cover and weren't freezing. Surely they went back to the auto. Just when she thought Rosy was asleep, he stirred and spoke again.

". . . raise 'em both. Bring 'em home."

After a while, he wheezed again and she thought to get more water, but her arms were around him and he held her hands and wouldn't let go. His words haunted her.

CHAPTER 27

The loss of warmth eased Nellie awake. At first, she was disoriented and could not find herself in time or place. Darkness surrounded her and no sound interrupted it. Gradually, she became aware of a soughing sound, like snow falling, and then the even softer sighs of someone breathing. She moved her legs and felt the weight of the dog at her feet. His breath.

Only then did she remember. "Rosy?" He should have been next to her. He hadn't died. "Rosy!" Her voice sounded hollow.

Still mostly clothed from the day before, Nellie scrambled out of the narrow bed. She felt her way to the kitchen area and brushed her hand over the table and the sideboard, almost tipping over the kerosene lamp base. She found matches and the bottle with the candle. The stub wasn't going to last long, but it shed enough light for her to search. She found Rosy upstairs on the lower bunk bed, curled into a ball for warmth. The Chinese robe wrapped around him. The fireplace chimney stood just outside this room and it retained some heat from the fire of the night before, but chill was seeping along the edges. His breathing had settled down from the earlier wheezing.

Nellie touched Rosy on the head, feeling responsible for his welfare, but not sure how to carry it out. She saved him from the cold. Could she save him from demons? No, only he could do that. She squatted down to study him in the low light.

Rosy opened his eyes and they stared at each other.

"I'm alive, ain't I?" he croaked.

"Barely."

"I'm thirsty. Musta turned my insides all out."

Nellie nodded. "It wasn't a pretty sight. Want to try re-filling?"

He thought that over and closed his eyes. After a while, Nellie pulled herself up by using the bed frame. Her body ached. She might as well let him sleep.

On the main floor, Nellie looked over the fuel situation. Half an inch of kerosene sloshed when she picked up the base. Morning crept through the windows, turning dark to gray and then daylight, muted with falling snow. Firewood was low.

What happened to Mrs. Smith and Sammy? If they had reached Ketchum, help would have arrived by now. She hoped they had not frozen on the trail north. Moonie clambered down from the bed and scratched at the back door. She opened it and snow fell in.

"Wait. I'll open the front. At least there's a porch." Moonie barked and followed her. Outside, he stepped into the shallow layer blown in by the wind. His paws left large petals for tracks. He looked over the field, sniffed the air, glanced back at Nellie with a puzzled expression, and took several more steps. "Difficult to know where to go, isn't it?" And what was she going to do? First, start a fire, then look for a chamber pot. The outhouse near the woods was not possible.

"We can't get out. We have to heat the cabin to wait out the storm."

A frisson of fear crawled up her back. They certainly had ample water if it didn't get too cold to melt the snow before they ran out of wood. She found as many containers as possible and filled them with snow, lining them up—cans on the stove, empty jars on the sideboard. She heated the coffee from the night before, taking a cup to Rosy. He still slept, snoring lightly, so she left the cup there.

Her camera pack and gear sat below the window where she'd first heard the dog tapping. Sammy must have rescued everything from the sled along the trail, because she had left it there to freeze. Bless that man. An idea came to her. She found the last lavender sachet in her coat pocket. There was enough left for a weak tea. She'd brew it up for Rosy. It was the only herb available to her and it might be better for him than coffee.

The crackling fire cheered Nellie and she hummed as she fed it, one stick at a time, and waited for water to boil. Many cans no longer had labels. Some were replaced with handwritten papers, but the rubber bands holding the labels were mostly rotten and broke when she touched them. Peaches. Pickles. Lamb. Applesauce. Each name in a pretty schooled script. No dates.

Apples seemed the best bet—they were acidic to begin with. She wondered how old they were. What had her mother told her about botulism? Painful death was all she recalled. Their rescuers, if anyone ever showed, might find three bodies: Rosy, Nellie, and Moonshine. Pickles sounded all right, too. The lamb—no, she wouldn't eat the meat. There were a few tins marked as green beans. She opened one and it was beans. That looked best of all. She dumped them in a pan to heat.

Upstairs, Rosy sat up, sipping cold coffee.

"Come down. I'm warming up some food and I've made lavender tea."

Rosy looked about as grizzled as the first day she met him, probably the day after all the tragedy there at the ranch, or maybe the same day. It seemed a lifetime ago, but it wasn't much more than three weeks or so. The moon would be full again soon.

"We been through the wringer. Leastways, I have."

"You look like it." She sat down beside him. "I have, too."

She patted his leg, feeling the silk of the Chinese gown. "This suits you."

"Think so?" He sat up straight.

"Let's go down and eat something."

"Where'd everybody go? Last I remember, Gladys was having hysterics all over the place and Sammy was gonna shoot me."

"For all I know, they're covered with snow. I'll catch you up. And you can catch me up."

One of Rosy's crafty looks crossed his face like a cloud over the sun. He sighed. "All right, girlie. Help me up. I'm an old, old man."

With the fire flickering low, Rosy confessed the sad tale to Nellie. Nellie freed Rosy from the guilty burden he'd been carrying: He didn't cause Jack's death. "Maybe Gladys killed Ah Kee, too, but I don't think we'll ever know, unless she confesses."

After Rosy ate and drank the tea, he laid on the couch and slept again. Night descended in the late afternoon. Nellie found another candle, placed it in the window upstairs, and checked on it every hour. When the yipping began outside, she knew the coyotes were back. The firewood was low, so she let the fire burn to bright embers before she placed more wood on it. This night would use the rest. When Moonie wanted out again, she waited in the doorway with the kerosene lamp. The snow had finally stopped. In the morning, she could try to make it to the road herself.

While she and Moonie sat by the fire, she let her mind wander. She would send her photos to San Francisco. She would try to implement some of the ideas she'd already conceived: photograph miners and sheepherders and men working. And women working. She forced herself to think about the scene with Mrs. Smith and what Rosy had said the night before. When Rosy took Jack to the cabin must have been when Gwynn

Campbell saw Ah Kee in the snow. Did he see Rosy too?

The boys. "Black ice" had become black eyes during the night. "Blue ice" and "black ice." Nellie surmised Charlie Azgo was the father of the first boy. Did he know? She could no longer think of him only as "the sheriff." He was, instead, a man. Maybe she and Goldie could talk Rosy into bringing the boys home. With two fathers, and a grandfather, there would be plenty of people to care for them.

The fire burned low and a sudden downward gust blew ashes into the cabin. A tendril of smoke leaked toward her, reminding her of another image the night of the moonshadows. She might never know the source of all she saw in the light of the moon.

Yipping from the coyotes drew closer. Nell retrieved the gun from beside the hearth where she'd left it. Although she had no idea how to fire any kind of weapon, perhaps a shot would scare them off. Through the window, she saw a dark shadow cross in front of the porch. "They're right there, Moonie!"

Nellie tugged the door open. She raised the gun high in both hands, pointing it straight out. "Get away!"

The explosion blasted her ears and the recoil shoved her back.

"No no, Missee! No shoot!"

Two bulky figures stomped across the porch and into the cabin. Sammy and Charlie. She didn't know which one to hug first.

CHAPTER 28

"The night before I went back out to Last Chance Ranch, I figured out some of what happened, although not all of it," Nellie admitted to her landlady after Sammy delivered her back to the boarding house. He took Rosy on to a medical clinic in Hailey. "The skis in Mrs. Smith's room told me she had been out there—I'd seen ski tracks when I went with the sheriff—and she and Rosy knew what happened. My first suppositions were wrong, of course. That maybe Gwynn killed the Chinese doctor and he wanted my negatives to throw blame on the sheriff, who took Ah Kee out there. Or that maybe the sheriff killed Three-Fingered Jack to throw blame on Rosy, wanting to get even with him for marrying his sweetheart. But as I grew to know Gwynn and the sheriff and talked with you and Rosy, I knew none of that was true. It was Jack who killed Ah Kee because he wanted opium and didn't get any. Finding the snow glasses gave me the last link. Gladys killed Jack and told Rosy that it was his fault. She could help him if he would hide the body's identity so no one would ever know Jack was dead, but just left town. My photograph ruined that plan."

The two sat by the fire in the dining room; the rest of the big old house was wrapped in silence. When Nellie arrived home, she'd begun shivering almost the minute she was in the door. Having Mrs. Bock care for her allowed Nellie to let down. She described finding Rosy and how Moonie had saved them from wild animals.

"I knew that woman suffered," Mrs. Bock said. "I knew she'd been to see Ah Kee, more than once. Jack deserved what he got." She was silent for a moment, shaking her head. "She shouldn't have blamed the doctor. Had to blame someone, I guess."

A log dropped in the fireplace. One of the housemates walked along the upper hall to the bathroom. Nellie shifted the blanket around her shoulders. "Why did Rosy let his sons go?"

Mrs. Bock shook her head. "He was afraid Gwynn would get them, I suppose." She rocked back and forth. "Without Lily, he was a lost soul.

"He was still Ross when she married him. Lily called him Rosy. Him and Lily got to be friends when Rosy came to eat four or five times a week. Whenever Lily and her pa had a blowup, she'd come stay and let it blow over. Rosy and her would play checkers by the fire and then she got him to playing chess and reading a book out loud to her 'til you wouldn't know he was just a miner. I knew he loved that girl."

Nellie listened. It was like hearing a storybook tale, a long, sad one.

"When Gwynn pulled Charlie and Lily outta Wyoming, fired Charlie and told him he'd kill him if he ever saw Lily again, Lily come here and moved in. Charlie went off to Boise City. Then one day, Lily comes to me and says she's marrying Rosy. Would I stand up for 'em? What could I do? I loved her and liked him. So we got the preacher in here and married 'em off. I gave her my old wedding dress."

The older woman sat quiet for a while. "They had those two boys and good boys they were. Then Lily got sick. Wouldn't tell nobody but me and Rosy and finally the Celestial, she called him. Brave, she was. I didn't think it was right though. Not telling her father. 'Course they hadn't talked for years."

With some hesitation, Nellie brought up what was foremost

in her mind. "Was one of those boys—" She stopped. Stirring the pot now might bring more heartbreak. "I mean, was the sheriff—?" Another log dropped, startling her. No, better to leave the subject alone.

"He told you." Mrs. Bock's statement was quiet but firm. "I'm not surprised. Rosy misses 'em somethin' terrible. It never mattered to him who fathered that first one."

"Maybe they should come home to Idaho."

Mrs. Bock frowned. "Doubt if Rosy'll change his mind."

"When he thought he was dying, he wanted Charlie to raise them."

"Land sakes." Mrs. Bock stopped rocking. "That'd be a pan of worms. Gwynn don't even know about Matt."

"Does Charlie?"

Mrs. Bock squirmed in her chair. "I think so." She was silent for a moment. "Let me think on this thing a bit. Now, young lady, you better get yourself to bed."

"Where *are* the boys?"

"Back East with Rosy's family."

CHAPTER 29

"Thought you knew everything, didn't you?" Gwynn Campbell met with Nellie in the living room of his mansion. Rosy and Mrs. Bock decided Nellie should visit Gwynn on her next trip. He was back to his gruff self.

"Yes," Nellie admitted. "I'm sorry, Mr. Campbell." How many times would she have to say it? On the other hand, he owed her. "If you hadn't attacked me, I wouldn't have been so certain that you were involved." Eating humble pie wasn't suiting her. "I have something else to talk with you about."

"I'm listening." Gwynn stood up and began to pace the room.

"At the ranch, after Rosy and I were stuck in the snowstorm, he talked about Lily and his two sons, Matt and—" She realized she didn't know the second son's name, only that he was like Gwynn.

The old man stopped pacing. "Campbell." He turned toward Nell and she saw the water in his eyes. "They named him Campbell. And I never saw him."

"Well, Rosy wants to bring them back to Idaho."

"Here? Can't believe he'd want that. Not after the way I treated him." He sat down again in the chair opposite Nellie. "Can't believe it."

"Not exactly 'here,' " Nellie said. "Back to Idaho."

"But I'm their grandfather. He can't take care of them, and he's broke besides. I have help here at the ranch. If they come back, they should live with me." He stood again. "I'll teach 'em

how to run sheep. They can take over the ranch." He straightened his shoulders.

This was much harder than she had envisioned it would be.
"No, you're not the only other living relative. At least, not for
one of them, not for Matt."

"What d'you mean?"

Better to get it over with. She stood up. "The sheriff is Matt's
father. Rosy wants the boys home and he wants the sheriff to
help him. Rosy has a job at the mine office now, the one Gladys
Smith used to have. He hasn't been drinking. He talked it over
with Sheriff Azgo and Mrs. Bock. Charlie already knew Matt
was his. He wants you to spend time with the boys, but they
wouldn't live with you." Her words ended in a rush.

The sound that came from Gwynn Campbell was akin to the
sounds she'd heard in the wild. He reached for her. Instinctively,
she stepped back.

"If you don't agree, you won't see them."

"They can't do that!"

"Yes, they can." She was moved to say she was sorry again,
but bit her tongue. "I'm leaving now. Think this over and call
Rosy." She gathered herself and stood as tall as she could. "Or
Charlie. It's time, don't you think?"

Nellie walked along the street toward the post office. April mud
was a sorry substitute for winter snow. It was a good thing
hemlines no longer swept the ground. Moonie trotted beside
her. She'd have to bathe his paws before letting him in the
boarding house. Under her arm was a large envelope with black
and white prints, her package of photographs to be mailed to
San Francisco. It had taken her the better part of two months
to make the decision as to which subjects and to finish the
prints she would send to the leader of the group, asking for his
critique and also to consider showing one or more in the gallery

he and others planned to open.

As she sorted through her winter work, each one reminded her of a piece of the story. The wheatgrass and aspens with the dark shadow in the background. The moon over Last Chance Ranch. The photo of Rosy, now titled "Miner from Triumph." The spread of clouds over a mountain butte: "Morning Glory." Was that too fanciful? And Mrs. Bock baking in "Goldie's Pies." There were others she had considered, including the two photos of dead men, but her courage didn't extend that far.

Gladys Smith had been sent to Twin Falls for trial. She hired a lawyer from Boise City who would argue that she acted in self-defense. The sheriff said that might have worked if Jack had only had a big bump on his head, most likely from the dog toy, but the coroner also found puncture wounds over his heart, thanks to Nellie's conjecture about the woman's hatpin. There wasn't just one. There were half-a-dozen. The trial would be held in the summer. In the meantime, Gladys was in jail. She had changed her name officially to Smith.

Rosy had left for Chicago a couple weeks earlier. He was nervous but determined to meet his sons again. He'd talk to them about what they wanted to do. It had taken Gwynn three weeks to make the call to Rosy and meet with him and Charlie. Nell would have liked to have heard that conversation.

The post office clerk weighed her package and sold her stamps to mail the photographs. Whatever the response, she knew she had found her work and her calling.

Outside, Moonie yipped. Nellie hurried back to him, afraid someone had thrown a stone or late season snowball at him. She found the sheriff squatted on his heels next to her dog, rubbing his neck and saying something to him in strange words.

"Hello, Sheriff." Nell hadn't seen him for a while. Mrs. Bock had been responsible for Rosy and the sheriff and Gwynn Campbell meeting. She was unsure how much to say, if anything.

"Good morning, Miss Burns." He looked up at her. "Do you think we know each other well enough now to use first names?"

Nellie blushed. "Yes, I think we do."

"Good. Nell, will you accompany me to the May Festival in Hailey next Saturday?" He stood, taking her hand on his way up.

Hands first, she recalled. "Yes, I would be honored." She ventured a small squeeze. "Charlie."

He nodded. "That's what Moonie said you would say."

ABOUT THE AUTHOR

Julie Weston grew up in Idaho and practiced law for many years in Seattle, Washington. Her short stories and essays have been published in *IDAHO Magazine, The Threepenny Review, River Styx,* and *Rocky Mountain Game & Fish,* among other journals and magazines, and in the anthology *Our Working Lives.* Her book, *The Good Times Are All Gone Now: Life, Death and Rebirth in an Idaho Mining Town* (University of Oklahoma Press, 2009) won Honorable Mention in the 2009 Idaho Book of the Year Award. She appeared on a C-Span2/Book TV interview in December, 2013. Both an essay and a short story were nominated for Pushcart Prizes. She and her husband, Gerry Morrison, now live in south-central Idaho where they ski, write, photograph, and enjoy the outdoors. www.juliewweston.com